For

Osman, Mehreen, Rayan & Maaneha

who continue to push me to follow my dreams.

I love you all.

SANIYA

SANIYA

Zara M

The
Book
Guild

First published in Great Britain in 2025 by
The Book Guild Ltd
Unit E2 Airfield Business Park,
Harrison Road, Market Harborough,
Leicestershire. LE16 7UL
Tel: 0116 2792299
www.bookguild.co.uk
Email: info@bookguild.co.uk
X: @bookguild

Typeset in 11pt Minion Pro

Printed and bound by CPI Group (UK) Ltd, Croydon, CR0 4YY

ISBN 978 1835741 115

British Library Cataloguing in Publication Data.
A catalogue record for this book is available from the British Library.

Prologue

It took one car ride on an ordinary day when I was eight years old for my life to change forever and turn me into the woman I am today. A part of me is trapped in that car, bleeding and broken, yet to be extricated from the wreck. That part is frozen in time, a reluctant witness of a catastrophic event that keeps rearing its head in different shapes and colours without forewarning. How could shopping for a dress become a life-defining event? If I had known the heavy price I would pay, I would have worn something old to the school's annual party.

1   *Therapist*

'I think my husband is having an affair with my best friend,' the curly haired twenty-five-year-old said quietly a few minutes into the first session.

'Oh,' I replied, unsure which emotion was prompted by this interjection other than a familiar unease in the stomach.

'You think your husband is having an affair?' I repeated her words, practising an essential counselling skill to emphasise the significance of her disclosure.

'That's what I said, isn't it?' Maria frowned and clutched her big ugly tote bag to her chest.

'Yes, you did. Tell me more.'

The first session was usually tricky, and the unease in my belly warned me that we had started off on the wrong foot.

She unceremoniously dumped the bag on the floor, and when she spoke, her voice wasn't quiet anymore. 'We've been married for a year, but he's not interested in me. Do you know that we've only had sex five or six times this year? I found several texts sent to my best friend. Sexual messages, if you know what I mean.' She broke eye contact as she added further evidence to her disclosure.

I leant forward, experiencing a slight disquiet within myself. 'That sounds like a tough place to be in, Maria.'

'Sounds like?' She laughed with a hint of bitterness. 'I know he's fucking her. Why wouldn't he?' There was a defiant expression on her face as she flicked away a lone tear.

I knew what she meant, but I asked anyway. 'What do you mean by that?'

'Saima is hot as hell, and look at me. How can my friend betray me this way?' She looked like a teenager with a new-found sense of adulthood. For a moment, another stubborn expression, a loud protest, and silent cry entered the periphery of my conscious mind as an old memory popped up. I deliberately shook it away, not realising I was shaking my head.

'Do you know what that's like?' she asked, running her fingers through the mass of thick curly hair.

'Have you confronted him or your friend?' I avoided the rhetorical but triggering question that had hit much closer to home than she had probably intended.

She frowned and folded her pale ringless hands across her chest. 'No. But I know it's true. Why would he not have sex with me if it wasn't true?'

'I'm sorry to hear that, Maria. How are you feeling right now as you share this?' A standard therapeutic question to save me from the apprehension in the belly that had converted into low-grade pain.

I had recently started working independently; this was the first time a client had sought therapy for sexual problems. I would be lying to myself if I said that I wasn't uncomfortable with this subject.

'This room is unlike the ones I've seen in films.' Maria's abrupt shift in conversation made me wonder if she had unconsciously sensed my discomfort. Her unexpected transition reminded me of the awful wagon drivers in Lahore who changed lanes at a whim.

'You don't like it?' I smiled as I looked around at the freshly painted ash-white walls that made this small room more significant than it was. Two sofas, two clocks, and two paintings faced each other, a wooden table on the side – cheap wood that fooled the buyer into believing it could be passed off as solid

2

wood – a therapist and a client. The paintings were the same size; abstract yet colourful images perhaps disturbed the white walls' spotlessness for some and added visual relief for others. A part of me liked the empty vibe of the room. I imagined an abyss waiting to be filled with stories of courage, loss, pain, joy, and so much more.

'Sorry, I wasn't trying to be rude.' Maria looked down at her hands that were in tight fists.

I looked at the vulnerable woman before me and murmured, 'I appreciate your candidness.'

'It hurts every time we have sex, and I wish I could…'

I held in an instant response and waited for her to say more. This time of hesitance was precious and created space for more unsaid conversations.

'I can tell he doesn't want it. And his text messages to her?' She looked up straight into my eyes. 'They think I don't know, and that makes it worse. I don't know how to explain it.'

Maria's face was flushed, and I could sense she was severely triggered.

'You don't have to explain it. I understand.' I blew out the candle on the table. Somehow it looked obscene in the backdrop of the intense conversation, creating a romantic aura mocking the energy of betrayal in the room.

'How could you ever understand what it is to be betrayed? They think they are keeping a secret from me,' she said, picking up her bag again and rummaging through, looking for something. Or nothing.

How could I understand? The unintended cruelty of her words provoked mild hurt within me. *How could I not understand?*

'I love my best friend. Do you know that?'

'I—' I started, but she cut me off mid-sentence.

'I feel as if I have to keep this secret to myself. I don't know how to confront them, and I don't expect you to understand.'

Her tone was cold and sterile and reminded me of doctors announcing the time of death.

'I can try to understand, Maria.'

Maria stopped and looked up as I reassured her. As if my vulnerable admission was the permission she had been looking for, a loud sob escaped her, and tears ran down her eyes.

'I wish I could explain to you.' After a few long seconds, she spoke, like a bus late to arrive. 'He never looks at me the way he looks at her. Am I not pretty enough?'

As her heart-shaped gentle face looked at me, anger filled every nook and corner of my being – anger at her husband for the self-doubt he had infused into this pretty young girl sitting before me. 'You are beautiful, Maria. His lack of interest isn't about you.'

She gave a wry smile. 'You are my therapist. Of course you'd say something like that.'

I knew better than to argue. How could I expect her to trust someone she had just met for the first time? Her husband's power in defining her view of herself was no surprise. A man could make or break a woman. I glanced at the clock; we had another twenty minutes.

We looked at each other. Quietly. The silence, like the thick fog in Lahore's winter mornings that left everything to muscle memory, was beginning to feel uncomfortable. For her or me, I couldn't say.

All of a sudden, she grabbed a few tissues to wipe another tear and said, 'Do you know we've never seen each other naked?' I wondered if Maria's repeated 'do you know' was a catchphrase or a deep longing for someone to know what she was going through.

'What do you mean? I assume you've been intimate a few times?' I asked for clarification.

'Duh!' Maria burst out laughing, but there was no humour

in it. 'It was always dark as he preferred that, and let's not call it intimacy, for crying out loud.'

Wrong question, I thought to myself.

She frowned and exhaled noisily through pursed lips. Was she disappointed in me?

'I'm sorry I assumed something there.' I did not want to lose Maria as a client. The session had taken a wrong turn, and there was an urgency within me to save the tender bond that had begun to form. 'It must be frustrating when others don't understand you.' I was hoping the validation of her experience might save the day. *Was I asking or telling her?* I wondered.

'I don't know.' Maria avoided eye contact and looked at the clock facing her. Damn. She wanted the session to be over. This was a red flag.

She took her mobile phone with a Garfield cover out of her bag and asked without looking up as she flipped through it, 'How long have you been practising for?'

I hesitated. 'I worked in a placement for a year or so but have been working as an independent practitioner since then.' I deliberately used the word practitioner to sound professional.

'Hmmm, so you're quite new at this.' She looked up, dropping the phone back in her bag.

I crossed my arms and replied, 'I've been working for some years.'

Maybe she won't return for another session because of all she has expressed today. *Did I ask too many questions? But she wanted to talk, didn't she?* I thought to myself as I shuffled my feet.

Many clients did not return after such a candid admission, overwhelmed by talking about parts of their lives they had consciously and unconsciously sworn never to talk about.

'Thank you for sharing, Maria.' I wanted to honour what she had done today. 'Would you like to schedule for next week?'

'I'll let you know.' She looked at me for a moment and added, 'Please don't tell my secret to anyone.'

'Oh, of course. Everything you shared today is confidential.'

'You didn't mention that at the start.' Her voice was flat, but her face was flushed, and a few seconds later, she abruptly got up and placed the fees on the cheap wooden table.

'My bad, Maria. Whatever you shared is—'

'I need to leave,' she cut me off mid-sentence again and got up and left the room.

I let out an audible sigh and sat motionless in my seat. My mouth was dry. *I don't believe it's my fault if she doesn't schedule next week*, I thought as I rubbed my neck. But how could I forget to tell her about confidentiality at the beginning of the session?

I shook my head as if to clear it and stretched my legs before the next session. Secrets were complicated. No one knew that better than I did.

2   *Child*

It was an ordinary day when it started, and I had woken up with excitement. Ami had promised to buy me a new dress for the annual school function because I was in the school dance, and although she hardly kept any promises, she was keeping this one. We hardly ever went shopping, and I was used to repeatedly wearing the few dresses stuffed in a single drawer in my wardrobe. It was a Friday, and running more than walking, I followed her towards the crowded shops in Liberty Market.

'Slow down, Saniya,' she scolded me in a tone that was never loud but made my heart skip many beats.

Ami scared me.

'Sorry,' I said and started taking slow steps so I wouldn't bump into her as she stopped at her tailor's shop. I never told her, but I believed one day she would lose me in a crowded place. It was a dream where I was lost in a big crowd, and Ami and Baba were nowhere to be found, and I remember waking up shaking and trembling.

The shops in Liberty Market reminded me of the living room sofa at Nana's home that had old and worn-out cushions in all colours and sizes, carelessly dumped, leaving almost no space for anyone to sit. These shops were nothing like the ones shown in one of my favourite films *Home Alone*. The malls in America were bright and beautiful. However, here, loud Indian music was blaring in some shops as if every shop owner was competing with the others to see who had the loudest sound system. I looked around, tapping my fingers on the tailor's table full of colourful fabrics whilst kicking it with my worn-out trainers. Ami turned around and gave me a dirty look that stopped my foot in mid-air. *Ugh! Why can't she get my dress first? What if she changes her mind?* But I knew better than to say anything. That would mean the end of this shopping trip before it had started. The foul-smelling rubbish lying beside the tailor's shop turned my stomach. I had not eaten since last night, but what was new about that?

'Ami, let's go.' I couldn't take the smell anymore. 'This place smells bad.'

'Stop it, Saniya,' Ami continued without looking at me.

'Sorry,' I whispered, grabbing her dupatta and covering my nose.

If I could have got a penny for the number of times I had apologised to Ami, I would be rich. The thought made me giggle, and Ami turned around.

'Stop it, Saniya. And look what you've done to the dupatta!' She snatched it from my hands and narrowed her eyes at me. I was in trouble. 'Should we go home?'

I peeked a glance at the tailor and saw him smiling at me. I turned around, feeling the heat in my cheeks, embarrassed and anxious. I hated for anyone to find out how Ami treated me. I wanted everyone to know that she loved me. She did love me, didn't she? Had the tailor seen the threat in Ami's face? Was the shopping trip over? But luck was on my side today, and Ami was forgiving.

'*Chalo*, let's get you a dress.'

I smiled tentatively, excited once again at the thought of a brand-new dress.

'Ami, I want bangles too,' I said in a sing-song voice as the shop ahead full of colourful bangles caught my eye. Was I pushing my luck? But blurting out thoughts without thinking wasn't a first for me.

8

'Let's get the dress first,' she said, walking through the narrow and crowded shops, almost bumping into a few people. A woman turned around with flared nostrils and pointed her finger at me, and I looked away. We found a shop with Eastern dresses, and I found a pink lehenga, a long skirt that reached the floor.

'I love this one. I don't want any other, Ami.' I loved how the silk felt between my fingers. The skirt had silver stars sewn all over, and I could bet they would glitter at night. The matching blouse had small silver-coloured flowers on the neckline, which complimented the colour of the stars.

'Theek hai. But let's look at some other shops too.' Ami was on her way out of the shop when I grabbed her dupatta again and, with eyes full of tears, begged her.

'Please, Ami, I want this one. Please.'

She looked at me and, to my surprise, replied, 'Fine. No need for the waterworks.' She turned towards the fat shopkeeper with a beard that was so big I could only see his eyes. 'How much is this?'

I am not crying, I lied to myself. Was this big man laughing at me? But no, he wasn't even looking at me. I hated when Ami scolded me in front of everyone. I should have been strong, and I was used to it, but at the same time, I felt embarrassed, and Ami would not stop anyway.

'*Chalo*, I got it. Happy?' Ami pushed the shopping bag into my hands, and I took the brown bag from the shopkeeper and followed her to the car where Uncle Uzair and Maheen were waiting.

'Ami, we didn't get anything for Maheen!' I had to yell at her, not sure if she could hear me in the noise of the loud music and the honking of the cars as we reached the parking spot.

She didn't even turn around as she replied, 'Now you show concern for your younger sister?'

I felt terrible. I loved Maheen, although she was just three and practically a baby. I loved to play with her.

'How was the shopping, girls?' Uncle Uzair teased with a

smile in his green eyes that reminded me of traffic lights. Ami's older cousin, whom Nana adopted when he lost his parents to a car accident, was not someone I was fond of. I did not know why, even though he would let me hand over the tools when he was fixing his car, his favourite pastime.

Was he even asking me? I didn't answer. I didn't like him and knew I was unfair, but I brushed the guilt away. I did not want to like him.

Ami smiled and sat in the front seat, looking at him as he turned the key in the ignition. Usually, she reminded me of the nun we met when we visited a local church on a school visit: unsmiling, although she did laugh when she watched *Tom & Jerry* cartoons with Maheen every morning. The only time Ami smiled was when Uncle Uzair was around.

I climbed into the back seat, holding the bag tightly to myself, and looked down at Maheen, who was sleeping, drool coming out of her mouth as she sucked her thumb. Maheen was a Barbie doll with big dark brown eyes, even though Barbie dolls did not have big eyes. She slept through any noise. How did she do that when I woke up even at the sound of Baba silently walking over to the kitchen in the middle of the night for water?

The car started moving towards Nana's home, where we were spending the weekend as Baba had gone to the village. I hardly remembered any weekend when we were not at Nana's.

'Put some music on, Uzair Uncle.' I pushed myself forward and started rummaging through the few CDs carelessly thrown in the space next to the car's shift gear.

'Wait, Sano.' Ami slapped my hand away. 'Why must you always be a nuisance? Can't you see Maheen is sleeping?'

'It's okay, Niggi,' Uzair Uncle whispered, but I could hear him. 'She's just a child. Don't scold her so much.'

I did not want him to worry for me. I did not like him or that he called Ami by her nickname. *Call her Nighat*, I ordered in my mind.

I rested my head on the seat, then jolted out of my slumber as I remembered the school party. I giggled and instantly covered my mouth so Maheen wouldn't wake up. The school was getting a merry-go-round for the first time, and I had never sat on one before. There was also a chocolate fountain, and Baba had promised extra money to spend on the day. I knew he would keep his promise, which is why I could not wait to go to school the next day.

I was about to lean forward again, wanting to see if we were close to home, when suddenly the brakes screeched, and my scrawny little body was thrown forward like a rag doll into the tiny space between the two front seats.

Along with the pain, a feeling of unease and dread coursed through me. Why was my tummy feeling funny? What was it? I was about to lean back when I saw it: Uzair Uncle tightly holding Ami's hand. His thumb stroked the back of her hand, drawing small circles. I could not look away, even though I wanted to. Why was he holding her hand? Ami never held Baba's hand. Was I imagining it? I closed my eyes and opened them again. The hands remained clasped together. His dark-skinned big hand. Her petite soft one.

I wanted him to remove his hand.

Stop it, will you? Let go of her hand. Please! I continued to scream these thoughts in my head, hoping Ami would heed them. *Why don't you listen to me, Ami?* When nothing worked, I stared out the car window at the noisy cars, but even then, I could not look away for long. They were still holding hands.

A rich, coppery taste filled my mouth, making me gag. I had been biting my lips again, an old habit that had started some time ago. Whenever I was worried, I would start biting my lips, unaware of the pain. I could not look away from these hands. *You are not supposed to touch her, Uncle Uzair.* My own hands felt cold, so I held Maheen's little hand.

'Mama…' Maheen cried out, waking up from her sleep. She

11

had decided to call Ami, 'Mama', when she had started talking. I had held her hand too tightly, so I let go.

'Ji, baby?' Ami turned around and replied softly.

Ami, show me both your hands, I pleaded, but she had already turned back. Why could she not hear me? I had heard of there being a connection between a mother and her children, but instead of a connection, it sometimes felt like there was a wall between us.

Please show me both your hands? My mind was running in circles, and I was finding it difficult to concentrate.

When I couldn't take the suspense any longer, I leant forward to check. Ami's hands were folded in her lap while Uzair Uncle held the car's steering wheel, looking ahead.

It was as if someone had untied the knot in my tummy as my own hands separated, and I started breathing more easily. Had it all been in my imagination? Probably. I snuggled against the headrest and shut my eyes. I did not want to open them again.

I wanted to sleep forever.

3   *Wife*

Some days I wished I wasn't married and had remained single. Relationships were hard work.

'Arsalan, how much longer?' I whispered to my husband, who had been talking to his mother for the last thirty-odd minutes and was walking in and out of the living room. He paused to look at me, pressed his lips together, and rubbed his left brow, that familiar gesture of his unsaid annoyance. I smiled sheepishly, and he turned around and continued. It was technically the entrance to our two-bed apartment, but we had thrown in a sofa and a TV and called it a lounge. How could he expect me to patiently wait around listening to random talk every other evening when he returned from work? This was my time with him, but saying it aloud would make me look bad, and I did not want to ruin my impression of being a loving and dutiful wife a year into our marriage.

'Ji, Amma... I'll try to visit tomorrow. You take care.' Arsalan finally ended the call as he entered the living room, but he was frowning. 'Yaar, why are you so impatient? You know how important my mother is to me.' Picking up the TV remote from the side table, he sank into the yellow sofa next to me. It was a used sofa that we'd bought from China Market. I didn't understand why it was called China Market with no hint of the land of the dragon, but I never bothered to ask. It was our first home purchase and had sentimental value for me.

'I know. I'm sorry. I was missing you more than usual today.' I inched closer and reached for his hand holding the remote. Tonight was the night I had planned for days.

He snatched his hand away and switched on the TV. 'You know I don't even see them that often, and they're only two streets away. And you have an issue with me talking to them.' His parents lived next to us, and we saw them three to four times a week, but apparently, it wasn't enough.

'That's not fair. I have no issue with you talking to Aunty. Why would I? I told you, I was just missing you.'

Arsalan rolled his eyes. 'Bring me some tea. I'm not in the mood for an argument.' He increased the volume and plopped his feet on the coffee table.

'I'm not arguing.' Unsure if he had heard me, I got up to make the tea, cringing inwardly at the sight of his dirty shoes on the table. Usually, I would point it out, but I didn't want to say anything to antagonise him further. Today was special.

I put the kettle on and took a long deep breath. Why were we like this? Bickering over the smallest things. Mistrusting and constantly misunderstanding each other.

We had been married for a year now. Arsalan was five years older than me, and we had met through mutual family friends. The attraction was instant; after two meetings, we gave the go-ahead to the families. I had recently completed my master's in English, and Ami was getting frantic looking for proposals. Arsalan – the only son of the Secretary Punjab, foreign qualified and working in investment banking – was a prize catch, and the fact that he was handsome was the icing on the cake. I believed I was the luckiest girl in the world.

Those who saw us saw a man and a woman: a husband and a wife. The man was taller than the woman. Tall, dark, and handsome, straight out of a Mills & Boon novel. The woman was a few inches shorter than him. Golden, light brown eyes, obviously pretty with a face she liked to think stayed in the viewer's mind for a few seconds longer once removed from sight.

We were *the* it couple. But in reality, we were more like two roommates who were friends, attempting to make love now and then with a platonic hug and an awkward reluctant union that felt forced by me.

I didn't feel I had been married for the past twelve months. We hardly ever had sex, and we barely kissed. Sex. I wouldn't call it lovemaking because feeling loved was the last thing I experienced in those few minutes of rough, hurried groping and painful penetration. There was no foreplay, nothing gentle or soft about the meeting between two bodies; desire was the last thing felt in that limited space.

Ever since we married, he hadn't asked me to have sex with him, not even once. During our time alone at home, we would watch films together, and many nights after dinner, as I would sit next to him, my body feeling the warmth coming from his, I would wait for him to kiss me or touch me. He was always keen to cuddle, but it never led to more, leaving me frustrated and resisting the bear hugs he was ready to offer. But that's all he ever wanted.

I thought it wasn't up to a woman to ask for sex. The man had to be in charge, and I was too shy to question why my husband wasn't touching me beyond a sporadic hug. Why did he turn his back on me every night? Excuses, one after another, followed about why we couldn't be intimate; sometimes he would say yes, and times were arranged for the next day or the weekend that were sometimes followed through, but mostly, I waited. It was as tedious as waiting long hours at a busy doctor's clinic, even after one was given an appointment.

Was I not desirable? Why didn't he kiss me? Why did he awkwardly turn away when I tried to touch him? The familiar anger reared its head at these questions. Why did he make me wait? Eventually, I asked him the questions. They were more or less variations of the same answer.

15

'I'm busy, Saniya.'

He had this response on autopilot; sometimes, he would interrupt me mid-question.

So, I did the best I could. I waited for him to be less busy, for passion to come knocking, and for Arsalan to agree to open that door with me by his side.

But I was hopeful that tonight was the night I would feel like a married woman, when we would kiss and touch and try to invite desire, which took as long as some VIPs did to arrive at an important event. I understood that sex was a conversation and could get better, but only if he was willing to participate. I wasn't the kind of woman men desired, but I was pretty enough. I wanted to believe that.

The rumbling of the kettle broke me out of my thoughts.

I carried the tea tray to the living room. 'Tea is ready, hubby dear,' I said in a forced sing-song voice.

'Thank you, begum.' Arsalan smiled and reached for the cup.

His smile calmed my nerves, and I sat down again beside him.

'Please stop watching.' The loud volume of the film was an antithesis to my calm mood, and it wasn't the first time I had pointed that out.

'Let me finish watching this scene.' Arsalan sipped the tea and returned to watching the film he'd selected for the evening. Since we'd been married, watching a film together had become an almost daily tradition, and most days, I enjoyed the process. Today was different.

I stayed quiet, feigning interest in the fight scene playing out. Why was the most natural act between a man and a woman so much work? I didn't even complain about how awful the sex was, but I was willing to explore and try; it's not as if I expected to be thrown against the wall and have passionate sex the way they showed in the films. That didn't seem real, but asking my husband to make love to me in the few minutes of 'sex' we had didn't feel right either. Arsalan did touch me lovingly now and then, I thought to myself, but a faint voice protested. *He didn't touch you but only did what you asked him to do.* The asking took the desire away and was a wearying process, as if asking a toddler to finish his food as he made faces and acted out, pushing the food away.

But I didn't dare tell him I'd never had an orgasm and was just happy to see him satisfied. The fact that he was comfortable was essential and made my marriage seem real to me.

I put my hand on his arm, stroking it. I liked that he was not very hairy.

'How was your day, begum?' he murmured.

Does he want to know? I wondered as his eyes remained glued to the action film.

I decided to play it safe. 'It was good. I missed you.' I waited for him to turn around even though I knew he wouldn't. This small talk was not new. Every day when he came back from work, drowning himself in mindless films was the first thing he did, and I would go and sit next to him; asking me how my day was was not feigned interest but a genuine need to know me. I kissed a tiny birthmark on his arm and waited for him to turn. He stayed where he was.

Lately, the realisation of Arsalan's single-track mind was hitting home, and right now, the violence in the film had all his attention. I was not the priority, but as long as he remembered that we were supposed to have sex tonight, it would all be alright. As long as he remembered...

That sounded bizarre, and before I said something that could threaten to spoil the mood of the evening, I abruptly got up. 'Going to change,' I announced, and left without expecting a response.

As I walked towards the bedroom, my shoulders were tense, and I could feel the heat on my cheeks. *Why can't he ever pursue me?* I thought and shut the door behind me. I bit into a clenched fist and took a deep breath. *Don't go down that road. Don't.*

I chose a backless lilac silk nightie with enough skin to tempt a priest. I had found it in one of those multi-brand shops, and it was a good find, costing me only two thousand rupees. I hoped he would like how it looked on me as I stared at myself in the full-length mirror. I turned around and tried to see how I looked from behind. It was a little sluttish. *Maybe I should change into my pyjamas*, I thought as I rubbed my clammy palms on the silk dress. The neckline was low and hinted at the cleavage. Was it screaming of desperation?

But I was desperate, and he was my husband. I lifted my chin and paid attention to my slim and curvy body.

You are pretty, I told myself and giggled aloud. I covered my mouth with my hands. I wasn't being crude. Getting compliments was not an alien idea for me, but the hunger for more, especially from Arsalan, was not satiated yet. My husband was as stingy with compliments as Midas's fist.

I jumped as the door opened, and Arsalan entered the room. 'I'm tired, yaar. I've eaten so much.' He burped aloud as he plopped himself on the bed. Our bed was a gift from Ami, along with the two wooden chairs upholstered in plain white, a small coffee table, and two lamps that added character to the room with their dimmed light when it was dark; the traditional bedroom furniture given by all Pakistani parents to their daughters.

I waited for him to notice me. He stretched his legs out, his eyes closed. My heart sank, falling like a skydiver pushed out a moment earlier than he was ready, and I felt the knot in my stomach.

I stood rooted to the spot, my hand on my stomach, waiting for him to open his eyes and see me.

He opened them after a few minutes.

'Wah, begum.' He smiled as he directly looked at me, and I broke eye contact, feeling the heat in my cheeks.

'Let me go and change.' He got up from the bed. The knots

loosened up more, almost close to being untangled, and with a big smile, I spun, feeling the silk against my legs.

I walked over to his side of the bed and got into the middle a few seconds before he returned.

'It was such a crazy day at work today. I need a break.' He switched off the bedroom lights, crawled next to me into his familiar place in the bed, and stretched his legs out.

The knots in my stomach started tightening again. I leant more towards him. 'Sounds like it was a tough day.'

'You have no idea. Unlike you, madam, I don't have the luxury of watching Oprah all day.' He laughed at his comment, although I found no humour in it. I laughed anyway.

I inched closer, bit by bit, close enough but still distant.

He slightly pushed my shoulder. 'Yaar, give me some space.'

His words stopped me.

'It was boiling today,' he added, picking up the air conditioning remote. The slight noise from the air conditioning alerted me to an increase in the cooling level of the AC.

I longed for him to touch me without me having to beg him.

He was slightly turned away from me and had picked up his mobile phone from the side table.

I snatched the phone away and turned his face towards me.

'How do I look?' I asked softly. 'Arsalan!' I called out again as he turned his face away. 'Look at me, please,' I lovingly pleaded, ignoring the tightness that was coming up in my neck now.

He cradled my face in his palm and replied, 'I'm exhausted, Saniya.' His voice was edgy as he snatched the phone from my hand.

'But you said we could have sex today,' I heard myself say, trying hard to dull the irritation and apprehension in my voice. This was how we used to plead to our maths teacher for extra marks in school.

He removed his hand from my face, and replied flatly, 'So? Is this a fucking business deal?'

19

My heart started to beat faster. This was not how I had envisioned our night to be. We had taken a wrong turn, and finding the way back today would be an uphill task. I could tell Arsalan was angry as I bit my lip. The vein in his neck was throbbing, and a minute later, he turned his back to me and started using his phone. I had wished to be a passionate lover tonight who tried to make love in a secluded corner with my husband. But instead, I was looking for that corner alone.

I leant forward and kissed him on the cheek, swallowing my pride and much more. *Don't cry*, I warned myself. He hated tears.

'Of course not, jaan. But it's been so long. Please?' I was openly begging now, a beggar who had moved past notions of self-respect and pride.

He moved further away from me. 'Why do you always make it a chore? Do you have to find a reason to be unhappy, be so needy?' He was shouting now. He slammed his phone hard on the table and sat up. His handsome face changed right before my eyes. His eye was squinted, and the throbbing vein in the neck was bulging more. I could see where the night was going, like one of those low-budget films where one knew the end as soon as the film began.

I noticed the candle I had lit up on the coffee table hastily melting away like ice cubes left out in the kitchen sink. Once frozen, it will thaw, and once melted, it will freeze again, but for now, it was melting away hope and desire and my dream of feeling like a woman, a wife desired by her husband for a night.

A man. A woman. We were living together, but that's all we were doing.

'I'm sorry.' I unashamedly reached out for him, trying to touch him to stop him. Stop him from getting angrier. Stop him from leaving. It was scary whenever he was angry because his face changed and he would resort to shouting and hurling abuse. Although he had never laid a finger on me in his anger, my gut alerted me to the possibility. I held my breath, knowing there was no U-turn.

'What is wrong with you? Stop acting like a bloody whore,' Arsalan shouted. He got out of the bed and grabbed his pillow and mobile phone from the table. He walked over and switched on all the lights in the room. The brightness shocked the room as if someone was shining a torch on a dead body's face.

'Please, Arsalan. Don't leave,' I was begging him, tears running down my face, my hands held together in an apology. I must have crossed a line for him to be so furious. The neighbours would hear the noise. Years later, the word 'whore' repeatedly used, like a child frequently calling out 'mama', would haunt me. He pointed the phone in my face and screamed louder.

'Now you want me to stop shouting, *chutiya aurat*? Your desperation is disgusting, Saniya. You expect me to make love to you when you behave like this?'

'I... I'm sorry,' I whispered, looking at my husband's flushed face. It was my fault. I should not have pushed him.

'Fuck your apology. You have ruined the night.' He left the room, banging the door hard and loud enough for me to feel my heart jump out of my body.

I stayed in bed, sitting motionless and holding my breath. I should have stayed quiet. My thoughts screamed at me. All I felt was the familiar panic that had been my trusted companion for as long as I could remember.

Why do you always push him so hard?

But... it's been five weeks...

So what?

I wanted to...

No! You did not want to...

I thought I wanted to...

The voices in my head grew louder, and I covered my ears with my hands and shut my eyes tightly. An image of a child in mismatched pyjamas popped into my mind, and I knew that the child had felt like the woman in the pretty gown.

'It will be okay. It will be…'

A few minutes must have passed when another loud bang came from outside and I heard his footsteps approaching. I trembled, startled out of my comatose sobbing state. I sat up, arranging my nightdress lest any part of my skin showed. The delicate nightie seemed so heavy on my body, and I wanted to rip it off. The room door opened, and he walked in, his face as flushed as when he had left.

'Do you always need to create some fucking issue? Can't you ever let us be happy?' he spat the words at me, little specks of saliva flying out of his mouth.

'I'm sorry. Please don't be angry,' I begged, hoping this would calm him down.

'The bloody air conditioning isn't working in the guest room. Why didn't you get it fixed?' he yelled.

I could not maintain eye contact and looked down.

'I did call the electrician, but he never showed up.' My palms were sweating now. I hoped this change of topic meant an end to his rage. I needed to stop apologising. I knew that annoyed him, but I never learnt, did I? How often had he told me it made him angry, and yet I continued to do it? Shame like a clinging vine was spreading all around me.

'Fucking excuses,' the verbal assault continued. He got into bed, turning away from me. '*Saari raat kharab ker di.*'

There was silence in the room after that, followed by gentle snoring from a man who was anything but peaceful. There was a soft hum from the air conditioning, or maybe it was my laboured breathing. I stretched my legs to rest on the bed as quietly as possible and stared at the ceiling. There was seepage in the corners. *We need to get it fixed*, I thought. Suddenly, it dawned on me that I was wearing the lilac silk nightdress. I shut my eyes, grabbed the corners of the silk, and crushed it with my hands.

A few minutes later, I opened my hands very slowly, as if the weight of the dress was crushing me; I got off the bed and went to the bathroom. Luckily, my everyday pyjamas were hanging there. Quiet as a mouse, I quickly changed into them and rolled the nightie into a ball, stuffing it in the toiletry rack, so it was out of sight. I tied my hair in a small knot and washed my face. Tears suddenly rushed into my eyes, and the wave within started building up again, threatening to upset the calm of the night. *Not now!*

I brushed my teeth, and returned to the bedroom within a few minutes. He was sleeping soundly, and my neck muscles eased a bit more. It was over. *Until next time*, I thought to myself. The roller coaster of thoughts was triggering, and I silently walked out of the bedroom into the little TV room. I was exhausted and didn't want to feel anything anymore.

I sat in the same spot my husband had been sitting in and found it to be warm still. That was definitely my imagination.

This was not the first time Arsalan had been angry and not the first time he had hurled abuse at me. However, this was the first time his handsome face had looked ugly as words flew out of his mouth. Is that how bullets were fired without a moment's hesitation in warfare? Did the enemy's pain not matter? But I was not his enemy. I was his wife. I didn't even understand some of the abusive words he used. I switched on the TV and lowered the volume. Some random film was playing on HBO. I tried to pay attention, but I dozed off, and when the doorbell rudely woke me up, I realised it was already morning, and our part-time helper had arrived.

I got up and switched off the TV. I looked at the clock, an ugly gift given by some random uncle at the wedding, showing 7:30am. I wondered if Arsalan too had woken up to the doorbell. Covering my mouth, I yawned and strolled towards the door.

'Salam, baaji,' Aamir greeted with a big grin on his acne-covered face. 'How are you doing on this fine morning?'

I was way too tired for small talk. '*Chalo kaam shuru kero*,' I replied, before turning around and walking over to the bedroom. Arsalan was still sleeping. I lay on the bed, turning sideways to face Arsalan's back. His capacity to sleep in one position for hours amazed me. Sadness welled in me, and I slapped away a disobedient tear that had slipped out without my permission as the memory of the night popped up.

I badly wanted to be held by him, just so I could be sure we were friends again and would not fight. Fighting with anyone made me nervous. His anger made me anxious, as I wasn't sure what it would lead to, and the not knowing made me nervous. I had been so sure that we would have sex last night. What did I do wrong? Maybe I was demanding? When was the exact moment I made a mistake? *Do I ask too much?*

But it had been so long. I cringed momentarily as I stared at his back in the yellow worn-out nightshirt. *You didn't feel like sleeping with him*, another voice said in my head. Lately, I had been wondering whether I demanded sex to tick a box or if I had any genuine attraction for my husband. I leant over and switched off the lamp on my side of the bed.

It will get better. One day it will.

It was the sun on my eyes that woke me. I slowly opened my eyes and saw Arsalan brushing his hair through the slightly ajar bathroom door. I had dozed off again.

'*As-salamu alaikum*,' I called out, sitting up. I hoped he was not angry; I silently prayed.

He turned around and smiled at me. 'You lazy bum, aren't you going to give me breakfast today?'

My handsome husband. The knot was almost untangled now; the strings were loosening up.

'Ji, Arsalan.' I jumped out of bed, walked over to the wardrobe, and pulled on my nightgown to wear over my pyjamas. I rushed to the kitchen and grabbed his oatmeal cereal, a spoon, and a bowl from the cupboard. I grabbed a table mat, laid down the white ceramic bowl and cereal box, and sat opposite Arsalan's chair. Aamir was washing the dishes.

'You are washing them now? What have you been up to all morning?' An unnecessary scolding, a mere distraction without any conviction in it. I couldn't have cared less what he had been doing all morning. He could have been flying kites for all I cared. Anger like a latecomer to the party had come knocking and I had to avoid opening the door.

'What's your plan for the day?' Arsalan asked, walking in and sitting at the table, placing his laptop bag on the floor beside him.

'Saniya! For goodness' sake, bring the milk too!' The edge returned to his loud voice.

I jumped in my seat, abruptly rushed to the fridge, and grabbed the milk carton.

'I'm sorry. I don't know what's wrong with me today,' I apologised and poured the cereal into his bowl.

He started eating, and I sat in my seat and looked at him, gulping down the food. If only he gave me half the attention he gave to his food.

He looked up at that moment, causing me to blush. Had he read my thoughts? I felt like a kid caught with her hand in a tin of biscuits. I smiled my big hearty smile. And lied. 'You look good in that shirt,' I complimented.

He got up. I followed.

'Yeah, yeah! You want to have sex tonight, don't you?' he whispered. It was like a harsh slap on my face. He was still smiling. That was cruel.

I stayed at the front door, my arms crossed over my chest. I wanted to throw up because I felt the hope again – one more time. I leant against the door for a long time, long enough not to remember how long it was after I had kissed him on the cheek before he left for work.

I was the designated choreographer that night, and ignoring the shame that filled every nook and cranny of my being, I turned towards Arsalan as we lay in bed.

'Are you in the mood?' I did not want to assume today.

'Sure. Give me a minute.' He turned over, picked up his mobile from the nightstand, and checked his messages.

I dug my nails into my palms. Did I want to have sex? No, I was an imposter who only asked for it because my mind told me that a happy marriage should have good sex involved.

'I'm all yours.' Arsalan lay on his back and stretched his legs out. He laughed as he said that, and I forced myself to smile while cringing inside. I took off my nightdress and left the panties on. I wasn't ready to bare it all. I started kissing him.

A moment later, he pushed me away. 'Slow down. You are too sloppy.'

'Oh, I'm sorry,' I said. I liked kissing him, but ever since he had told me how bad I was at it, I felt guarded and ashamed of my uncontained way of kissing him. I needed to slow down and not force myself onto him. Wasn't that what passion was, however?

I leant into him once more and started kissing. 'Is it okay?' I stopped to ask.

'Yaar, stop talking and asking stupid questions. Just do what you want to,' Arsalan replied with a familiar annoyance.

'Sorry. What do you want me to do?' I asked and instantly regretted asking another question. *Stop talking*, I admonished myself. I felt the sweat under my armpits and bit into my lower lip. What was happening?

He turned over, and with rough hands, he fondled my breasts as I lay trapped under his body. I never liked the feel of his hands; they hurt me, but I didn't dare say that. He was rough and disinterested. I could deny everything to myself, but my body knew I didn't turn on my husband. Neither did he provoke any desire in me. We were part of a play and poorly acted out the script.

'You like that?' He looked straight into my eyes.

'I love it… don't stop…' I mumbled.

That was all the cue he needed. He ripped the panties off a few minutes later and penetrated deep within me. I grabbed the end of the qulit, trying my best not to let my face show signs of the physical pain I was going through. His eyes were luckily closed for the few minutes of painful penetration that was burning my skin, and I clenched the bedsheet more tightly as I tasted blood in my mouth from biting into my lower lip.

I looked up at my husband's face. His eyes were closed as he thrust deep within me. Did he not care how dry I was and how much pain I was in?

'I'm about to come…' the great warrior announced.

'Me too,' I lied with as much force as I could muster to validate his act of passion that wasn't contagious.

He opened his eyes and looked at me with a triumphant smile.

It was over before it started.

He rushed to the bathroom immediately afterwards. There was no holding each other or any words of love exchanged. I dried the tears that had been shed unannounced. I never wanted him to know how it felt. At least he was happy, and I could tell myself I was married.

'Are you happy, madam?' he asked as he returned in a freshly ironed set of blue pyjamas.

I smiled. A big one that used the last shred of energy my battered body was feeling.

'Thank you,' I replied and got up to change.

'Shower, please. I don't like how you smell afterwards.' He laughed. Did he believe that he was funny? I sometimes wondered if he knew he was the only one who laughed at his own bad jokes.

I closed the bathroom door behind me and lay down on the floor. Shame, anger, pain, and more unidentified emotions overwhelmed me. How could he be so cold and cruel? This was sex for him. My husband, who claimed to know me so well, could not sense the physical and emotional pain he caused me in the few minutes of hurried lovemaking granted after days of begging. Loud sobs racked my body as I covered my mouth with the white towel. I showered and crawled into bed beside my husband, who snored away that night.

A husband and a wife.

We had sex, or that's what we told ourselves that night.

A man and a woman. Married. The man slept with his eyes closed. The woman slept too, but with her eyes open.

4 *Mother*

My children were the best thing to have happened to me. The thought made me smile as I looked at my son, busy playing with his shiny blue car, the latest addition to his toy car collection, while my one-year-old daughter crushed the biscuit in her pudgy hands.

'Nyle, you have to take a shower, baby. Hurry up,' I called out to my three-year-old. He was a handful and growing bigger by the minute.

Nyle picked up his car and ran out of the kitchen. 'No, Mama. No, Mama, I don't want to.'

Great. I took a long, deep breath and closed my eyes. Bathing him would be an uphill task today.

Neha clapped her chubby hands together, her little legs swinging in the high chair where I had been trying to feed her lunch. She was a demanding eater, unlike her brother.

'Bhai is funny, is he?' I smiled, cleaning her face with the wet towel and picking her up from the high chair. She had eaten most of the chicken and rice, and I didn't have the strength to force-feed her the rest today.

'Let's take a shower, baby.' I kissed the top of her head and left the dishes for the cook to clear later.

'Zubaida, please bring Nyle to the bathroom. I'm late!' I yelled out to my trusted helper, a godsend arranged by my friend, Fatima. Zubaida was a childless widow, and it was selfish of me to feel relief in the knowledge that she didn't have any liabilities or never took any holiday time. She was a maternal figure for all of us, even though she was the same age as me.

She entered the kitchen, collected the dishes, and piled them in the sink. Short and slightly plump, she had a friendly, open face that made me comfortable. 'Baaji, I will give them a shower.'

'Let Majid clear the kitchen, then, and you can come and help me with the kids.' Luckily, Majid, the cook, was also a good find, sent by Arsalan's mother, and after months of different kitchen helpers, I now had a team of reliable house help.

'Let me bring Nyle, our naughty kid. *Barra shararti hai.*' She laughed. I liked how warm and loving she was with my children and could understand how she vicariously fulfilled her maternal instincts through Nyle and Neha.

It took me an hour to get the kids showered, changed, and fed, and now they were happily watching Barney on TV and ready for their afternoon nap. Zubaida was trustworthy, but I was an anxious mother who preferred doing everything independently. I didn't want to neglect the children. I never wanted them to think that I wasn't there for them. How working women found the courage to leave their kids for hours was a mystery; for me, a trip to the salon gave me crippling guilt.

'Baaji, your phone is ringing.' Zubaida entered my room as I picked up my big brown tote to head out.

I started, realising that my phone was, indeed, ringing.

'Hello.' Arsalan's voice at the other end was chirpy.

That's surprising, I thought, as I balanced the mobile between my ear and shoulder and unlocked the front door.

'What's up?' I asked. In the background, there was the sound of loud traffic, and I thought I heard a female voice. He was supposed to be at the office. 'Where are you?'

'Walking back to my car. I stepped out for lunch.'

'Oh. Lunch?' I asked, trying to tame a few stray strands of hair.

'Yes. Is that a problem?' His voice carried an edge to it.

'No, of course not. Business lunch?' I instantly regretted asking him.

'For God's sake. Why are you interrogating me?' The chirpiness was replaced by a steely edge. 'Be ready by seven-thirty,' he added.

'I know, but let's leave at eight. I want to put the kids to bed first.'

'Yaar, why the hell do we have a nanny? You need to learn to let go.'

'Please don't tell me how to raise the kids.' I felt attacked. 'You be here by seven-thirty. Knowing you, we won't leave by eight anyway.'

'I will be,' he replied in a curt tone.

I bristled. 'But you always make us late, and I don't want to be the last one to arrive at the party.' I hated how my sense of punctuality got compromised because of him.

'Yaar, stop repeating everything. I said I will come early, and you're the one who wants to go late.' His voice was harsher, and although some part of me knew he would still be late, I decided to let go of this moot point.

'Fine. I'll leave with the driver if you're not here.' *Why couldn't I just let it go?*

In the three years of my marriage, I was beginning to find my voice in sporadic moments where an impulsive, defiant part of me didn't care or wanted to remember the ugliness of his temper or how intimidating it was for me. I eventually paid the price for triggering him, but somehow silencing my voice seemed harder as time passed, and it seemed to have developed a mind of its own. In all fairness, I did have a habit of repeating and controlling things, and even though Arsalan would politely tell me to stop, I would keep pushing until he lost his temper. That's why, after every angry episode, he would say, 'You never listen,' and I would apologise. I just didn't trust him.

31

As it were, he hung up without saying goodbye, and I could sense that I had struck a sensitive nerve.

Ignoring my apprehension, I left the house to finish my nails and hair for dinner. Arsalan was a senior manager at a private bank now and the Pakistani definition of a settled man: good job, a modest home, kids, and so one wasn't expected to aspire for more. We rented a four-bedroom house a few streets away from from his parents' house and far away from my mother's home. Arsalan preferred staying with his parents, so getting a place close to them and living independently was a good compromise for both of us. Being the only son, I wondered about the motivation behind his regular visits. Was it attachment to the family or the guilt that was inculcated by religion and culture that demanded his need for proximity?

I was inclined to believe that it was the latter. No matter how much they hid behind the persona of modernism, the typical Pakistani family was deeply rooted in expectations, especially the son and the only son. At times, I wondered if Arsalan was the kind of man who could experience complex emotions in any relationship.

Ami and I, on the other hand, had an estranged relationship, and her critical side had gone into overdrive since she became a grandmother. She loved my children to death, but she was critical and controlling of my parenting skills, and the only way I could cope was by avoiding her and going to her place at weekends only. That was an experience that took me a few days to recover from. However, Arsalan loved her and always took some time out to have lunch or dinner at her place. Naturally, he was treated like a prince, typical of Punjabi households where the son-in-law was placed on a pedestal.

Life was good for the most part, though, but it depended on what 'good' meant. There was financial liberty. We travelled, hosted dinners, enjoyed our children, and had families that got along well with each other. Some things remained unchanged, but I tried not to let them blind me to the goodness between us on most days.

It always overwhelmed me when I began to realise how, even after several years of our marriage, we continued to experience intimacy. My husband no longer cared to address it, physically or in a conversation, and his verbal abuse and anger issues were always uninvited guests to the party we called our marriage. In a way, we were stuck like limpets to the stones of the past.

I shook my head, trying to snap out of unwelcome memories of the past, and left for the bank, the first stop on my day's agenda, followed by the salon where a few hours of tender, loving care washed away many worries. A couple of hours later, as I returned home, I felt like a new person.

The children were asleep in their room. The sight of sleeping kids did beautiful things to a mother's heart. I leant over and kissed them. Both had inherited dark, thick hair from their father and fair skin from me, and the combination had produced two good-looking children. I knew I was biased, but still.

'Baaji, they need to be woken up now,' Zubaida announced as she entered the room and put the ironed laundry in her hands in the wardrobe. 'Any more, and they won't sleep at night.'

'No, let them sleep,' I said. 'Tomorrow is Sunday so they can stay up late. Please make me tea.'

'Ji, baaji.' She nodded and walked towards the kitchen. I followed her into our small but chic kitchen, the house's most well-lit room. The power of the sunlight always left me in awe; the clout it carried in lifting one's mood and distracting one from the darkness outside and within oneself.

Since we had been invited out for dinner, I was looking forward to spending time with Arsalan, even if it wasn't time alone with him. I wanted to pamper myself and dress up and look pretty for him. After becoming a mother, the most significant change within myself was how my children were never far from my thoughts. They came knocking at the door of my mind, sometimes uninvited, other times with an invitation, but they knocked frequently. I wondered if the worry would ever stop. For now, Nyle and Neha happily consumed my days and nights.

By around 7:30pm, I was all spruced up, the kids had been fed, and I could feel the excitement of meeting new people and taking a break from motherhood and home duties for an evening.

'Hello. What's up?' Arsalan asked as he put his laptop bag on the living room sofa. I winced a little as my OCD around the laptop bag placed on the recently upholstered sofa got triggered, but I said nothing.

'Baba is here, kiddos,' I yelled out at Nyle and Neha, who had been waiting to greet Arsalan.

'Baba, Baba.' Four little legs ran towards Arsalan, and he picked them up in his arms and started to twirl. I placed my hands on my chest as my gaze fixed on the scene before my eyes. I was a lucky woman to be married to a man who was a great dad.

The screaming and cuddling continued for a few minutes, and eventually, Nyle and Neha, after offering me a quick hug, went to their rooms.

'Zubaida, please put them to sleep.' Without waiting for her response, I picked up Arsalan's bag and walked over to his study to put it away.

I could hear him singing in the shower as I entered the bedroom. I had started packing my evening bag and put a few sweets – my hidden poison – and my compact powder for retouching in when he came out of the shower.

My handsome husband, I thought as I looked at his wet hair and shaved face.

'I had good business meetings today,' he shared as he started putting on his underwear.

There was a stirring in my body. I was turned on and, for a moment, imagined Arsalan tossing me onto the bed for a quickie.

'*Mashallah*. I'm proud of you.' I turned around to look at my reflection in the full-length mirror.

Arsalan started singing an old Indian song as he finished dressing up. He couldn't carry a tune to save his life, but my heart felt warm at his voice, like snuggling into a blanket on a cold winter evening.

I wore a black, embroidered, open-front, mid-length shirt adorned with bright ethnic buttons and chose nude heels to go with it; I added diamond studs to complete a formal look. Arsalan had gifted them to me the week before, and I loved them. When it came to money, he was a generous man, and that was one of the things I loved about him. It served to reassure me in moments of sheer unhappiness and frustration.

Sweat threatened to stain my underarms, so I moved in front of the air conditioning and lifted my arms. 'Honestly, Lahore is so hot.'

Without warning, I laughed out loud. This city made me feel like a misfit, almost like an imposter, and I wondered if I would ever truly belong somewhere.

'What are you laughing about?'

I stepped aside as he stood before the mirror, brushing his hair. 'An old joke,' I replied, smiling. If only he knew all that I thought of. I hoped we could get close enough one day, that he wouldn't even have to ask me what I was thinking. Not everything though. There were some things I didn't want him to know.

He turned towards me. '*Bachay so gaye?*'

'Yes. The kids are sleeping.' I was anticipating a compliment for all the hard work I had put into getting ready that night. I knew I looked lovely; black was my colour.

Hope was alive in my heart.

He walked over to the two-seater suede green sofa and started to put on his shoes.

'How do I look?' I finally asked.

'Great!' he replied without looking up as he continued to tie his shoelaces.

'Arsalan. *Aap ne dekha bhi nahin mujhe.* Look at me, please. Why can't you ever compliment me on your own?' I let out a sigh as I played with my ring finger. I knew I was complaining and sounding needy, but then I was needy.

He looked up at me, stood up, and rolled his eyes. 'Please grow up, Saniya. You always look pretty, so why must you hear it from me?'

At that moment, I wanted to pick up the ashtray on the table next to the bed and throw it at him. Without responding to him, I rushed out of the room, shocked at my violent impulse.

Because you're my husband, I wanted to scream at him. I went and sat in the living room and took a few deep breaths. I didn't know what was worse: stay and tell him how I felt, or walk away. Why could he not see that I needed him to see me? So many times, I had felt invisible to him, wronged. But like so many times, the fear that I would open my mouth and surrender to the overwhelming impulse within me to scream at him kept me silent. I hated fighting with Arsalan.

And walk away I did, like many other times in my married life and the life before, when I felt invisible, wronged, and so deeply hurt that I wished to vanish. Yet, he was blind to all the emotions that were so powerful and alive within me.

Anger was the only emotion that scared me. For the longest time, I had fooled myself into believing nothing made me angry, and anyone who knew me vouched for it. But for the last year or so, I had been forced to swallow my anger like a spoon of bitter medicine and make a conscious decision not to go down the road where I would end up experiencing the immense sadness that had accompanied the neglect of all these years with my husband. Years of almost no intimacy, his busy work, the occasional dinner where he was on his mobile phone unless I screamed in his face. So much loneliness. But now wasn't the time to go to that dark place that had become darker with each passing year, and if I wasn't careful, it could swallow me whole. I abruptly got up and slapped my cheeks with my hands. *It will be fine, Saniya. Try to have a good time tonight.*

I offered my most radiant smile to Arsalan as he entered the hall.

'Let's go, babe,' he announced, apparently not noticing that his ignorance had hurt me enough to leave the room. I sighed. Nothing new about that.

Not for the first time, I wondered if I was married to the patronising male of a few minutes ago or the smiling, caring man who just called out to me lovingly. Sometimes it felt like being married to two people. Did he care, however? Or had I just settled for his crumbs?

We were quiet on the way to our close friends Asma and Wasi's party. Wasi was a colleague at Arsalan's workplace, and they had known each other for many years. He and his wife married a year after we did but could not conceive children despite three rounds of IVF. My heart ached for my dear friend, Asma, who had so much love to offer and had to live with this painful reality every minute of her life. We had instantly connected, and now, many years later, we were a close-knit group that met almost every weekend. If the hubbies were travelling, we girls hung out on our own. *Girls! Why the hell not? Age is just a number,* or that's what I liked to tell myself.

Dinner was being served outside on Wasi's sprawling lawn with enough trees that it could pass as a rainforest, and even though it was a bit hot, the beautiful garden and the elaborate array of food made up for it. Little lanterns were hanging from the trees, creating an exotic ambiance. The smell of fresh BBQ being grilled filled my nostrils, and I looked up at the sky and realised it was a full moon. What a beautiful night. I grabbed a can of coke and moved to the corner of the garden where most couples sat. Some were sitting on the other side of the garden drinking from the bar. Some of them I knew, and some I had not met before.

I approached a young lady with a pretty face. 'Hi, I'm Saniya.' Her left eyebrow was pierced with something silver, and she wore bold red lipstick.

I had never seen anyone with a piercing before.

She got up and, to my surprise, hugged me before replying, 'I'm Rabia.'

'Are you friends of Asma or Wasi?'

'Both. Our husbands worked together.' I took a big gulp of my chilled drink, still reeling from a total stranger's spontaneous show of affection.

We instantly connected, and the conversation moved from the crazy traffic in Lahore to politics to upcoming dress designers, everything, and nothing. I didn't remember the last time I had such an engaging conversation.

'So are you...' It wasn't nice to ask if she was single or married, but my curiosity was piqued.

'Am I what?' She was smiling as she responded, almost teasing me.

I hesitated. I didn't want to offend her; somehow, it was always important that others were pleased with me.

'I'm single, babe.' She got up abruptly and lifted her arms in the air.

I bit my lip. 'I'm sorry. I didn't mean to offend you.' I didn't know what else to say.

'Come on... nothing offensive about it. Relax!' Shrugging her shoulders, she walked away.

Heat rose in my cheeks, and I took another sip of the bitter Coke. I looked around, hoping to catch Arsalan's eye.

You made her leave.

But I only asked a question... A faint protest.

You always end up pushing people away.

Do I? I did apologise.

You're sitting here alone, aren't you?

But I only...

Rabia unceremoniously plopped back on the chair.

'Hey. I'm back. My bladder was bursting.'

My eyes widened, and I felt the heat in my cheeks again. She didn't catch onto the surprise and relief I was experiencing. The conversation started again, and I made a mental note to be more careful about what to ask her. I liked her, and I wanted to stay in her good books. She was different, and right now, that's exactly what I needed.

As we continued to chat, I learnt that she was training to be a psychotherapist and had almost completed her degree.

'Intriguing,' I said.

Rabia beamed. 'Oh yes, it's an interesting line of work for sure.'

Unlike her, I had studied psychology only briefly at university. Although I had loved it, for some inexplicable reason I didn't remember, I did my master's in English. But my brief love affair with psychology left me pining for more. The human mind fascinated me with its conflicting thoughts, emotions, and behaviours it wanted to act upon.

I asked her more questions about where she was training, the fees, and other details and decided to talk to Arsalan that night. I wanted to explore the option of studying again. I was optimistic, an unrecognisable excitement about the possibility of something new, to read the next chapter in the book of my life that might be more interesting than the previous chapters that had kept me stuck, not allowing me to read on. I couldn't remember the last time I'd felt this adrenaline rush, an emotion that had been a long-lost friend I realised I missed. The last time I had been this excited was when I met Arsalan.

I got up to look for Arsalan. I wanted to be close to him, an impulse that sought the proximity of my husband.

He was standing with his friends. 'Haanji! Having fun?' He had already started dinner, perhaps the first to kick-start the buffet.

'Yes. Let me get my plate,' I replied as I checked out the night's offerings.

As I took small bites of the chicken rice and Russian salad, I thought of how to bring up the course with Arsalan.

He had always encouraged me to work, so there was nothing to worry about, but he could consider this as neglecting the children, and that was a cause for worry.

Stop overthinking.

'Earth to Saniya!'

I was startled as I heard Arsalan call out my name.

'Sorry,' I responded sheepishly.

He leant towards me and whispered, 'Let's go home.'

My heart skipped a beat, a familiar stirring in my body at this gesture. That was twice in one day. Hormones... slow down...

I hooked my arm in his, and after thanking our guests, we headed home.

Once we were back home and done with our night routines, which included getting water and kissing our sleeping children, we settled in bed.

Arsalan was playing Candy Crush on his phone, a virtual game that made no sense to me.

'It was a lovely dinner,' I said, putting cream on my feet and gently massaging them. They hurt like hell, thanks to the lovely heels I had worn.

'Yeah,' came the distracted response, his eyes glued to his phone screen.

It irritated me. I craved our time alone, and when we did get some, his needs always got in the way.

'Can you put your phone away?' I wanted his attention. 'I need to discuss something with you.'

No response.

Silence.

Such passion for a stupid game. Why did he ignore me so blatantly? It was so bloody dismissive. I clenched my fists. All those times in our married life when I had wanted the same passion from him, a look of desire, a touch that would consume his attention beyond anything else, came back to me. All those times I had been thwarted for something silly like a game. We should have been lovers, passionately intertwined like strings of yarn to make a warm scarf, and yet here we were… virtual strangers in bed.

I tried again. 'I have something important to discuss. There is a counselling course I want to do.'

'So do it,' he responded, without stopping the game or looking up. 'You do everything independently and now suddenly want my input?' He grunted out the words as if nothing mattered to him.

What the hell was wrong with him? Did I always have to beg for everything? I was seeing red now.

'Listen to me, please.' I touched his arm and softened my voice.

'Please take it easy, Saniya. I'm tired. We can talk tomorrow,' came the response as he continued to use his mobile.

'I want to talk about it,' I snapped in a high-pitched voice. 'Can you leave your phone, for God's sake.' I wanted to snatch the iPhone from his hand.

He finally looked up and put the phone away. 'What the fuck is wrong with you? Where is this coming from? Stop nagging me.' His face was red, the familiar aggression clear in his voice. It always came on quickly, like a hungry lion feigning sleep but waiting to be alerted to prey.

My heart was hammering in my chest, but I didn't want to back down today. 'You never have time for me. Never. Why do I have to ask for everything? Sex, your attention, your time, your care?'

'*Laanat hai tumhaare pe.* You have no shame whatsoever.' He turned around and looked at me, the veins on his neck bulging. The lion was fully awake now.

I had made a mistake, and I rubbed the tense muscles of my neck. But I still didn't want to back down. 'I need attention,' I cried out in a pleading tone. 'I need your time, Arsalan. Is that too much to ask?'

The question remained unanswered between us. My voice lost its last resolve; my heart was heavy as if a big slab of cement was sitting on my chest. It felt as if I couldn't move or breathe.

It wasn't the first time that I had lost my anger. Each time I connected to my anger as a child, teenager, or adult, something inexplicable got triggered; an alarm bell within me that started ringing loudly, screaming at me to lose the angry voice and frustration and hide in the corner again. Anger made me feel I would lose control, and that scared me no end.

When would the storm raging inside me be allowed to roar and howl? Something told me that this anger must have its way before I could find the place of stillness in me, the calm, the peace I had been searching for for a long time now...

'You are an ungrateful bitch,' Arsalan snarled, spit flying from his mouth.

'Don't swear at me.' My voice was almost a whisper. I was openly crying now, willing him to stop with tears that I didn't want to wipe.

'Cut this drama. You just need an excuse to be unhappy.' After slapping the phone hard on the table, he rose from the bed and started walking back and forth.

'That's not true. I don't find reasons to be unhappy.' I followed him in standing up, facing him, wringing my hands. Something drove me not to stand down, and I wanted to be heard. I wasn't willing to settle.

He came close to my face and, pointing a finger in my face, shouted, 'You ungrateful bitch. Last month I took you on holiday. This week I bought you those fucking earrings. Nothing makes you happy.'

'Please don't scream. We can discuss calmly,' I pleaded and touched his arm. 'I appreciate the gifts, but I want your attention too, Arsalan.' The more his voice rose, the more nervous I felt, hoping he could hear me begging for his love and care.

He slapped my hand away. He was sweating at this point, and I noticed he was breathing hard. 'Do you have any idea how much I tolerate about you?'

I took a step back. I had pushed too hard. My legs started to shake.

'I know I repeat a lot and interfere, but I'm working on it. Promise.'

'Shut up. Cut your drama.' He stabbed a finger on my forehead and slightly pushed me.

'Please stop. I'm not creating any drama. I just wanted your attention for a moment.' I thought I was going to faint. I walked over to the sofa, sat down, and started crying.

'Great. Now be a victim. I'm so sick of you.' He walked over and stood over me.

My heart was still racing. I hadn't realised he would be so severely triggered.

'The kids will wake up. Please, Arsalan.' I got up, deciding to leave the room, the only possible way this could stop. He never raised his voice in front of Nyle and Neha. I had just reached the door when I felt him behind me; his hand grabbed my arm, his grip firm and forceful.

'Now you're worried about the kids, *haraamzaadi!*' he roared. 'All you ever do is complain. You think anyone wants to touch a woman like you?' His face, voice, and touch all looked so scary now.

'I'm sorry. Please stop.' I was sure he was going to hit me. His face was inches away from mine. I looked at the floral painting behind him and prayed that he would stop. An apology mostly worked.

'Why can't you ever be happy? *Chutiya aurat.*' He put more pressure on my arm as his spit sprayed my face.

'You're hurting me; please let go of my arm.' I tried to pull away. 'I feel like I'm going to faint.'

'For the last time, cut your drama. *Insaan ki Bachi ban jaao!*' He shouted the last words in my ear before letting go of my arm. 'I can't share a room with you right now. You've ruined my entire day, and tomorrow I have such an important meeting.' He stormed out of the room, slamming the door so hard I could have bet the hinges had loosened.

I stayed rooted to the spot for I don't know how long. A short time later, I rushed to the bathroom and turned on the tap. As I rolled my sleeves up, an ugly bruise bloomed where he had held my arm. A fresh wave of tears filled my eyes, and I bent to wash my face. I hated crying.

What if he came back? I went back to the bedroom and put my ear to the door to see if he was outside in the living room.

How did a pleasant evening end in such ugliness? The aftermath of these fights left me numb, almost frozen. Unfeeling. Like victims of calamities, who are unsure if they can trust that the worst is over. Staying still lest they made a wrong move again. This wasn't the first time and wouldn't be the last. Four years and there had been countless such altercations where something trivial had progressed into screaming and verbal abuse. Today, physical abuse had been added to the list.

I consoled myself that he had never beat me in anger. *Be grateful. You have all the freedom in the world. You have a home, house help, and money.*

You asked for it, the voice continued in my head.

Did I ask for it because I grew up with a mother who hit me and hurled abuse at me whenever she wanted to? Didn't she also say the same things? 'Saniya, there is no other way to get through to you.'

Why was I so difficult? Why was I too much for others with my neediness, my call for attention, and my ungratefulness? Why did I ask for it? My mind would give me many reasons to be convinced of the reality my husband rubbed in my face, the reality of a demanding and difficult woman, but what about that timid voice deep down that defended me?

That timid, trembling voice protested that I didn't invite his anger and abuse. That I had been trying so hard to change over the years, to adjust my expectations according to his needs. And then, as these thoughts kept coming one after another, that faint-hearted voice gained some strength and spoke a little more loudly.

Look at all the changes you have brought in yourself. You no longer open his wallet without his permission. You don't tell him to drive the car slowly when it races so fast, even if you hold your seat tightly on the nerve-wracking car ride. You don't tell him not to stay out late with his friends. You don't send multiple text messages if he doesn't respond and annoy him with your distress.

I was no saint. I knew that. I knew I was controlling. Early in our marriage, I always needed to know where he was. I would panic if I didn't hear from him, imagining him lying dead in some ditch. I would endlessly seek his attention and resent his private time for himself.

Was that love? Or was it fear of ending up in my mother's home again? The thought alarmed me even as I thought of it now, at this very moment. I would look forward to seeing him after his business trips. I would miss his presence at night, being able to touch his feet with mine; that brief contact made me feel as if I had reached home after a long and tiresome journey. But slowly and gradually, I took his remarks seriously and worked on my behaviour.

It's asking that frustrates you, isn't it? the familiar voice challenged again. The voice became louder and louder a few months into the marriage.

No! Stop it! What if I ask?

But he never asks you. He forgets that you're there.

He's always busy; how can he remember me?

And Arsalan does remember me when I remind him, doesn't he?

But I knew, he mostly responded and hardly ever took the initiative. When we would be sitting in the living room, he would only look up when I called out his name and wanted to speak to him.

Aren't you tired? The annoying, persistent voice again.

No! I'm not. What is there to be tired of? That's how men are, didn't Ami say so?

Out of nowhere, a memory from my childhood popped up. I had reached out to my mother as she had held my sister in her lap, posing for Maheen's first birthday picture. I inched closer, moving my scrawny little body next to Ami, so I could feel some of her warmth and get comfort. She didn't open her arms to take me in the circle of that warmth. I waited. And I waited some more. And then I asked, 'Would you hug me too, Ami?'

No response.

She was trying to settle Maheen, who was fidgeting in her lap. She wanted to; she was just busy, I reassured myself.

'Ami,' I called out again, trying to pull at her arm now, and that was when she finally looked up, startled by the force, and then her arms opened up, and I had entered the little circle of her loving embrace. I was safe. This was home.

Haven't I mostly asked? I had to ask for love and attention, to be seen by her. Now, I had to ask for a compliment from my husband, a hug, a comforting hand, or simply for him to turn around and see me.

Why couldn't he ever see me? I knew I was pretty. I had charm, I spoke well, and any place I went, I did get attention, even when I wasn't begging for it. I made friends quickly. Shopkeepers offered me discounts. I did recognise something in me that drew attention and care and a special something that made it hard for people to turn away. A vulnerability, some pain that shone through, and a hint of helplessness made others want to rescue me. Yet, my loved ones ignored all that so effortlessly, almost callously.

I was constantly told how I should work on becoming a better version of myself.

Don't repeat. Don't control. Only call a few times at work. Wait to ask what time he will return.

And I had protested and questioned it but eventually stopped as the insults were hurled my way. For days, I would feel shaken and oddly ashamed, like I had committed a sin, but then, I wasn't allowed to be sad for long either and was called out! He was the saint, and I was the sinner.

Once I got pregnant, I had hoped our life would be more peaceful. One change that immediately took place was that we stopped having sex entirely. Arsalan said he feared that he would hurt the baby.

I immediately bought that explanation. It was a relief to know that there was a genuine reason for him saying no and that it wasn't because of me. I thought what a great father he would be, already being so protective.

If truth be told, I could never connect to my physical needs. Slowly and gradually, my body started to go numb, and the need for intimacy was more mental than sexual. I think I had desensitised myself to it and rationalszed my relationship's limitations. The year I was pregnant was a good one for the most part. I was given more care and allowance and I felt closer to Arsalan than ever before. He was patient for the most part, would fulfil my night cravings, and I would get an occasional back rub, too, if I asked enough. I would also occasionally think that we fought less because sex was no longer the cause of conflict and I should maybe let go of it entirely if it meant the abuse would stop.

But I was unable to accept it, and it was almost six months after childbirth before I asked my husband why we weren't intimate anymore, and like clockwork, excuses followed. Eventually, we resumed the joke that was called our marriage. By then, I had almost lost hope, and it was more like a task that I would fulfil by reaching out to him every few weeks. His excuse of being exhausted also failed, as even on our few holidays, he would always have some plausible reason.

I was happy to have a daughter when Neha was born but overwhelmed with caring for two kids despite having good help. Like me, Arsalan was busier than ever, and I would be snoring away when he returned home.

Now that the baby had just turned one, I felt I could change something about my relationship. The counselling course ignited new-found hope towards life.

Shame on you, I admonished myself for calling my life a dark tunnel.

How ungrateful you are! said the familiar bashing voice.

Sometimes it was as if my mother was talking to me. Did she not always say how ungrateful I was? That I was a brat, a rebel? And Maheen was the good one! The one who was comfortable holding onto Ami's dupatta or roaming around the house with her rag doll whose hair was messy and one eyeball had popped out of the socket.

This was my life. I was a happy mother but an unhappy wife and a lonely individual. I wanted to do something. Resume my teaching or a part-time job, to add more meaning to my life beyond taking care of the children and home.

Exhausted with the endless train of thoughts, I shook my head, trying to clear it, and went to the children's room to see if the noise had awakened them. My heart skipped when I saw a sliver of light from the guest room's door. I had hoped that he would be sleeping by now. It was always so hard for me to sit with this anxiety post-conflict, and, in most cases, I would impulsively act because the consequences of the action were more bearable than this knot in my stomach. In the children's room, I felt calm. I had always experienced safety in this room. Arsalan avoided fighting in front of the children, although they probably did hear the shouting and cursing. And because my babies were my happy place, an unexpected bright sun shone on a rainy, cold day. Their soft skin and warm hands distracted me from the coldness and sense of doom that was a permanent resident in the home with me.

The kids' room was decorated in shades of yellow and cream. There was a single bed for Nyle, with his favourite Lightning McQueen duvet cover, and next to the bed was Neha's cot, a white-coloured one made of pinewood. A pink cot mobile with little ballerinas hung over above, and soft music played. I never had a room of my own growing up, and moving from Baba's home to Nana's every weekend perpetually made me feel like I was homeless. There were hardly any toys for Maheen and me, and we were never spoilt. I wanted my kids to think that they belonged and owned their space. I wanted to spoil them rotten.

At that moment, the only sound in the room was the gentle snoring of my precious babies and the little louder one of Zubaida's that was oddly comforting.

She lay on a mattress in one corner of the room. Although I felt comfortable knowing she slept in the same room as the children, I still had a baby monitor, so if a slight sound came from either of the children, I would jump out of bed, operating on autopilot.

I read the 'Ayat al Kursi' on the children again, one of my favourite prayers, and even though I was tempted to wake them up and hug them tight, I settled with just looking at them. I didn't want them to have the childhood I had. I had never been able to count on my Ami or Baba when it came to sharing anything that bothered me. I was on my own. I wanted my babies to know that I had their back no matter what. But would it be enough to prevent the emotional scars they would have, witnessing the relationship their parents had? The last thing I wanted was for my children to feel as unsafe as I did, but somehow, the environment at home was turning into that. Would I be able to make good human beings out of them? I wondered what they made of the shouting and screaming that they heard. Were they damaged? I stood in their room for a minute longer and then, mustering all my courage, I struggled towards the guest room, each step carrying the weight of the last few hours, but I had to do it. It felt like walking through wet, dirty mud, where taking each step was an uphill task. I opened the door and found my husband on his phone.

No surprise there.

'May I come in?' I asked very softly. My hands were clammy. Could he hear my fast breathing or that I was on the verge of crying?

He didn't answer.

I waited. *Don't ask again.*

A few seconds, or many minutes passed, and he looked up from the phone.

'What do you want?' he said, irritated but not as angry as before.

That was all the cue I needed. I rushed over and lay down next to him, holding him tightly. A few seconds later, I felt his arms around me, and then I couldn't take it anymore. I started crying, sobs bursting out of my body; I pushed my face harder into his chest. 'I'm sorry.'

'Stop crying,' he gently replied, his arms still around me.

'Why do you want to fight? Why do you want to make yourself unhappy and us unhappy?'

I had no answer. After my crying subsided, I didn't want to move. I felt loved and safe. This was my husband; I needed to make sure he was happy; I made a stronger resolve in my heart. He was my home.

I could see how loving he was and how much he did to provide us with a good home. I needed to stop complaining. I had to practise more gratitude and stop trying to control the relationship. He was a man, and men got angrier than women. Ami used to say that all the time.

After a few minutes, I lifted my face from the corner of his neck and sat up. A long-forgotten stirring moved my body; I wanted him to kiss me.

'Let's go to our room,' I whispered.

'Nahin, let's just sleep here; the room is cold now,' he said, his voice drowsy.

'Theek hai. Let me go and switch off the lights in there.' When I came back, Arsalan was half asleep, the phone finally charging, and I no longer had to compete with an inanimate object for my husband's attention.

My voice trembled, but I tried again to discuss the course with him. 'There is a counselling diploma, a once-a-week class. Shall I join it?'

'Sure. When have I ever stopped you?' My caring husband, understanding as ever.

'Thank you.' *I am so lucky*, I thought. I needed to stop being so sensitive and overthinking everything. It was so simple, and I felt guilty for causing such a big argument over nothing. What else could a woman ask for?

Intimacy was just one part of marriage. Why make such a big deal out of it?

'It sounds fascinating. I could even become a therapist, you know.'

51

He laughed out loud. 'You're like a little child who starts believing everything. You haven't even started this course and you already see yourself as a therapist. It's not an easy year. *Tum to khud Pagal ho*, how will you treat other crazy people when you're crazy yourself?'

I ignored the familiar unease in my stomach.

Yeah, I was a dreamer. If I dreamed again and again, it could be real. I knew it could happen, and I mumbled as much under my breath.

Arsalan rolled away from me. 'Switch off the lights now. I'm exhausted.'

'Of course.' I was back to being the obedient and caring wife.

5   *Student*

'Nothing is exciting in my personal life,' I said, unable to make eye contact with my group members or the two tutors whose facial expressions questioned my statement's validity. I started to fumble with the open notebook in my lap. 'I mean it. There's hardly anything to say.' I wanted to sound convincing despite the slight quaver in my voice. It was my first class, and I was invited to express my feelings after everyone had had their turn. Little did they know that this was the last thing I wanted.

Joining this self-awareness class had turned me into a nervous wreck all day, and I had imagined all kinds of catastrophic events that would make me miss the evening class. What if the children fell sick or Arsalan got upset over something? Carrying that apprehension, I had planned everything for those four hours, from the evening meal to entertainment options for the children. Arsalan's mother was kind enough to offer to look after Neha and Nyle for the class duration.

'Will you be eating at home or Aunty's home?' I asked Arsalan as he was getting ready. He stood preening himself before the full-length mirror in our bedroom.

'I'll go to Amma straight from work and be there for dinner.' He started brushing his thick hair. Sometimes I ran my fingers through it, and he liked it.

'That's great. I won't be worried knowing you're there. Please do keep an eye on the kids.' I picked up the white chicken kari suit I had chosen to wear for the class and slipped it over my arms.

'You've already reminded me about that so stop repeating yourself.' He was frowning.

I mumbled a customary apology and, half-dressed, I leant forward and kissed him. The contact of my bare chest against his turned me on, but I ignored the tingling in my body and stepped away.

'Allah Hafiz.' Arsalan hugged me quickly and left the room.

I liked my reflection in the mirror once I was dressed. When I felt nervous, dressing up helped calm my jitters. The more worried I was about any challenging event, the more attention I would give to my physical appearance. Again, the world would see an immaculately dressed, attractive woman with a beaming smile, not the shaky person who was sure she would somehow make a fool of herself.

After marriage, I became more modern in my choice of clothes, finally free of Ami's conservative clutches. Arsalan allowed me to explore my sense of style. My in-laws were more progressive, and it was as if I could breathe under an open sky rather than being locked in a small wardrobe. That's what the years under Ami's roof had been like, especially when university started, and she became more rigid and controlling. A part of me appreciated Arsalan giving me space and the freedom to be however I wanted, which was liberating. But then another part of me wondered, if Arsalan loved me, why didn't he care enough to ask me why I hadn't returned by midnight after an evening out with friends?

I was putting the kids in the car when my mobile started ringing. It was Ami.

'Ji, Ami.' I picked up the call and buckled Nyle's seat. Neha was sleeping in Zubaida's lap.

'Busy ho?' she asked in a tone that I recognised too well. A tone that made my insides recoil.

Starting the car, while tapping my fingers on the steering wheel, I replied, 'About to drop the kids at Aunty's.' It was an obligation to answer Ami's calls, but it made me anxious and more so because they were unavoidable. I could predict the next line of questioning.

'Where are you going at this time?' The interrogation had begun.

'I start a weekly class today, Ami.' I put the key in the ignition and started reversing the car.

'Weekly class?'

'Ji, Ami,' I replied as patiently as I could, taking long, deep breaths. 'It's a self-awareness class.'

'How many hours? And what do you mean "self-awareness"?' she asked in a high-pitched voice.

'It's for around four hours. Aunty will look after the kids.' Could she not hear how irritated I was?

'Kids are too young. I don't understand why you do this.' There was accusation in her voice, and I rubbed my neck with one hand as I turned right onto Aunty's street.

'Please don't start. I don't have time to argue with you right now.' Lately, I reacted whenever she blamed me for everything she imagined I'd done wrong in life, and I didn't want to ruin my mood because of her. 'I need to go, Ami,' I said more calmly now, and ended the call without saying goodbye. We had almost reached our destination anyway.

'Mama, I want ice cream,' Nyle called out from the back seat, his little legs hitting my seat.

'Sure, baby. I will ask Dadi to get it for you. Stop kicking, though,' I scolded light-heartedly. Arsalan thought that I spoilt the children, and maybe he was right. I didn't want to be like my mother. Loving Nyle and Neha was all I wanted to do.

I was blessed to have such understanding in-laws. Aunty was encouraging and promised to look after the kids every week. I trusted Zubaida, but knowing Aunty was there allowed me to worry less during my class. Despite their support, I was initially assaulted by the guilt of abandoning Nyle and Neha to pursue my interest. And now that Ami knew, her constant berating of me for taking this course would add to the maternal guilt that felt like something born during childbirth that grew with time. The difference between Aunty and Ami was so stark. Where the former was warm, nurturing, and non-judgmental, the latter was like a military general whose only communication was to order what she thought was best for others. However, she was warm with Nyle and Neha and revealed a side of her that I hadn't been a beneficiary of as a daughter.

My mother, of course, played a critical role in my life. She was the villain in my story, getting more potent and malicious with time.

My mother ironically believed that a mother should always be available for her children, and if motherhood was not all-consuming for her, she was not fit to be a mother. Her hypocrisy baffled me.

Where were you, Ami, when I needed you? I don't remember you smiling at me. Why do you hate me?

I wasn't ready to answer those questions, even though I knew the answer, and neither could I ever imagine asking her these questions. I also couldn't wrap my head around her expectation that I connect with her daily – was she not be aware of the reality of our relationship?

'Look what other daughters do for their mothers. There's them, and then there's you,' she said to me more or less every day.

It infuriated me. Some days, I was unaffected. On others, I wanted to say something that would hurt her.

My mother. This one word was difficult to utter and even harder to internalise as a permanent part of my life. But she was my mother, and so, tied against my will by the bonds of blood, I would muster up any sense of calm I had in me to call her every day and ask her, 'How are you, Ami?' and then let her rant and give me unwelcome advice on all aspects of my life and how I could be a better Muslim and a better human being. She also reminded me that my chances of ending up in hell were very high unless I redeemed myself fast. She would be critical of the smallest of things, like me putting a photo on Facebook or spending an evening out with my girlfriends.

I would grudgingly visit Ami every week because not meeting her would invite melodrama and guilt-inducing shame that would almost convince me that I was a terrible daughter and had no justification for disliking Ami. I wish Maheen were living in Lahore. Maheen, my baby sister, and her five-year-old son, an adorable male version of my baby sister, wrapped me around their fingers. Especially Musa, whenever he called me 'Sano' Maasi, my heart would melt. It was strange to say it, but sometimes I thought he was more like a brother than a nephew. I had always wanted a brother throughout my childhood, with an enduring fantasy of him protecting me from the childhood I had. Was I unprotected, or had I made everything bigger in my head, and my lack of love and connection to Ami was my fault? Weren't all desi mothers like Ami – overinvolved in their married daughters' and sons' lives and offering unsolicited advice continuously? So why did I react the way I did? Why did I not miss Ami at all? I wasn't sure the reasons I gave myself were valid enough to justify the disobedient and unloving daughter I was.

Maheen was the bridge between us, and she was the appointed mediator when things got ugly or to the point of me blocking Ami for weeks on end. I hardly had any friends in the city, and I was perpetually hungry to talk to Maheen. Whenever we spoke, she shared her life story about her friends, her married life, etc. She was content, and I took heart from that. She had no idea about my battles, my marriage troubles, their origin, the complexity of my relationship, none of it, and I never wanted thst to change.

Never.

I reached Healing Matters half an hour before the class started, wanting to get a sense of the place before the students arrived. Having already missed the first two classes, I was nervous about making up for lost time. How would I catch up? I wish I'd known about this course earlier, but there was nothing to be done about that now. Healing Matters was a decade-old psychotherapy training and mental health services centre that offered a four-year programme that qualified one to become a psychotherapist. It was affiliated with the American Board of Psychotherapy; they designed all the coursework taught by locally trained therapists and visiting faculty for a few courses twice a year. The centre was in a commercial building with a sterile, cold vibe that added to my anxiety.

When I entered the classroom, a few students were already seated in the big room on chairs in a semicircle. There were two chairs at the head of the room.

'Hello,' I said to the two men chatting with a woman. They stopped and looked up from what looked like an animated conversation.

A bald man, in baggy pants and a floral half-tucked shirt, shook my hand. 'Hello. I'm Haris.' I found out later that he was in his mid-forties, divorced after fifteen years of marriage.

'I'm Saniya.' I smiled as I shook his warm, sweaty hand.

'Welcome. First class today, haan? Nervous?'

He talked fast, asking all sorts of questions, most of which I didn't manage to catch.

I smiled back, and replied, 'Ji. First day and yes, a little bit nervous.' I sat in his seat, and he took the empty one opposite me. Oh! I shouldn't have taken his seat, but it was too late. *So much for first impressions, Saniya.*

'This is Saqib.' He pointed towards a young guy in a white shirt and black blazer, with hair reaching his shoulders and freckles that covered his entire nose. He was busy on his phone and looked up at the greeting, momentarily distracted.

'He's a lawyer, so anytime you want to sue someone, that's your guy.' Haris laughed, reminding me a bit of Samuel L. Jackson.

I admired people who dared to laugh at their jokes, even the lame ones. *This is a friendly bunch*, I thought, my anxiety dissipating.

'And this is Aisha, the lady who brings us the yummiest homemade biscuits every Friday.'

Aisha laughed, and what beautiful, wholesome laughter it was. She was a short, slightly overweight young woman, perhaps in her late thirties.

'Yaar, there is more to me than just making biscuits.' I sensed a little edge in her tone. *'Tum ne to bawaarchi hi bana diya!* I'm more than a cook, you know.'

'Aisha, not *bawaarchi*, chef! You're a chef,' Haris clarified, laughing out loud, once again filling the silence in the room.

'Whatever. *Tomayto*, tomato!' she retorted with a scowl on her face.

'Don't be upset, yaar,' Haris added, leaning over and patting Aisha on her knee. 'Saniya, this young woman here is the mother of two teenage boys too. You happy now, Aisha?'

She looked so young. Unsure of how to respond, and judging by Aisha's scowl, I just politely smiled.

It didn't take long for me to realise that these people had a bond. They were close, and this banter between them was normal.

And so began the most profound journey of my life, and I couldn't wait from one Friday to another.

The class was divided into two parts. The theory was taught first, followed by group therapy, called the 'process'. In the latter half of the class, the 'process' was where the students talked about their issues. Listening to others' stories of trauma and loss made me apprehensive but curious too. There appeared to be an unsaid expectation, like the elephant in the room, that everyone must confess. Every time the process started, I would worry about being made to share pieces of my life. How could I ever do that? What if Ami found out? The tutors insisted that we maintain confidentiality, but saying that wasn't enough. My heart would start pounding; my palms would feel sweaty even when someone else was talking; and my legs would have this restless feeling, an overwhelming urge to get up and run out of the room. I feared it wouldn't be long before all heads in the room would turn towards me, and I would be forced to say something.

Share my secret.

The class had fourteen students: three men and eleven women; the gender inequality was loud and blaring in the room. There were two more stay-at-home mothers like me, one a single mother who had a part-time business and joined the class to find her feet in a chaotic world that could easily forget her. The diversity in the class was enriching, and we were unified by the scars not seen but felt. We wanted the chance to be heard and seen without judgment and sympathy.

And then there were the tutors. I remember the first day Ahad entered, wearing a worn-out pair of blue jeans and a plain black T-shirt. He was lanky, towering over 6ft, a bearded man in his mid-thirties with pale skin and short, dark, curly hair. He wasn't classically good-looking, but the kindness in his deep-set eyes evoked something in me. I mostly sat next to him, which made me feel safe from the prying eyes of my classmates.

I studied beforehand to ensure that I had answers to all the possible academic questions. I submitted my work on time. In many ways, I was still the kid in school who was scared of other children and found it safer to be the teacher's pet. I wanted him to admire me and always be on my team.

My other tutor, Maha, was also very loving and intelligent. She had a master's degree in counselling from Australia and had worked for a few years in New York before landing in Healing Matters.

Maha had a disarming smile on her heart-shaped face with small, light-green, wide-set eyes that glittered with intelligence. She had a very petite frame, almost fragile, yet her knowledge more than made up for this obvious delicateness. A lover of cats, we would often find her feeding stray cats during our break.

I looked up to her and respected her presence in the class, but whenever I got emotional, it was Ahad I fantasised about; Ahad whom I wanted to hold my hand. I was ashamed of this and how his presence dulled the gnawing ache in my tummy that hadn't left me alone for almost three decades. Ahad became the man of my fantasies who would hug and hold me. The first time I realised this, shame entered every cell in my body. I didn't attend class that week. It was difficult to imagine sitting before him, and I feared that he would find out what I thought of him. He was a therapist, wasn't he? I felt vulgar and ashamed. But I couldn't stop imagining his arms around me.

I remember how devastated I felt when he announced in class that he would be taking two weeks off.

During our break, I cornered him. He was holding his big blue coffee cup outside. 'You'll be back after two weeks, won't you?' I couldn't speak properly and stared at the plate in my hands with a lonely biscuit staring back at me.

'Of course. I'll be back by then.' He leant in as he said that and patted my arm.

Taking a small bite from the dark chocolate biscuit, I tried to behave as if this was all very casual. 'I was wondering, is all. That's all.' It was a wonder, though, that I managed to stand upright as my legs threatened to give way completely. In order to distract myself, I looked up, and that's when I saw him smiling, the skin around his eyes crinkling.

'I'm happy you cared enough to ask. I'll be back, I promise.'

'Thank you.' I smiled back, my face feeling hot. *Great. Now I'm blushing like a teenager.*

Those weeks were the beginning of a tumultuous journey. There was a growing attachment to Ahad, and the thought of seeing him every week kept me going. The distress in my marriage took a back seat for a while, and nothing mattered but my time at Healing Matters. Week after week, my classmates narrated their personal stories. Those stories were heart-wrenching to listen to. We grieved for lost relationships, endless emotional pain, and missed opportunities. I learnt about Saqib, for example, who was good as a lawyer but suffered from low self-esteem about how he looked. He told us how being a middle child made him feel invisible, and the same freckles that I found cute made him feel self-conscious of his face as friends in his teens had bullied him over them.

In one class, Aisha took the entire ninety minutes of the process session, sharing that she was sent to the Murree Convent at age six after her mother died in a road accident because it was a family tradition that all girls went to Convent. Although it was one of the best schools in the country and she had friends, she never recovered from leaving the safety of her home and seeing her father so rarely. It was as if she had lost both her parents in that accident.

In the process, she shared her sense of abandonment and how she suffered back then and later in life. She became overprotective of her children and clingy sometimes; she was now trying to process and understand this behaviour in the class.

Maha responded to that, saying, 'It almost feels like your maternal instinct sees your younger self in your children. You're afraid to let go of your inner wounded child.'

I was intrigued by that analysis. Did the past impact our present life choices? How does one undo the past, then? Could I change now?

Aisha expressed how she would get separation anxiety from her children. It was why she never worked, although she had a master's in economics. For her, this class was a massive step towards growth. Initially, she was anxious, constantly calling and checking on her thirteen-year-old twin boys. Her husband worked in a construction company in Dubai, and she lived in Lahore with her in-laws. I saw an anxious woman with a beautiful smile that reached everyone's heart but not her eyes. I saw two hazel-coloured eyes where now and then lonely tears would come up but somehow didn't have permission to spill over. She brought biscuits, samosas, rolls, and other things for all of us at tea break, and when we would eat all the scrumptious food and rave about her culinary skills, a rare smile would appear.

Before I knew it, one year had already passed, almost like a roller-coaster ride. The theory part excited me as much as the process scared me. All the theoretical ideas about boundaries, strong skills, and attachment patterns excited my mind, and I was curious to discover them. I was interested in exploring what that meant in my life. Did I have any boundaries with my family and friends? Was I passive or aggressive, and did I even know how to be assertive?

All of this was so new. It enhanced my self-awareness, but I was still left frustrated and helpless when I thought of Arsalan and how difficult it was to share this learning with him. I had started to hope, inspired by Maha and Ahad, that if we worked on ourselves, other people would also change. What did that even mean? How was that possible? I wanted to believe that changing myself would make Arsalan behave differently. The idea of my husband abadoning his screaming and shouting was as novel an idea as a nun going to a club. A part of me was excited to participate in this journey of inner work, but a much bigger part of me knew that some people never changed.

Process, or group therapy, provided a safe space for all the students to talk about their wounds, and it was a requirement to maintain the confidentiality of these sessions. It was our little world where anyone and everyone was encouraged to be congruent and give authentic feedback to each other – a place where pain, when expressed, was seen and held by others. I wasn't congruent though. It was upsetting to recognise that I was mostly dishonest with Arsalan and tried to be a version of myself that I thought he preferred.

One day, I would have a different, honest story to tell.

The process was particularly intense on the Friday of half-term, when we were only a few months away from the end of the course.

Saqib, the grouchy young lawyer, asked too many questions as Amna shared her conflict.

She was patient until she snapped, 'You're so intrusive. Why do you harass others with so many questions?' Her face was red, and she was frowning.

'I was asking out of concern,' he said, folding his arms across his chest.

'Concern? Is that how you show it, by interrogating? Crap!' Amna got up abruptly from her seat, her hands on her hips.

In almost a whisper, Ahad said to her, 'Sit down, Amna.' There was a pause for a few minutes where Amna looked at Ahad and sat down, letting out a breath that was audible to all.

Ahad turned in his seat and faced her directly. 'What's triggering you?'

Amna picked up her bottle from the floor beside her and started drinking water. A few minutes later, she replied in a brittle voice, 'He reminds me of my mother, Ahad. I feel I have to justify what I'm feeling. Do I have to give evidence of it?'

'Is it possible you're projecting some of your feelings for your mother onto him, Amna?'

'Maybe,' came an exhausted reply.

'How about you give Saqib the same feedback but in an assertive and non-aggressive way?'

There was silence in the class. Hot-headed Amna was bound to get upset. But surprisingly, she took the feedback well.

Amna turned towards Saqib and looked directly at him. 'I get overwhelmed when you ask so many questions, Saqib. I know you mean well, but could you allow me, and maybe others, to explore our feelings a bit more before answering questions?'

Saqib adjusted his thin, rimless glasses and responded softly, 'Fair enough. I'm sorry that you felt interrupted.'

I loved witnessing that, amazed at how the choice of words could evoke such a changed sentiment in people. Saqib took the feedback well, and Amna shared that she didn't feel guilty afterwards, unlike with her earlier direct and blunt response.

Something important I learnt was that, when commenting on someone or expressing something, it was essential to start with an 'I' rather than a 'you' because a 'you' would make people feel confronted and criticised. These were important realisations that I was learning. I felt like a child in a toy shop for the first time who could buy anything they liked. Those few hours were the most exciting time of the week, and I lived my life waiting from one class to another.

Every week when the process would start, Ahad or Maha would ask their customary question, 'Who would like to process?' Nervous and scared, it felt like someone from the group could get into my mind and heart and fish out all my secrets. I would stare down at my clenched hands and pretend that no one could see me if I couldn't see them. I believed Ahad understood that, and he would protect me from exposing myself.

But a time came when Maha put me on the spot and challenged me to talk about myself. I protested, saying my ordinary life needed no processing; my heart screamed and begged Ahad, my idealised protector, to step in and stop her. The unfaltering gaze of my classmates provided a pressure I hadn't felt before.

I was so uncomfortable, hoping to be magically transported from my classroom to somewhere else. Anywhere that didn't make me so uneasy. It was as if I was being forced to remove bandages that covered wounds that were still bleeding, with pus oozing out of them, and made to look at those wounds. I wasn't ready to show them to anyone.

Even though no one was forced to talk about themselves, the shared space of talking about our deepest, darkest emotions made me nervous. I often wanted to cry or scream, and neither option was acceptable. I wondered whose acceptance I was seeking.

I looked around at the group of familiar people, yet they all looked like strangers.

'I have nothing to share,' I repeated.

'Maybe you can tell us about your early years? Or tell us about your present life?' Maha pressed on.

'How are you feeling right now, Saniya?' Maryam, another lawyer in the class, asked, and it felt like an interrogation. She was a pretty, fair Pathan girl with light-blue eyes and a shoulder-length mass of ebony permed hair. She hardly smiled, but it lit up her entire face when she did.

Who the hell was she to ask me such a big question so casually? Did she have any idea what she just asked? Could she not see that I died a thousand deaths in less than a minute as she blurted out that question while chewing gum? What kind of group therapy was this? It felt like wounds were ripped open and left to bleed.

'I have one younger sister,' I said in a measured voice. 'I had a happy childhood and am now happily married for almost five years. I have a son and daughter, and I can't thank Allah enough for his blessings.' My palms were sweaty, and I wanted to wipe them dry on the sofa chair I was sitting on. I didn't do it. *Please don't move. Don't blink. Let them buy this truth and wait. Wait for them to move on.* I'd overused the word 'happy'.

'Seems like you have a perfect life, Saniya.' Maha leant towards me with a knowing smile. 'Tell me what makes you sad?'

I was paralysed. Maybe for less than a minute, but it seemed like forever. The eyes of my classmates bore holes in me, multiple drills going through my heart, into my soul: so much blood, so much pain, so much chaos, and confusion. I looked at Ahad and quickly looked away. He knew. He always did.

'I know you're scared. I know you're terrified, but you can let us in. Just get up and open the door.' His soft voice pierced through the fuzzy feeling in my head.

Ahad's gentle voice shook me out of my comatose state. My eyes were wet before I could stop them, rebellious tears falling from my eyes. I sobbed loudly, shocking myself, and looked up at him. It was terrifying as I found myself shaking. My mind and body had their own will, and I couldn't stop them from rebelling against me. Somehow, all my deeply buried secrets were about to be yanked out of me with a crowbar. How would I face the shame of it all? No one would talk to me again. Some would feel sorry for me. Some would judge me. They would no longer be able to see the smiling, well-put-together woman but a mass of broken, ugly pieces, disintegrating and falling all over the floor. I felt like a fancy wine glass slammed against the wall and shattered into countless pieces.

A gentle hand patting my arm. 'Take a tissue,' a comforting female voice called.

I had no idea who this was; that thought was followed by anger. I picked up the tissue box and unthinkingly threw it in the air and ran out of the room. My notebook fell on the floor. I didn't stop to see if the forceful throw of that tissue box had hit someone. Somehow that box of tissues made my tears real. That gentle hand made me feel weak, and I hated being weak. I was strong. Isn't that what was expected of me? So why change that now?

I dashed straight to the bathroom and quickly locked the door behind me, fearing that someone would follow and make me cry again and talk and expose it all. *No, I won't let them. I won't.* I could never tell a living soul about Ami. How could anyone think that I could share that secret? I was ashamed to be Ami's daughter. And Arsalan calling me a bitch and a whore weren't honorary titles that had to be shared. And why was I obliged to share because everyone else was? No. It was my choice, and dammit, others couldn't control me.

Dropping to the bathroom floor, loud sobs followed; this moment was heavy and overwhelming. I covered my mouth tightly with my hands and ran the basin tap so that the sound of running water could drown out the sound of my mourning.

Grief. That's what I felt. That's what I always felt. As if someone close to me, someone within me, had died. It had always felt like the death of a moment, a relationship, love, a lifetime.

Sitting on that bathroom floor, I didn't know what was coming.

6   *Little Girl*

The birthday party ended differently from how it had started. I could hear the sound of laughter and sniggering coming from the room next to Nana's. It was a small room, the size of a storeroom, that Nana had converted into a playroom for Maheen and me. It was my favourite room in his house, with its bright pink walls, oversized cushions on the floor, and a few toys and books that mostly Nana had bought us. I loved lying on the cushions and reading for as long as Ami allowed me to while Maheen played with toys.

'Open the door,' I yelled, hoping my voice could be heard above the shrieking as I tried the door handle. 'Ami has told us rooms cannot be locked, Maheen.'

When there was no answer, I started knocking.

The giggling continued, which made me knock even harder, even though I was half smiling. Maheen was my reason to smile every day, like the daily cartoons she and I watched whilst finishing our breakfast before going to school. Even when they were on repeat, they still invoked spontaneous bouts of laughter from both of us. She was only four years younger than me, but I was very protective of her. There was an unspoken rule in the house: Maheen had to be looked after at all costs – the precious baby of the family.

It was Maheen's seventh birthday, and she had invited a few of her school friends. I had been allowed to invite a friend, and

Sara – my bestie – had promised she would come but had yet to arrive. Sara and I had been together since nursery school, and Ami and Baba knew her parents well. She had two older brothers and was fiercely loved and protected by them, and her dad was a policeman... a fact that continued to amaze me. Police officers were real-life heroes. They were powerful and saved lives, weren't they? Uncle Azhar looked scary and strict until he smiled, and what a radiant smile he had. It reminded me of the rainbow that appeared after a rainy day. But his smile and seeing Sara running into his open arms made me want to cry hard. Why did it make me want to cry? Why did my tummy hurt when I saw Sara and Uncle together? My mind was overflowing with more questions than answers almost all the time. If only there was an on/off switch...

Baba, in his white doctor's coat, made me proud too, but he wasn't as strong as Uncle Azhar. He would let me play with the stethoscope hanging from his neck for hours, and secretly, I wished I could become a doctor like him. But he studied such big, thick books. I tried picking one of them up once, and it was heavy, so hard. How could one learn everything inside?

Maheen refused to open the door, so I went into the garden, where there was lots of space to explore and look for hidden clues and secrets.

Secrets. I hated them, especially my secrets. But I loved adventures, yes. Sometimes I would climb a big old tree in the back garden and stay there for almost an hour, reading my favourite novels that Baba bought me once a month from the cute little bookshop in Main Market. It was my happiest memory. The front garden had a big apple tree, and Maheen and I loved when it was ripe with juicy apples that we would pick from the ground, and Ami would make apple jelly for us. Ami cooked yummy things for both of us, and that's why I knew she loved me. There were small hiding corners where Sara and I played hide-and-seek when she was visiting me. Oh, that was a happy memory too. Maybe I only thought of the sad things, which is why I was always sad.

The few adults who were invited were all busy chatting with each other. A few of Ami and Baba's friends were invited as well as the family. I rubbed my bare arms in the simple cotton T-shirt I was wearing for that evening and looked down at my naked feet in my sandals. I needed socks or maybe a cotton jumper. Autumn had arrived earlier than the year before. There was a big bouncy castle that had been pre-ordered for the party. At the moment, it was unused and reminded me of the new girl in a school everyone else was initially wary of being friends with. The seat next to Nana was empty, so I sat on the white plastic chair. I wished Sara would turn up to make the party more fun. I needed a familiar face in this little crowd.

Maheen came rushing out a few minutes later, followed by her friends. It was crazy after that as the girls jumped onto the bouncy castle, and shrieks and screams followed. The screaming seemed like a ritual all children had to perform, whether there was an actual need or not.

'Beti, you go and play too.' Nana nudged me, pushing me towards it.

'Nana… but it's for little girls… not for me,' I protested. No way was I going to be found in the proximity of easily excitable screaming seven-year-olds. I was tempted to surround myself with their infectious energy, but at eleven, it seemed like too frivolous a thing to do. I didn't feel I was eleven anyway. Was I not already reading books that my neighbour Hajira Apa, who was at university, was reading? That's why my creative writing skills and vocabulary were good. I already used big words that other children my age didn't understand half the time.

Nana didn't ask again and turned his chair towards the children, smiling as he smoked his pipe with his big hands. I believed Nana loved Maheen more than me, but then everyone loved her more. Even I loved my baby sister more than I loved myself.

Baba was busy talking to his friends while Ami was laying the plates and glasses on the table, being helped by Uzair Uncle, who passed her the paper plates and cutlery. Seeing them made me want to throw up, so I looked away.

However, I couldn't ignore the fact that I was starving, not knowing when the cake would be cut and the pizza served. I walked towards the kitchen. It was almost 4:00pm, and I hadn't eaten lunch. Had I even had breakfast?

No one was in the kitchen, but food ready to be served was on the counter. There were sandwiches and burgers, chips, and more. I was about to grab a burger when the tiny cupcakes on Ami's favourite white serving plate on the top shelf caught my eye. My sweet tooth could not be distracted by anything savoury now. Cupcakes, it would be.

I grabbed the little stool in the kitchen corner and moved it closer to the shelf. It was an old kitchen with straight shelves and counters that screamed of decades of neglect. I didn't remember Nani, as she had died before I was born, but I had heard from my aunt that the house was well maintained when she was alive. After her death, the neglect started, and Ami and her only sibling Hafsa Khala could not keep up with Nani's living standards. The kitchen and the rest of the house were a testament to that.

I missed my aunt, whom I hardly saw now that she was married.

Making a solid resolve that I would take only one cupcake, I climbed the red stool. No one would have to find out. The pink cupcake was calling out to me. 'Eat me, Saniya, eat me', and a little giggle burst out. I quickly covered my mouth so that no one would hear me. Getting caught was the last thing I wanted while my stomach was grumbling. So often, I laughed at my jokes. But they were funny. I knew I was funny because my friends told me so.

Pink was my favourite colour, and the chocolate cupcake topped with its pink cream frosting and little silver edible balls on was all I wanted. There were twelve cupcakes in a perfect circle on the fancy white plate Ami had told me was Nani's and which was considered a family heirloom passed on by Ami's grandmother. I could never understand the value people attached to things and not human beings. There was so much I didn't understand, but I wanted to.

Without thinking, I shifted my weight on one leg while deciding on which cupcake to choose and the stool wobbled. I grabbed the shelf for balance. There was a loud crash, and to my horror, the cupcakes were lying unceremoniously on the floor. Oh God! I grabbed the plate instead of the shelf to catch my balance. My legs started to shake. I was going to fall from the stool. Without a moment's delay, I climbed down. I was rooted to the spot as I looked at the spoilt cupcakes.

What should I do? Should I dump them in the bin with the broken plate, or should I run for it and deny all charges? I started to cry, feeling increasingly scared, when I heard her footsteps. *No, Allah Mian, don't let that be Ami*, but it was. There was no place to hide.

I could always tell it was Ami from her footsteps and the familiar tapping of the wedges she always wore at home.

'What is this?' she screamed as she entered the kitchen, and before I could say anything, I got a slap on my face – another one followed on my head, and another. I cried loudly as I tried to free my arm from her grasp. There wasn't even a moment's pause as she continued hitting.

'I'm sorry... I was hungry, Ami...' I was stammering, my legs trembling, and I knew any minute I would fall down.

'*Haraamzaadi!* Do you always have to ruin everything?'

I tried to get away, but she punched me in the back.

'Please, Ami, stop!' A few more slaps landed on my face and head; it wasn't stopping. 'I'm sorry, please, *Maaf ker dein.*' A drop of pee came out, and I quickly pressed my legs together. That's the last thing I wanted, to pee in my pants and invite more of her beating.

Suddenly Baba turned up at the door as she raised her hand again.

'*Maar do gi kiya iss ko?*' Baba shouted and pulled me from Ami's grasp. 'Are you trying to kill her?'

'Look at what she's done!' She grabbed the broken pieces of the plate and threw them hard on the shelf.

'I'm sorry, Ami… I…' What else could I say?

'Go to your room, Saniya!' Baba ordered, cutting me short.

Hold me, Baba, I silently begged him as heaving sobs wracked out of me. I was hurting all over.

'Did you not hear me? Go, clean up,' he repeated, his voice sterner and louder now. Baba had never raised his hand against me, but who knew when he would follow Ami's lead. I believed Ami could make him do anything and he would hit me one day.

I turned around and ran towards my room next to Nana's. I locked the door behind me and threw myself on the bed as heavy sobs rocked my body. Every part of me was crying with pain; even those that Ami had not hurt.

Baba's rescue had left me feeling more unprotected than ever – never a hug, a loving touch, or words of comfort. Just an order like an army officer, cold and matter of fact. *Go to your room, Saniya.*

He would ask Ami to stop and me to disappear, a neutral mediator between a mother and daughter. Should he not be fair and pick a side sometimes? Fathers were meant to protect us, whereas Baba was just submissive and went along with whatever Ami decided for us. Yes, he mostly stopped her from hitting me, but was that enough? Why did he not question her, or even better, make her stop completely? And to add insult to injury, he never bothered to check up on me later. I'm sure he assumed it was my fault, and making Ami stop temporarily was enough.

It's enough, Baba. I want to be picked up in your arms and held, and I never want to be scared.

After a few minutes I sat up and looked around at the dull, white-washed room with high ceilings, a simple bed, and two dilapidated side tables. The only attraction in the room was the big window behind the bedpost that overlooked Nana's big back garden, with at least two or three stray cats roaming around at any given time.

For a long time, Ami sent me to sleep downstairs in this ugly room with Maheen, while she slept upstairs. I hated it! Why did she send me here? Why would she leave both of us alone downstairs whilst she was alone upstairs?

A fresh wave of panic gripped me as a memory popped up. In the middle of the night, a nightmare, a walk up the stairs, light under her door, but Ami not in the room. Ami was not in her room.

No! Nothing! Nothing! Don't go there, Saniya.

I lay down again and covered myself with the thin, faded blanket, hiding entirely underneath it. I cried for a long time and eventually dozed off. A loud bang on the door rudely woke me up sometime later. Shocked, I sat up, my heart pounding. What time was it? There were faint voices outside.

Oh, how much had I slept? A maximum of a few minutes? My breathing quickened as I heard the loud banging again and Ami's impatient voice.

'Open the door, Saniya! How often have I told you, you cannot lock the door.'

With trembling legs, I quickly rushed to open the door. I bit into my lip and replied in a whisper, 'I'm sorry. I didn't realise I'd locked it, and then I fell asleep. I'm sorry.' I retreated inside.

'Come outside. We're about to cut the cake,' she replied with an exasperated sigh; her eyes were narrowed. 'Wash your face first. *Kia halat banayi hui hai.*' She wrinkled her nose and left the room.

'Ji!' came my meek reply. I must have smelt. She wouldn't have hugged me anyway, so no surprise there. Not a loving touch. Nothing. As if nothing had happened.

My head hurts, Ami. My face is still burning; my chest is so heavy, Ami. It feels like there are rocks in my chest. Hold me, would you? I want to hide in your arms like Maheen does when she's upset. I want you to wipe my tears and tell me you love me. You do love me, don't you, Ami? I read somewhere that all mothers love their children, so I know you love me too. Why won't you show it then? You get angry with me over everything and nothing. Do you wish I hadn't been born?

Stop, Saniya! These thoughts were making my tummy hurt. I rushed to the bathroom and started washing my face, my hands frenzied as I kept throwing water on my face. I picked up the comb on the shelf and tried to untangle my messy hair.

'Ouch!' I cried as the comb brushed against my scalp.

That was where Ami had slapped me, again and again and again.

Tears welled up in my eyes again as I winced at the pain, but I pushed them down. I slammed the comb hard on the basin. No more crying.

Crying was for the weak. I'd heard Sara's dad saying that many times. Sometimes the crying made Ami hit me more. I couldn't let her see I was weak; for some odd reason, she was less angry when I was angry. I needed my anger; it was the only weapon I had that made me feel less helpless in my life, even if that weapon was a cap gun that didn't shoot bullets.

I hated Ami. She was the worst human being on the face of this earth. Worse than Uncle Uzair; they could have a competition with each other as to which one of them I hated more. I picked up the comb and tried to brush my matted and messy hair once again, finally managing to look presentable. My white T-shirt was crumpled, but this wasn't the time to ask Ami to fetch me something new from the suitcase upstairs. I wondered why she didn't leave any clothes at Nana's house. My head and back hurt, and I could feel Ami's fingers biting into my scrawny arms. I changed my underwear which showed signs of the earlier pee accident and opened the door slightly to check if anyone was outside. The hallway was empty. The last thing I wanted was for someone to discover what had transpired here. Ami never shied away from scolding or hitting in front of other people, but I didn't want to be embarrassed today in front of Maheen's friends. It was too much. I wiped away the disobedient tears and rubbed my hands on the new black jeans Hafsa Khala had sent from Dubai.

Nana's home was built over a large plot of land, but it wasn't a very big house. I slowly walked out once again. The sound of laughter from outside betrayed what had happened. Everyone looked happy. I prayed and hoped that Ami hadn't told them.

She was putting candles on the chocolate cake on the table as Uncle Uzair stood beside her, handing her the candles individually. I looked away. She should ask Baba to help her. Did she not love Baba anymore? Baba was becoming so fat. Maybe that was why. Then she should do it herself, and Uncle Uzair needed to leave her alone. It really annoyed me! I looked around quickly, feeling the heat rising in my cheeks. No one could read my mind, could they?

Wanting to be close to Baba, I found him smoking away, silent as always. He hardly ever talked, but Uzair Uncle talked a lot and laughed a lot too. Why could he not see that he needed to take care of himself and look smart like Uzair Uncle?

He was so handsome. His black hair reminded me of a TV actor's; I thought hard, but the name didn't come to me.

I was biting my lips again; the taste of blood felt yucky. I needed to stop.

Nana was in his usual place, in the middle, surrounded by people. He was always smiling, sometimes even when he was sleeping.

The screams from the bouncy castle diverted my attention; the little girls were happily jumping and falling without a care in the world. How lucky they were. Maheen was adorable, laughing away along with four of her friends. *Allah Mian, please always make her smile and laugh like this. Don't let her know... don't let her...*

I approached Baba and stood beside him as close as I could. He was staring at something, and I followed his gaze, but nothing was there.

When I was little, I would run towards Ami, and she would raise her hand and say, '*Peechay hatto.*' Did Ami do it deliberately, or was it a thoughtless action? I wanted to believe it was the latter. I sometimes cried, but I stopped running towards her at some point. I couldn't remember when Ami hugged or kissed me last, but I would find her hugging Maheen.

Many nights I stayed up trying to think of reasons for her not liking me. I wasn't a naughty kid. I did well in school and hardly got in her face. Did I not say yes, Ami, and did most of the things she asked me to do? I got her water whenever she asked, and I looked after Maheen. Other mums got angry, but did they hit their children like Ami? There must have been something wrong with me. There must. She said I never listened to her; God knows I'd tried. I had to try harder.

And then there was Nana, who might not hold me in his lap like he held Maheen, but he loved me. I knew that, and if I did hug him, he always kissed my forehead. I needed that today, but somehow, I couldn't hug him.

Why was life so hard?

After what felt like hours, food was served, and the cake was cut. Starving, I cut myself a big piece and went and sat as far away as I could from Ami's prying eyes. I turned my chair around, facing the bouncy castle, so my back was towards all the adults. Maheen and her friends were back, carelessly bouncing away, with no sign of exhaustion. Was I as happy when I'd been her age? I didn't remember. Was I happy now?

After everyone had left, the noise of a heated argument from the hall caught my attention. I was in the TV room lying on the sofa and could hear Ami and Baba arguing while Maheen was sleeping.

'Take Saniya with you,' she told Baba, who was returning home.

'Why? Keep her here with Maheen,' he argued. 'You need to be less strict with her.'

'*Kia Matlab?* Please stop telling me how to be her mother. Can you not see how difficult she is becoming, and you're telling me to be less strict?'

Baba gave up and left, which made me anxious. I wished we'd left with him or he'd stayed back. I'd changed into my pyjamas, the ones with the cartoon characters all over. I had no choice. But I was eleven. And I shouldn't have had to wear something so childish.

Uncle Uzair came out of Nana's room and sat beside me on the big sofa facing the TV. 'Give me the remote,' he asked nicely. I handed it over silently. I wasn't watching anything anyway.

He switched on the TV and called out to Ami, standing in the doorway. 'Come and rest.'

How long had she been standing there? I sat at the far end of the sofa, waiting for Ami's reply. *Go to sleep, please, Ami*, I thought, playing with my hair. I wanted to get up and leave the room, yet I also wanted to stay. I wouldn't say I liked this moment; there were so many of them now. Moments of something I didn't have the words to describe.

Ami stood at the door for a few minutes with a big smile that was as rare as Maheen and I getting ice cream before bedtime.

'Okay, sir,' she said, and came and sat down between Uncle Uzair and me. Her hair was down, and she looked pretty, unlike when she wore her usual angry bun. Her voice was different from how she had been talking to Baba.

I stared at the TV screen. I couldn't breathe. Why wasn't she sitting on the other sofa in the room?

'Tired?' he asked her softly, but I could hear him. I kept staring at the TV where a random advertisement was playing. Was it a sports product ad? My hands were cold. I could not move. Ami was sitting too close to him. I closed my eyes. Should I leave the room? No, I needed to stay.

'Haan, Uzi! Long day,' she responded, leaning her head back on the sofa, and from the corner of my eye, I could see her head touching his shoulder.

I closed my eyes. I swallowed hard and tried opening my mouth to say something to distract Ami, but it was as if someone was choking me. I needed to stop this.

Don't, Saniya. Don't say a word.

I was going to scream. I turned my head and saw that her eyes were closed. Her head was resting completely on his shoulder now, and Uncle Uzair was texting on his phone. Unable to hold in the urge anymore, I sat up and almost screamed.

'Ami!'

She instantly opened her eyes and sat up. Her face was red, just like Maheen's when she was caught with her hand in the biscuit tin. 'What is wrong with you? Stop screaming.' She fixed her dupatta and turned towards me. 'Why are you here? I mean why are you up?' She had a tight-lipped smile, but her voice was soft.

Now she remembered that I was here.

'Are you hungry? Did you eat anything?' she asked, gently touching my arm. Who was this woman? The one who hit me day in day out, the woman who disappeared in the middle of the night, or the one who was talking to me like mums usually talked to their kids? So, she did know how to be a mother.

'Ji, Ami. I did.' I didn't want to see how closely she was sitting next to Uzair Uncle, her leg touching his. They never sat like this when Baba or Nana was around. My tummy had started to hurt.

I was old enough to know now that there was something wrong with how Uncle Uzair and Ami were with each other, but I didn't have a name for it. It was confusing.

'Go and sleep then. Why are you still here?' Her tone changed, as if she'd read my thoughts.

'I don't want to sleep.'

'I'm not asking you. Get up right now. You have school tomorrow,' she ordered.

'You want to go up in five minutes, Saniya?' Uncle Uzair asked.

I got up. I didn't want to answer him. I hated him. I didn't want any favours from him. I hated him when he gave me chocolates, hugged me, or sometimes picked me up from school with Ami sitting next to him, and I hated him now as her legs almost touched his. *Why are you still sitting there, Uncle Uzair? Get up and take some other seat.*

I stormed into the guest room. Maheen was already asleep, with the blanket I had used earlier covering her body. I didn't want to brush my teeth, so very slowly, leaving the door ajar, I went and lay down next to Maheen, holding her body. I touched her tiny feet with mine and closed my eyes. This felt good. Safe. Rubbing my eyes, I suppressed a yawn.

I don't know how long I'd slept for when loud laughter rudely woke me up. Had I even slept at all? I pulled Maheen closer to me as I stared into space. Was Ami laughing? No, it was Uncle Uzair's deep laugh. I kissed Maheen on her cheek and sat up. What now? I switched on the bedside lamp to check the time. It was midnight. I ran my fingers through my messy hair before walking over to the door to place my ear against it. There was some noise, but I wasn't sure what it was.

I had to do something to stop it. *Stop what?* I asked myself, but I didn't have an answer. I knew I didn't want Ami to be alone with Uncle Uzair. I got up, left the room, and immediately turned around.

Uncle Uzair's arms were around her, and he was leaning into her and speaking softly; her hand was on his chest and her face cuddled into his neck. This was scary, and I immediately turned around and shut the bedroom door loudly.

What to do now? After a few seconds, I opened the door again.

Ami was sitting up, and she turned towards me. She was scowling, but I didn't care at this point.

'Why were you making so much noise? What's the problem?' Uncle Uzair turned towards the TV that was switched off.

I wasn't scared. 'I'm hungry.'

'But you just said you ate. Why can't you ever let me rest?'

'I'm thirsty, too,' I protested.

'*Dafa ho!* Go get a drink from the kitchen.'

Slowly, taking small steps, I walked towards the kitchen. She followed me and I wondered if she would start hitting me again. I found that I didn't care.

I removed the water bottle from the fridge and poured it into the glass she handed me from the shelf. I poured the water slowly, taking as much time as possible. She was tapping her fingers on the kitchen counter.

'More please,' I requested.

She poured me some more, her pretty face starting to change colour.

I wasn't scared.

As long as she stayed here with me, I wasn't scared. She could hit me if she liked. As long as she was here, I could breathe.

'I want to eat something.'

'Why didn't you eat when everyone else was eating?' she asked loudly and turned towards the fridge, taking out the rest of the cake left from the birthday and slamming the plate hard on the kitchen counter.

'I did eat then. But I'm so hungry I can't sleep.'

My stomach was full of something that almost made me feel like throwing up, but I would eat the cake. I had to eat the cake.

I ate little bites from the large piece she had cut out for me. If only I could keep her with me for longer.

'Where will you sleep, Ami?' I didn't want to hear the answer. 'Please sleep with me today.'

'Stop being a baby. Even Maheen doesn't ask me that now. Hurry up, would you?' she said, her fingernails tapping the kitchen counter again. She had pretty hands.

Before I could take the last bite, she pulled the plate away and ordered me to go to my room.

How was I supposed to stop it? But what was I stopping?

I walked out and didn't look towards the lounge where Uncle Uzair was sitting. Waiting. Why was he waiting? *Don't ask that question when you don't have the courage to know the answer.*

I knew they weren't watching TV. *Stop!* A fresh wave of nausea hit me, and I swallowed hard. Ami followed me to my room.

'Don't get up now. I am warning you,' she said and slammed the door hard. I ran towards the bed and closed my eyes.

Why could I not stop her? Why could I never stop her? I had to stop her for Maheen's sake. For Baba's sake.

My stomach was hurting as if a big tight ball had been placed inside my body, like the red one Sara's brothers played cricket with.

What was Ami doing upstairs? It was all Baba's fault. He should have been here on weekends with his family instead of dumping us at Nana's all the time. He hardly had time for us or Ami in the week, and the moment he was free, he rushed over to the village where Dada and Dadi lived. I know Baba missed his parents, but then why couldn't he take us with him? Something told me that Ami didn't like them. I had once heard her call them *paindu* and old-fashioned.

The following day when I woke up, Maheen was not in the room. I got up and, half asleep, stepped out of the room. She was in the TV room having a glass of milk in her favourite Barbie cup and watching Donald Duck cartoons.

Where was Ami? Suddenly I remembered I had school today. She wasn't in the kitchen. I knew where she was but wanted to go elsewhere.

I was thinking about what to do next when I saw her descending the stairs. She was smiling, and Uncle Uzair was behind her. He suddenly pushed her onto the stairs and held her arm when she was about to fall forward.

'Uzi! *Batameez!*' she cried, before laughing. How pretty she looked when she laughed. *Who was this woman?*

She stopped as she saw me looking at her. For a moment, everything stopped. In that little moment where we looked at each other, we saw each other. That's all. We saw each other.

'Go get ready for school!'

'Where is my uniform?' I asked, feeling the sudden urge to scream.

'It's where it always is, Sano,' she curtly replied. 'Go check the wardrobe; I'm getting your breakfast ready.'

'Uzair, please call Chacha inside,' she requested Uncle Uzair.

'Yes, ma'am.' He bowed, which made Ami smile. Why did Nana sleep so late? He needed to keep an eye on things happening in his home, I thought, frowning.

I picked up my cereal bowl and sat in the TV room too. Uncle Uzair walked in, picked up Maheen and started tickling her.

'Whose baby are you?' he asked.

'Ami's!' she shrieked.

He started tickling her more and repeated the question. 'Whose baby are you?'

Maheen started shrieking with laughter. 'Ami and Uncle Uziiii's.'

He stopped then and hugged her.

I hated him. Why did Maheen call him that? She didn't like him when he hugged her. She didn't like how happy Ami looked when he did that. He suddenly saw me.

'Saniya, are you ready, beta?'

I didn't reply and quickly gulped the milk down, got ready and went to sit in the car, waiting for Ami. There was a time when I loved going out with Uncle Uzair. I loved when he tickled me too, but then it all changed. She changed. He changed. Everything changed.

Nazeer Chacha, Nana's old driver, was waiting in the driveway. With his white beard and red shalwar kameez, he looked like Father Christmas to me. I wanted to go inside and ask Ami why she wasn't coming to drop me at school.

Forget it. Just leave.

School wasn't the same when we stayed at Nana's home. I would be worried all day, my thoughts on Ami and Uncle Uzair. Were they together? What were they doing? A part of me wanted to keep an eye on them and another never wanted to know what was happening between them. I didn't have a choice. I had to be with Ami. I needed to. I only liked school when I was at home, and Baba was there. That's when I enjoyed the English class, the games, and my friends. When we were staying with Nana and Ami was there, I couldn't pay attention. I just couldn't. *Dear God, make Uncle Uzair disappear from our life.*

When Ami was at Nana's home, I couldn't eat. I couldn't sleep. I couldn't breathe…

I didn't know why my tummy hurt all the time. I didn't want to close my eyes even when sleeping. I felt scared when I didn't find Ami in her room. *Where do you go when I close my eyes? Where do you go when I'm afraid? Where do you go?*

7   *Client*

The idea of spending an hour alone with Ahad had kept me up for the better half of the night. I had mixed emotions like a jar full of assorted sweets: excitement, anxiety, curiosity, mistrust, and more. My first therapy session was scheduled for 11:00am, and as always, I arrived ten minutes early. I had left my mobile at home in a rush, and the idea of arriving early to calm my jittery nerves wasn't working. What if Arsalan called or the children needed me? In the end, I just decided to take a deep breath. Arsalan and the kids could survive without me for a couple of hours.

I rubbed my bare arms in the short-cuffed yellow shirt, shivering in the cold. No one was present today except the receptionist, who was busy tapping away on her keyboard. *Healing Matters has become a second home*, I thought as I paced up and down, trying my best to avoid the blast of the air conditioning. The counselling rooms were unfamiliar territory, and I'd never needed to open the doors to any of the four session rooms. One the one hand, I was scared of being locked away in a room for an hour; on the other, the prospect of spending that time with Ahad, someone I cared for deeply, excited me. At this moment, Ahad meant a lot to me, a fact that constantly surprised me.

After a few minutes, I sat down on one of the empty, dilapidated chairs. Why was Ahad not here yet? Had he forgotten about the session?

'You can go and wait inside the room, Saniya.'

I was jolted out of my deep thoughts when I saw the admin assistant looming over me.

'Okay. Thank you, Shehryar,' I replied with high-pitched laughter, hoping to elicit a friendly response from the grumpy man who had a reputation for never smiling. He was certainly upholding it today.

Taking a long, deep breath, I walked towards the counselling room. It was like entering a doctor's clinic as they waited to jab you with a painful needle. Why did these doctors smile as they held a scary injection that would hurt like nobody's business? It was almost like they took some sadistic pleasure in hurting their patients.

I often thought that my limitless imagination was like an untamed horse that galloped to all the places it could – a terrifying thought. I didn't know how to break this horse in yet. At times I wondered if there was something wrong with my brain. I had dark thoughts that overwhelmed me, thoughts about physically hurting Ami or Arsalan. And thoughts that were sunshine and rainbows: Ahad and me, two people who cared deeply for each other. I often lived in my fantasy world; the weirdest ideas plagued my mind in the wrong places at the wrong time. I had read that a thin line exists between sanity and insanity. Should I ask Ahad if it was true?

After fidgeting with the straps of my red leather tote for a few minutes, I dropped it on the floor and leant back, shutting my eyes. *How will I make eye contact with Ahad?* It was challenging enough to be around him and hide how I felt about him. What would I talk about? I couldn't talk about Ami; discussing Arsalan would be a bit premature. Maybe I could discuss future career options?

Feeling sweat gathering in my armpits, I stood directly under the fast-moving fan. *Great. Sweat stains*, I thought as I raised my arms in the air. I hadn't been with any man other than

Arsalan alone. I'd dreamt of spending an hour with Ahad, who took up enough space in my psyche for me to feel like a nun in a strip club, but now that that moment had arrived, I felt nervous. I hoped I wouldn't start blushing.

As part of our certificate class, we were offered one therapy session with the tutor of our choice. Afterwards, we had to start personal therapy with someone else, as continuing to see our teachers in therapy was a conflict of interest. It would have represented a dual relationship and been counterproductive for therapy to be effective. I understood it was a rule and a conflict of interest, but it didn't make sense that I couldn't talk to my tutor, whom I was already comfortable with. Who made these illogical rules, anyway?

The room needed some revamping. It was small to the point of being claustrophobic, with its empty white walls and no window to look outside.

I loved big glass windows, even those without a view to behold. There were two mud-coloured plain leather sofa chairs and a small round table. The leather felt hot, despite the air conditioning, and the table had a lonely box of tissues. Was it a given that clients cried?

The room's cold and sterile emptiness reminded me of a hospital waiting room. Wasn't a therapy room meant to be comforting and carry a vibe that would evoke emotions and hidden truths in an air of empathy and positivity?

This was a sad little room. There was a Hollywood film where the protagonist went to therapy. Now, that was a beautiful room. *Good Will Hunting*, I think. It was a massive room with big comfortable sofas and yellow sunflowers on the table. Flowers made a difference with their softness and reminded some of love, warmth, and hope. I considered whether I should have brought flowers for this room but dismissed the thought the next moment. Healing Matters made enough money with their high fees, so this was the least they could do.

Forget it, Saniya, I scolded myself. *Stop trying to be the rescuer.* Feeling restless, I moved the small table away, almost touching the wall. I didn't want this box of tissues.

Suddenly, the door opened, and I abruptly stopped as if I was caught red-handed. A smile broke acorss my face as Ahad entered the room.

'Hello, Ahad.' My legs were weak, and my breathing shallow. Could he tell?

'You're smiling. What's the joke?' Ahad sat down, the familiar smile on his face. My heart felt warm and cared for whenever I looked at that smiling face. The room felt less lonely.

'Oh, just something I remembered,' I replied. Were my legs shaking? I put both my hands on my knees. This was Ahad, someone I had grown to trust. Why was I so uncomfortable? Could he see that? I dug my heels firmly into the hard floor, hoping to stop this betrayal by my body, but being betrayed by my own was not unfamiliar to me.

'Tell me?' He pushed a little. As a newbie therapist in training, I was vigilant, feeling defensive towards this gentle probing.

'I don't remember now,' I lied and looked down at the floor. It was a plain white tiled floor with cracks at the edges, broken like me. Ahad was sitting too close for comfort. His feet almost touched mine, so I pulled my legs towards myself the minute I noticed. Did he see the abrupt action?

'Whatever you tell me, Saniya, it will stay between us.' His gentle voice knocked at the door, the door within that was so tightly locked and shut. *I won't open it,* I promised myself, *not yet.* I wasn't ready to.

'I know that,' I said, looking up. It was so hard to look into his eyes. They saw too much. I looked away. I looked at him again and saw that his intense gaze had not wavered from my face.

'Stop looking at me.' I laughed.

'What happens to you if I keep looking?' he challenged with a serious expression in his eyes.

'I feel I won't be able to talk,' I replied, my voice dropping to a whisper as I folded my arms and averted his gaze. 'I won't be able to say anything.'

Apart from wanting to keep looking at him, finding comfort in this man who, from the beginning of entering my world, had held me with those kind eyes and warm smile, I felt special. That was it. That's why I always felt as if I'd been singled out from the rest of the class, the beneficiary of that compassion I was hungry for.

He leant forward then. 'I know this is scary. You don't have to say anything if you're not ready. Or you can choose to say anything you feel like.' His voice dropped to a whisper too. 'There is no rush. You choose, okay?'

I started shaking all over. That invitation was all I had needed to hear all these years. The space to make a choice. To be heard and seen. Did I get to choose? Was that even possible, and did I even know what to choose? Choose between continuing to hold my pain in or finally letting someone witness it but at the price of sharing secrets that filled my entire being with shame. This choice was like being in a confession box where one was dying to confess to the carnal truths but at the risk and fear of being judged.

I couldn't look away this time, and I silently started crying, neither worried about him looking at me nor caring what it looked like. I couldn't stop or look away from his compassionate gaze.

He shifted a little, reaching out for the lonely box of tissues on the table, and I snapped at him.

'Do not offer me that box of tissues,' I warned. Did he not know by now how much I hated crying? I was a strong woman, and breaking down before anyone was the last thing I wanted to do. The weak ones cried, and the strong ones fought. Isn't that what Baba had taught me and Maheen?

He stopped and smiled at me. 'All right,' he said, and leant back in his seat.

'Good!' I raised my chin, defiant and victorious, as if a little battle had been won just then. But a voice reminded me that I didn't want to fight with him. He was on my team. He was the only one on my team.

'I don't know where to start,' I murmured and looked down at my ringless hands. I had taken off my wedding ring. 'I don't know where to start.' The tears seemed to have stopped on their own. For that, I was grateful.

'What are those tears expressing, Saniya?' His sincere voice instantly made me look up. I always found my way back to him, no matter where I was.

'What do you mean?' I rubbed my eyes and sat up straight.

'Are you happy?' He asked a different question, but was it?

'Why the hell do you keep asking me this? Stop asking me that when I've already told you I'm happy.' I could feel my face warming up. Was it anger, or did I feel caught out? Anger was an uninvited guest, but this time, I wanted it to give me the strength to appear strong.

He kept looking at me without saying a word and leant back further in his chair, if possible, almost as if my anger had physically pushed him back. Dead silence followed.

I felt unnerved; the uncanny silence was the last thing I needed.

'Please stop asking me that,' I almost shouted, running my hands through my hair. 'I'm sorry for being rude.' I hadn't raised my voice like that in such a long time.

'You are angry,' Ahad observed.

'Is that a problem? What does your analysis say about that?' My hands were in fists, the nails biting into my palms. Would they leave a mark? But then, did temporary scars matter? It was the wounds to the heart that left permanent scars. I had a sudden urge to punch something.

Not him. Something.

So many emotions were coming and going, and I was tired. But somewhere deep within, there was a slight gentle push and a little girl's voice finding the courage to say something. To finally share her secret with one person, at least.

You've been carrying it alone for too long; tell him.

I don't know how to.

Have you lost your mind? Was it not shameful enough to be a witness to it for you to now make it real by telling the world about it?

But I'm only telling him.

Don't listen to anyone. Trust him. Tell him.

I want to. I'm so tired of keeping it in. But what if something happens?

Yes. Don't tell anyone. Don't ever. It's so shameful.

I felt the tears well up in my eyes again and started to shiver once more. My mind was running in circles. 'I want to share something, but I don't know how to,' I said in a shaky voice, looking straight at Ahad.

I wanted to, though, badly.

'Would you hold my hand?' I asked quietly.

Maybe he heard me and wanted to, but he just sat there, motionless, his hands in his lap, palms upwards as if waiting to receive my pain. I yearned to hold empathy and compassion in those hands.

'Is it something that happened when you were a child, Saniya?'

He knew how to go straight for the jugular. I unexpectedly experienced a rush of courage, and I nodded.

'I can't say it, though,' I babbled.

'Fair enough. I can imagine how difficult this is for you.' His kind, warm face was closer. Was it?

'I feel ashamed telling you what it is.' *Slow down... slow down...*

'Do you think I'll judge you?'

'I believe you will. I believe everyone will. You'll think I'm like her!' Why wouldn't my legs stop shaking? I restlessly stretched them out in front of me and realised they were close to Ahad's. I pulled them back once again.

'You don't want to be like your mother?'

It was as if he had slapped my face hard.

'What are you talking about? How did my mother come into this conversation?' I abruptly got up and grabbed the bag lying next to the chair.

'Please sit down,' Ahad requested.

'What kind of therapy is this? Will you tell me about my life?' I argued. 'Aren't you supposed to ask me questions?'

I walked towards the door and then turned around. His back faced me, and he asked me again without turning around.

'Please come and sit down, Saniya.'

I opened the door and left without saying anything. Outside, the cold blast of the air conditioning almost felt like another slap, but I didn't care. I walked fast, left the foyer, and quickly dashed towards the main gate, almost fearing that Ahad would follow and make me sit and confess to it all.

My armpits were sweaty again, and I felt I would stop breathing if I stayed a minute longer in this place. I needed to escape. Once in the car, I turned up the air conditioning, turning the vent towards my face.

I grabbed the car steering wheel tightly with both hands as waves and waves of uncontrollable sobbing hit me, making it difficult to find my bearings. I wasn't sure how long I sat crying with my head on the steering wheel. I didn't care if anyone was watching.

The pain had seeped into every nook and corner of my body. It was so difficult to hold it in now. I wanted to let it out so badly, but another strong thought followed, and then I felt rage. *Why the hell do I have to keep it in? Why? I won't!* I grabbed the tissue box lying aimlessly on the dashboard, took out a few tissues, and callously wiped my tears. I got out of the car and slammed the door hard.

And I walked back on the same path. I had to. It was high time I did.

I didn't care to knock on the door. I knew he would be there waiting; I didn't know how, but I just did.

He didn't even turn around. How did he know I would be back? I crumpled on the sofa and looked into his eyes, daring, pleading with him, hoping he would understand. He would call it out, the reality, and be my voice for what I had not allowed myself to acknowledge, even in many isolated and not-so-isolated moments of my life.

I stayed quiet for a few minutes, and then I decided. It was time.

'My mother.' Two words captured the story of my life.

'Your mother?'

'Yes.'

'Yes' was a small three-letter word that carried so much power. We said yes to so many things. Yes, I want coffee today; yes, I will help you with your homework, son; yes, I will go out with you; yes, I will continue to stay with you even when you hurt me; and yes, it was about my mother.

I finally said it. Yes! It was, is, and always would be about my mother. It started with her, and maybe it would end with her too.

'Tell me more…' Ahad encouraged me in a low voice.

'I don't know how to say it,' I muttered, rocking back and forth.

'I hear you. Take a deep breath…'

'My mother cheated on my father.' Oh, God! Had I just said it out loud? I had, hadn't I?

'My mother cheated on my father for a long time,' I repeated, covering my face with my hands a moment later.

'I am so sorry, Saniya. Could you look at me please?' The calm voice, indulgent like a warm hug on a cold winter evening.

'What are you sorry for?' I challenged him as I uncovered my face.

'For what you have gone through.' He leant forward, and his eyes were wet. 'I cannot even imagine how traumatic that must have been for you,' he added.

'It was,' I admitted, tears welling up in my eyes again.

An eight-year-old's voice, trapped in a car. A teenager's anxious one in school, imagining various scenes at home. A young adult slapped and spat at when she would try to follow her mother lest she disappeared to places the young adult couldn't imagine going to. An empty bed at night. *Ami, where do you keep disappearing to?*

Years and years of being a secret keeper and to date continuing to be one…

Ahad joined me in the silence as I tried to escape the memories. Why did Ahad stay silent? The silence was unbearable, so empty. Was it my responsibility to fill it?

'It stopped when I was almost twenty, I think. She used to hit me a lot too, but that also stopped. I chose to stop it.'

I raised my chin in defiance, finding the familiar but often missed innate strength in me.

'I told her I would beat her black and blue if she ever touched me again.'

He didn't ask me any questions. I would have run away again had he asked any questions.

'How come there is no water in here? It is so hot,' I complained.

'I'm sorry for that. Do you want me to get some?' he asked, almost getting up.

I shook my head. 'It's fine.' I clasped my hands over my head and closed my eyes.

'How much time is left?' I asked a few minutes later, opening my eyes and looking straight into his warm brown ones. I blinked back tears as I saw the compassion in his eyes. *Stop crying, Saniya!*

'Another fifteen minutes, but we can wrap up earlier if that's what you want?' he said in a soft tone.

'What I want? Did you seriously ask me that?' I wrapped my arms around my body. 'You're tired of me now, are you?'

'No! I'm not, Saniya, but I thought this was too much for you. I didn't want to push you more.'

'So, you want to quit on me now? Already tired, are you?' I picked up my bag. I wanted to leave.

I could feel my face heating up and my hands clenched in fists. I wanted to break something so badly.

'Hey!' Ahad got up as if wanting to block my exit. 'There is nothing more I want and nowhere else I'd rather be than here. To be here for you.'

I wanted to believe his words. Should I? I sat down again and whispered, 'Stay here, then.'

'I'm not going anywhere. I'm here for you as long as you want me to be,' he promised.

'But we only have fifteen minutes left…'

'You don't have to worry about that. I'm here for as long as you want me to be,' he repeated.

We looked at each other; the promise in the space awakened a speck of hope in me. Hope that I wished would grow.

'Would you like to come again tomorrow?' Ahad asked. 'I'm free around noon.'

'But I thought I could only see you once?' I questioned.

'It's okay. This is important. You are important. So, noon tomorrow?'

'Yes!' I smiled as bright as a sun coming out in its full glory after heavy rain.

And that was how it started. A therapeutic relationship

that promised more than what I could have asked for. Week after week, Ahad and I met for sessions sometimes twice a week. I shared everything with him; bit by bit, the box of pain hidden away was opened and Ahad was let into my inner world. Ahad promised healing to me, and it was the first time I had experienced love and care. In class, I would notice him smiling at me, and once or twice when a peer challenged me in class, he stepped in and took my side. Ahad was my guardian angel, and I no longer cared for Arsalan and his erratic behaviour.

I wasn't alone anymore.

8   *Wife*

I was browsing my Instagram page when I came across this quote by Daniel Keyes, and the timing and relevance of it bowled me over.

I don't know what's worse: not to know what you are and be happy, or to become what you have always wanted to be and feel alone.

How did social media know about my journey? Arsalan once told me it was a social media algorithm, but I wasn't curious to learn more about it. My knowledge of the world was limited, to say the least, and for some unexplainable reason, I had no motivation to gain more. For now, my love affair with the human psyche had converted into a lifelong commitment, and my curiosity was satiated by psychotherapy.

I was no longer the person I had been for the last thirty-five years of my life, and I knew that the movement within could not be contained. The thought brought a smile to my face. Despite no change in my married life, becoming a therapist changed me significantly, not only professionally but also as a person. Professionally, I was working with different clients over the years, and the stories of pain and loss, success, and struggle were fascinating but also difficult to process. I never knew the resilience of the human spirit in the face of traumatic adversity before I joined this field.

Therapeutic work required me to be self-aware and to meet

parts of me I had not met before. I was learning to slow down and examine facets of my personality that triggered Arsalan. I knew I had compulsive habits and my need to control could be overwhelming for him, so I started to sit with anxiety and not surrender to the impulse that wanted me to be at the helm of everything. Unlike before when I had to have the last word regarding children or home running, or financial decisions, I was learning to let go of my perfectionist script and trust Arsalan and his viewpoint. It came to my attention that these habits were the trigger for him, but I also learnt that it still didn't justify his abusive behaviour.

Was this process pain-free? Far from it. Did I sometimes wonder if that place of dark inner struggling was easier to cope with than this growing understanding of who I was and what I wanted from myself and others? I paid a heavy price for this new-found understanding as I could no longer stay in denial and distract myself from my ever-growing pain and frustration of being a young woman whose physical and emotional needs remained unmet, who was lonely and was drifting away from her most intimate relationships.

After five years of training to be a therapist and being an independent practitioner for almost a year, I knew that feeling self-assured and self-doubt were both critical. One needed to be open and curious about these inner states. I was learning not to allow the harsh inner critic to shame me for any feelings or thoughts emerging within me but to be open to the process. I often wondered with some trepidation where I was heading, a feeling similar to that of waiting for the result of a critical exam.

Stop the session, would you? I ordered the internal therapist.

It was Arsalan's fortieth birthday, and I had thrown a formal dinner in the evening, and the most exciting news was that Maheen was visiting after a year from London.

For me, that was the highlight of the cold December evening. I had invited fifty-odd people, primarily close family and friends.

Maheen had travelled alone to Pakistan with Ahmed, who was ten now. He was two years older than Nyle, and although they didn't see each other more than twice a year, they bonded over a game of *Fortnite*. All children bonded well over iPads, TV screens, and video games, and it looked like the days of playing tag outside or sitting around talking to each other were *history*.

Stop overthinking and get to work, Saniya.

It was 9:00am, and with Maheen and Ahmed still sleeping due to jet lag, I walked over to Nyle and Neha's room and silently opened the door, afraid to wake them up a moment before they were supposed to. Sleeping children were a sight for any mother's sore eyes and the peace that came with it was a bonus.

To my surprise, they were up and huddled together in Nyle's bed, watching something on the iPad.

'Mama!' they both screamed in unison, bringing a big smile to my face.

'Oh, you're both up.' And, of course, unlike their ongoing squabbles, an iPad reminded them of the bonds of blood.

They laughed, as if their grand plan had been busted. I slid into the bed with them, almost falling off, but I desperately wanted to hug my babies.

'Bas, beta, no more iPad.' I gently tried to remove the device from the chubby fingers holding it for their dear lives. *Sofia the First* was playing, which was Neha's current favourite. *Why was Nyle watching this?* I thought and immediately squashed this gender-biased thought with the same impulse that I killed a cockroach under my foot the minute I saw it.

'No, Mama! No, Mama!' they shouted; the protest was loud and clear about the possibility of being deprived of their beloved gadget.

Finally, I tickled them so they would let go of the iPad, bringing another round of screams and shrieking.

'Shhhhh! Khala will wake up,' I warned them, but it was falling on deaf ears.

Suddenly, they both jumped out of bed and ran towards Arsalan, who had just entered the room.

'Baba, look what Mama is doing!' Neha, the telltale, got into action.

'Tell me. What is she doing?' He picked up Neha and pulled Nyle towards him in an embrace.

'She took our iPad. We had just started, Baba.'

'Really? Are you sure you both had just started?' We exchanged a knowing smile, amused by the accusation.

'Let's have breakfast, little monsters,' he roared and carried them out.

I took the iPad from underneath the bed, tucked it under my arm, and followed them into the kitchen.

Arsalan was a loving father, which was one of the reasons I cared for him or, more importantly, could push away other, more unsettling, thoughts and continue to compromise. Nyle and Neha deserved a stable home.

'We want cereal. We want cereal!' they both started chanting in unison.

It was noon by the time the little human beings were fed, showered, and plopped before another Disney film. Today was not the day for parenting 101, I assured myself. I had a long day ahead and couldn't care less how much screen time they had as long as they were out of the way. Maheen and I spent the morning getting our facials and nails done. I had engaged with a small event management company that was relatively new to manage the dinner, giving me more time. The week had been hectic between work and family, and I was looking forward to indulging myself.

While we were driving back home, Maheen suddenly turned towards me. 'I'm not sure if you're happy, apa.'

Woah! Where did that come from?

'What do you mean by that?' I asked her in a curt tone as I continued to drive.

101

'I don't know how to explain it, but you look sad more often than not.'

The combination of sadness and inquisitiveness in her voice made me want to punch something. I held the steering wheel tightly, turned around for a moment, and gave an exasperated sigh. 'What the hell is wrong with you?'

'Relax, apa. I'm asking out of concern, that's all.' She reached out and patted my hand, but I swatted it away.

'Well, you've made such a huge statement, so now explain what you mean by it.' I could feel the heat in my face – to be asked questions that I was not fully able to answer was triggering as hell. Why did everyone question my happiness all the fucking time! 'So go on, explain what made you think that.' My voice was raised, and I started tapping the steering wheel with my fingers. I wasn't planning to let her off the hook.

'How does one explain a feeling? You're the therapist. You should know better than to ask that question.'

I peeked a glance at her and saw that she was frowning. My defensiveness was contagious enough to infect her.

'Oh, wow. Are you going to use the therapist card now? My dear sister, feelings don't grow out of thin air.' I took a deep breath and parked the car on the side of the road. Why was I fighting with her when she had asked a question out of concern? A question not far from the bitter truth.

'I take back what I said,' she said, turning away and looking out the window.

'I'm sorry,' I said more gently. 'I didn't mean to jump on you, but I wondered what made you ask now and not before.'

'What do you mean?' She turned to look at me; her expression was of disbelief, laced with some curiosity.

'It's just that you notice my happiness, or lack of it, now, Maheen. What about all those years in Ami-Baba's home? Why did you never ask me if I was happy then?' I had a sudden urge to wail.

'What do you mean?' She stared at me wide-eyed. 'There was no reason for you to be unhappy back then until—'

'Let's drop this,' I interrupted her, not letting her complete her sentence. 'Let's talk about it some other time.'

There was silence after that, filled with the weight of unanswered questions, but as the evening approached, the discomfort between Maheen and me dissipated. That was the beauty of life. It mostly succeeded in distracting from harsh realities rather than causing further distress.

The dinner was a huge success. Arsalan had a big smile, and I loved his compliments that were expressed publicly for the first time. After the cake was cut, he gave me a sideways hug and made a little speech, showing his appreciation for the effort I had put in. I mirrored his feelings, and hope ignited once more, a tiny bud that could possibly grow. Maybe something had shifted between us, and I had been so wrapped up in kids and work that I had missed it. Later on, as I was sitting in my room taking my shoes off, I started to feel guilty over neglecting Arsalan and the kids and working overtime. Luckily, Arsalan, who was taking a shower in the bathroom, interrupted the unfounded or deserving guilt.

'Let's sit in the lounge and have coffee. Let's ask Maheen to join.'

'Sure. You call her and I'll get your coffee, sir.' I kissed him on the cheek, and even though my feet hurt from walking in high heels, I made myself walk over to the kitchen, thinking that maybe making coffee could partly compensate for the guilt. I carried the tray with three bright mugs filled with hot coffee, the nutty aroma filling my nostrils.

Some random English song was playing in the living room, a little too loud for my taste.

'I am the official DJ for the evening, ladies,' Arsalan claimed as he fiddled with his phone, having connected it to the TV; that was why the volume was higher than usual. He was in a good mood, and I smiled at him. I liked this version of my husband which almost made me forget the other one. The ugly, angry one.

'Play something else, please,' I requested as I handed him his coffee and sat beside him. Maybe today we could be intimate. He was in a great mood, and it had been a couple of months since I had asked. I was hungry for even the few minutes of intimacy we called sex. Maybe if I asked him after Maheen left, he wouldn't say no?

Don't get too hopeful. He is tired, isn't he?

'Was that Neha?' I asked as I thought I heard her crying. 'Please go check on her,' I requested Arsalan, who had changed the music to old Indian songs.

'Aye, aye, Captain,' he said and immediately got up.

'Arsalan Bhai! Please teach Adnan a few things, too. He's lazy.' Maheen wasn't impressed by her husband's habits of being a couch potato after coming home from work.

'Don't be impressed, Maheen. Your brother here hardly moves a muscle otherwise.'

'Ah! That's not true, begum.' Arsalan laughed, heading towards the bedrooms to check on the kids.

I was enjoying an old Lata Mangeshkar number when a loud ping from Arsalan's phone broke the song's rhythm.

A WhatsApp text popped up on the screen and then disappeared. Without thinking, I picked up his phone and opened his text messages.

Happy birthday. I miss you, love.

It was from 'Laiba', a name unknown to me, and as I zoomed into the WhatsApp display photo, a pretty face looked back at me. My heart started to beat so fast that, for a moment, I felt I would faint.

'What is it, apa?' Maheen put the coffee mug on the table and came and sat down next to me. I handed over the phone with lifeless hands, put my arms around my torso, and started rocking back and forth. Who was Laiba? How long had this been going on for?

'Apa. Please relax. It could be a random message,' Maheen said as she quickly put the phone down and tried to hug me.

'Stop, Maheen.' I pushed her arm away. I didn't want her here trying to make me feel better. I was sick of people pulling me into a web of denial.

'She's fine. Was just a little restless but has gone back to sleep,' Arsalan announced as he entered the room, his tone light and cheery.

'I'm tired. I'm going to sleep,' Maheen said and leant in and whispered in my ear, 'Please don't say anything right now.'

'Come on, Maheen. Now that the children are all settled, do you want to sleep? I'm the birthday boy. You can't leave the party, sis.' Arsalan picked up the coffee mug and sat down next to me.

'I'm tired, bhai,' Maheen meekly protested and left the room.

Her absence left a void in the room, which I didn't know how to fill. Wave after wave of agony warned me that I couldn't hold my silence for much longer. This uneasiness and turmoil weren't new to me. Was I not familiar with secret relationships and whisperings on discreet nights? Was it not something that had defined my existence and distracted me from happiness and peace throughout my life? The idea that my husband was also cheating on me was too much to imagine, and before I could slow down to ask without the anger that was building, I blurted out, 'Who is Laiba?'

'Excuse me?' He picked up his phone from the table. The gesture was not lost on me.

'I asked you something. Who is Laiba?'

'Where is this coming from?' Arsalan said, his voice a mix of nervousness and false confidence. Or was I imagining it?

'I asked you a simple question. Who is she?' I could hear my voice getting louder, but I didn't care what the consequences of that would be.

'Where is this question coming from?' Arsalan put his coffee mug down; the irritation in his voice was crystal clear.

'Why the hell did she text you at this hour? Who is she?'

'Lower your voice and calm the fuck down.'

'No, I will not calm down today. Tell me, who is she?'

'Why did you snoop on my phone?'

'Don't change the topic,' I screamed.

'She's a business colleague. Works at another company.' He tried to hold my hand, but I pushed it away.

'Why did she say she missed you?'

'How would I know, yaar?' He had a pleading look in his eyes that confirmed my doubt. How could he make a fool of me with these blatant lies? How many times would I be made a fool of?

'Open your WhatsApp and read out her text,' I ordered loudly.

I was indifferent to Arsalan's anger, to my fear of him. I was like a car speeding on a highway with failing brakes.

'I'm not doing any such damn thing. I don't know what you think you read, but she's just a social acquaintance.'

'Oh really? A social acquaintance who tells you she misses you on your birthday at midnight? Stop lying. How long has this been going on? Tell me,' I screamed. 'Who the fuck is she?' I was trembling at this point. I couldn't sit anymore and started walking back and forth.

I was beyond caring and wanted to break something.

'Why the hell is this music still playing?' I picked up the remote to switch it off and threw it hard on the table. It missed it and fell on the floor with a loud bang.

'Calm down, Saniya!' He got up and barged towards me.

I stopped in my tracks and pushed Arsalan with all the force I had.

'Get away from me. Don't you dare come close to me.' I was crying and screaming at the same time.

'Stop screaming, you bitch.' Arsalan tried to cover my mouth with his hands, but I pushed them away and stepped back.

'Don't you dare call me that. Don't you ever call me that! You don't touch me. You don't even fucking hold my hand, and now I know why! How long have you been fucking her?'

'What the fuck is wrong with you? *Pagal ho gayi ho?* If she texted me, how is it my fault?' His tone kept oscillating between high and low.

'Are you telling me that this isn't your fault? You didn't make her feel it was okay to text you at midnight with loving texts? I don't fucking believe it.' I laughed without a tinge of humour.

'Calm down. There are guests in the house. The children will get upset. We can discuss this in the morning.' He tried the polite route, but I was done. I was done with this man, his lies, and his treatment of me. I hated him with all the energy I had in me in that moment.

'You want me to calm down,' I lowered my voice. Almost inaudible…

'Yes,' he answered.

'Then tell me the truth.'

'As I said, she's working for another company. I've met her a few times, and we're friends, that's all.'

'Friends?' I yelled out. 'Why did you not tell me?'

'What is there to tell you, dumb woman? It's not like I'm having an affair with her.'

His eyes were bloodshot now, and for a moment, I felt nervous, but then another moment took me to another night and another time. Held hands… two people… more than hands… the discovery of it… the unease… the denial… and yet all of it was true. No one was ever just friends, were they? A man and a woman were always more than that.

'Friends do not send such intimate texts at midnight. Call her now, and I want to talk to her.'

'Have you lost your fucking mind? Stop this nonsense right now.' He walked up to me and grabbed my arms.

'No, I won't! You haven't touched me for years, and you go around being friends with other women? Let go of my arms. You are hurting me.'

But he did not budge.

I was shaking with rage and pain. Rage that had been anger once, unspent and rooted in helplessness.

'I'm warning you, Saniya. Stop this!'

His face was contorted into an ugly mass of bones and flesh, and spit particles flew out of his mouth as he shouted, *'Maar khaao gi, bata raha hoon!'*

How could a good-looking man turn into this easily forgettable face, a face that made me feel disgusted in that moment?

'How many times have you met her alone?'

'I am not answering any of these questions. Get lost, bitch.' He let go of me and was about to leave the room when I grabbed his arm.

'Give me your phone.'

'I am warning you, Saniya. You are pushing my limits here.'

'Oh, you know about limits now, do you? I want to know!' I shouted as a hard slap hit my cheek and grazed my ear. I couldn't move for a moment.

I was still reeling with the shock of the slap when he pushed me hard and tried to leave the room again. I ran towards him and started punching him on his back. He turned around and grabbed my wrists, but I was unable to stop myself as wave after wave of grief and anger hit me.

'I hate you!'

He exerted pressure on my wrists as I tasted the tears running down my face.

'You're hurting me,' I bawled and tried to bite into his hand.

'What the fuck! You crazy bitch,' he cried and pushed me back with force.

The last thing I remembered was falling on the floor, holding my tummy with my hands, and screaming and wailing. Amidst all of it, I remember another slap and being spat on when I said, 'I'll tell Baba everything.'

That slap by Ami was as brutal as this one, imprinted on my face for many years, seen only by my eyes and its sting burning into my skin at unexpected times.

I opened my eyes and felt Maheen's hand gently rubbing my forehead. The room was a little dark, but I could see the clock hanging on the wall in front of me. Was its ticking always this loud? What was happening?

'Are you okay?' she asked.

'My head hurts a lot. What's wrong with me?'

'You had a nervous breakdown. It was so scary, apa. The doctor gave you some sedatives.'

'How long have I been out?'

'For more than a day.'

I tried to sit up, but my body felt weak. My head was throbbing.

'Please get me some Panadol,' I said. My tongue felt like sandpaper.

She left the room, and I closed my eyes. I felt confused. Nervous breakdown? What did that mean? The last few hours were fuzzy in my mind, but then images started popping up and I quickly opened my eyes as my breathing quickened. The memory of the evening came rushing back, all at once. A few moments later, Maheen returned with the medicine and a glass of water. I quickly gulped down the water and looked at her.

'Where is he?'

'He's outside with Neha and Nyle. He's very upset.'

I let out high-pitched laughter. 'He's upset? Wow! I didn't ask if he was worried. Are the kids fine?' I stopped laughing and wiped my eyes.

'As fine as they can be, apa. We told them you're a little unwell.'

'I want to see them.'

Maheen didn't say a word, and a few minutes later, both the children entered the room, walking behind their aunt.

'Mama, are you sick?' Nyle climbed on the bed, followed by Neha.

'I'm fine, meri jaan,' I said, and hugged the kids tightly. I had a strong urge to cry but I swallowed hard. I didn't want to worry them.

'Why don't you go and play with Ahmed, and I'll order pizza for dinner?' I forced a smile on my face and successfully pushed down the tsunami of tears threatening to burst out of me. The innocent smile on my children's faces and how easily pizza could divert them from the harsh realities of life made me extremely sad.

The children left, but Maheen stayed at the door.

'Apa, I'm sending Arsalan Bhai inside. Please relax now and try not to be insecure about a casual friendship. You and only you are his wife, and you should know that he loves you.'

Her voice shook with unspent tears. She was shaken badly, evident on her pale face and trembling hands, so I stayed quiet even though her questions were triggering. How did I know that I was the wife?

I had always been insecure about other women since we got married. Arsalan was always friendly towards women, and I didn't mind that, but I had drawn a boundary from the get-go where I didn't want him to talk or meet any of his colleagues alone. For many years I took the blame for being narrow-minded and mistrusting him. But after five years in personal therapy, I knew exactly what the trigger was and why I had reacted so badly. Firstly, I felt like a friend in the marriage, so any indication of his alliance with another woman got alarm bells ringing in my mind. Secondly, exposure to the trauma of knowing that my mother had cheated caused me to mistrust my significant relationships. I knew it was my baggage, but could my husband not help me to carry it?

Sometimes I wanted to share my story with him, but I didn't trust him. How could I feel safe in a sexless, emotionally dead, and abusive marriage? And today, the verbal abuse had taken another turn with the hard slap. He had hit me, and I didn't know where to go from here. Should I tell Ami? Or ask his parents to intervene? But what would that achieve? I didn't want to go and live with Ami. That thought was enough to give me nightmares. I had no home to go to.

He slapped you once. Don't make a big deal out of it.

But what if it's the first of many more to come?

There you go. Feeling sorry for yourself. Stop being the victim.

But I am one!

The headache was getting worse, and the meds weren't working. I shut my eyes and tucked the quilt closely under my chin.

What was happening to us? We were different species. I was the woman who jumped into the middle of the sea on our honeymoon, and he was the man who didn't like the feel of sand under his feet. At my core, I was reckless, loved adventure, and wanted a partner as passionate in the bedroom as he was about embracing life with open arms, whereas Arsalan liked to play it safe in almost all aspects of his life. Yet he made his marriage unsafe with his temperament issues.

I wanted to be loved and desired wholeheartedly, and the last thing I wanted was for my husband to be friendly with other women. Yes, they were platonic interactions, just a few professional meetups and chats during the day, but everything was always done without my knowledge. This wasn't professional. I just knew it.

How could I tell him how scary it was for me when I found out such a truth? How unbearable this was for me, more painful than childbirth. It was being stabbed in a wound that had never stopped bleeding: my childhood wound. I couldn't tell him about Ami because telling him would mean he would look at me differently. He would judge me.

And even if I parked this bitter reality of my life, I would always fight with him over the fact that he treated me like a platonic friend, so him having other female friends made me insecure. I felt threatened. He would say, 'It's your issue that you're so insecure.' But post-therapy, I realised it was partly his job to make me feel secure. Wasn't sex an essential part of a marriage for a woman to feel secure in her husband's need and desire for her? His lack of attention made me feel invisible.

A rude knock on the door shook me out of my thoughts and, without waiting for a response, he entered the room. He crept towards me slowly, as if he feared I would lose control again. 'How are you feeling now?' he asked in an unfamiliar soft tone and sat down in the same spot Maheen had been sitting in.

I was unable to look at him. I could feel the slap on my face, burning my skin. Why was I feeling ashamed?

'You hit me, Arsalan.'

'I'm sorry for raising my hand, Saniya. But you pushed me against a wall.'

I took a deep breath and stayed quiet. I knew what he was doing now. The lack of ownership of his actions, the gaslighting, and then being beaten to a pulp narrative, 'you made me do it' served his view of himself and perhaps suppressed any healthy shame he should be feeling. It helped him not to see himself as the abusive man he was. I didn't respond to the apology. I was unsure how to respond to an apology that blamed me for his actions. But for now, the woman was a bigger concern for me than him hitting me.

'You scared us all. *Ab bas ker do…*'

'I should stop? Stop what?' I asked, looking directly at him, my shoulders stiffening up and my breathing becoming rapid. I was getting scared of the angry impulse that had a life of its own and was not dying down. What was happening to me?

'Look, she means nothing. And if it helps, I will limit my interaction with her even more.'

'And who will be next?' I asked hopelessly. 'You'll end up being friends with someone again.' I didn't trust him but didn't want to say it out loud. There was no more fight left in me. 'I don't know how to explain this to you, Arsalan. It's too much for me to accept.' I started to cry at this point.

'Acha, relax. I'm not exactly looking to make friends.' He then leant forward to hug me.

I felt my body tightening, resisting his touch. Still, he held on, and slowly I found my resistance crumbling away at the familiarity of his arms and his touch.

This was my husband, a man I had madly loved once upon a time. A part of me still loved him and always would, wouldn't I? I put my arms around him and put my head on his shoulder.

'Sssshhh… bas… no more…' He rubbed my back as I continued crying.

'Promise me you won't ever be friends with any woman again, please…'

'I've heard you. Now let it go, please.'

I didn't respond, holding onto him tightly. We had good loving moments like this in our marriage. Laughter, joy, romance, little pockets of all of it… trips together… beautiful children together… families who respected each other… didn't we? Yes, significant parts were missing, and a lot of hurt and pain had accumulated over the years, but there was a lot that was good too, and I was also at fault for many things that I'd tried my best to change over the years. I was less controlling and was learning to give him more space. But it failed to work, and maybe that's why it was hard to hold onto the good. I tried my best to remember the happy moments, but lately they were fading away and were hard to retain in my memory.

Hope came knocking again as my husband held me and kissed my head. Hope was scary, but hope kept us going, didn't it...?

It was hope that had kept me going in a decade-old marriage that carried enough pain to drown anyone, and it was the same hope that bonded us together. I had challenged myself time and again to extend my empathy for my clients towards my husband, see his lack of desire as a shortcoming, and was learning to accept it, but some days my needs were overpowering and I knew I was justified in my expectation. I needed reassurance, and against my better judgment, I leant back and, still in his arms, looked at him and said, 'Promise me you will never make friends with anyone again.'

'Anyone? Not even men?' he teased, smiling with an effortless charm that had made me fall in love with him in the first place.

'You know what I mean.'

'No, I don't.' He continued to tease.

'Please. I need you to say the words.' I was apprehensive again at his deflection.

'What words?' The smile never left his face as he continued, and for a moment, it felt bizarre to integrate his warm smile with the avoidance his words exhibited.

'Please, Arsalan.' I was begging.

'You want me to stop talking to half the population of the world?'

'Forget it.' I tried to move out of his arms, but he held on.

'Relax. I don't intentionally make friends with anyone.'

'Are we back to arguing about that? Why can't you ever accept your faults?'

'It's not my fault. There is a fundamental difference in how you look at things and how I do.'

Hope slipped away again. Could we never move towards rainbows after a dark storm had ended and the sun was finally out?

I swallowed my disappointment. 'It's fine. I don't think you'll change. And I won't carry the burden of this marriage alone anymore.' I took the risk of saying what I had only imagined I would.

'You're overreacting. I've heard you. Just drop it now.'

'Then say the words dammit! Make the fucking promise, would you?'

'Calm down. Fine, I promise. Happy now?' He got up as soon as the words jumped out of his mouth. The moment of intimacy had begun to die, and all I could do was watch it go. 'Now take it easy. The children are upset,' he said and abruptly left the room.

And once more I returned to life.

9   *Student*

'Saniya. Come back to us.'

I snapped out of my daydream and saw Ahad's smiling face. My heart skipped a beat. He never failed to warm up every inch of my being.

'I'm here,' I responded, but couldn't maintain eye contact for long. Some of my classmates started laughing. Why did people laugh at the most banal things?

It was the last month of this certificate class, following which, my diploma would continue with new tutors. The idea of not seeing Maha, Ahad, and some of my group members who were not continuing was sad. Healing Matters was my happy place, my family.

However, it was the thought of not seeing Ahad every week that was unimaginable, and even though I had weekly sessions with him, the class was the cherry on top, and for some reason, it was important to know that I mattered to him more than others. I believe I did.

He was the calm to the raging storm within, and I felt content and secure sitting in my chair beside him. His warmth and empathy were a balm on all the wounded and scarred parts of my soul, and his presence distracted me from what was happening in my personal life.

At times my growing emotions towards Ahad overwhelmed me. What if one day he stopped reciprocating? I also experienced moments of doubt when I wondered if he was in fact reciprocating or I was just imagining more than what reality was offering. I didn't have a name for these emotions. They were unlike anything I had ever experienced. Maybe I had experienced them with Arsalan but not with the same intensity as I did with Ahad. Would I call it love? I didn't know, but my feelings towards Ahad had a distinct, novel, and pleasantly new flavour that made me smile without a reason, and after many years, I felt like I was at peace. Ahad saw me for who I was, with all the broken parts, my secrets, and life traumas.

I don't remember ever being as content as I was in those days. Healing Matters made me feel like a homeless person on the street who had finally been taken in and given shelter, food, and warm clothes. The three and a half hours I spent with my group were like being with family, and I was learning safety and love. Safe enough to know I could choose to express myself if I wanted to and to know that even if I hadn't shared my story with anyone as yet, the occasional faraway sad look in my eyes or the tears that ran down my cheeks when someone else was processing, didn't go unnoticed. Even if no one asked or said anything, the class allowed me to express my emotions in silence.

This course was changing me. I wasn't as triggered by Ami's critical attacks as before. My need for attention from Arsalan had gone down a significant notch. The human psyche became my first love, and between home duties and socialising demands, I would spend hours reading books on psychology. I was curious and fascinated by the theories we had been taught. I would submit all my assignments on time, do extra reading, and ask all the right questions, a classic teacher's pet. I would do anything to get attention and, it was attention I got. I was hungry for it all the time, almost crippled by it, because no matter how much I got it, my appetite for it seemed insatiable.

Despite being the firstborn, it was always Maheen who got the undivided care and the hugs and kisses as a child. Why Ami always made me feel unwanted was a question I never found the answer to. It was easier for her to slap me rather than hold me. There wasn't a single snapshot in my mind's eye that exuded the warmth of a mother's embrace, and although I knew it wasn't possible that she had never held me, in my conscious memory, no matter how hard I tried, I couldn't think of a single time.

I would go through old albums and always see Ami with Maheen in her lap. I would be standing next to her with a forlorn expression. There was one photograph of my first birthday, though, where she was smiling and holding me in her arms. I had that photograph tucked behind a credit card in my purse, and sometimes, I would take it out and look at it with longing, but before long, anger and grief would follow, and I would put it away. The two strong opposing emotions were like two opponents on the battlefield, and I had yet to find out who the winner was, if there was one.

Arsalan's sporadic abuse had started to affect me less. As always, I would stay silent in the face of his screaming, but unlike before when post-altercation would be spent crying and feeling confused and upset, I was now able to, at times, move on as best I could by busying myself with the kids or my studies. Mostly I still curled up in a ball and cried and howled, but this class had lowered the shame and responsibility I had been carrying for causing his anger.

Therapy and this class made me realise that his defence, 'You make me do it,' and refusal to own his anger and blame me for it was gaslighting. This behaviour belonged to him alone, and even though I would trigger him now and then with my idiosyncrasies and control, I didn't deserve the reaction I got. Especially when I was willing to listen and address my issues. He had stripped me of my fundamental right as a woman and wife, and he neither accepted it as his fault or did anything to resolve his sexual or aggresive problems. There was no remorse or empathy for the frustration and helplessness I lived with daily. I had no idea why he never experienced desire for me, and I was losing interest in finding out.

I hadn't found the courage to share this in my therapy class. It was too much information. I chose to present a particular side of myself to the world and wasn't ready to take off the mask I had deliberately adorned, a persona I wanted to maintain for my sanity.

When I had no choice but to continue the life I had to live, what was the point of telling anyone how unhappy I was? To the outside world, we were a handsome, educated couple with two adorable babies, a well-established life with a comfortable house, and every piece of evidence pointed to a regular, stable life.

The outside world only saw an educated, smiling man. They didn't listen to the filth coming out of his mouth or see his wife begging him for days to look at her, notice her, and make an effort to be intimate with her. It was sad even to imagine that my husband had to try to be close to me. Was I not a desirable woman? It wasn't about being pretty. I knew there was something deep within me that men were not sexually attuned to, but I deserved *some* physical love. I didn't expect Arsalan to feel desire for me all the time, but expecting it once a month at least wasn't too much to ask for, was it?

The world didn't know how difficult it was to listen to my husband speak to me lovingly in front of others and privately use cruel and harsh words.

Filthy words like 'chutiya', 'bitch', and 'messed up' stayed in my system longer than drugs remained in the blood. It was hard to forget the taste of those words, a bitter aftertaste that left me feeling confused, ashamed, and in a cloud of chaos for days that seemed longer than they were.

The sad truth of my life was that, in so many ways, my husband was a carbon copy of my mother. Just like her, he was verbally abusive, withheld physical love, and made me feel ashamed of my need for love and attention. Ami, over the span of my early years, would repeatedly say, 'Jaan *chor do*,' to get me to leave her alone when I expressed a need to her, whether it be physical, for example food, or emotional, like wanting to sleep with her at Nana's home. She would raise her hand to stop me from coming closer, and in the same way, my husband complained about my nagging and need to connect and for his attention. Ami's hand got imprinted in my psyche, and Arsalan further deepened that handprint with his rejection of me.

As a woman and mother, I could not understand how a parent could say something so harsh to her children and where she expected me to go after leaving her alone. How did she expect me to self-soothe when I was very young? As a mum, I ensured I was present for my children, and whenever they needed my attention, they became the focus and everything else faded. Initially, it was a polar opposite parenting stance from my mum's, and everything was about Nyle and Neha, but with time, I learnt to be present for them but also put my needs to the forefront and work towards striking a balance.

I hadn't realised until I started this course that Arsalan often said something similar about leaving him alone: 'You're always running after me,' when I would pursue him for a kiss, chat, or just for him to look at me. But in the last year, I was learning not to ask or wait for him as much as I did before for a kiss, sex, or attention.

I learnt how to cope. Silence helped. Telling myself it was happening to someone else helped even more. I remembered how, in the first year of my marriage, fantasy became my go-to place. One day, after Arsalan left for work after another episode of fighting and shouting, I saw a man holding a woman in his arms on some random film on HBO. I imagined myself as that woman and felt a fluttering within my belly. It was a light sensation that left me feeling warm and something I didn't have a name for. I closed my eyes and imagined myself sinking into that man's arms, my face in the nape of his neck, being held so tightly that I almost felt breathless in a pleasurable way so I dared not wriggle out of his arms.

Alarmed, I snapped my eyes open. Why was I fantasising about another man? What was happening to me? It was just a moment, that's all it was. But a few days later, out of nowhere, I imagined my fantasised lover's arms around me again and felt the same sensation more strongly. Did it make me feel happy? Was it sexual? I couldn't place it. His embrace was like experiencing warmth after being out in the cold for a long time. And then, as time passed, I started going into this fantasy whenever I felt down or distressed. I also remembered that when I was little, and Ami used to hit me, I would imagine Baba hugging and kissing me. But he was a silent spectator, and I had stopped thinking of him as my rescuer. It was odd that after so many years, I had started to draw on the same protection: the comfort of loving arms around me and feeling like the most precious thing to the man who held me like a sweet and beloved porcelain doll. My fantasy became my go-to place in times of tension and turmoil.

And now that fantasy had a face.

Ahad.

The thought of Ahad looking at me with understanding and empathy, checking up on me now and then, and the once-a-week session were all I needed to feel I mattered in my world.

Throughout my life, the most prominent constant was the deep gnawing ache in the middle of my tummy that came rushing in like unannounced monsoon rains. It played like a very low-key song in the background, and when I was distressed or anxious, the song would get louder and make me sit up straight. I got it checked many times, but no painkillers or antacids could remove the pain.

And then, of all the places and all the times in the world, a moment arrived when the web of knots in my tummy released, one by one, untangled, fighting each other to take the lead in coming apart.

It was during my third class. My classmate Umber, an upcoming freelance photographer, was processing. She was short, with a long mane of silky red hair that acted as a ruse, distracting from her plump body. She told the class how she had struggled with polycystic ovaries for a long time and was fat shamed. Suddenly, she changed course like an impulsive driver who switches lanes without giving any indication.

'I was raped when I was five,' she said and leant forward, partially covering her face with a hand, her loose hair dropping down and covering the rest.

Maha was absent that day, and Ahad was taking the class alone. He shifted his sofa chair to turn towards her but didn't utter a word.

'So sorry to hear that,' Musa, the young university student, interrupted.

'Let her talk,' Ahad reprimanded him, raising his hand in mid-air but in his habitual gentle tone.

'It was Ata Bhai, my neighbour's son.' She continued to look down and then started crying, the heart-wrenching soft cries of an adult and a little five-year-old girl, helpless to what she had been exposed to. Her pain was palpable, spreading through the room like a thick fog, hiding everything in the periphery.

I suddenly had a strong urge to run away from the room. A part of me admired her courage to share her deep pain without prompt, yet another part wanted to run away from listening to more of this.

'It must have been so scary for you,' Ahad said calmly.

'He touched me. Everywhere. It hurt so much! So much...' She abruptly got up and walked towards the back of the room, where a floral-themed vibrant jug of water was placed on a big dining table. The colours seemed obscene in light of what was unfolding in the room, a tad too bright and jarring to the senses.

Nida and Shahmeen were crying; the rest of the class were silent and sombre. It was as if we were attending someone's funeral, the pungent smell of death in the room. It was a death of childhood, the age of innocence; at five years old, she was robbed of her days of being carefree and frivolous.

I felt restless, my legs itching to get up and run. Such processes evoked thoughts and emotions in my mind and heart that I never felt ready to address.

Umber came and sat back in the seat. 'I'm done for today.'

There was complete silence for a few moments, and then my classmates fidgeted and chatted in their seats, an air of disquiet mixed with the heaviness of meeting another's pain so intimately. Others mirrored the turmoil I was experiencing in my mind, an urge to escape one's pain that had come alive by meeting its companion in another person.

Whenever someone processed, it activated a lot for others; personal traumas slowly waking up, wounds that had been silently bleeding becoming loud, and deeply buried thoughts threatening to come up.

There was a moment as students started shifting when I looked up and caught Ahad's warm eyes, and then, for a flash, he held my gaze. That look alone said a lot to me.

At that moment, my tummy expanded inside, releasing the knots of a lifetime intertwined with pain and turmoil. It felt like Ahad held one end of the knotted rope, and bit by bit, he untangled it.

During the break, I stepped out. I wanted to be alone. I sat in one of the garden chairs, leant my head back, and shut my eyes.

'Are you okay?' Ahad's voice jolted me out of my reverie, and I sat up. He noticed that.

'Sorry, I didn't mean to startle you.' He pulled a chair close to mine. Too close.

He was holding the rope again, untangling it bit by bit.

123

'No, it's okay, I'm fine.' I wished he would hold me.

'Why are you not having tea?' he asked in his typical soft voice laced with something that made my heart skip. Every time.

'I'm not thirsty.'

'You want to talk about it?' He was looking at me like he always did, his gaze almost reaching the dark recesses of my mind, heart, and soul to places no one had been to before.

'I don't know. I can discuss it in our session. I feel sad for Umber.' I looked up and held his gaze.

He didn't say anything but reached forward and patted my hand for a brief moment. A current ran through my body, but I didn't move my hand away in the hope that he would hold it. This was the first time he had touched me. That brief touch carried so much power, and I silently protested its abandonment so soon.

'Come on. I want you to eat something.'

'I don't feel like it.'

'I'm not asking; I'm telling you. Let's go.'

To my surprise, he stretched his hand towards me. Was it really happening? I had fantasised about Ahad holding my hand so many times that for a moment I froze. But then I took his hand and got up. He let go of it after a tight squeeze. What a lovely gesture this was, and I felt my throat choking up, and before I could stop them, my tears betrayed me once more and filled my eyes.

Ahad didn't say anything but stood close as I quietly cried. I wanted to lean into him and be inside his warm embrace. It had been so long since I had been held. Arsalan and I hadn't touched each other for months, not even a hug or gentle handholding. And more than that, what alarmed me was that I no longer felt the need for it from him. Whenever he came in close proximity, it triggered me, and my body recoiled and protested that invasion.

For the next few weeks, I continued to see Ahad in therapy. That hour was my happiest hour, more so than the counselling class. I felt seen, met, and loved by this tall, warm person and felt deeply attached to him. It did feel like love. Between sessions, I would have a fantasy where I was in pain or hurting, and he was the one who, like a knight in shining armour, saved the day for me. That day in the garden froze in time for me, and I would imagine myself scared and confused and him coming forward and holding me in his arms. He would kiss the top of my head and tell me he would be my friend forever and never leave me alone. I could come to him for anything. I realised I wanted more than friendship. I wanted love.

What surprised me was how my fantasy was this platonic image and nothing more than that. Considering I had unmet sexual needs, and he was attractive, I never felt that temptation for him. He was like coming home after a long, arduous journey.

After many sessions, I was ready to talk more about my mother. I was prepared to risk exploring it.

'How are you?' my smiling and warm-hearted therapist asked me.

'I'm good. What about you?' I responded with an equally heartfelt smile, as if we were sharing some secret that only we knew about.

'What would you like to talk about?' Ahad leant back in the uncomfortable Healing Matters chair. Ahad's energy was heartfelt, unlike Arsalan's aggression, like marshmallows slowly cooked over the fire on a winter evening.

'I want to discuss, you know...' I looked at him, urging him to read and complete my thoughts.

'You want to discuss your mother?'

'And my marriage. But I need to say out loud what I still find hard to even think about on my own, Ahad.' I was anxious the minute the words left my mouth. There was a heavy rock lodged in the middle of my chest, and I felt suffocated.

'I can't breathe.' I started shaking.

'Take long, slow breaths. Tell me what you're feeling.'

'There is this huge rock right here,' I cried out, hitting my chest in small, abrupt movements. 'I can't breathe.'

'You're having a panic attack.' He took my clammy hand in his.

'Take it out, will you?'

I grabbed onto his hand with both of mine, refusing to let go. My heartbeat slowed down and so did the tears on my cheeks, but I didn't want to let go of his hand. A voice warned me that it was wrong to touch him, but I didn't know how to let go of his hand. He had offered it himself, hadn't he?

'I want to share all that's happened, but it's hard…' I began.

'It's okay. There's no rush. Take a long, deep breath….' His hand squeezed mine, and I sensed he wanted to withdraw it. I instantly let go and grabbed a few tissues from the box and wiped my tear-streaked face.

'She didn't love Baba at all. She cheated on him for so many years.' I was feeling distraught as images popped into my mind. Baba always trying to please her, and she dismissing him with her habitual coldness that only melted to something warm when Uncle Uzair was around.

'It went on for years and years, Ahad.' I looked up at him at that point, trying to find some evidence of shock or judgment. All I saw was limitless compassion and understanding of the pain and shame I was experiencing. 'I feel so ashamed,' I added.

'It's her shame that you're experiencing. It belongs to her and no one else.'

'What do you mean?'

'She should feel ashamed for making your home so unsafe. Her actions have nothing to do with you, Saniya.'

His words landed somewhere in the deep recesses of my psyche. Did her actions have nothing to do with me? But what if I ended up like her? I was also thinking about another man. I had just held his hand, and would I have stopped if he had offered more? I was beginning to feel uneasy with where my mind was taking me. I started playing with my hair and avoided looking at him.

'Did your father know of this? Anyone else in the family?' Ahad's questions stopped me from going further into that darkness full of difficult questions.

'No. I made sure no one knew. I made sure of that.' I crossed my arms and leant back. 'Only I knew, and now you know. Please don't share it with anyone. Please promise me that.' I no longer had any control over the secret I had been a custodian of for over three decades.

'Of course. Anything you tell me stays between us, Saniya. You never have to worry about that.'

'It went on for years and years until he left Pakistan. Every time we would go to Nana's house, they would...' I didn't dare to complete the sentence. 'I feel so ashamed,' I repeated without thinking.

'As I said, it's not your shame. What happened to you was horrible, and no child should have to carry the burden of their mother's actions. I can't imagine how you held it in for so long, but you kept your parents' marriage intact by keeping this to yourself.'

It hit me how true that was. Had I shared the burden of that ugly truth, Baba would have left Ami.

I rested my head on the sofa and shut my eyes. I didn't have the energy to voice all the thoughts roaming around, swimming through the stream of my consciousness. An image popped up in my head. My mother was sitting on the bed, his head in her lap, her fingers running through his hair, and her face close to his... so close.

I abruptly opened my eyes and sat up. It was unbearable to think of that. It was painful to think of images like these. He secretly held her feet under the blanket as we watched TV on the lounge sofa. A lipstick mark stained his cheek as he came out of the kitchen, matching my mother's lip colour. So many nights on the weekends, I woke up to find her missing from the bedroom. I stayed up for hours, comforting Maheen so she didn't wake up and feigning sleep as I discovered Ami sneaking quietly back into her room. Somewhere. I was protecting her too. Could she not see that? I was afraid to tell her that I knew. I didn't want her to feel ashamed.

No one knew of all these clandestine moments or how heavily they weighed on the little child, the teenager, the young adult, and even the grown-up woman. Because, for all of them, that woman who cheated on her husband was her mother, and somehow, she believed that it would define how the world would perceive her, and she didn't know how to assuage her fears.

'I hate her,' I said, slamming my fist on my knees. I repeated the movement and Ahad took hold of my fist and gently opened my fingers one by one and put my hand on my knee.

We looked at each other in silence, and the urge to ask him for a hug was overwhelming. 'I'm tired; I don't want to talk anymore,' I said quietly.

'That doesn't mean you have to leave sooner.' So I stayed and secretly wished I could stay around him for the rest of my life. My heart reassured me that he would always be around. He had told me once that he had been working with clients for many years, and I knew I was more than a client, even if we didn't admit that to each other.

That evening, one of my classmates called me while I was getting ready for bed. The children had long gone to bed, and Arsalan was attending a business dinner.

Shahzen had joined Healing Matters just a few months before me, and although she was in her early twenties, we were close.

'*Kaisi hain aap*, madam?' The chirpy smile in her voice always made me laugh, even on a day like today, where I could still feel the aftershocks of an earthquake that had lasted for many years of my early life. The session had left me with heaviness in my mind and body.

'I'm good. A little overwhelmed, Shahzen.'

'Why? Tell me about it.'

'Therapy is tough. The session was exhausting.' I tried to adjust the pillow under my neck. Since the session, I had been experiencing stiffness and shoulder pain.

'I didn't know you were having therapy. Since when? Who are you seeing?' She blurted out a parade of questions, sounding more like an investigating officer than a friend who was simply curious.

I laughed at her inquisitiveness and the bombardment of questions. 'Aren't we all having therapy? Isn't that part of the course requirement?'

'It was, but I don't think anyone has continued with it after that one session we all took. But good for you.'

'Well, I'm having sessions with Ahad. I've been seeing him for weeks now,' I proudly announced, as if being Ahad's client was an honour that had only been bestowed upon me.

'What do you mean, Ahad? How can he be your therapist?'

Was she upset, or was I overreading her emotions. 'What do you mean? Why can't he be?'

'He's our tutor. He's only supposed to offer one session.' She sounded pretty angry; the emotion was no longer a mere hint.

'It doesn't make sense to me. Why only one?' I feigned innocence and regretted sharing what I had. I knew about the one-session policy, but when Ahad had confirmed it wasn't a problem, why would anyone else have an issue with it?

'Because it's a dual relationship and a rule of the organisation. Didn't you know that?'

I sat up in bed and hugged the pillow. This conversation wasn't going to be our typical leisurely exchange of words that flowed from one topic to another like a meandering river. I felt as if something was breaking in that moment.

'No, I didn't know that, and he offered it to me, Shahzen.'

I started to feel my full-blown defensiveness at that point. Why was she blaming me? It was Ahad's choice, I reassured myself.

'I don't know what's happening here, but this is not okay.'

'I didn't know. Why are you blaming me?'

'I'm not blaming you, but I asked for one extra session, and he flat out told me no.'

'I don't know why he said no, and maybe there are others who are seeing him or Maha. I don't understand why this is a big deal,' I added.

She ignored my words and asked, 'How long has this been going on for?'

I felt caught between a rock and a hard place. I didn't want to divulge any more information, but I had to. I swallowed hard and replied, 'A few sessions. Yaar, I really don't understand why you're reacting like this.'

'Because it matters. I'm still trying to process what you've just shared.'

My body was fully activated at that point with a gnawing foreboding sensation. Her reaction was alarming, and I could feel my breathing quicken.

'Anyway, I need to go, but this is very disturbing. How could he favour you like that?' Her voice sounded choked with unshed tears. What was happening? What had I missed?

'What favour, yaar?' I almost cried out.

'Stop acting so naïve! Did you not hear that it's against the rules? I asked him for one extra session, and he refused, and here you have been meeting him for weeks.'

'Not meeting him! Taking therapy sessions, for fuck's sake.' I threw the pillow on the floor and got out of bed.

'I can't talk to you anymore,' Shahzen abruptly said and hung up on me without me saying anything.

I threw the mobile on the bed and went to the kitchen to get a glass of water.

The first thought that hit me was that Shahzen shared my feelings for Ahad. I wasn't entirely sure what feelings I had, but I could hear her voice's loud and clear anger, jealousy, and betrayal.

This was horrible. Shahzen had turned a nurturing and significant life experience into a dark, dirty secret. He was my therapist, and I should be expected to feel attached to my therapist. I felt as if I had lost something. I didn't know what it was. Yet, the feeling was strong and loud. Should I go and discuss this with Maha? Had I done something wrong? That night I was restless and kept waking up until Arsalan's irritated voice admonished me to be still. *God, please fix this.* I could not lose him.

In the morning, I texted Maha and requested to meet her urgently. She invited me to her place. I was certain she had picked up the distress and urgency in my voice. Class was still two days away, but I couldn't hold in this anxiety. I kept reassuring myself that I was making a mountain out of a molehill, and this wasn't a problem at all. After all, Ahad was a professional, and if he had continued to work with me, he must have thought through his decision.

At noon, I waited for Maha in her comfy and casual living room. It had green walls with quite a few paintings of all sizes on the walls. My eyes darted from one art piece to another, but I was lost, and her walls reminded me of how I felt at the Sunday bazaar, where one could get everything at wholesale rates in a place of utter chaos.

A maid offered me a glass of mango juice. I gulped it down, thirsty and almost dizzy. Was this how one felt sitting before a confession box in a church? But here, the priest knew who I was. What was I confessing to though?

Maha entered the room smiling and calm as always. That's the energy she always brought to a room, but it did nothing for my jittery nerves today.

'How are you, Saniya?' Her voice, face, and energy were all serene, like sitting under a big old tree on a hot summer's day. My throat was choked, but I gulped down what was coming up and wiped my sticky hands on the blue denim I was wearing.

'I wanted to share something.'

'Sure. Tell me.' She got up from the seat opposite me to sit next to me. She could sense that I was upset. She was emotionally attuned to others.

'You know how you and Ahad offered us a session each?'

'Yeah, I know. Do you want one with me?'

'No. I already took mine with Ahad,' I replied and looked away. I liked the lamp that was standing in the corner of the room, alone but glorious with its mosaic design, and that was the beauty of it in a crowded room.

'That's good. He is a good therapist.' She confirmed what I already knew.

'Well, I am still taking sessions with him. It's been more than two months now.'

'What do you mean you're still taking them?' She tilted her head and looked at me with narrowed eyes.

'I know we were told we could have one session, but Ahad said I could go on.' My voice was breaking, and I hated being vulnerable before her. What if she figured out how important Ahad was to me?

She stayed quiet for a few moments. Too long.

'It's not your fault, Saniya. Ahad should have known better.' Maha was frowning.

'I don't understand, Maha.' Tears rolled down my cheeks. What was happening?

'You will have to make a call, Saniya.'

'What kind of call?'

'You can either continue the class or therapy.'

She had just pushed me quietly into the pool's deep end.

132

Did she not know that I was scared of the water? Did she not know I didn't know how to swim?

'It's a dual relationship, and this is against the rules. You are an outstanding student, and I would hate to see you go. But if you want to choose therapy, I respect that too.'

'But our classes are ending anyway, so can't I continue?' I protested. There had to be a way out of this.

'No. A rule was broken and it's not fair to make an exception for a student,' Maha replied with a tight-lipped smile. Was she softening the blow?

I heard what she said. I understood the choice she was nudging me to take, but I didn't want to listen to any of it.

'Take your time to think about it and let me know by Friday. If you choose to continue class, you must have one termination session with Ahad as soon as possible.'

There was disappointment in her voice every time she spoke his name. And every time my heart dropped lower and lower to a place where it might be impossible to retrieve it. I had lost him. It was over. Termination.

I blinked away the tears and looked straight into her disappointed face.

'I will continue the class. I don't need time to think about that. Please let me know when I can have the termination session,' I responded with all the courage I could muster.

I could hear the sobs, loud and angry, pulsating within with a force that was hard to diffuse, but with all my will, I placed a heavy boundary in front of it. I didn't want Maha to know how close I was to Ahad. I knew she would judge me for having feelings for my therapist. I bowed my head and looked at my pale hands.

'Good call, Saniya. You have the potential to be a good therapist. I understand this must be difficult for you, but remember, this wasn't your fault.'

Stop blaming him. Stop it, please.

'Thank you for your time, Maha.'

'You're welcome. I appreciate your honesty and you coming forward.'

'Yeah. I had an idea about this rule, but Ahad said it wasn't an issue. I'm sorry.' I felt guilty for blaming the man I cared for with every cell in my body.

'I'm proud of you for coming forward with it. I will recommend another therapist to you too. This has been going on for too long as it is.'

A sob escaped me, and I abruptly got up, but she had seen the tears spilling uncontrollably.

I said, 'Thank you,' and without turning back, I rushed out.

After decades and decades of unimaginable, gut-wrenching pain that was an unwanted companion, I finally had a space where I felt understood and was able to heal, and I knew I was important to someone in this world. And now, Maha was telling me that it takes a long time to heal and that there would be more pain to navigate through. How could she know how emotionally dependent I was on Ahad? The thought of not seeing him was devastating.

Later in the evening, I texted Ahad asking for a session. He had told me that I could ask for an extra session beyond our scheduled one.

The word 'termination' was a death sentence, and I couldn't stop thinking about it. Minutes passed, turning into half an hour, and then one hour turned into more hours, but no response came. I checked my WhatsApp; the blue ticks indicated that he had seen my text.

Why wasn't he responding to me? I turned the phone upside down and a minute later looked at it again. *Relax! He's probably just busy.*

I heard Neha and Nyle arguing in the TV room.

'Nyle! Neha! Stop screaming,' I yelled out, but the noise didn't dissipate. 'Zubaida,' I screamed again. 'Leave everything and attend to the kids.'

I got up and shut the bedroom door and fell on the bed upside down.

Hours passed without any response. I sent him a few more texts.

Please reply to me... Have I done something? When can I see you? But no response came. I was unable to sit still so grabbed the car keys and went for a drive.

Around 10:00am the next morning, I got a text from Maha.

Saniya. You are scheduled for your last session with Ahad at four tomorrow afternoon.

Why did she arrange the session? She must have talked to Ahad. Was he angry at me and that's why he hadn't replied to me? I started rolling my stiff shoulders. It was alright. I hadn't done anything for him to be mad at me. I did tell Maha that it was Ahad's choice, though, but I wasn't blaming him. I would tell him that I wasn't blaming him. Ahad would fix this.

And with that hope and faith I had in Ahad, the safety I had come to trust in his care for me, I entered the therapy room the next day to meet my protector, who I knew wouldn't stop taking care of me.

10 *Therapist*

'Can we be friends if I terminate therapy?' Taha enquired as he put a half-empty glass of water on the table beside him. He had been my client for two years, and we shared a grand working alliance, a term exclusively used for the therapeutic relationship between a client and therapist. His journey had been quite transformative, and I had loved being a part of it; an empathic witness to this young man's resilience to change himself. He had sought therapy to treat his addiction to cocaine and suicidal attempts, and gradually, the will to live had taken over, and he had stopped trying to harm himself. He was now a life coach for adolescents who suffered from addiction, and for me, it was a miracle that he had choreographed this recovery and continued to inspire himself and others.

I smiled at the sweet question. 'No, even if we terminate therapy, we won't be able to be friends.'

'Why not?' he asked with a smile that reminded me of Nyle's preschool friend Musa who had the same expression that melted my heart.

'It will affect the work we've done in therapy, and I would rather keep the sanctity of our therapeutic relationship intact and honour the work we've done.'

'So, are you telling me I have to pay you for the rest of my life just to see you?' His caramel-coloured eyes had a mischievous twinkle.

I burst out laughing.

'Yes, Taha. You got it!'

After he left, the room carried the remnants of shared laughter and trust and a journey between a healer and healed. Sometimes I wondered which one I was, the former or the latter, as I too was healing with the love and validation I got from the clients. Taha's desire to be friends with me was a profound healing moment. Having always run after loved ones for attention and care, to be pursued now was a novel and sometimes overwhelming experience that I was learning to get used to. I was worthy of being loved and my clients reminded me of that daily. I had a purpose in my life now, and I was valued.

Lately, I had started to question if considering myself as a healer for my clients was indulging in a God complex and putting myself on a pedestal. The challenge with this self-image was that, often, when I worked with clients who didn't have a success story like Taha or never returned to therapy after a session or two, I experienced a sense of failure and would keep questioning myself.

But the good news was that I was aware of this and had been exploring it with my supervisor every week. Ah! My supervisor. Every therapist's go-to person to understand our blind spots and understand the client's process.

I was grateful for this incredible and fulfilling profession I had found my way into and felt humbled by the love of my clients and the risk they took in trusting me, granting me permission to enter their inner worlds, furnished by wounds and pain, walls adorned by incredible stories of trauma and human endurance.

I got up and stretched and felt a piercing pain in my lower back. I had to slow down. I was working long hours, and between Nyle and Neha, the demands of home duties, and Arsalan, I was exhausted more often than not. It felt like I'd signed up for a cross-country race with no pre-defined distance or duration.

I needed to take time out for myself but guilt, with as many shades as a colour palette, kept me trapped. A Pakistani woman's work was considered her 'me time'. Maybe it would change one day, but today wasn't that day, and I experienced guilt from the fulfillment and joy I found in my work and how sometimes it invaded my consciousness more than the thoughts of my husband and children.

My last session that day was with a thirty-year-old single dentist with a severe history of physical abuse by her father, who had been in therapy for around six months. She lived with him, and he had complete control over her life.

We had explored her past trauma, the dysfunctional relationship with the abusive father, what her mother's silence and inability to protect her meant for her, and how it all manifested in her adult relationships. She moved from one man to another and unconsciously always sought abusive men, and then left them.

Through therapy, she had come to a realisation that, in searching for a safe, loving relationship, she unconsciously chose men who were similar to her father and invoked familiar feelings of abuse and rejection.

Zoe arrived a few minutes late, rushing in, and after dumping her handbag on the floor, she sat down, putting her feet up, cross-legged on the sofa.

'Hi, Saniya.' Without waiting for a response, she picked up the handbag she had thrown down a moment ago and started rummaging through it, looking for something but taking out nothing.

'How are you, Zoe?' I began. 'How was your week?'

'I hate him. Why does he control me so much?' She threw the bag on the floor again and started picking the cuticles of her nails. Her restless energy was palpable in the room, and I sensed an unease within myself. She was mostly highly strung in the beginning of every session and settled towards the end.

She had big, lost eyes that dominated her face, distracting the viewer from her other facial features. She was a very skinny woman who, as a child, would stop eating when she struggled with any overwhelming emotion, be it fear or anger, or helplessness. Her eating disorder had carried on as an adult too. We had explored her relationship with eating in many sessions, and she understood it was something she could control in a world where she experienced powerlessness against her harsh father. She had made progress and had a healthier lifestyle now.

We also processed the helplessness she had internalised from her mother, a weak figure, dependent on her father, unable to stand up for her rights as a wife, and who couldn't protect Zoe. For her, the abandonment from her mum was as damaging and painful as the abuse from the father.

'You know he's waiting outside? When will he let me go?' She put her legs down and started looking around the room. 'Wasn't there a red floor cushion here, Saniya?'

'No. So tell me, what does him letting go of you mean for you?' I was familiar with how her train of thoughts ran all over the place and knew how to bring her mindfully to the moment.

'I want to be free of him. Don't you understand that? I am a thirty-year-old adult, for fuck's sake.' Her voice rose, cracking with a mixture of frustration and helplessness.

'Are you?' I challenged. It was time to put the foot on the accelerator.

'Am I what?' Her head tilted towards me.

'Are you an adult?'

'What kind of question is that?' She rolled her eyes. 'Don't go Freudian on me.'

I smiled at her remark. Her wry humour was a part of her I looked forward to meeting. 'What stopped you from telling him today that you wanted to come on your own for the session?'

'I don't know. He told me he would bring me here.'

'He told you? And you agreed?' I smiled to soften the challenge.

'I didn't know therapists were allowed to be sarcastic?'

'I'm sorry if you felt like that.' She didn't take it well.

She shrugged and looked away and delayed answering my question. 'What choice do I have? He can get furious.'

I let out a deep breath. Thank God she wasn't seriously offended. 'And what does him being angry mean for you, Zoe?'

'It means he'll shout and scream. I hate it.' She yelled the last words out and slammed her fist on the table next to her.

'When he starts doing that, can you walk away? Or tell him that you cannot accept it?'

'I can't say that to him. I can't move.' Her voice had dropped to a whisper, and she buried her face in her hands. A scared little girl sitting in a woman's body, and I had an impulse to get up and hug her. I stayed in my seat.

'Who is talking right now, Zoe?'

She stayed silent and did not respond. 'It's the little girl who can't speak up. She seems to be frozen in time.' She looked up at me, with quivering lips.

'Zoe, your inner child is so scared of your father that she cannot move when he starts shouting. She quietly sat in the car today and came over here.'

Hearing that, she burst into tears. After a few minutes she started talking. 'Something happens to me when he starts shouting. I get scared. As if any minute he will get up and start hitting me.'

'I know. I hear you. But you're not that girl anymore. You are an empowered woman who earns for herself and can get up and walk away any minute. Zoe, he knows that, but you don't know that yet.'

'That's true. I can stand up to him now, but I freeze when he gets mad.'

'That's your trauma response to all that you went through as a child. Have you heard of fight, freeze, and flight?'

'Yes, and yes, when he's upset, my hands get cold and my body is so stiff it can't move. My heart rate is so slow, Saniya, and at times I can't breathe.'

I nodded. 'I understand. Your nervous system perceives the threat and responds how it always has. Breathe for now and honour yourself for how far you've come. It's not easy to stand up to all that fear and pain. But you're trying so hard and have come a long way.'

I encouraged and acknowledged the internalised little girl's pain and the adult woman's strength. I was holding the role of the mother in the room, providing love and assurance and encouraging her to stand up to the abusive father. I wondered, though, if I could protect her.

'I can never say anything to him,' she said, dejected and hopeless.

'You also couldn't say out loud that he'd hurt you. You thought it was your fault all these years, right?' I reminded her of the early weeks of therapy when it was difficult for her to express how hurt she had been by her father. To come to terms with the knowledge that the father she loved was also the father she hated.

'Let's try something,' I suggested to her. 'It's called the empty chair experiment.'

'What do I need to do?' she asked, immediately in her habitual mode, the good girl who can't say no to an authority figure. As I was the perceived nurturing mother in the room, I knew a part of her psyche unconsciously feared when I would become like the aggressive father or the passive mother and abandon her. She had become a people pleaser, especially in her intimate relationships. I was aware of my conflicting position where my advice as her therapist, who had more power than her in the therapeutic relationship, could be seen as controlling, like her father. But I also appeared as the mother she didn't have who encouraged her to stand up to the abuse and believed in her.

I sat on the floor, leaving my sofa chair empty before her. 'I want you to imagine your father sitting in that chair, and whatever you feel like saying to him, you can say it.'

'This feels so weird. I can't speak to an empty chair.' She laughed, playing with her bleached hair. Her face had lost colour. Was I pushing her too soon?

'Take your time; if you're not ready for this, we can try it some other day.' I rested my head against the wall. My back was hurting; the concrete fence added to the painful pressure in the middle of my back rather than relieving it.

This experiment was used as an intervention, and the timing of it mattered. If done too soon, it could negatively impact the client. In my years of work, I saw most people struggling with mental health issues because of their parents, be it physical beating, which was a common practice and culturally accepted, or parents' unhappy marriages, which was again expected to be acknowledged with a pinch of salt. And even though these issues deeply hurt my clients, they found it very hard to accept that their parents had played a damaging role. They would rather believe that they caused it, and denying the reality of their parents was easier than admitting it.

The sound of Zoe pouring water into a glass shook me out of my reverie. Guilt pierced through me for neglecting her, but I didn't let it grow and nipped it in the bud. I couldn't expect myself not to zone out at times.

The energy in the room had changed. I saw it on my client's face. She would look at the empty chair and then look away. Her breathing changed. My body felt the pressure of unspoken words, long repressed and forgotten like a precious item in some cupboard in the house, lost but quickly found when thought about.

She started to speak. 'Who the hell do you think you are?' Her face was flushed and sweaty.

She had jumped right in.

'Why are you waiting outside for me? Why did you hit me over nothing?' She paused and looked at me and turned her head towards the empty chair again. 'I hated you when you started shouting at me in front of everyone. I was so embarrassed, Abu.' A sob escaped her. She tried to resist it, but the tears pushed forward. The tension in her body had become a force felt in every nook and corner of the room. 'I can't do this anymore.' She covered her face with her hands.

I got up from the floor. This was beyond her window of tolerance.

Her shoulders slumped and sobs wracked her body. It was difficult to see her pain, but it had been granted permission to escape, like a prisoner who was told his sentence had been reduced and he could leave.

'You don't have to. Take it easy. You did great.'

In moments like these, I would fully experience my helplessness at multiple levels. A therapist who could not take this pain away even if she tried, who was part of a world that brew hurt and anguish in one way or another. I wished I had a magic wand to help those who walked into my world. I was beginning to learn that healing did not mean escaping one's pain or solving problems and that the way to recovery was through pain.

I reclaimed my chair. She needed to see her father was not in the room. I patted her leg, mindful of how physical contact between clients and therapists was looked down upon in therapy, but at that point, I didn't care; the little girl in my mind's eye needed to be touched and validated.

'I'm sorry for what you went through when you were young and what you continue to go through.'

She looked up as I said those words and a smile lit up her face. That moment was odd. That radiant smile pushed the cascades of tears and sorrow away, standing bright and tall. It was unexpected but heartfelt to watch.

'I feel so light,' she announced, cleaning her tear-streaked face with the back of her hands, removing any evidence of their presence and what they meant, victorious in the little shift that had come within her.

'I know I will stand up to him one day,' she said, lifting her face. I knew she would.

'I believe in you, Zoe. You have come such a long way.'

Our eyes locked in a moment of shared hope. This intervention could have backfired, but saying she could stand up to her father was enough. It would take a few months of therapy before she could arrive at that place where she could actually stand up to her father, but it was a start. I wanted to take my time with it and hoped she would continue to show up.

Tired but content with the work, I left for home and put some music on to disengage from the clients' processes.

As I entered the house, I was greeted with loud screams.

'Mama!' Nyle and Neha came running towards me and hugged me. *Awww... my babies...*

'Yes, Mama *ki jaan*.' I kissed the top of their heads. 'Stop screaming, you two. What's up?'

'Mama, I want to order pizza but Nyle is saying I can't.' Neha started bawling, and before I could get a word in, Nyle yelled out.

'Mama, she's lying. I never said that.' He slapped Neha on her back and her cries turned into high-volume screaming. She was a loud crier.

'Stop it, both of you. Or no ordering in.'

Instantly there was silence, followed by two pairs of legs running towards the living room. Threats worked every time, and I wasn't proud of this parenting tactic, but it had been a long day, and I had no bandwidth to try some other way to calm them down.

I looked at my reflection in the mirror in the lounge and noticed my grey hair which Arsalan had jokingly pointed out in the morning.

'*Buddhi!* You're old, madam.'

He could be hilarious when he was relaxed and spontaneous, and for him to notice even the grey in my hair was a welcome moment. Any attention was better than none at all.

At present, things were smooth at home. He was busy as always, but for a change, I had no time either to think about my marriage troubles, and I was content. We were no longer drowning in our suffering and dragging each other down, and I hoped this could be the first step towards more peace. But that's what our marriage had always been like. There were good and bad days, and we were making an effort with each other. I was calm and grounded and in a good space in my life. Work was my happy place.

I was pretty ambitious, and since becoming an independent practitioner, I had worked hard to build my practice. Healing Matters no longer referred clients to me, and I was dependent on client referrals or my colleagues. Unfortunately, there was not a sense of community among the therapists and, at times, there would be days without any work. The fear of failure would blind me to the fact that I hadn't long been in this profession, and I would have nightmares about not having any clients to work with. That was one of the reasons I said yes to anyone who reached out for therapy and ended up working weekends.

I asked Arsalan to go out for dinner in the evening. I was resilient, and I didn't like giving up, and the session with Zoe had rejuvenated my hope for the human spirit and strength to work and bring change. I kept oscillating between hope and hopelessness, falling and getting up again, giving up and trying again. I held these opposing forces within with the same compassion and acceptance for both. Today I wanted to find my way back to my husband, and as things were relatively calm, I wanted to use the opportunity to connect with him. Yes, my marriage was turbulent and empty, but there were also seeds of friendship and care. Maybe there was still a chance to grow those seeds into plants and, eventually, trees. Perhaps they needed a different kind of nurturing and love.

Around 8:30pm, I was ready and dressed to kill in a black jumpsuit with a chunky gold necklace that matched the golden eyeliner I had experimented with.

'You look pretty, babe,' Arsalan complimented me as he entered the room, back from the office.

'A rare compliment from my husband!' I laughed and stepped forward and put my arms around him. At that moment, I remembered the rush of falling in love in those initial days of marrying him. It was all I needed, a little acknowledgement that I existed and all the pain could dissolve.

'Really? I think I always compliment you!' he teased, hugging me back.

'Yeah, right. And I'm Angelina Jolie's twin sister.'

'I wish you were.' He laughed and bent forward and, to my surprise, kissed me on the forehead. A strong surge of emotion came up, and I stepped closer to kiss him on the lips when the door opened with a loud bang.

'Mama and Baba are kissing,' Nyle screamed as Neha joined in, laughing, and ran forward to hug us. Arsalan opened his arms, pulling us into a tight embrace. It was one of the happiest moments of my life. I wished that this moment could freeze in time, to become the blueprint of my remaining years of life.

'We want to go with you too,' Nyle demanded. He was a handsome boy, a good mixture of us both, and tall for his age.

'No, Nyle,' Neha argued. 'They're going on a date. You dumbo!' My six-year-old little madam was mature beyond her age, which sometimes worried me. Her ponytail bobbed as she struggled to get out of the tight embrace.

'Mama, she called me dumbo!' Nyle wailed.

'Crybaby.' Neha wasn't going to back off and managed to free herself and started jumping.

'Enough!' I laughed and disengaged from the group hug, reassuring them with the thought of pizza arriving.

Arsalan withdrew and went to the bathroom to freshen up after kissing them both.

The dinner was one of the best I'd had in many years. We didn't argue. We chose the same place to eat and stopped at our friend's post-dinner for coffee.

After we came back, he pulled me towards him and cuddled me. There was a moment where I had hoped there would be more, a kiss at least, but I didn't want to ruin the space between us that was new and so tender, like a newborn that has to be held gently and with utmost care. He was tired, I reminded myself and settled for a hug and dozed off.

It must have been an hour later when I was jolted out of my sleep. I had no idea what prompted it, but my heart was racing. I turned over to hold Arsalan and found the bed to be empty. Where was he? I looked at my phone and it was 2:00am.

I looked towards the bathroom, but there was no light switched on. Maybe he had gone to get a drink of water, although he never did that.

Slowly, I slipped out of bed and crept towards the guest bedroom, which Arsalan now used as an office when working from home. I somehow knew he was there, but I didn't know how. I wiped my clammy hands on my nightdress; it was one of those moments when you just know, deep within your body, an instinct one deeply trusted.

A flashback came at that moment. Another night, I'd woken up to a closed door and muffled voices, which caused me so much distress and unease about what was going on behind the door, yet the fear of opening them was greater. I shook my head and took a long, deep breath. Take it easy. He must be working.

As I crept closer to the door, I heard voices. Arsalan was talking and laughing. I put my ear next to the door. Who was he

147

talking to at this hour? I couldn't breathe, and my legs started to shake.

'The day went well. I tried calling you before, but I think you were sleeping.' A moment later. 'I miss you too.' His voice was different. Loving. Seductive. This was not how I had ever heard him talk.

I listened for the next few minutes, his voice drifting away. I couldn't move, rooted to the spot, numb, feeling my legs might give out at any minute.

I went back to my room, closed the door behind me, and went back to bed. My heart broke into a million pieces, and I knew in that moment those pieces couldn't be found or repaired again. I decided not to confront him. It wouldn't change anything.

A lonely tear escaped my eye, and I covered my face with the duvet cover. My marriage was over.

11 *Girl*

'Hurry up, find your other shoe,' I scolded myself, with a heart that was running a mile a minute as I feared Ami would leave me.

Again.

She never waited for me when we had to go somewhere and left without warning if I wasn't ready on time. She was waiting in the car now with Maheen and constantly honking, the noise starting to pound in my skull. Where were we even going and why could I not remember? I knew I had to go with her or she would... what? I was getting more confused and overwhelmed as the honking continued. Wiping the beads of sweat from my forehead with the back of my hand, I started running around the room looking for the other shoe.

Why could she not stop honking and help me look for it?

I cried out loud as I looked under the bed, under the table, but I couldn't find it. Suddenly the honking stopped. I paused. Ami! She was leaving. I ran outside holding on tightly to the one shoe. In the rush, I tripped and fell face down on the hard driveway. And to my greatest horror, I saw the red Corolla speeding away with Maheen's face plastered to the rear window, waving at me. I got up and ran as fast as I could, screaming at the top of my lungs.

'Ami! Stop!' I was crying but the car didn't stop and soon vanished.

I snapped open my eyes. My heart was thumping loud enough to hear it, or was I imagining it? It was pitch dark, and I adjusted to the darkness after a few moments had passed and the ceiling fan caught my attention. I turned my head and heard the old clock on the wall. *Tick-tock. Tick-tock.* Oh God! It was a dream. I was in my bed at Nana's home. I touched my face and found my cheeks to be wet. Had I been crying in my sleep? What a strange and horrible dream it was. Turning on my side, I found Maheen lying at the far end of the bed. I sat up and dragged her dead weight by her legs towards me, afraid she would fall. God, she was heavy!

What a terrible dream, I thought again as I wiped the tears and hugged Maheen tightly. Why couldn't we ever be at home on weekends? I frowned, thinking of my room at home, missing my books and my favourite pink cushion that my best friend had given me for my birthday. There was nothing to do here, and unlike my younger days when I could spend hours outside, I was bored and restless now. Nana was old, too, and he hardly listened to anything we said. He had some issues with his hearing, and everything had to be repeated, but Ami said it was because I spoke too fast, a mile a minute, according to her. Ami was hardly to be seen when we were at Nana's, and then there was Uzair Uncle whom I hated with every fibre of my being.

Last night I was upset, so in protest, I skipped dinner even though I loved chicken biryani. My stomach grumbled in hunger, and I hoped there was some left over.

The bathroom light was on. Ami must be in there. I waited for her to come out, to get her permission before getting food from the kitchen. For a change, she had started sleeping downstairs with us, unlike before when she would be in the room next to Uncle Uzair, and those were the nights when I could hardly sleep a wink. That contributed to the dark circles under my eyes which Baba thought was because of watching TV. When Ami slept with us, it felt safe, and I could sleep without any worry.

I hoped Ami wouldn't get mad at me for wanting food at this hour. A long time ago, I had woken up in the middle of the night and started watching TV, and Ami had lost her temper. She had woken up Baba too, and Maheen with the yelling and scolding and a harsh slap on my back that had hurt.

I was terrified of her anger. Her face changed. Her eyes would bulge, and she would give an icy stare that could mean anything. I knew in my heart that she didn't like me, but sometimes she smiled at me, and when she did, it would make me happy and hope that the smile would never disappear from her face. I wanted that experience more often. But lately, her anger was contagious, and for no rhyme or reason, I wanted to break things and scream at the top of my lungs, and the energy it took to ensure that it didn't happen was tiring. Maheen and I were never asked how we were doing like my friend's mum asked her every day after school. Ami was a robot who served us food and clothes, and Baba was a silent figure who followed her lead. Was that how mums and dads were?

I couldn't ask her any of that. I loved her but I hated her too. How did that work? When I thought of her and that man, my head hurt as images came up. A few days back I had seen them standing and hugging in Nana's kitchen. I had run out of the room, breathless and terrified. Had they seen me run? I never wanted Ami to find out that I knew her secret. I didn't understand why not, but it was something I felt strongly about. My heart wished she would stop without anyone finding out what she'd done, because the day this terrible secret came out, she would leave us. I believed that. I had to keep her secret safe. My mind was confused thinking about the nature of what she was hiding.

I looked towards the bathroom again. Why wasn't she coming out? That was odd. I got up and put my ear against the bathroom door. Silence. There was no sound coming from inside. I tried the door handle, and the door opened up to an empty bathroom.

My heart sank. She was gone again. Shutting the door closed, I went back to bed. Would she ever stop? Bile came into my mouth, but I didn't throw up. A few minutes later, the room door opened, and I heard her tiptoe into the room. I wasn't planning to let her know I was up, but without thinking, I got up and looked at her.

'Where were you?'

'Why are you up? Don't you know how late it is?' Her face was flushed, and she wasn't wearing a dupatta. I could see she wasn't wearing a bra either. I noticed things like that now.

I felt a strange sensation in my belly. It was new, unlike the one I had experienced since that fateful day in the car.

'Where were you?' I repeated. I knew my voice was raised and she could hear how angry I was.

'Go back to bed, and I don't want to hear a single sound.'

'Where did you go?' I didn't realise I was yelling until Ami lunged forward and spat on my face.

'How dare you shout like this? Who are you to ask me anything?' A harsh slap followed, and I fell on the bed. I got up again and walked up to her and thrust my face into hers.

'Behave yourself.' She slapped me again and pulled my hair, but I couldn't feel the pain.

Something snapped inside me. I pushed her with all my force. 'Don't hit me again, or I will tell Baba.'

Her hand stopped in mid-air. I covered my mouth with my hands. Oh God! What had I just said? My legs started to shake. She would kill me now. Why did I say it? How could I embarrass her like that? *Shame on you*, a voice said to me.

'I'm sorry, Ami. Sorry…' I stammered and started crying.

She looked at me with a strange expression for a moment and went to lie down next to Maheen without uttering a word.

I stood for a minute trying to calm down, then went to my side of the bed and turned towards the wall. I couldn't look at her, hating myself for what I had threatened her with. How could I say that to Ami? This would change everything. She would leave us.

Nothing changed, but it was the last time Ami ever hit me. She stopped talking to me. She would instruct me about food and studies and typical mum things, but she would hardly get angry or hit me. She ignored me, and it was as if I had stopped existing for her. The silent treatment was unbearable for me. In some ways, it was worse than the beatings.

As time passed, I learnt to accept Ami as she was. I found joy in school and loved my teachers and friends. Baba was a happy distraction, and even though he was very busy with his patients, he was like Father Christmas, showing up with hugs and gifts, but more than once a year.

My teenage years were a mixed bag. I loved my school life and friends and worked hard so my teachers would notice and give me the attention I was so hungry for. At home, Baba became more loving, until Ami tattled on me and then he scolded me. I could see his heart wasn't in it, but maybe I wanted to convince myself that he didn't mean it. I thought he went some way in compensating for Ami's cold and harsh treatment towards me. There were days at Nana's home I hated and was scared of running into Ami and that man in ways that haunted me for days afterwards, but maybe it was all a bad dream. I didn't catch her with Uncle Uzair again. Either she was more discreet or she had believed my threat.

I might have just made it all up in my mind. I had no way of being sure.

In school, I was a teacher's pet. I was also the girl who said yes to everything, even when I wanted to say no. I was always smiling and was liked by almost everyone. I was told that I was pretty and intelligent, but it felt awkward, and it was hard to believe the compliments, although I did say thank you to them. Ami never told me any of that, and it bothered me that her opinion meant more to me than anyone else's.

Baba sometimes said, *piyari beti*, but it was rare. He always said it to Maheen, but why didn't he say it to me? Yes, Maheen was the cutest little girl ever, but so was I, wasn't I?

I wanted attention, so I entertained my friends with funny jokes and agreed to anything they said. I pleased my teachers by working hard and getting good grades. I offered to carry their books to the staffroom. But something inside me didn't sit well with how I behaved towards others. Even when I was all smiles, like a clown, I was angry inside for saying something I didn't believe in and took it out on everyone at home in bits and pieces, sometimes even on Maheen, which earned me more silence from Ami.

It was my last year of O levels when life took an unexpected turn. I was in my maths class when the principal came to the classroom. Maths was a nightmare, and my mind went into a frenzy whenever a new concept was taught. I couldn't understand it for the life of me, and under our desks, my friend Naila and I were writing little notes to each other. She wasn't my best friend, but I liked her a lot. She was the most easy-going girl amongst us, and whilst other friends made me nervous, she didn't. I could be myself with her and didn't have to seek her attention.

'Saniya Beta, please get your bag and come with me.'

The school principal was looking down at me with an odd expression. She was a big woman; if Father Christmas was female, that's what she would look like.

I grabbed my books and triumphantly looked at my friends, happy to head home sooner. I was glad not to be studying the boring maths class, that's all.

'Miss, why do I need to go early?' I asked the principal. She didn't reply and accompanied me to the gate. Something was wrong. As I reached the gate, I saw Uncle Uzair had come to pick me up. I hated him, and today wasn't Friday, so why was he here? He only came on Fridays because we went to Nana's home straight from school.

Today was Thursday, and Baba came on Thursdays. He always came to pick us up and would take us for ice cream afterwards. It was a weekly ritual that Ami didn't know about; it was our little secret. After lunch on Friday, he would return to the village and come back late on Sunday.

'Take care of yourself. Be strong.' Ms Shaista patted my head and hugged me. What was happening?

When I approached the car, Maheen was sitting in the back seat.

'Why are we going early?' I asked Uzair Uncle.

'Get in the car. It's all good.' He hurriedly got us in the car. I opened the back door to sit next to Maheen.

'Come and sit in the front seat,' Uzair Uncle said.

No! I hate you!

'No, it's fine. Let's go home,' I said in a quiet voice. 'Maheen, do you know why we're going early?' I whispered into my younger sister's ear. She didn't seem bothered.

'I don't know, apa. I want to go home and sleep.' She yawned and put her head on my shoulder.

I put my arms around her. Everything was better when Maheen was with me. As we got close to our home, there were a lot of cars outside. I was old enough to know what that meant. Something had happened to Nana. This many people only came to weddings or funerals, but why were they at our house, not his?

'Is it Nana?' I asked Uzair Uncle. As I walked up to the house, Nana was sitting in the front garden, looking older and more tired than ever. That's when I knew.

I stopped in my tracks, my legs too heavy and weak even to take one step forward. Somehow, Maheen pulled me forward and I started walking.

There were so many people standing on our little front lawn. As I stepped forward, I saw Nana was crying. The front door was open, and there were piles of shoes at the door. The room was full of women crying or whispering in each other's ears.

Where was Ami? Had something happened to Ami?

'Apa...' Maheen whispered, pushing herself closer to me. Ami's friend, Sidra Khala, ushered us inside when she saw us both standing in the doorway and brought us into a hug. She was crying loudly. She abruptly picked up Maheen, although Maheen was too old to be picked up.

I knew it then. Ami was dead. My heart started to slow down. It would be okay. It would be fine. I could take care of Maheen. Baba would take care of us. If Ami was no longer there, I wouldn't have to take care of her secret anymore. How awful of me to think that.

Suddenly, Ami and Baba's bedroom door opened, and Ami rushed out. She ran towards us, crying loudly. She was so loud. I had never seen her like that.

She grabbed me and hugged me tightly. Maheen struggled out of Sidra Khala's arms, and Ami wrapped her arms around her. 'You both have to be brave. I have to tell you something.' She leant back and looked at us, wiping the tears from her face. Sidra Khala put her hand on Ami's head and started patting it.

'Baba had an accident,' she said in a whisper, almost as if she didn't want us to hear it.

I looked at her with wide eyes. Did she say accident? I clutched Maheen's hand tightly. It was cold. I started to tremble. Why was the room so cold?

She started crying again. 'He's gone, meri beti, he's gone.'

'Gone where?' I asked. 'Is he in the hospital?' Silly question. Where else would he be?

Ami didn't reply and continued to wail.

A sudden movement caught my eye, and I saw Uzair Uncle and Baba's friends enter the living room.

They passed by us and went into Ami's room. Why were they going in there? There was a little voice that perhaps told me what was happening, but I didn't understand the words it was using.

And then the world stopped. That's how I would describe it. I saw all the men outside go inside the room and come out carrying a bedstead, and then I saw him. Clad in all white with his face showing was my father. My baba.

I had seen enough films to know what a dead body looked like, but this was my first time seeing one in real life.

My baba.

I wriggled out of Ami's grasp and ran outside. I rushed past someone, colliding with them, hearing Ami's and Khala's voices, but I couldn't stop. I went to the back of the house and took the rusty stairs to the terrace upstairs: my usual hiding spot – a little shaded corner that was my safe place. I pulled my legs up towards my chest and hid my face as I sat down. I couldn't cry. I knew what had happened, but why wasn't I crying?

So many thoughts came rushing like greedy children running towards the ice-cream truck that came to our street every afternoon. Were we poor now? Where would we live? Ami would marry Uzair Uncle now. Why was Ami crying? She didn't care for him. *He's out of your way now, isn't he, Ami? So celebrate now, would you?* The man I hated would be a permanent part of my life, and my baba, the only person who loved me in this world, was gone.

My last thought before I dozed off on that dirty floor was that everything would change now, and it did.

12   *Client*

I waited for Ahad for what was to be our last session together.
I was numb as I sat in the same room where I'd had many
sessions with him. I had come early, and luckily, the space had
been vacant. Ahad was with another client, so I waited for him
in the therapy room that he always booked for our sessions. It
was different today. The room no longer exuded the warmth
and openness it had unconditionally offered for many weeks, or
maybe I was different today. Ahad had already warned me about
the impending change with his lack of response to my texts. Was
he angry with me because I had gone to meet Maha without
informing him? I regretted doing that, but after Shahzen's
reaction to finding out I was seeing him in therapy, I just went
on autopilot. Maybe I didn't want to get into trouble, which had
triggered me to act impulsively, or maybe I had blind trust in
Ahad that he would would fix this problem. He would figure out
a way for us to continue to see each other.

There was a part of me that wanted to be the 'good girl'
who followed rules, but in my shadow was a rule breaker who
didn't care about right and wrong. The thought of wanting to
continue therapy in secret made me uneasy. Was I turning into
Ami? The thought almost overwhelmed me. She was the last
person I wanted to emulate, but this unfamiliar temptation to
cross a line because of my attachment to Ahad shocked me to
my core.

The night before had been one of the most agonising nights of my life. More painful than watching my mother leave our bedroom at night to be with Uncle Uzair, more excruciating than sleeping alone in our home for the first night when Baba died, more painful than childbirth, and even more hurtful than the many nights spent with Arsalan sleeping with his back turned towards me. Guilt about the overwhelming pain threatened to throw me to the bottom of a deep, dark hole from which there was no way out. I had no idea why Ahad had become so significant in my life after spending only a few hours a week with him. The idea of not having that intimate emotional space with him made me want to die. I didn't even care at this moment how Nyle and Neha would be impacted if I wasn't around.

I had laughed and cried with him and found the freedom to express and experience so many emotions; it was like meeting a new part of myself every time I had a session. I could text him any time I wanted to, and he would always respond and sometimes even call back if I was having a rough day.

Until now.

This was the first time he hadn't responded to me. An image of a little girl, playing alone on a terrace for hours, came to me then, and I felt devastatingly alone again.

It was a dark day today, and the universe seemed to have picked up on that. I looked outside through the little murky window that hadn't been cleaned for months. The sun, which had been shining so brightly in the morning, seemed to have given up, and in its spot were dark and gloomy clouds. The dilapidated wall clock announced that Ahad would be here in five minutes.

Today, I would go back to being invisible again, back to being someone who hid her thoughts, feelings, anguish, and pain from the world. It wasn't just that one hour. It was more than that. I had carried him in my heart all the time, day and night, knowing that in my world, there was someone to whom I mattered. He was like a silent song playing at the edge of my consciousness all the time, a soothing, strangely comforting, song. I had mattered enough for him to feel my pain when I cried inconsolably. It was evident on his face, the endless compassion and love for me. I knew I hadn't imagined it all. His infectious laughter at my good, and bad, jokes had allowed my more spontaneous side to emerge. He would look at me intently as I shared my thoughts and ideas, would effortlessly understand me, and make me believe that every word that came out of my mouth in that one hour was precious, like every diamond strung together on a necklace worn by a princess.

'Hi, Saniya,' Ahad greeted me as he entered the room and abruptly sat down in a sudden movement opposite me. He wasn't smiling today. Was he not supposed to knock? But when had he sought my permission before barging into my heart?

'Hello,' I greeted him back in a whisper, my voice faltering, nails biting into the palms of my hand in clenched fists.

My breathing was rapid as I looked away from the piercing look in his eyes. Why were the veins in his neck throbbing? What was happening?

'How are you doing today?'

How was I?

'I don't know,' I whispered and looked at his face. 'Why did you not reply to my text? Are you annoyed with me?' I had asked too many questions; I knew none would be answered today. I started fidgeting with the plain gold band on my ring finger. It was a gift from Khala.

'I understand that this is a tough time for you.'

Why did he avoid my questions? Was his voice distant and cold, or was I reading into everything too much?

'I don't know what to say, Ahad,' I said finally. I tried to make eye contact with him, but it was getting increasingly difficult as he was giving me a cold-eyed stare. His icy attitude was spreading through the room and reminded me of the creepers that slowly grow on walls and cover them inch by inch.

'You don't have to say anything. But I would still invite you to express how you feel,' he said in the same monotone he had started the session with.

'Feel about what?' I finally looked him straight in the eye this time, my voice sharp. I turned my head away from that familiar yet unfamiliar gaze and looked at my hands folded in my lap. What did he want me to express? That I felt like dying? That five minutes had already passed, and I only had fifty-five more to go before this was over. Before I went back to hiding once more?

'I wish you hadn't offered this special space to me,' I whispered. 'It's very, very hard. You should have offered me one session like everyone else,' I added, trembling as the unspent anxiety of the last few hours caught up with me. Why was he washing his hands of me?

Don't be ungrateful, a voice whispered in my head, dissipating the emerging anger rising within me. 'I'm grateful to you for giving me this extra time, but what do I do now?' I said softly, looking up at him with eyes that begged him to take us back to where we had been.

'I will refer you to another therapist,' he suggested dispassionately.

'Are you serious? I can't share everything all over again.' I stood up abruptly, sobs racking my body. I wanted to punch the wall next to me.

'Sit down,' he said in a stern voice, and I immediately sat down. He carried on in the same tone. 'I understand it's difficult, Saniya, but clients often change therapists.' The cold, professional drone continued, like a newscaster presenting the weather forecast.

His impersonal tone and the emphasis on the word 'client' was as agonising to my ears as a patient listening to their terminal prognosis. But then I was a client, wasn't I? Whom did

I imagine I was in reality? His lover? Best friend? Soulmate? I was always a client, and he reminded me of that today.

'Why did you offer more when you couldn't stay?' Was the hurt discernible in my voice, or could he not listen to my pain anymore?

'Saniya, your need was so strong that I simply couldn't say no to you.' His eyes narrowed, and the cold, flat tone in which he uttered these words jolted me as if a strong current had passed through my body. I felt as if he had suddenly slapped me hard across the face. My need was so strong that he couldn't say no? It was my fault?

I shut my eyes, and I felt the tears rolling down my face.

There was nothing more left to say. Had Arsalan not said the same thing? That I should 'stop being so needy'. Had Ami not also used words that meant the same? 'Will you stop following me all the time,' she would scream when I followed her around the house seeking her attention.

Knowing I had made him break a rule and I had been blaming him made me ashamed of myself. 'I'm sorry. You're right. I don't take your care for granted. It's just that…' I wasn't sure of what I wanted to say. When would I change and stop being needy?

'There's nothing to be sorry about. Let's move forward now.' It was the same dismissive tone that I deserved to hear, and why wouldn't he be dismissive? I'd put him in a difficult position, and here I was imagining I was the one who'd been wronged. For a moment, I thought about the man who had started to fill every painful reality of my life with pale shades of love, but maybe it was all an illusion. It was my fault that I had cast him as the main lead of my life story.

'I will refer you to another therapist, Saniya,' he said, his voice becoming quieter, almost as if he didn't want me to hear this bad news. *Stop assuming he cares for you!*

'I don't want therapy anymore. I won't go to anyone again.' I lifted my chin, even though I knew I was to be blamed for this predicament. But in that moment, I made a silent promise to never be vulnerable again.

'You have started a critical process. It would be best if you didn't stop it,' he argued, and for the first time, I saw the Ahad I knew. The one who was invested in my well-being.

'If it's not you, it doesn't matter.' I was about to say more but realised how needy I sounded again.

'It's up to you, then. I can't force you. It's your decision.' The cold tone again.

My mind was racing. He didn't care anymore. I had pushed him to this point. *It's alright, Saniya. You will survive.* I was conflicted between begging him to stay and trying to mirror his feelings and let him leave without a protest.

'Yes, it is my decision. Thank you for your suggestion.' I tried to make my voice more grown-up.

There was silence after that. For how long, I don't recall. I looked at the clock above his head; half an hour was still left. Half an hour more of my neediness that he couldn't say no to.

I started crying loudly and unashamedly. I couldn't hold it in anymore.

He said nothing. He no longer offered any comfort with either his words or his silence. I looked at him through glistening eyes and saw my therapist, who no longer wanted to work with me, care for me, and wasn't the man I had bared my soul to. He was the first person I had shared everything of my life with unabashedly. I could never trust anyone again.

I was ashamed and torn and regretted ever opening up to him, broken into minute pieces that could never be assembled again. Where would I hide now? No one would ever see my inner world. I was going to shut the doors and never allow anyone to make me vulnerable. *Be strong, Saniya, and smile like you always do.*

I wouldn't ever let myself be seen again! I would no longer allow anyone to let me feel so much.

Never again, I promised myself silently. I stood abruptly, then grabbed a handful of tissues from the torn rose petal box on the table. I wasn't too fond of this worn-out tissue box, a constant reminder of tears shed and a sign of sheer weakness.

'Thank you, Ahad, for your time, and my apologies again for putting you in this uncomfortable position.'

I left the room without waiting for him to reply, knowing too well that there was still time for me to be needy. Right then, in that life-defining moment, I decided I no longer had any needs. It was time to hide again.

13   *Woman*

A quote popped up on my Facebook account as I waited for the last session of the day. It was one by Rumi that said, 'Lovers don't finally meet somewhere. They are in each other all along.'

Lovers.

I was a stranger to the concept and could never imagine being anyone's lover. I wasn't the type of woman men fell in love with, and despite many years of therapy, this conviction was still deeply ingrained in me, almost as if it had become a part of me. I was the girl next door and, at best, a friend, and I had accepted that. Or at least made my peace with it.

After the session, I was going to get my hair done for a party later that night that I had been looking forward to attending. My last client of the day was a rather special one as he reminded me of myself. He was twenty-nine years old and shunned by a narcissistic father for supporting his mother in the face of his verbal and emotional abuse. How traumatic it must be for a son to be rejected by his father for protecting his mother. He was the manager of his parents' relationship like I had been, and through therapy, we worked on how he could quit this responsibility that was never his to begin with.

I still remembered our first session. I had felt so much pain: his and mine combined, and the shared wounds we had experienced. He believed he wasn't important to anyone, invisible to others, a wound woefully familiar to me. He initially resisted hard to connect with me or trust me. His long-term girlfriend had ended the relationship and a few more similar experiences had made him believe that he wasn't loveable and that *everyone left*. I couldn't tell him that, for this hour every week, I would always be here. I would never hurt him like Ahad had hurt me. I knew I was identifying with him, projecting my experience, but I had been exploring this in supervision to understand the dynamic within therapy.

'Hi, Saniya.'

His entry snapped me out of my thoughts. Although he was 6ft 5in, his presence never intimidated me.

I smiled and returned his greeting, feeling comforted by his presence. It was like having a friend in the room. In my years in personal therapy, I had realised that the little girl in me wanted to be protected by a father figure.

I had lovely female friends, but even though I had deep-seated trust issues with men, I was looking for emotional support from a man, support that my father didn't provide in the face of my mother's issues, then my husband, and finally Ahad, whom I had trusted so deeply. My fantasies around a man had always been platonic, though – an image of a protector who would stand by my side and be my go-to person for anything and everything. 'How are you?' I asked finally.

'I'm good,' he replied, stretching his very long legs before him. At times, I was tempted to call him 'leggy', but I wasn't sure how he would receive it. Wearing the therapist badge, one questioned everything.

I began by asking him what he wanted to talk about.

'Nothing special. You tell?' He sent the ball flying into the court like he did every week.

I laughed out loud. 'You are a real pro at this, aren't you? Well, I'm throwing the ball back at you.'

'I don't know what to talk about,' he protested with a mischievous grin on his bearded face.

A few minutes passed, and we sat smiling at each other. He would look away and then back again, and there was emerging tension in the room. I experienced a strong impulse to fill that silence, but I held back. Silence always paved the way for deep melodious noise.

'I don't think I will ever find anyone who will stay,' he said quietly, revealing his biggest fear.

I thanked myself for not succumbing to the pressure of saying something banal to fill the silence. 'I hear you. But it will change...' I spoke slowly but with an undertone of a gentle challenge.

'How can you be sure?' he asked in a low, wary tone, doubt evident on his face.

'Has it not already changed?'

'How has it changed? All the girls I've ever enjoyed dating have just disconnected whenever they felt like it. They all leave.' He shifted in his seat and his left leg started to shake.

I looked directly at him. 'Do you not see me?'

'What do you mean?' he asked as he slightly tilted his head.

'Don't I count? Have I not stayed ever since you walked through this door?'

His eyes widened and colour rose in his face. He pulled his legs towards himself, and the leg stopped shaking. 'But you're my therapist. You have to stay.'

'And you're also thinking, paid to stay?'

His silence answered my question. It was a defensive move to remind himself that this was a professional relationship and not to get too attached, but then therapy took place within the space of an attachment bond. I wished I had remembered that with Ahad and not been as ashamed as I was back then and continued to be.

'Yes, I am your therapist, and you pay me. But you know that I care for you, and within this session, I stay with you throughout. And you also know that no matter what, I am here whenever you need me within the limitations of our therapeutic relationship. I choose you every time.'

He started scratching his chin and looked at me with an unfocused gaze. What was he thinking? Maybe he was thinking about how I always said yes to an urgent session, offered a fee discount so that he didn't have to miss sessions, and was an empathetic witness to his journey.

I had stayed.

'I'm not sure if you'll stay.'

I took a few moments before replying. 'I don't think that's your fear.' His real fear was something else, as I had suspected for a while.

'Why do you say that?' he asked, frown lines on his forehead again.

'I think your real fear is not that I will leave but that I will stay.' I laid down the final card on the table.

He shifted in his seat, moving his legs back and forth. The room's energy was thick with anxiety and conflict like the early morning fog in Lahore.

I stayed quiet, letting it sink in that he was worthy of being cared for, and I wouldn't reject him as his father or the other people in his life had.

The session ended on that note, and he quietly left the room. But just before leaving, he turned around and said, 'Take care of yourself.'

Had he stayed, he would have seen the tears in my eyes. I also wasn't sure that someone would stay for me, that someone would ask me to take care of myself.

After the session, I rushed over to get myself prepped for the party, and by the time I was back home, I was absolutely fraught. I managed to do everything, but anxiety came visiting unannounced like a childhood friend. I put an old Indian song on I loved and started getting ready.

I looked in the mirror as I finished dressing up and admired myself in an all-black jumpsuit with high heels and my almost waist-length hair tied up in a messy bun. The kohl eye look suited my face and was striking against the paleness of my skin. I chose a soft lip to draw attention to my dark eyes. I paused as I realised I had dressed up for myself tonight, almost as if I was single. I parked this bizarre thought and rushed to get the children out of the house.

'Get ready. We're running late,' I cried at Nyle and Neha who were glued to their iPad and hadn't put their shoes on.

They protested, but I was adamant. 'I'm leaving in five minutes.'

'I'm coming, Mama... don't go!' Neha cried from her room and appeared in the hall in less than a minute. It always worked, and tonight, I didn't want to second guess my parenting and what it would mean for my children's mental health.

'Let's go, kids.' I locked the front door behind me, and we headed for Zoya's house. She was a university friend I had recently connected with after she had moved back to Lahore from Amsterdam. Her husband was in the foreign service, and my children and hers were luckily in the same age group. Since she'd moved back, we would seek each other's help for babysitting services if we had to go out. She had good support at home and was a very attentive mother, which made it easier for me to drop my children at her place. I knew they would be taken care of.

Ami was always an option, but the children got bored there, so I preferred Zoya and no longer had the energy to explain my life's short-term plans to my mother. I felt interrogated, and despite years of processing my complicated relationship with my mother, I always got pulled into a war of words with her. Her power to trigger me was mind-boggling.

That night I was planning to attend a charity ball with my friend Maria from Healing Matters. She was a senior therapist, but we had connected well in a few workshops we had taken together. She had free passes to the event and had offered me one. Single and attractive, Maria turned heads wherever she went.

Arsalan was in Malaysia attending a golf tournament with his friends, and I was the happiest when he was away. I experienced a sense of freedom, connecting to this new-found sense of singlehood, which was an odd way to feel when married. Our relationship had arrived at a place where we oscillated from two polite strangers to sometimes long-lost friends, and as long as one of us didn't get triggered, there was harmony.

But we were hardly husband and wife. We didn't touch each other. We slept at the far edge of the bed, wary of even mistakenly touching each other in our slumber. It had got to the point where I had finally dared to stand up to him and explicitly warn him that I wouldn't take his abuse. I would walk out. I didn't leave, however. I didn't know how to, and a part of me knew that this warning meant nothing.

Things were sort of settled between us, or was it simply because we were too busy in our lives to fight? A part of me believed that how I was changing also impacted Arsalan's behaviour and he was less aggressive, or maybe he was trying hard to control himself as well. We had both learnt how to float after drowning after so many years. Our issues were now unspoken conversations between us. Lack of sex, his infidelity, my unforgiving withdrawal from the marriage, my coldness and fierce independence.

We were doing our best to survive for our children, parents, society, and ourselves. In my zeal to let go of controlling Arsalan or trying to manage the marriage, I had withdrawn into my world of work and kids and friends, and I was somewhat at peace; it had been a couple of months since there had been a fight. That triggered self-doubt in me at times, and I blamed myself for all the earlier abusive interactions, but then an inner voice reminded me of so many times when Arsalan had shouted and hurled abuse over nothing, and the fact remained that he was a full-time father but a part-time husband, and that's not how marriages thrived.

'Mama. You've missed Zoya Khala's gate,' Nyle pointed out with his little finger and shook me out of my painful reflections.

I took a deep breath and reversed the car to park in front of Zoya's home. The kids didn't even wait for the vehicle to stop and excitedly ran out. This was their favourite place to be, and this knowledge helped me with my mother's guilt. I got out of the car to ensure that they were safely inside.

I waved off Zoya's invitation to come inside. It would just make me late for the party, and I hated being late. Having dropped off the kids, I felt like I could breathe easy. After the stress at work, this was a welcome change.

Although I was gaining a reputation for my work as my practice grew, on the personal front my loved ones mocked my profession at every given opportunity. Ami dismissed it by saying, 'You're so crazy yourself. How can you heal others?' Arsalan's disregard for my profession was more potent. He was indifferent to it and hardly ever asked about my work.

I took out my phone to call Maria as I reached Pearl-Continental Hotel while searching for some change in my purse for the valet. I was in no mood to find a parking spot and walk more than I had to in high heels. Today was the day to pamper myself.

'I've reached the hotel, Maria. Where are you?'

'Babe, at the entrance with our passes.'

'Aye, aye, Captain!' I experienced a sudden rush of excitement I hadn't felt in a long time. I walked towards the event, confident in my stride, aware of how I looked and the attention I was getting. I was hungry for it.

'OMG. You look gorgeous, Saniya,' Maria cried, accompanied by her typical boisterous laugh.

I silently wished she was a little less loud, but it came with the territory of being her friend.

'Let's find our tables,' she said and grabbed my hand, pulling me along. After a few seconds, I discreetly untangled my hand from her slightly moist one. Physical touch was not my cup of tea, and my body rejected any contact, male or female, other than Nyle and Neha, whose touch I craved, probably because they had both been inhabitants of my body, a part of me that I loved fiercely and felt safe with. We reached our table, where three seats were vacant. It was a table of six, and three people were already sitting and chatting with each other. They were young, two men and a pretty girl. I wondered if they were actual friends. The girl's short haircut with bangs almost touching her eyes intrigued me, and her pierced lip with a silver ring shocked me further. I was sure there was a tattoo somewhere on that body.

There was a dance floor, and two Lebanese singers were singing English songs in the middle of the room. It was an odd combination – the singers, the choice of songs, the disco lights – almost as if the organisers had been trying too hard to turn this into a fancy affair.

'I'm going to grab some wine. Do you want some?' Maria asked, getting up from the table.

'You know I don't drink. Get me some Coke, please.' A part of me was judging the casual consumption of alcohol and women wearing off-shoulder and minidresses. It hit me that I was turning into my mother.

'The drink or the drug?' she asked, laughing loudly at her joke.

'Ha! Ha! Very funny!' I replied with a smile but no humour in my tone.

I leant forward and grabbed the bowl of peanuts. I was hungry, and no one else seemed interested in them. I was disconnected from the entire scenario, but that always happened. I would be super excited to socialise, but once I reached the place, I would disconnect, feeling low and wanting nothing more than to head back home to get into my PJs and cuddle with my babies.

I had closed my eyes just for a minute when I heard him.

'You're bored.'

A shock wave passed through my system as I found myself face to face with a man sitting too close in the seat next to me.

'Sorry,' I said, an apology in my smile.

'Hi. I'm Gordon, and I'm sorry for bringing you back to this boring ball.'

I laughed at that. 'It's not boring at all!'

'Are you sure? You can tell me.' His voice, with its thick British accent, dropped to a whisper, and he leant into me as if we were sharing a secret.

'Yes, I am.' I was still smiling. I leant forward and poured water into my glass, the oldest trick to deflect discomfort.

'Are you alone here?' he asked.

I slowly took a sip of water before replying to him.

'No, with a friend. I'm Saniya.' I shook his hand.

'What do you do, Saniya?'

'I'm a therapist,' I replied before turning in my seat to look at the singers on the stage. I needed to figure out where he was going with these questions, but then it occurred to me that maybe there wasn't anything unsavoury about his intentions.

'You are kidding me,' Gordon continued. 'That's wonderful.' He looked at me as if he was awestruck.

'What's so wonderful about it?' I shrugged my shoulders, but inside I was intrigued by his excitement.

His face assumed a faraway look. 'It is such a powerful profession. The ability to heal people and comfort them.'

That pleasantly surprised me. 'Thank you. We're not healers, but I get what you mean.' Hardly anyone understood what we did or appreciated it. In my part of the world, men had low emotional intelligence and there was stigma attached to mental health issues.

I asked him what he did, wondering if I was asking out of politeness or genuine curiosity.

'I'm a motivational speaker, an avid traveller, and more...' He smiled again, a dimple in his left cheek.

'And what do you motivate people to do?' Was I teasing him? Something about him made me feel at ease, and I was quite enjoying our playful banter.

It seemed like he was too because he smiled. 'I motivate them to do what you motivate them to do.'

'And what is that?'

'To breathe, hope, and remember there is always a choice available.'

What a wonderful response. His emotional intelligence made me want to continue our conversation, but I stayed quiet. Something about Gordon was unsettling me, but in an exciting sort of way. Like a new beginning.

He saw me looking at white patches on his arms. 'Vitiligo.'

I felt caught as if with my hand in the biscuit tin. He had read my thoughts.

'I'm sorry.' I noticed he didn't have it on his face.

'For—' Gordon was in mid-sentence when he was interrupted by my friend, who reminded me of unannounced hurricanes that somehow escaped the watchful eyes of the meteorological department.

'Babe, sorry it took so long!' Maria was back. Great, I needed her noise right now. The energy between Gordon and me was electrifying and one one hand it was stimulating me, but on the other hand, it was making me retreat. What a strange feeling.

Maria greeted Gordon, but then abruptly turned to me, as if Gordon wasn't even there anymore.

'Hello, Maria,' Gordon began, but then turned to me. 'So, how long have you been practising for, Saniya?'

This man knew how to dismiss and engage at the same time.

I raised an eyebrow. 'For two years, including my training. Just getting started, I would say.'

'Do you like what you do?'

'I love it. It's the best thing that could have happened to me.' I stopped myself from getting too excited. Where was this going? I got up then. I needed an excuse to take a break from this. But what was *this*?

'Where are you off to?' Maria enquired whilst gulping down her drink.

'Coming back...' I answered vaguely, feeling out of breath.

The ladies' room was vacant. I looked at my flushed face in the mirror. My black mascara was partially smudged and was threatening to travel further down. I grabbed a tissue and ran a few drops of water over it to clean my under-eye area.

Breathe... slow down... I shushed my internal therapist and walked out of the room.

When I stepped back into the party, the music was louder; people were chatting more exuberantly; and laughter was coming from everywhere. As someone who preferred quiet spaces, this was overwhelming for me.

I turned around to leave, but then decided to wait for dinner to be served, and that was when I heard footsteps behind me.

'Are you leaving already?'

It was Gordon.

'No.' I turned back and smiled. 'Are you stalking me?'

He burst out laughing. 'Gotcha.'

Damn. Did I say that? Did it qualify as flirting? *Stop.* I needed to stop overthinking and let myself be.

'I'm trying to find a place to sit and wait for dinner to be served,' he said. 'I'm starving.'

'Me too,' I replied as we walked together and found a little alcove in the lobby. To have something to say, I asked him where he was from.

There were tons of people in the lobby, but this corner we

had found felt intimate with its two small leather chairs and a painting of horses on the wall.

'I'm from England. South,' he replied with a bright-eyed look, as if the thought of home had cheered him up.

'And what brings you here?'

He didn't reply and watched me playing with my hair.

I immediately stopped and folded my hands in my lap.

After what seemed like an eternity, he said, 'I travel around for a series of workshops I conduct. I've been to Pakistan before and love it.' He had a big smile on his face that made me blush.

'I wonder when dinner will be served,' I replied, blushing at how silly I sounded and taking out my phone to look at the time. What was happening here? I needed to get up and leave.

'Married?' He seemed to have an endless list of questions like tricks from a magician's hat, and I felt compelled to reply.

'Yes. Two kids. A girl and a boy.' I took out my purse and showed him a photo of Nyle and Neha. Good. He should know I was a mother.

His face softened. 'They're beautiful. You must be a good mother.'

There was a fluttering inside me upon hearing this. No one had ever told me that. I momentarily looked away, not sure how to respond to it.

'Do you not believe that, Saniya?'

He said my name with such familiarity.

'I try my best.' I turned my head to look at him, and for some odd reason, I almost choked.

'That sounds perfect. Can I ask you a personal question?'

'Now you ask for my permission!' I laughed out loud, happy to be distracted from all the emotions I was experiencing. 'After interrogating me all this time.'

He laughed to, but he was still watching me intently... as if he cared. Why would he care about a random stranger?

'I hear you! Can I have your number in case I need to refer someone?'

I hesitated, but only for a moment. This was ridiculous. Gordon was perfectly nice. 'Sure,' I said. 'Give me yours, and I'll forward my official number.' Why did I ask him for his number? I could have just given mine. Could I not? Something was happening here that seemed to have a life of its own, and I didn't want it to stop. Or did I?

The music changed in the background, and a slower Celine Dion number started playing. It was my favourite.

'You have a lovely voice.'

'What?' I frowned at this off-hand comment. I hadn't realised that I had been humming along. 'Hmm yeah, it's not bad,' I said dismissively. I always did that.

'Why do you put yourself down so much?' he challenged. Was he reading my thoughts now?

'It's a fact!'

'Well, I think it's lovely. Do you sing?'

'Not really. I thought of learning a long time back, but then…' I had to leave. This was getting a bit much.

'Why don't you learn now?' His unfaltering gaze and stream of the right questions were wrong in the moment. I was feeling exposed.

'Hmm, I don't have time for it… I do love singing, though,' I said quietly, almost as if I didn't want to admit it to myself.

'You don't have time to indulge your passion?'

I bristled. Who was he to say such direct things? I got up abruptly. 'I'm going to find Maria.'

He didn't say a word. Didn't move from his seat.

I stopped and turned around. 'It was lovely meeting you, Gordon. Hope the rest of your stay in Pakistan goes well.'

That's when he stood up and stepped closer. My heart started to race. Was he going to hug me?

Instead, he extended his hand, and without thinking, I took

it, feeling a sudden urge to cry. Why was I feeling so emotional? He squeezed my hand warmly. 'The pleasure is all mine. I hope we get to see each other again.'

Without replying, I scooped my hand out of his grip and started walking fast. What had just happened?

I hadn't told anyone about my singing or that I used to sing in school competitions and my teachers sometimes called me to the staffroom to sing for them. I stopped singing after Baba died. He was the only one who praised me for it and encouraged me to keep singing.

He took many things with him when he left. Someone who had faith in me, who loved me and made me feel I had a parent I could go to for minor issues like maths homework or a scraped knee.

'Why are you so quiet?' Maria asked, as we turned into her street. Even having Maria in the car wasn't enough to distract me.

'Am I?' It always helped to reply with a question when I wanted to avoid an answer. I wasn't sure why I was quiet, but I didn't feel like talking.

'Tired?' she asked in a quiet tone, a rare occurrence that revealed the real Maria who hid behind the boisterous energy and loud mannerisms.

'Not really. I had a good time.' I looked ahead and hoped that the conversation had ended. There was noise in my mind tonight and I was exhausted.

Maria joined me in my silence, probably reluctantly, as she was quite the talker. I liked talking too, but silence was my go-to place ever since I had started therapy. I had discovered an introvert in me who liked her own company as much as others'.

Later, after the kids had been tucked into bed, I made a cup of tea and sat in the lounge. I put on Netflix and randomly clicked on a season of *Friends*. Despite having watched it many times, this show never failed to calm me.

Gordon is attractive, I thought, stroking my arm as I remembered some of his comments. *He is funny too.* I smiled as I remembered some of his comments. I wanted to talk to him. Would he reach out? Feeling a bit restless, I silenced the TV and started humming.

It was one of my favourite Lata Mangeshkar songs. At what time I started singing, I did not know, but bit by bit, I found my voice getting louder and opening up the song within me. I could feel myself smiling as I continued to sing one song after another.

Feeling self-indulgent, I grabbed my phone and recorded a tiny part of the song and sent it to Maria.

A few minutes later, the WhatsApp ping alerted me to a voice note in Maria's chirpy voice. 'Babe. You have a beautiful voice. Where have you been hiding it?'

I laughed out loud in a surge of energy and decided to look up singing lessons. The most legitimate class was one the Aaafi brothers taught, as part of a well-known classical music teaching group in Lahore.

Damn. The classes began tomorrow, and I had therapy sessions and a birthday party to take the children to. It was exciting and worrying at the same time as I thought about another hat that I wanted to wear.

Too excited to let my busy schedule dampen my spirits, I took a screenshot of the contact details and went to bed. I was going to sing! Yaaay!

A few days later, I was catching my breath between therapy sessions when a ping alerted me to a new WhatsApp message. I mindlessly opened it, expecting a client's text for appointment.

How is the healing coming along?

I jumped from my seat when I saw from the display photo that it was him. He had reached out. I was grinning from ear to ear.

As well as the motivational talking is going? I quickly responded. Was I too eager?

I had saved his number as Gordon Motivation. I didn't care for surnames. I cared for what that person's presence in my life meant.

I referred a client to you, came the response.

Thank you... I appreciate that.

How is your family?

They are well. As well as one can be.

How are you? he asked.

Me?

Yes. You.

I'm fine. What else would I be? I couldn't remember being asked that in a long time.

I looked at the time and put the phone aside because the next client was about to arrive. Ugh! I wanted to chat longer.

I had been lucky with the office space. It was a private firm located fifteen minutes away from my home. They gave me a nice big room on the ground floor. Most of their offices were on the first floor and the basement; the only inhabitants on my floor were the admin, the photocopy room, and a little café/kitchenette. It was quiet here, so I took the space. The rent was affordable too and covered the amenities.

Over the next couple of days, Gordon and I started chatting every day. I wasn't quite sure where our conversations were heading, but they were still meaningful and challenging. I liked our conversations: he asked me daily how I was, and I was learning to respond by saying, *I feel low today. I had five sessions today. Children are acting out. Arsalan seems to be busier than ever. My mum is unbearable.* We started to talk about anything and everything. Not everything, though. I never wanted to tell anyone about Ami or Arsalan's rejection again.

A few days earlier, Arsalan had thanked me for supporting his work routine and not demanding any time, and that made me feel guilty. Was I helping or just grateful to have more time for myself? Or more time to connect with Gordon?

Ma'am, how is the day treating you? The ping broke me out of my guilt.

I'm good, sir! Did I ever thank you for pushing me towards singing? I asked, loving that I was flirting and slowly embracing this side of me.

No, you did not! Go ahead...

Well, thank you. I love the singing lessons! I'm pretty good, If I may say so myself!

You may and you should. It makes me truly happy that you said that. X

What is with the big X? I asked.

It's a sign of affection! he texted back.

Ohh! Is it a British thing?

Very much so, came the quick response.

Thank you! I was warm and fuzzy inside.

What are you thanking me for? he asked.

I don't know! I didn't know what I was grateful for. Him making me sing, or being a companion in my loneliness, or making me learn how to trust again. But that was how we connected. We flowed without a beginning or an end, connecting when we wanted to and disconnecting when we wanted to.

My dad is unwell, he informed me one day.

What happened? I could sense he was upset. Gordon was an only child and had lost his mother to a car accident when he was just three years old. He was very close to his father, the only parent he had ever known. The parent who never remarried and cared for his little boy all his life despite being a vet and having a hectic life. Gordon's obsession and love for animals stemmed from his father's profession and the many summers interning at the animal clinic his father owned.

He doesn't take care of himself. His thyroid is acting up... I

181

could sense his worry and fear. *I want to see him soon. As soon as these workshops are over.*

I hear you, my friend. I will pray for him. Eat now. It's almost dinner time.

I put the phone away. There was a dinner at Arsalan's parents' house, and he had asked me and the kids to be prepared to travel there ourselves. He was going there directly from his meetings.

Thank God Zubaida was with me. What a relief it was to have such good help.

In the middle of getting ready, I realised I had saved my chat with Gordon. Feeling this unease, I picked up the phone from the dresser and thought about deleting the conversation.

Why did I have to delete it? Why did I feel as if I was doing something wrong? He was simply a friend. Why could I not have one if Arsalan could have countless female friends?

No. I would not go down this road. I had nothing to feel guilty about. I put the phone down and let the chats be. Gordon and I had something special between us, and feeling guilty made it feel like a cheap affair. It was a bond, unspoken conversations, bleeding wounds, and more. It was a shared space of being cared for and seen... I needed to live too.

14 *Girl*

Ami never left our room again after Baba died. She slept with Maheen and me throughout the night. I would get up many times to check on her; my body was so attuned to the fearful expectation of her leaving us for a place that didn't make sense to me. I knew what transpired behind closed doors at night; I saw the little interactions in the day, like a forbidden touch, but imagining my mother with another man tied my insides in a knot that was impossible to untangle. The tummy aches would start. I would wake up in the middle of the night with nausea, and I lost my appetite more often than not. Once, Ami had to take me to the doctor, and he told her that I was developing ulcers because of bad eating habits and stress. I still remember how stunned I had felt when Ami had said, 'What would she be stressed about?'

I was shocked to realise my mother had no idea how miserable I was. I also remembered how kind the doctor had been and how his response surprised me even more. He turned towards Ami and said, 'She looks stressed and unhappy, yet you know nothing about it?'

Ami went red in the face, as he was the first person who had stood up to her like that. He was tall, fat, and had this big moustache and the sweetest smile. I had so badly wanted him to hug me, and for many weeks, I fantasised that he was my father and would protect me as he had at that moment. That thought troubled me. Why did I imagine that when I loved Baba? Sometimes, I got furious at Baba for not knowing what was happening under his nose, for being so weak, and for allowing Ami to bully him. Baba wasn't strong, and that made me angry. I loved him, but I never felt I could reach out to him.

We moved into Nana's house a few weeks after Baba's death. It was the worst day of my life. I imagined nights and days filled with seeing what my eyes did not want to see, and that thought made my insides churn. I had stopped eating and sleeping. My clothes were hanging off me, but Ami didn't notice any of that. She was busy packing my home away or pampering Maheen, who had become clingier than ever. I had lost my father too, but somehow, that fact had gone unnoticed by people around me. Uncle Uzair would visit every day, bearing books, chocolates, and fruit for us, but his care made my insides recoil, and the minute he would enter the house, I would run away to hide on the terrace.

I hated him with all the hate I could muster, and when the day finally arrived for us to leave home, I felt like I had been sold off. The idea of leaving the only home I had ever known was gut-wrenching. Even Maheen was more pleased and comfortable when we were in our home, which made me wonder if she knew about Ami and Uzair Uncle too. But I didn't dare ask her and tarnish her little mind with a reality she couldn't digest. It was like feeding too much food to a baby who had just started experimenting with solid food.

I started having nightmares after Baba died that repeated every other night. In my nightmare, I was in school. Baba was coming to pick me up, and then, as I was waiting for my parents outside the school sitting next to the guard, I saw a car pass by with Ami and Uncle Uzair in the front seats, so happy and laughing and not seeing me waving my bony arms to make them stop. I would wake up drenched in sweat at times, wanting Ami so severely, wanting her to come and hold me. But I didn't know how to ask her, nor did she ever hold me.

I hated that my home was breaking right before my eyes, and I couldn't do anything. I screamed and fought Ami the day Baba's possessions were cruelly given away. In my mind, I would say to her face, 'I hate you, Ami. I will always hate you for what you did to Baba. I don't like it when you cry as if you cared for him. You are a bad woman!'

Due to all my shouting and protest, she kept a big comfy sofa chair that Baba always sat in, his wallet, his stethoscope, and a briefcase I had hidden away from Ami's sight. It was his sofa seat, and many times after his death, I would sit in the middle and remember my baba. Maheen was lost too. I often found her crying in her sleep and Ami rushing over to comfort her. She would always know when Maheen was upset. She would lie down next to her, holding her in her arms, running her long fingers through Maheen's hair as I peeked through my blanket.

Why do you hate me so much, Ami? I have my reasons, but what are yours? Why can't you hold me too?

I sometimes wondered if Ami hated me because I knew about her affair, but then I remembered that she was strict with me before that day in the car when I saw them holding hands. My earliest memories of her were feeding me and changing my clothes but never of her playing with me or hugging or kissing me like she did with Maheen. *Did you not want me, Ami?* Until Maheen was born, I thought it was because she wanted a son, but then she was a mother hen with Maheen, so that theory didn't apply.

The day we closed the door to our home to leave for Nana's house, Uncle Uzair came to pick us up. It was the longest ride of my life. That car reminded me of another time when my life had altered, as I had witnessed two held hands that didn't belong with each other. And here I was, back in that car again. *Will Ami marry him now? Will I have to call him Baba?* I had a tight knot in my tummy, so I reached for Maheen's hand. I felt more scared then than at any other time in our lives as I imagined the possibility of Uncle Uzair as my baba.

'Apa! You are squeezing it too tightly!' Maheen whined.

'Saniya! *Tang mat kero*,' Ami called out from the front seat.

'She's not doing anything. Maheen, be kind to your sister.' Uncle Uzair came to my defence.

'I was. You don't have to scold Maheen. Sorry, Maheen.' I let go of her hand. I hated him. Why did he talk to me? Could he not see that I hated him from the bottom of my heart?

'*Batameezi mat kero*, Saniya,' Ami scolded again, now coming to his defence in her typical loud, angry voice.

When we arrived at Nana's, he was standing at the doorway for us with tears running down his face that he hadn't bothered to wipe away. He held his arms out, and we rushed into them. Ami walked up closer, too, and started sobbing. I didn't want to see her, so I pressed my face further into Nana's arms. He smelt of an aftershave Baba used – Old Spice. I started crying at that point. A moment later, I felt Ami grabbing my hand.

'Acha, be quiet now. It's okay. You're worrying Nana now, Sano.' It was an unfamiliarly soft tone. Her hand was warm, and I was about to squeeze it when she let go. Too soon.

Hold it longer, Ami.

Her hand had a familiar feeling, and in the moment, I felt devastated as she removed it from my grasp.

That night Ami slept between Maheen and me. We all shared the big bed in her room on the upper floor, not in the guest room where we were usually asked to sleep. I leant closer to her after she had gone to sleep and put my hand on her arm. She smelt of fruity shampoo, the kind my friend used at times. Maheen had her leg on top of Ami. Twice I got up to check if our door was locked, and it was. I dozed off and woke up in alarm, fearful that Ami would not be with us. She was with us that night and all the nights after that. She never left the room again.

Uncle Uzair moved to Canada a few months after we moved into Nana's house. I never knew why he went, and I don't remember saying goodbye to him. I'm sure I didn't. But one morning, I found Ami sitting in the garden crying, and I thought maybe she did love Baba to miss him so much. But it was Uncle Uzair's departure that made her cry so much. I still remember that moment. I felt pure hate like never before. I promised myself that I would never call her Ami directly. She was not my mother. That day I told myself that I was an orphan. It was as if a huge rock had been dislodged from my chest as I no longer had to keep an eye on Ami. I was cheated of my time to grieve for my baba, and I hated Ami for that.

Hafsa Khala also moved back to Pakistan to live with us. Because of Ami, I couldn't initially trust her, and as I had never spent any time with her, I expected her to be like Ami, but she wasn't, and I ended up having a surrogate mother for a few years.

Khala was funny and very warm towards me. She would challenge Ami, too, when Ami would scold me. She loved me, and that made me happy.

I did worry for Nana, however. He looked older after Baba died and even more so after Uncle Uzair left. It made me think that he lost two sons back to back. But the day Uncle Uzair left, my life changed.

Once again.

From there onwards were the happiest years of my life and I started to trust that life would be different even though I missed Baba.

I was finally at peace, but I was not as confident a person as I thought I wanted to be. I would please my friends so they would like me back, but everyone in school had a best friend; I was the odd one out who moved from one group of friends to another.

I would come home to Maheen and tell her every day that she was my best friend until one day she said, 'But, apa,

Laiba is my best friend. You're my older sister!' She frowned as she reminded me of my role in her life. Her voice sounded impatient, and I was embarrassed that I was needy for my sister's acceptance of us as best buddies.

'So, we can be sisters and best friends too!' I put on a brave smile, but I was blushing.

She frowned again and said, 'So if we're best friends, we should tell each other all our secrets. That's the rule, apa.'

My mouth opened to utter a response, but I stayed quiet. At that moment, I knew I could never have a best friend. How could I tell anyone my secrets? My most significant and most shameful secret. I blinked back tears and, in a chirpy tone, replied, 'You're right, Maheen. We are sisters.'

'Yes, apa! Yes,' and she hugged me as if relieved from the responsibility of being my best friend. Maybe I was my own best friend?

School life, even with my struggles to make close friends, was fun. I loved studying and got straight As in my O levels. I was one of seven girls who got them, and Ami was ecstatic. That day she hugged me, kissed my cheek, and told me she was proud of me. She also gave me a gold chain that Nani had given her. That was one of the most unforgettable, special moments with Ami, and I missed Baba that day. He would have been so proud of me. I spent the night in his chair, missing him and feeling angry at Allah for taking my only parent away.

That day, hating Ami was a bit harder, but I didn't want to stop trying. I felt guilty as I imagined hating her less. Shame on me for softening up with the woman who had hurt my baba the most. I was betraying him. I felt I would betray Baba if I allowed myself to love Ami.

But you do love Ami, a soft voice whispered in my ear.

All our friends decided to go out for our farewell dinner, even those who got Bs and Cs. I asked Ami, and she had too many questions until Khala interjected, and I got permission to go. Nana gave me three thousand rupees for my grades, and my hands trembled as I held the money in my scrawny hands. I believed I was the wealthiest sixteen-year-old in the world. Ami, to my surprise, bought me a pretty red dress from a boutique. Luckily for me, she ended up listening to Khala.

That day was also the day I met the love of my life, or that's what I believed as a naïve teenager. We were all waiting to be picked up, sitting outside Café Zouk on the pavement after dinner. Giggling at silly jokes, dismissing the fact that we might not be together again, as what were the chances of all of us ending up at the same university? Some of us felt sad and others anxious, thinking about university and the unknown new transition in life. I was worried whether I would make good friends but also hopeful that university would mean more freedom.

Asifa was going to drop me home that day as she lived close to Nana's. I was listening to her and Zubia as they continued cracking bad jokes when I heard him.

'Asifa, let's go!'

I looked up to see a tall guy in a red T-shirt wearing cool sunglasses. There were instant butterflies in my tummy. A different kind from the usual tight, painful knots that had only slowly begun to ease since Uzair Uncle had left.

'Bhai. Come meet my friends!' Asifa got up, grabbed her brother's hand, and pulled him towards where we were all sitting.

'And this is Saniya. Can we drop her home? I have promised her.' She was jumping from one foot to another.

'Of course, we can,' the cute brother promised, with a beaming smile that showed perfect white teeth. Oh my! He was handsome.

I followed them to their car. It was big, silver and shiny – a Civic maybe. I didn't know much about cars, but I fancied big vehicles and wondered how rich people lived their lives. We were from a working-class background and money was always tight. I didn't like our small Suzuki, and I tried my best to get dropped far away from the school gate so no one saw me getting out of it. Most of my friends were affluent, and I secretly envied them. Was that why they looked happier?

Sitting in the back seat of the car, I sneakily glanced at Asifa's bother now and then. I liked how he drove fast but with authority. Like he'd been doing this for a long time.

'Bhai, did you know Saniya got all As?' Asifa proudly announced as if my As could distract him from her Bs, Cs, and Ds.

'That's great to know. Your parents must be very proud of you,' the brother said, looking briefly in the rear-view mirror where my gaze met his. I hurriedly looked away, feeling the blood rush to my cheeks.

'Thank you,' I timidly replied. He had a fair complexion, clean-shaven but with very dark hair, almost like Tom Cruise.

Asifa turned around to face me. 'Saniya, why don't you come to our place?'

'I didn't get permission.'

'Let's go to my home, and I'll call Aunty and seek her permission. Please, chalo…'

'Theek hai,' I agreed, breaking into a smile. I couldn't help it. I loved it when someone wanted me like this. It was so rare, and it made me so happy.

While Asifa phoned Ami, I sat in the living room, self-conscious and shy. He was sitting right across from me, looking at his mobile. I wondered how old he was.

Suddenly he looked up at me. 'So other than studies, what do you like doing?' he asked.

I was tongue-tied and started fumbling with the bag in my lap. Before I could answer, Asifa barged in. 'She likes to sing, Adnan Bhai.'

So, his name was Adnan.

'I don't like to sing,' I protested and clutched the bag tightly. My heart was racing. Was he going to ask me to sing? Did I want to sing?

'Why don't you sing something, Saniya?'

I knew it. I hated to be put on the spot.

'Yes. Please sing that Nazia Hassan song you sing so often.'

'Which one is that?' Adnan asked.

'"Teri Yaad". She sings like Nazia, bhai…' Asifa grabbed a toffee from the bowl on the centre table and threw one at me.

'I'm not singing,' I said, picking the toffee up from the floor. I was never good at catching anything. I wanted to hit Asifa at that moment.

'Why not?' Adnan Bhai challenged and looked at me intently.

I didn't know what to say other than smile and look away.

Soon, they gave up, and we went to Asifa's room. There I learnt that her brother was doing his undergrad at Yale and was twenty-one years old.

That night I started dating my crush in my mind. I saw us sitting for hours on the terrace of Baba's home in my secret corner. He would laugh at my jokes and listen to everything I had to say as if it was the most important thing he had ever heard. I would sing for him too.

And I happily dozed off, in love for the first time.

I carried him around in my thoughts all the time. He would hug me when Ami would scream at me. He would sit quietly next to me when I would miss Baba. His face would soothe me when I would be up many nights out of habit, all those years of worrying about Ami.

I started visiting Asifa more and would run into him now and then. He would chat, smile, tease me, and ask me when I would sing for him. And giggling and excited, I promised I would do it one day. I was convinced in my heart that he liked me too.

And then one day I found out he was getting engaged to Khala's daughter. I remember crying that night, and I missed Baba more than ever. And more than anything, I lost my fantasy and could no longer carry him around in my heart.

That last summer before university was bittersweet. An incomplete summer romance, although I knew I wouldn't have dared to talk to Adnan Bhai.

I was so stupid. I was scared of Ami, and although she had never sat me down and told me not to have a boyfriend, I just instinctively knew it wasn't okay. It would upset Baba. But I wished that Adnan had stayed longer, chatted more, and made me sing.

I wanted to sing. I asked Ami if I could take singing lessons.

'Have you lost your mind?' The veins in her neck were throbbing.

'Why can't I?' I protested although her anger made my hands clammy.

'Besharmi key kaam! We don't do such things in our family.' She went on to enlighten me about our Khaandani values.

I burst out laughing, and the laughter turned into crying at some point. She was talking about family values?

'Pagal ho gayi ho! Batameez!'

'Ji. I have lost my mind. But you're right, Ami. It is shameful to sing. Such things don't happen in our family.'

I left the room quietly, but that was the last time I sang, even alone. In my room, I thought I would choke with all the emotion. I wanted to scream in her face and ask if cheating on one's husband was allowed according to our family values. I was old enough to know that Ami had been cheating on Baba. I had a word for what she had been doing.

I started punching the pillows as hard as I could. I could feel my face getting hot and sweaty. I hated her so much. Why couldn't she have died? Why did it have to be Baba? If she had died, Baba could have married Khala, and we would have been happier.

Khala made me feel less alone. She would take me to bookshops and let me buy whatever I wanted to read. I was hooked on *Sweet Dreams*, a girly romance that Ami had forbidden me to read. But Khala could challenge Ami on that too, so she stopped scolding me, and I spent my entire summer reading books. I loved playing badminton with her, and after work, she would play with me sometimes. Maheen would come and spoil our game because if madam Maheen wanted to play, we had to let her. I did feel jealous of her sometimes, but I loved her too.

Why did Ami love her more? As I grew older, I felt it was worse than before. At night sometimes, I would find Ami sitting alone in the lounge, staring at the switched-off TV. I would find my heart pounding when I saw her. A part of me wanted to hug her because she looked so sad. But then the question that would upset me would be: who is she feeling sad for?

In my mind, I had conversations with her.

Ami, are you sad for Baba, or are you sad for him? *If you're sorry Baba died, I want to come and hug you even if you don't like my hugs. But if it's* him, *then I wish you stay unhappy forever. I want you to hurt as much as I hurt, Ami.*

Maheen was the only one who brought a smile to Ami's face, and I was jealous of the bond they shared. Maheen was younger and missed Baba and had started crying over every little thing, so we had to make sure we kept her happy. But then, what was my fault? Why did I have to suffer so much?

After the summer came to an end, it was time to start applying for university. I got into all of them as my grades were so good. I decided to go for arts, although Ami wanted me to be a doctor. A part of me wanted to carry on Baba's legacy, go to his city, and work at the free clinic. Ever since he died, I hadn't even seen Dada and Dadi, my paternal grandparents. There was some issue between Ami and them, and we never saw them again. I don't think they liked Ami, and I once heard from Hafsa

Khala that Dada and Dadi found Ami's family to be too liberal, and that's why we saw them less and less over the years. But did they not love Maheen and me?

Baba was the only son. Why did they not see us? But even when Baba was alive, we would hardly see them. Baba and Ami had a love marriage, and I don't think Dada and Dadi accepted it. They had met through some friends, and the rest was history. I was fifteen when I came to know all of this. I still couldn't understand why, if Ami loved Baba, she carried on with Uncle Uzair? What changed? There were so many unanswered questions and only one person had the answers, and it was the one person I couldn't ask.

I took up English literature and psychology at the university of my choice, feeling excited about what lay ahead. The night before university, Khala made pasta for me. She had taken me out earlier and had bought me new university supplies. Nana had also given me extra money for food to spend at university. Ami was silently observing all of this, lost in her thoughts. Maheen was more excited than I was. She took Ami shopping and bought me a pretty satchel for my books. It was a dark brown leather bag with a big button. I thought Ami had bought it for me, and for a moment, I felt a familiar feeling of want and care for her, but then I learnt that Maheen had suggested it.

'Apa, are you a grown-up now?' Maheen asked innocently at the dinner table.

I laughed at her naïve assumption. 'Yes, I suppose I am,' I responded, smiling at her and leaning forward to kiss her on the cheek.

I spent the night before university tossing and turning. I missed Baba. He would have been so excited. He was always happy when I did well in academics. I was feeling nervous about the girls I would meet the next day. Would I be able to make friends or even a best friend?

Am I a grown-up now? I thought of Maheen's question again and felt sad. I grew up in that car many years ago. I grew up when I wasn't supposed to. I didn't get to be a child. I lost all my years of being carefree to protecting my parents' marriage.

I had to stay inside and watch, Ami, while you played, Maheen. I was busy guarding Ami's secret lest it got out, which would have done so much harm. I knew it would break Baba's heart and Nana's.

Many years later, I realised I didn't want my mother to feel the shame of being exposed. I had been protecting her, but rather than appreciate me, my mother had resented me for being the child who wouldn't leave her alone so she could spend time with Uncle Uzair.

The last thought I had before sleeping was that, one day, someone would love me unconditionally and make the lost little girl feel loved and found.

15   *Woman*

The night I heard Arsalan chatting away with someone, it was as if there was a loud crash within me. I knew my heart, or a big chunk of it that still leant towards my husband, was broken at that moment and I would never be able to find its pieces again. As a budding therapist in training, it was hypocritical to be so hopeless, to believe that I could never heal from this hurt, while I inspired and encouraged my clients to think and feel otherwise. But that night, I was drowning. I could no longer excavate any remnants of hope for my marriage from within me. After years of doing this dance, I was tired. Heartbroken. Hopeless.

That night, I shut the door of my heart, mind, and soul to my husband, and I knew I wouldn't ever open it for him again. And I, more than anyone else, knew how to shut doors. Had I not closed one for my mother, and to date, it remained closed? There was a bizarre sense of emptiness within, as if a few organs within the body had been extracted, but rather than making me feel light, the emptiness elicited a sense of heaviness.

Every once in a while, one had to disappear, not out of sight but behind another face that suited others – a false self. The wife in me had to disappear and check out. I no longer wanted to be available to him in any way other than as a robot that performed all the functional wifely duties that a 'good wife' was expected to perform. Run the house smoothly, take care of the children, be attentive to the in-laws, show up for social events with a smile, and that was that.

This time I didn't even harbour any interest in questioning him about who the woman was or what the nature of their relationship was. I didn't know when I'd stopped caring, but it was apparent that now I had. I just had to learn to make peace with the new me.

It was a busy year for both of us. Arsalan had been promoted to the country manager position; he had been travelling more and, generally, was in a happy, stable state of mind. Somehow, my lack of interest in a relationship with him had made him more amenable. Sex was already a taboo topic, and unlike before when, after a month or two, he would respond to my reaching out for a few minutes of physical contact that he called 'lovemaking', and I got my confirmation that I was still married, I was no longer asking him for sex either. We shared a bed, rooted in our corners, distracted by our phones until we slept. Time and again, the reality hit me that because I had withdrawn from the relationship, he was more settled, and if he had ever wanted more from me, his lack of attention to the change in me proved that his understanding of marriage was limited to a functional household with kids that could maintain social graces. The man did not understand intimacy, and I doubted if the connection I thought we had earlier in our life was real or a projection of my idealised fantasy of a relationship.

I knew that my demand for sex after a few months had been a response to a panic I would feel rising within me that demanded some evidence to define me as a married woman. It wasn't sexual drive that made me text him seeking an appointment. Sometimes, it was triggered by remembering an old, forgotten rush of need for his embrace and touch. Sometimes, it would be an erotic scene in a film or a friend mentioning that her husband couldn't get enough of her. So, I reached out, and usually, after weeks and some reminders, we would have intimacy. He would immediately get up to shower with an expression that demanded gratitude from me. His sex drive was very low, and despite my subtle encouragement for him to get his blood work done or seek therapy, nothing really changed. Everything fell on deaf ears. He didn't care for my frustration or needs. He would complain that I didn't fulfill his need for companionship: a coffee evening or watching a film he liked, which could lead to a sexual encounter, but there was a resistance in me that was either harboured from the cycle of abuse or, lately, I was beginning to admit that we were two very different people with hardly anything in common. And there had been countless times when I had started spending time with him the way he liked, but it never led to any initiative from him. Through therapy, I understood that it wasn't normal for a man not to have a desire for his wife in a decade. He hid behind countless excuses, and I no longer believed them.

Sex didn't give me any pleasure. Never had, really, and how could it when my husband didn't ever touch me in a way that reeked of desire? He performed it as a task that his 'needy' wife kept forcing on him. What a sham those five minutes were where I ground my teeth with the pain while faking being in the throes of pleasure to further affirm to him that he was indeed a man. Man enough for me, that is.

I was an unhappily married woman, which added another secret to my bucket of secrets. But I daren't let the world or my children know that. It was enough that Maheen knew it, and I had made her swear that she would never disclose the reality of my marriage to anyone, especially Ami.

I didn't expect empathy from my cold-hearted mother, and God forbid if she expressed any care, I wouldn't be able to receive it. I didn't know how to, and I felt like throwing up at the thought.

An educated woman without kids could walk out of a marriage, but a mother of two would be shunned by society. The justification for divorce had to be catastrophic, like physical abuse that could harm one's life, and anything less than that wasn't a good enough reason to end a marriage.

I counted the reasons: a rare episode of being choked, and countless occasions of being screamed at and verbally abused; a sexless marriage where my husband would recoil from offering me a kiss, let alone more; and now, I was at a point where I finally knew that I was a vibrant, alive woman with healthy needs who deserved much more.

I clammed up in more than one way in my marriage, and Arsalan noticed none of it. We would meet our families, take our children out, and watch a film together, and we would smile and laugh in a shared space of friendship, but I was disconnected. Any residual feelings of attachment I had in me were more around the father of my children rather than my husband. He was a good father, which made me feel more trapped than ever.

One morning, before leaving for his work trip to Amsterdam, Arsalan asked me a strange question. He was brushing his hair in the mirror and smiling and humming something. I was sipping my tea and looking at him. Today, I had my diploma class and was in a good mood. Healing Matters was my happy place.

'Are you happy, Saniya?'

I froze, the cup of tea suspended in mid-air. 'What do you mean?' I felt nervous, as if I had been caught cheating.

'It's a simple question. Are you happy?' He turned away from the mirror to look at me.

'You have never asked me before.'

'So, I am asking you now.'

'I don't know how to answer that question.' I picked up my cup of tea and started sipping it but stopped, losing my morning craving.

'What do you mean? Why would you take so long to answer just a basic question?' He seemed genuinely perplexed and irritated. I could feel the resistance in me. I also wanted to scream in my husband's face and tell him I was unhappy. Another part of me wanted to rescue my friend, of sorts, and the father of my children whom I cared for and felt partly attached to.

'Sab theek hai.' I felt stuck.

'Obviously, I know that. But your reaction makes me think you're not happy.'

'I didn't say—'

'What would you be unhappy about?' He didn't let me finish. 'A beautiful home, lovely children, and money to buy shit aren't enough for Your Highness? And a husband who doesn't interfere in your life,' he added. 'Learn to be grateful.'

'You mean, who isn't interested in my life,' I mumbled under my breath.

'Say that again?' He had an interrogative tone bordering on aggression. I experienced a familiar nervousness.

'Nothing. Relax. Get ready; you have a flight to catch, remember?'

'Whatever! You've spoilt my mood,' he complained and turned towards the mirror, spraying aftershave. The smell of Hugo Boss filled the air. It was a potent scent.

I was tempted to make amends by lying and telling him I was teasing him, but something stopped me. I no longer wanted to hide behind my fear of what would happen if he got angry. 'When do you return?' I asked instead.

'I told you, but you never listen. Check your email and find out.'

'Why can't you just tell me?'

'No, I'm not interested. Bashir!' he yelled out to the cook to carry his bags to the car.

He was so mean at times.

Nyle and Neha came rushing in, and just before hugging Arsalan, they stopped.

'Are you fighting?' Nyle asked.

I was shocked. He had never asked this question before. Today was a day of some very tough questions.

'No, we're not, baby,' I replied lovingly and opened my arms to hug him. He ignored them and turned towards his father. Neha ran into my arms, my baby girl, my protector who somehow knew when I felt sad and knew the exact moment to hug me and make me feel better, for the moment, at least.

'Baba, what will you bring us?' Nyle always asked this question about Arsalan's business trips. And he replied like he always did.

'It's a surprise, son.' He hugged Nyle and kissed Neha's head and, ignoring me, rushed out the door.

My eyes welled up with tears. His capacity to hurt me amazed me.

'Mama, why were you and Baba fighting?' Neha, these days, automatically repeated anything Nyle said.

'No, Neha, we weren't.' I picked her up in my lap and called out to Nyle.

'Nyle, come to Mama.'

I knew well not to hug one child while the other was looking. I knew what that other child felt while waiting for their turn.

'No, Mama. Not with her. I hate her!' Nyle screamed, standing at the door.

'Nyle. You don't speak to your sister like that.' Where was all this anger coming from? I was shocked at this outburst. Nyle was a naughty boy, but he never gave me any trouble when it came to his temperament.

'I hate you too. You make Baba leave, and then you go too.' He was in tears.

I felt gutted hearing these words. What was happening to my son? I felt an alarm in my body, an inexplicable unease.

201

I turned to Neha. 'Neha, janu, go to Maasi. You can take the iPad. I need to talk to bhai.'

She jumped from my lap at the magical word 'iPad' and ran out of the room. It was a moment of parenting failure where I had to use something I knew wasn't suitable for my child, but I didn't care. I had to speak to Nyle.

'Nyle come here, janu.' I held him. He resisted initially, trying hard not to cry, his emerging manhood being threatened. I had been cautious not to subject my son to the 'boys don't cry' stereotype, but somehow, it had still been internalised.

'Why do you say I send Baba away?' I gently asked him, ruffling his hair.

'You do!' He slapped the hand away, red in the face with big tears in his eyes.

'I hear that. Tell me, what makes you say that, baby?'

I could hear his reluctance, but I wanted to get to the bottom of this before it became a part of the story he made up and began to define his life choices. I had studied enough psychology by now to know how crucial childhood was in shaping the adult personality. Sometimes it scared me too, because I knew I was making many mistakes. I lowered my voice to a whisper. 'I'm sorry that you're hurting. Tell me, Nyle.'

'You're always fighting before he goes, and you always smile more when he's not here,' he whispered, all the fight gone from his little body.

I felt as if someone had stabbed me in my gut. My little boy had noticed so much, and I had been fooling myself in thinking that my children were protected from my pain and the farce of a marriage that Arsalan and I had created.

'That's not true, baby,' I coaxed. 'Baba and I are very happy.' He was too young to hear the truth.

'But you fight...'

'When did we? Tell me?'

'Just now! I heard Baba speaking loudly...' He seemed pretty upset and convinced of his reality, which was more accurate than he realised.

I closed my eyes for a moment before opening them. 'Nyle, when Baba has to say something important, he speaks loudly. That doesn't mean he's angry.' I felt like crying too, but I took a deep breath to hold back my tears. My son needed a parent at the moment, not another broken child.

After a few more minutes of convincing him, he seemed to be placated, and for the time being, I felt I had prevented my child from feeling damaged by his parents' actions.

That night I cried a lot. I somehow believed that having experienced adversity growing up, I would be compensated through my marriage. Why was God so unfair to me? I didn't deserve this.

For the longest time, I cursed myself for not having enough gratitude for the life I had, but I could no longer lie to myself.

I was grateful for my husband's support in my journey as a therapist. I was thankful to him for providing me with a home and stability. But I had also been hurting for a decade in my loneliness, in my unmet needs, in my invisibility, and the abuse that I had to tolerate, and that still threatened to meet me around the corner. I finally realised that gratitude for the former did not compensate for the latter's pain.

My diploma class was the next day, so I dropped the children off with Ami. Despite my feelings for her, I couldn't help but feel that she too was lonely in that big old house. Relationships were so strange. So many layers and shades of the same colour constantly oscillated between hurt and healing.

The class was in the evening, but with Arsalan out of the city, I decided to visit Ami in the morning and stay overnight. I felt like doing that after so many years. Therapy had started to soften me towards Ami, and I wanted to work towards having a relationship that may not be ideal but could be comforting for both of us and for my kids. One of my biggest regrets in life was that two of my most significant relationships were so dysfunctional and my kids were aware of it.

The children were excited as they loved Ami's house, which had once been Nana's, with its big rooms, which offered plenty of hiding places as well as room to enact 'The Famous Five'. Seeing them running around happy and giggling, the mother in me felt joy and peace for their happy childhood, but the little girl in me felt immensely sad for all those years of confusion and chaos I had felt. In the years I should have been giggling away and running after butterflies, I had been shadowing my mother to stop her from *that*. It was still difficult to say out loud that my mother was having an affair with another man right under her husband's nose. She cared for Uzair in a way that blinded her to her children's needs. She became another man's lover and no longer my mum.

As I drove over with the kids happily chatting, I deliberately pushed away the doleful thoughts and mustered up a smile. Nana's home was also where we had celebrated our birthdays once a year, so I leant towards those happy memories of bouncy castles and balloons and lots and lots of ice cream. However, just like any other memory, they also reminded me of my most significant loss. Baba was always so happy at those parties, gently challenging Ami's obsessive-compulsive habits of wanting everything perfectly organised or cleaned while the party was ongoing and winking at us, reassuring us that all would be okay. A memory of Baba scolding me and sending me to my room popped up, but I immediately dismissed it. Today wasn't the day for it.

Oh, and I missed Khala. She had been my rock after Baba died, but after a year, she moved to Dubai, and she had been happily settled there for the most part. I didn't blame her. It wasn't easy to live with Ami.

'Nano.' Nyle jumped out of the car and ran towards Ami, who was waiting at the main door. It was now old and washed out, but at one time, the solid wood spoke of prosperous days when Nana had money that displayed class.

'Nyle. You have to wait for the car to stop,' I scolded him.

'I want to go too. Open the door!' Neha started hitting my seat with her legs.

'Stop it, Neha.' God, what was wrong with these children? Behaving perfectly, then the minute we reached Ami's, they gave her the perfect ammunition to shoot me in the head.

I took a long, deep breath and got out of the car, helping Neha untangle her seat belt, after which she bolted out as if she had been in jail.

Ami was smiling as she came forward and picked her up.

'Maheen, meri jaan,' Ami gushed, not realising what she had just said.

'Nano, I'm Neha! You're so silly.'

Ami started laughing. I looked at the scene before me and a profound sense of loss hit me before sadness took its place. Who was this woman who loved my children with such abandon? Her referring to Neha as Maheen wasn't lost on me either, and it hurt me every time she made that mistake. *Ami, did you never love me at all?*

I took a deep breath as tears choked me, gulping down my need to cry. Instead, I brightened my voice and said, 'Salam, Ami.' I had very rarely shown my vulnerable side to my mother, and I wasn't starting today.

Without meeting my eye, she greeted me, turned around, and entered the house.

Perfect. I'm home!

An hour before I had to head out for class, it started again – the interrogation.

'*Kab tak chale ga yeh sab?*' Ami asked casually while sipping coffee from an 'I love you, Mum' mug that Maheen had bought her last winter. She and Ami were still very close, but then, it was much easier to love Maheen.

205

'What are you talking about?' I asked, feigning innocence.

Kill me now; here she goes.

'How long will these classes take? The kids are getting badly neglected.'

I started feeling agitation in my body, but unlike all the other times when I would storm out of Ami's home sooner than I was supposed to, I took a long breath and told myself to take it easy. I was trying hard not to let Ami trigger an aggressive reaction from me. Through therapy, I was learning to contain these impulses and learning self-regulation and grounding. I didn't want to give this power to anyone – the power to upset me in a way that would bring me to my knees.

'It's not just a class, Ami. I'm training to be a therapist.' I tried to invite the adult in her to have a rational discussion.

She slammed the mug on the side table a little more forcefully than necessary. 'Then give these children up for adoption. Can't you ever be responsible?'

I couldn't hold it in any longer, but I tried again. 'You're being very unfair. One class a week doesn't affect the children. There are many working mothers.' I could feel the protest intensifying within me.

'There are so many women who do not have children. You are so lucky, yet you take all of it for granted.'

'How am I taking it for granted?' Despite myself, my voice rose.

'Nyle was telling me that you argued with Arsalan also?' The blame took another turn.

I started to lose it at this point. 'You mean you asked him? Why do you ask such things from the children?'

'Your husband works so hard. You're so lucky; I don't know why you can't have more gratitude for such a perfect life.'

'And a perfect childhood too?' I challenged her, instantly regretting it as I added, 'And you, the perfect mother!' I started laughing until tears started rolling down my face.

'What was wrong with your childhood, and what is with this sarcasm? *Hamesha se hi besharam aur batameez ho.*'

'Please mind your language. I'm not going to tolerate it.'

'So, this is what this once-a-week class is teaching you? You will regret this attitude when your children do this to you!' She was practically shouting now.

'Please don't shout. Neha and Nyle have heard enough of it in their life.'

'Why do you shout at them, then?' The attack continued.

'Why do you always assume it's me? Why do you always blame me?' I was on the verge of crying, but I would never give her that satisfaction.

'Stop making up stories. Arsalan has never raised his voice.' She began tossing around the TV remote on the sofa.

There was no point. I closed my eyes and took a deep breath. This was a losing battle. 'Don't let them play outside. They've already changed into their pyjamas.'

I left the room, not waiting to hear her reply. I didn't even say goodbye to the kids because another minute in her presence and I would have started screaming.

However, in the car, I just broke down. I thought of my friends' relationships with their mothers, and my heart filled with longing.

I slapped the tears away and clutched the steering wheel with all the force I had. I wanted to scream, but I shut my eyes for a few minutes and then started the car. I had been looking forward to this weekend, especially today's class. We had an international tutor taking our class, and he would be doing a few live therapy sessions as well. We were in the final year before we were assigned clients, and I was nervous and eager to learn as much as possible before sitting in front of someone who looked towards me for help and healing. Just imagining it scared the daylights out of me when I had so much of my own trauma to process.

I got in before the workshop started. Around thirty people were attending, and I scanned the room, looking for my classmates, wanting the comfort of their presence on a day like this. Unfortunately, most of the seats were taken, with just a front-row seat next to Ross available. Never shying away from being at the forefront, I made my way there and grabbed the seat before it was taken too.

Ross Kenneth had been coming to conduct training and workshops for a few years now. He was an experienced psychotherapist who lived in Virginia, taught psychodynamic theories at the local university, and worked in private practice. I awaited his yearly trips, always sensing a strange comfort in his presence. He was in his mid-fifties, tall and well built.

After greeting me quickly, he rose and made his way to the front of the room. The session started, and he quickly announced he would be doing a fishbowl, a live counselling session in front of the entire group.

'I need a volunteer, though,' he said, scanning the crowd. 'Who is going to be brave enough to share themselves in front of strangers and people they know?' Discomfort echoed loudly in the collective laughter.

My heart began to race, and I was driven by a strong impulse to challenge myself and take a session from this experienced therapist. A part of me wanted the attention, and it wasn't the first time in my life where, despite being anxious and scared, I had taken the risk of exploring a new experience in life. Whether it was offering to be a guinea pig for a magician at a birthday party when I was a child or dancing in the front row at a friend's wedding despite having two left feet. I saw myself raising my hand, a hand that seemed to have a mind of its own.

'Great!' Ross exclaimed, rubbing his palms together.

I smiled and walked towards one of the chairs in the middle, my legs wobbling. I immediately regretted my decision, as I looked at all the faces around me. For two years, since joining Healing Matters, I had never participated in my process in class. Ever since I had terminated my sessions with Ahad, my silent resolve to never discuss my pain had continued, but somehow, Ross drew me towards breaking that promise.

I looked down at my hands and had an impulse to start crying; my pain seemed to be spilling out of me uncontrollably. I didn't know what was happening, but Ami, Arsalan, Ahad, and everyone else's faces started swimming before my eyes. All the people who had hurt me.

'Everyone, please put your phones on silent. This will be an hour's session.'

I almost decided to get up and excuse myself. I had a strange metallic taste in my mouth.

'Hey, Saniya!' He smiled and greeted me. 'Are you already regretting sitting here?'

I laughed. 'Yes.'

'What makes you regret it?'

'I just feel very nervous.'

'I get that. You don't have to share anything you are uncomfortable with, though.'

I tried to think of a safe thing to discuss, but there was this wave of despair, almost, telling me to share it all. There was something about Ross that was screaming that he cared for me. What if I told him everything?

'I hate my mother.' Shock waves passed through my body at my confession. I abruptly got up from the chair. Ross didn't say anything. I sat down again. 'I mean I don't hate her, but I don't like her...' I tried to make amends, but the cat was already out of the bag.

I looked around the room, startled, and looked down again as I felt all eyes on me, eyes outside and eyes within.

'What would it mean for you if you said you hate her again?' Ross gently pushed, taking a seat himself.

I looked up at his kind face. 'Everyone will judge me,' I whispered.

'Everyone will judge you?'

'Yes. What kind of daughter hates her mother?'

'The kind that has been hurt by her mother, perhaps?'

I kept looking at him. I needed to keep looking at him.

'It wasn't that bad.'

'But it wasn't good either, was it?'

'I'm tired, Ross…' At that point, I started crying. I didn't care who was watching. 'My mother hit me a lot. I don't think she wanted me.'

He stayed silent, playing with the ring on his finger.

'What's the point of sharing it now? Where was anyone when she did that, haan?' I couldn't believe how quickly I had dived into the session and how much I was sharing. Words seemed to be pouring out of my mouth, maybe because I had bottled everything in since Ahad.

'You sound angry, Saniya!'

'I am angry. Why, is it a crime?' I didn't know what was happening to me, but I was beyond caring.

Ross raised his eyebrows. 'You tell me. Who are you angry at?'

'What kind of question is that?' I wanted to add stupid, but I had been raised to be polite.

'It's a question. Who are you angry at?'

'My mother, of course. Who the fuck else would I be angry at?' I was about to get up again, my legs itching to move.

Ross got up, put another chair next to him and sat in it, leaving the one opposite me empty.

I shook my head. 'No, I'm not doing this. I'm not talking to the stupid chair.'

'Tell your mother how badly she has hurt you…' he said, his voice gentle.

I stayed quiet for a few seconds. I avoided looking at the chair.

210

And then, out of nowhere, a memory popped up where she had slapped me hard across my face in the middle of a grocery shop for accidentally dropping a Mitchell's ketchup bottle on the floor. The bottle hadn't broken, but she'd still struck me. I was twelve and mortified. I had picked up the bottle, quickly putting it back on the shelf, and hid behind the cereal box I had picked up just so no one could see the red mark on my face.

'Why Ami? Why did you not love me?' My anger had dissipated, and I felt like sobbing aloud, my entire body shaking with tension. 'I needed you, but you kept leaving. I was tired of stopping you, Ami.' The sobs broke out, and I covered my face with my hands.

I didn't know how much time had passed. Ross put a comforting hand on my knee. 'You're tired, aren't you?'

'I am,' I replied in a little girl's voice. I was so tired.

'I can imagine how traumatic it must have been for you to be unloved and abused by your mother,' he said, his voice lined with some unidentified pain, maybe his and mine both.

'How can you imagine that?' I threw out the retort.

'Do you see this?' He pointed to a scar beneath his eyebrow.

'Yeah…' I didn't know where this was going.

'That's my mother, Saniya.'

Our eyes locked, a shared pool of pain, two unwanted, unloved, beaten-up children.

'I don't know what to say.'

'Would you like to lie down?' he offered.

A little laugh disguised as a sob broke out. 'Why do I need to lie down?'

'You don't have to stop her from leaving anymore, sweet.' His kind words were too much to bear. Suddenly, out of nowhere, Ahad's face popped up before me.

'What are you shaking your head for?' Ross enquired.

'I don't need to rest. I don't need anything.' I had broken the promise I had made a year ago; I was back to needing again.

And here I was, expressing my burning need to be cared for in front of the world.

'I think I want to stop now. I don't want to go on…' I wiped the tears away and took a long, deep breath.

'I hear you. You don't want to go on, do you?' The implicit meaning of his response to my literal here-and-now feeling wasn't lost on me. He wasn't just giving me the option to stop now but had connected deeply to a part of me that wanted to run away from the painful realities of my life.

I was tired and didn't want to go on. I was tired of making any more effort. My heart had already withdrawn from my husband, and I finally let my mother go then too. Or I thought I did.

'You are courageous, and I am honoured that you let me witness your pain.' Ross had the perfect words, as always.

'Thank you. I appreciate it.' I got up and went back to my seat.

I looked around to see kind and loving faces. I felt I had done something important for myself – something crucial for others. I didn't listen as Ross went on discussing the session. How, without even knowing the story, a client could be given space to express their hurt and be held never failed to amaze me.

As I drove home, it dawned on me that I had taken another turn in my journey. I had worn my wounds with pride and no longer believed I was responsible for realities that didn't belong to me. I realised that to heal others, I didn't have to hide my wounds.

I had met the wounded healer today.

16   *Wife*

I was exhausted, and I badly needed a break. While it was good that my practice was growing, the extra hours were beginning to take a toll on my mental health.

Since becoming an independent practitioner, I had slowly become popular and now got referrals from everywhere. Sitting in the office today, I wondered if I ought to use these precious few minutes I had to check on the kids, but before I could do that, the door opened.

'*As-salamu alaikum*, Saniya.'

I looked at the handsome man standing in my office with a half-smile on his face.

I sat up straight, feeling a bit nervous. 'Hello, please have a seat.'

Why am I nervous?

'Thank you. Sorry, I'm a little late.' This client had a deep, husky voice and, along with being well built and handsome, he was also quite tall. I thought he looked like Arjun Rampal, my all-time favourite Bollywood crush. Of course, that made me a bit self-conscious of my own drab appearance: a Batman T-shirt with worn-out jeans. I had been feeling under the weather and hadn't bothered with dressing up this morning.

I decided to take the upper hand. 'So let me explain how this works. Anything that you share is confidential. Lahore is smaller than we imagine, and we might socially have mutual contacts. Rest assured, if I know of any contact, I will let you know, and confidentiality will not be compromised.'

The client nodded. 'Thank you. That's good to hear.' He had piercing eyes, and they were fixated on me. The room felt smaller than before, and I remained strangely nervous.

'Tell me a bit about yourself,' I said, trying to break the tension.

Be a professional woman! This is not Arjun!

I felt like an imposter playing therapist as, in that moment, I would have liked nothing more than to be sitting across from this good-looking man in a coffee shop. Why was I behaving like a giddy teenager? Sometimes I felt that my lack of dating experience contributed to this innate shyness and awkwardness I had around men, especially those I suspected had an interest in me.

'I'm forty-five, a lawyer, and single,' he began. 'And this is my first time in therapy, and I'm unsure if I need it.'

'Well, that's the right place to start,' I replied, smiling.

Are you flirting, Saniya? He's your client! Stop it!

I changed tack. This man had an intimidating presence that filled every nook and corner of the room. 'So, what brings you here?'

'That's exactly what I was thinking. And I wasn't expecting such a pretty therapist.' He leant forward as he said it. 'You don't have a WhatsApp DP to warn your clients.'

I noticed his body language, and it was as if he was creeping more and more into my personal space.

'Thank you. So, what brings you here?' I didn't acknowledge the compliment although I was sure he saw the redness in my cheeks. I hated it when I started blushing.

'You already asked that.' He was smiling now. What was happening here?

I started to get uncomfortable – an exciting discomfort. I was used to being complimented by men, but this was something else, an intensity I was unprepared for.

I was about to say something, but I let the silence be.

He said nothing and kept looking until I had to look away. I was aware of the control that this man had taken the minute he had entered the room.

'Has anyone told you that you have a powerful sex appeal?'

'What does it mean for you to tell me that?' I challenged him and looked straight into his eyes, slightly agitated by this blatant onslaught of his masculinity.

My palms were sweaty. This was the first time in my life that someone had told me I was sexy. Even Gordon hadn't used those words, although I could strongly sense he found me attractive. I had convinced myself that, although the lack of intimacy in our marriage was Arsalan's fault, I must not be good enough for him, hence the lack of desire. I always saw myself, despite being considered pretty, as a girl-next-door type. My words belied the tension I was experiencing in my body.

He started laughing. 'You got me.'

I smiled at his words. So, this was a deliberate game of charm he had been playing.

'I think I have commitment phobia. And my mother no longer has the patience for it.'

'What do you understand commitment phobia to be?'

'Hmm, well, I'm forty-five and still single; it's pretty clear what it means.'

Slow down, you overconfident arse!

'Yes, you shared that. I would still invite you to think about it. What is your understanding of these two words: commitment and phobia?' I felt more confident now that I was on familiar ground.

He was pensive, and the energy shifted in the room. 'I've had many relationships, but when settling down, I'm shit scared. I can't be responsible for another person in my life.' His voice caught with some unidentified emotion.

'Tell me about your parents, your siblings.' I needed to explore his primary relationships. It always started with that.

He seemed uncomfortable now. 'Nothing special. I'm an only son. My father left us when I was two.'

215

'Left?'

'Yes, left. He remarried.' He shifted in his seat.

I wasn't nervous at all now. A power shift had just happened in the room.

To an outsider, it might look like his initial flirting wasn't therapy, but it was all part of the process. Everything that entered the therapeutic field was information about the client.

'They are still married, but he stopped existing for us.' His voice was sombre now. He was a heartbroken little boy trying his best to make light of his bleeding wound hiding behind the persona of a charming man. The rejected daughter in me wanted to reach out to this abandoned son; a moment of heightened pain filled the room.

I took a long, deep breath and asked, 'When you were young, who was your go-to person if something happened in school, for example?'

It was a very pertinent question. Who had made this little boy feel safe?

'I wouldn't worry my mother. She was in depression for years after he left.'

I noticed how he said 'he' and not Daddy or Abu… just like for me, Ami mainly was a 'she', wasn't she?

'I had to take care of her,' he added.

He shared a few instances of his early years and the worry he experienced for his mother in school, where he was scolded for always being late in submitting his homework. He didn't know how to tell the teachers he had too much on his plate when he was home to focus on his work. It was only after his A levels that his mother decided to go and live with her brother, who had lost his wife, and that's when he went abroad to university and started turning his life around.

'Well, we are coming to the end of the session for now. Thank you for sharing today.'

'I don't know how I managed to say all this. I want to come

again, but I fear...' he deliberately left his sentence unfinished.

'You fear?' Somehow, I knew the answer already.

'I fear I will fall for you,' the confident Casanova said. 'A gorgeous, smart woman who listens is a lethal combination!' He was back to being the charming male. I now knew it was a defence mechanism that protected the little boy's pain.

I confidently smiled. 'Well, considering that you have commitment phobia, it shouldn't be an issue.'

He laughed, a spontaneous laugh that seemed authentic and had no power play.

'Pretty and funny? Damn. See you next week, then. Can I pay online?'

'Sure. I'll share the details. Take care.'

I stayed in the office a bit longer. I had enjoyed the session, and his compliment hadn't gone unnoticed. I had never imagined that I could be perceived as sexy by a man. It was ironic that clients came to therapy with a fantasy of seeking something but unknowingly offered so much.

That evening we were invited for dinner at Arsalan's parents' home. I was exhausted, but I was looking forward to it too. They were good people, and I felt guilty for not spending enough time with them. The kids were super excited for all the goodies waiting for them at Dada and Dadi's home.

'How is your practice going, beta?' Uncle asked after dinner as we sat down with cups of green tea.

'Alhamdulillah. Pretty well, Uncle.'

'It must get emotionally very draining,' Aunty stated. 'I can't imagine sitting for hours listening to other people's sad stories.'

'Yes, but it...' I couldn't complete my sentence as Arsalan jumped in.

'*Baith ker sunana hi hai.* How difficult is it to sit and listen for an hour and get paid?'

The familiar resistance came up in me. I hated how my work was mocked and made light of.

'It's not just sitting and listening. It's much more.'

He laughed. The laughter made it worse. It had no humour – a feeble attempt to sweeten the bitterness. I suddenly remembered a line from the film *The Holiday*: 'I understand… how it can actually ache in places you didn't know you had inside you'. My mind was strange. It was an all-time favourite of mine because it promised the possibility of love in the most unexpected places. My soul was even more bizarre. The unfolding within just kept emerging in the wrong places all the time.

Arsalan turned towards me. 'There is a two-day trip to Dubai coming up. Chalo? The kids can stay here.'

I wasn't prepared for this. Where had this come from? Hope came knocking rudely on the door that had been shut. Suddenly, Gordon's face appeared before my eyes. *Don't go there.*

'I don't know. The kids haven't stayed alone before,' I tried protesting, but a part of me was happy to be invited and about his interest in me. It wasn't that he wasn't committed in his own way, but what he didn't understand was that, despite his sincerity towards me, his anger kept bringing us back to the starting line.

'You both must go. We would be more than happy to take care of them. I will take time off from the hospital,' Aunty assured me. I had started to suspect that she had an idea that our marriage was on the rocks. I wasn't sure how because we had never fought in front of her, but she was a mature, insightful woman, and it was no surprise that she could sense the energy between us.

'Neha, Nyle, come here!' Arsalan called out to the children.

They left the TV and came running, plopping themselves abruptly in their dad's lap.

'Are you guys ready for an adventure?' he asked them in a whisper.

Arsalan's love for the children and his playful, warm attitude always made me feel thrilled and sad at the same time. I was pleased as a mother to see my children thriving, but I felt low as a wife who was the recipient of anger and abuse.

'Do you want a two-day sleepover here?' he asked the children.

'Yes! Yes!' They both started screaming in unison.

Everyone started laughing.

'Will we get McDonald's?' Nyle asked. His life's purpose started and ended with a Happy Meal.

'Yes. And we will also go to Playland,' Uncle promised.

'We can take the kids with us, Arsalan?' I hesitatingly suggested.

'Don't give that option in front of them. What's wrong with you?' he scolded in a loud voice.

What was wrong with me? Isn't that what I had always wanted? For my husband to take an interest in me?

So, without time to think, I was ambushed into a two-day trip when I was conflicted and unprepared to spend time so closely with him. I wanted to spend my time talking to Gordon. But a lingering half-dead fragment of hope had come alive with Arsalan's invitation. Maybe this was the beginning of my marriage that I had always fantasised about?

The next couple of days were spent packing and preparing for the trip. I deliberately withdrew from chatting with Gordon. I liked how my request for space was always respected, although I felt rejected too, at the ease with which he was ready to give me space. While the adult appreciated that, the inner child didn't want to be left alone. But whenever we connected, it felt like two childhood best friends. Talking to him felt like talking to myself. Gordon was like coming home after a long, tiring day.

A day before we had to leave for Dubai, he called. I was

rushing back from the salon and picked up the call without looking at who the caller was.

'Hey, stranger.' A warm voice beckoned to me on the other end.

'Hi!' I smiled, always happy to hear the warm, comforting voice on the other end.

'I've been thinking of you. You doing well?'

How was he so attuned to my emotional self? 'I'm okay. What makes you ask?'

'You've been missing. I haven't heard from you for four days now.'

'Is that so? Are you keeping count, Gordon?'

His deep laughter broke out on the other end of the call.

'And why am I always expected to be the one to reach out?' I felt a little angry as I said it.

'No, you're not,' he replied softly in a voice full of compassion that touched parts of me that craved this care.

A sudden urge to cry and a tear slipped down my cheek. The little bugger, constantly betraying me!

'Saniya?'

'Yeah?' I responded in a little girl's voice. I found myself shrinking.

'Talk to me.'

'It's fine.'

'It always is. Tell me.'

'Nothing to tell. I need to go.'

A few seconds passed and I felt strangely comforted by the silence.

'I'm going to Dubai for a few days. I'll call you when I'm back.' I closed my eyes.

'Okay. Are you looking forward to going?'

Was I looking forward to spending time with Arsalan? I didn't know. But I knew that I wanted to meet Gordon and he was in my thoughts often.

'How are you, Gordon? All good with you?'

'Yes. Take care, and I hope you're singing, my dearest friend.'

I wanted to cry. The words 'my dearest friend' made me feel I belonged somewhere.

'Thank you,' I whispered. 'And thank you for calling.' I loved that he understood when I didn't want to respond to his question and didn't push me. The ease and comfort I found in my friendship with him brought me so much relief.

I couldn't continue with my singing classes. Life had got in the way. I could sing for myself, but the songs were lost somewhere. My voice was lost somewhere. I did find it. I found it when I screamed in my husband's face a few years back when I found out about another one of his friendships. I found it in Healing Matters. I found it with Ami, where I no longer allowed her to walk over me. I still found it with Arsalan, where my silence spoke louder than my words.

I deliberately escaped this space and encouraged myself to look forward to the trip. He had taken a step forward, and I felt that I needed to reciprocate, even if I felt more alone than ever before. Even though this trip wouldn't resolve the issues between us, maybe it could be a step in the right direction?

But where did Gordon fit in with all of this? Maybe I was drawn towards him out of anger at my husband's past and ongoing shenanigans. I wasn't sleeping with him, but was this emotional cheating, then? What was I doing? Was I drawn towards Gordon to spite my husband? Did that mean that I still cared for Arsalan? Yes, I did care for him even when I tried to convince myself of the contrary. But Gordon was much more than an avenue for revenge. The word revenge didn't even sit well with me. I just wasn't that person.

Gordon was familiar even though I hardly knew him. That's all I could think of. It didn't feel wrong to be drawn to him. To feel cared for by him or to miss him too at times. He made me think in ways I hadn't known how to. How could I explain to anyone who he was when I didn't know fully myself? Most importantly, he showed respect to me in a way that made me take pride in being a woman, that made me feel I mattered.

I didn't want to have an affair with him. Somehow that thought repulsed me. It didn't do justice to the unique space we both shared.

On the day of the flight, I woke up with the feeling I used to have when I had an exam. It was the first time I was leaving my babies alone, and I was a nervous wreck. The thought sent an alarm through my body. Suddenly, a flashback came of Maheen and me sitting in the car, holding hands after we were picked up from school… on our way to experiencing the biggest change of our lives: Baba. I didn't want my children to ever go through the trauma of losing a parent. It was the most devastating and painful feeling in the world.

I rushed straight to Nyle and Neha's room. They were not in the room. My body went into an unexplainable panic, and I ran to the living room. Both were in their pyjamas, half asleep, lying on the sofa watching TV.

'Nyle. Neha,' I called out, plopping myself between them and grabbing them both. I wanted to hold them for as long as I could.

'Mama. You're squishing me.' Neha, ever the drama queen. Why did children cry so much these days? Probably all the screen time hyper-activated their nervous systems.

'Yes, I am! I am!' I started tickling them. Nyle managed to pull himself out of my arms and run off. Neha took the cue and did the same. I just chased them.

'I'm going to catch you,' I screamed after them, laughing along with them. It was our little game.

They both went straight to Arsalan's room and jumped on the bed.

'Woah! What's happening here?' Arsalan called out in a happy and sleepy voice.

'Mama is trying to get us,' Neha, the informant, replied.

Arsalan grabbed both of them and tucked them under the blanket. 'Now Mama can't get you.'

My heart skipped a beat before Arsalan stretched his arm and pulled me into the loving embrace. Despite myself, I felt warm, fuzzy, and happy.

We all tucked in together, holding each other, and I was happy. Nothing mattered at that moment. My pain, unmet needs, our fights, nothing mattered.

I closed my eyes for a moment and made a silent prayer.

Ya, Allah! Please help me find a way back to him. Let my heart open up again.

Despite making a promise with myself that I wouldn't cry, I couldn't help but tear up when I left my kids alone for the first time.

'Excited?' Arsalan asked me as we settled in the back of the car.

I reached out and held his hand. Something in me made me want to touch him. 'Yes, I am quite excited.'

He squeezed back, but then withdrew his hand and started doing something on his phone. For a moment, I felt the deep, familiar ache in my heart, but then I shook my head and told myself to be grateful for what was and not grieve for what wasn't. That's the resolve I had made to myself after the therapy session I had taken the day before the trip.

I had been in therapy with Yasir for a year, and it had been an exciting journey. After Ahad, I saw a few female therapists, but after a few sessions, I began to resist opening up to them. With Yasir, we had come to understand that, at some point, I ended up perceiving female therapists as my mother, which made it difficult for me to trust them. A man had wounded me, and I wanted my emotional needs to be met by a man. And the inner child tried finding Baba in men for the protection he could not provide. I loved him for the love he had showered on me, but a part of me never forgave him for not standing up to Ami.

My therapist became the father figure in the room for me. I finally poured my heart out and shared my childhood trauma and the pain of my married life. He heard, validated, and helped me have a different perspective on my married life. He helped me see Arsalan as someone who had his own language of love, whether through his unconditional support of my work, generosity, or blind trust in me. But he never dismissed his abuse or lack of desire for me as an excruciating reality and encouraged me to see myself beyond a wife and mother. We had also been working on having better boundaries with Arsalan and being more assertive in letting him know I wouldn't tolerate abuse. I was trying my best.

Last night's session had helped me strengthen my resolve to give my marriage the best shot. After all, I was the strong one. Despite giving up so many times and telling myself I was done, I was never really done fighting for a better relationship with Arsalan.

Dubai turned out to be a good break. Arsalan had meetings during the day, but we spent the evenings together. We met some of his colleagues the first night, and I enjoyed the food and the banter. His colleague had a villa on the beachside, and for me, it was a perfect moment as I stepped out on his private beach and looked at the calm waves across the dark blue sky and a half moon peeping through the clouds. Arsalan walked up behind me and put his arm around my shoulders. 'Are you having a good time?'

'Yes.' I snuggled a bit more into him and closed my eyes. My husband. Things seemed to be turning around. I promised myself again that it was time to let go of the past. A sudden doubt crept up again. Who was he friends with these days? Was he with someone? And again, I brushed it away and reminded myself that at the end of the day, I was his wife, and a few platonic casual friendships couldn't replace my position in his life.

That night when I reached out to him, he didn't protest, and we became intimate after months. I made the move, as always, but this was one of the few times he didn't say no. I felt like the happiest woman alive on the earth. These last few months, ever since that night when I heard him on the phone with someone, I had withdrawn from the relationship. I had stopped asking him to be intimate with me, and it was no surprise that he never questioned months of abstinence. That was the headline of our marriage, anyway. It was one of the happiest nights of my life. Nothing mattered. No one mattered.

The next day, I spent time shopping, getting stuff for the children, gifts for Uncle, Aunty, and Ami, and a few things for myself. I had lunch by myself and felt at peace. The occasional thoughts of Gordon didn't last for more than a few minutes. We went for a desert safari in the afternoon, again with his colleagues. I was looking forward to the night, seeing the beginning of the new dawn, but I could see that Arsalan was tired. So, as much as I wanted my husband, I decided not to put him in a difficult position, and I quietly hugged his back and went off to sleep.

'Can you try coming early today? And let's not meet anyone tonight,' I suggested as he prepared to leave for work on our last day in Dubai.

'I might not be free before seven, but I'll tell the team I won't be available afterwards.' He kissed me on the forehead and left the hotel room.

I felt like singing, so I did. I decided to pamper myself and went and got a jumpsuit from my favourite clothing shop, Zara. He had been busy every day, coming in late at night, but I didn't want to be the nagging wife and wanted to look forward to the evening. I got us a dinner booking at Zuma, a fancy restaurant a friend had recommended. I wanted the night to be special and so, around 7:00pm, I was all dressed up. I had already packed the rest of the stuff as we had an early flight the next day. I hadn't missed the children as much as I had thought I would, but I was excited to see them and more excited to see their reaction to a bag full of their favourite toys and sweets. Neha had asked me to wrap up all her gifts, so the afternoon had been spent doing that for both her and Nyle.

Arsalan entered our hotel room, a large fancy room we were blessed to stay in. I was grateful for all these luxuries that life had thrown my way. 'Yaar, we will have to have dinner with the team. I couldn't say no,' he announced and collapsed on the bed with his shoes on.

'Arsalan, yaar, that's not fair. I wanted us to spend time alone.'

'I know, but this team dinner is important. I might meet some prospective new clients too.' He said it all in a matter-of-fact tone.

'I got us a table at Zuma. Please try to get out of it. Please,' I stubbornly insisted.

'Saniya, yaar, try to understand. I can't say no at the last minute.' He picked up his mobile and started browsing through it.

I felt angry. Betrayed. 'You can say no to me, but you can't say no to them? This entire trip has been about them.' I went and sat on the sofa chair opposite the bed and took my shoes off. 'I'm not going for this dinner.' I felt all the excitement of the evening rushing out of me, coupled with disappointment and frustration.

'*Yeh kiya bakwaas hai!*' He sounded agitated now and sat up on the bed.

I felt the unease in my belly, and I could feel my heart starting to beat so fast I could almost hear it. 'I'm not upset.

Once you're back, we can spend some time together.' I was scared and knew where this was heading, and like all the other times, I knew there was no stopping him. I could only hope that, as we were in a hotel, he wouldn't be as loud as he always was.

'What do you mean once I'm back? Why the fuck would you not attend the dinner?' he said, his voice rising.

'Keep it low, Arsalan. I don't want us to fight. Fine, I'll come.' But it was too late. His face was a familiar red and contorted in aggression.

'For fuck's sake, stop being a complaint box. I brought you on this trip. You've been shopping your arse off, yet you can't be happy. *Dafa Raho yahaan hi.* I'm not taking you now.' And he jumped off the bed and started changing his shirt.

'Why are you overreacting so much? Is there something else that you're upset about and projecting onto me?'

'I'm overreacting? You bitch. Shove your analysis up your arse!'

'Don't speak to me like that. I told you I won't tolerate this language anymore.' My heart sank, but this time I wasn't willing to compromise on the boundaries I had tried so hard to define.

'Nothing makes you happy. *Izzat raas Nahin aati tumhain...*' He seemed like a hungry animal, unleashed.

'You're being unfair. I'm grateful that you brought me here. I just wanted us to spend time together alone, and I don't think it's unreasonable to ask.' I started to cry at this point, but there was a new-found strength that made me want to stick to my opinion and not end up apologising as I had always done in the past.

'Grateful? Are you going to fucking lie to my face?'

'I'm not lying. I'm not.' I put my shoes aside.

He walked towards me and shouted again, inches away from my face as I sat on the edge of the chair. 'I'm done with you. For ten years, all I've heard are complaints. Sometimes it's sex, then it's other women, then it's... oh, you don't give me time!

227

Nothing can make you happy because you're just an ungrateful bitch who wants to play the victim all the fucking time. I feel sorry for you.' He pushed me back with his hand on my chest, sharp and cold.

My body went into shock. I had never expected him to push me. I was numb and frozen. A few minutes later, he grabbed his wallet and phone and left the room, banging the hotel door hard behind him.

I curled up without moving from the chair, as loud sobs racked my body and, once again, I helplessly watched my marriage falling apart. It wasn't working, and it was time to let go of hope and accept the reality of another failed relationship in my life. Growing up, I had hoped and believed that my husband would make up for Ami's cruelty and he would be my companion for life. Coming to terms with the truth of the loneliness and my loveless life was as hard, if not more so, than childbirth, and the last thought I had before I slept was that, if Gordon left me too, how would I survive?

17   *Daughter*

I had a secret that I was ashamed of.

No, that wasn't true. I had more than one secret that I regretted sharing. The biggest one was about my mother's affair. It wasn't that my mother had an illicit relationship with a man we all trusted for years – I sometimes wondered how she got away with it without anyone finding out – but it was the fact that I was chosen by the universe to walk into something I wished every day I had not. Why couldn't I have carried on living my life in ignorance like Nana, Hafsa Khala, Baba, and Maheen?

Why me?

Why was I selected to be part of this darkness that no amount of light could ever minimise?

Another secret that remained untold was the relief I experienced during the events that unfolded after Baba left us forever. Somehow, his death became the catalyst to bringing an end to my active trauma, a bloodthirsty truth that had sucked all the life out of my childhood. Baba's death had also kicked Uncle Uzair out of our lives, and how that impacted me was more profound than any words could explain or my young mind could even comprehend.

When he was alive, I had to continuously live with the guilt of not telling him what my young eyes witnessed. Every time I was in the same room as Ami, Baba and Uncle Uzair as they discussed a game of cricket, my heart would be pounding so hard that it surprised me that no one could hear it. My wretched heart would beat with anger and helplessness as I saw what a lie was being lived right before my eyes, and was too scared to share the truth. I was overwhelmed because I was constantly betraying Baba, and the sad part was that Ami had no idea how much toll this was taking on me. I had chosen her and was protecting her, but she had no idea.

I didn't know what to believe. I saw how Uzair Uncle touched her feet under the dining table with his own, or how Ami thought that we wouldn't notice the lipstick marks on Uzair Uncle's cheek or his hand on her back while she cooked. No one else noticed because they weren't looking. But I was always looking and saw more than my eyes could bear.

I feared the consequences if I ever confronted Ami. There was no one to help me understand it all, and I was always anxious. My tummy would be in knots, and I had no appetite, biting my lips until they were dry and bleeding.

Ami and I didn't have a relationship. We just lived together. I called her Ami. She called me Saniya on rare occasions.

After Baba died, it became even more evident that we were two strangers whom the world knew as mother and daughter. Khala was the closest thing I had to a mother, but for Maheen, Ami was a good mother. I had mixed feelings when I saw the bond they shared. I was confused. I was jealous. I was disconnected. Weren't parents supposed to love all their children equally?

Ami and I hardly talked. We would talk about unavoidable functional things like when the car would be available or what to make for lunch, but there were no conversations. Somewhere, I had this strong feeling that she resented me for Uzair Uncle moving to Canada, almost as if she had found out how often I had wished for that to happen. I was already carrying enough guilt to last me a lifetime ever since I realised that maybe Baba had to die for Uzair to leave Ami alone. Many nights I trembled with pain, questioning myself as to whether I had wished Baba's death. Maybe Uncle Uzair also felt guilty for betraying Baba. It all got very confusing in my head at times.

Ami and I only coexisted. I didn't tell her when I won a trophy in the inter-university debates or when I acted as a beautiful 'Anarkali' in the university play. I didn't tell her when I cried for hours after I heard of the Father's Day plans being discussed by my friends.

My mother provided a home for me and put food on the table, but she never made me feel loved or nurtured or as if I mattered to her in this world.

I found Ami in my teachers. I found her in my friends' mothers. I tried to find her everywhere, but the wounds inside were bleeding – all the time. I needed my mother. I wanted her to put oil in my hair. Take me out shopping. Tease me about boys. My friends would tell me how their mothers were more like their friends than their parents.

I had neither a parent nor a friend.

When Arsalan's proposal came, Hafsa Khala told me about it. I had immersed myself in university life and, unlike some of my friends, was neither dating nor paying much attention to the men around me. Did I not find someone attractive when I went out? Sure, I did. But it wasn't enough to hold my attention for long. Asifa's brother, my school crush, was the last guy who had interested me. I knew now that it had meant nothing. It was just a random moment that didn't last for long. I just didn't trust men.

I met Arsalan for the first time during our informal engagement. Before that, a photo had been shared with me. I liked how he looked, and I didn't think of asking anything else. By that time, the discussion of my marriage had been had so many times, and many prospective suitors explored, that I was pretty sick of the topic. I was ready to say yes even before I saw Arsalan's photo.

I asked Khala, 'Why is Ami kicking me out?'

She tutted. 'Come on, Saniya. That's not true.'

'Then what's the rush? I've just finished university.'

'Meri jaan, we are just exploring our options.'

'I want to do my master's.'

Hafsa Khala cupped my cheek in her palm. '*Shaaadi ke baad ker lena, beta.*'

'No, Khala. I want to do it before.'

I knew she'd support me, but nobody could do anything once Ami had decided something.

Apparently, Arsalan's mother had seen me at a wedding I attended with Ami and Khala and liked me. I remember wearing a plain pink silk suit with a mukesh ka dupatta. I was wearing light make-up and had let my hair down, straightened by Hafsa Khala. I knew this preparation was with the hope of some *rishta* coming, and luckily for my mother, who was convinced I would die an old maid, a proposal came for me.

Arsalan's father was a bureaucrat, and his mother was a general physician. He was the only son. My friends thought I was crazy to say yes without meeting him. But then, he too, hadn't met me. I saw it as a romantic thing and sent a photo of mine from a university event. I wore a black shalwar kameez, which my friends unanimously recommended. I was wearing make-up, too, and I knew I looked pretty. Black was my colour and looked striking against my fair complexion.

Only two of my friends were allowed to attend the engagement. Ami was acting out and nervous about the entire extravaganza. She wanted it to be a simple affair. She didn't wish for any *Halla Gulla*. I wasn't surprised. I expected nothing more from her. Why would this be any different when she had been so stingy in celebrating the essential critical moments of my life? But I would be lying to myself if I didn't admit that, somehow, I had hoped this would be different.

The first thought that came to my mind when I looked at Arsalan and shyly looked away again was, *he's handsome!* My immediate next thought was, *why did he say yes to me?* Ami had done an excellent job of making me believe I wasn't good enough in more ways than one.

I was wearing a light-yellow shadow work kurta with the same-coloured dupatta and a white shalwar. Ami had lent me her gold earrings, and I was asked to wear light make-up. I was so nervous.

The event was simple but lovely. Arsalan and I sat together, surrounded by family and friends. Ami had thrown a lavish high tea, and Maheen was giggling like a teenager. Throughout the event, I was only thinking of Baba. I missed him. I missed Nana too. Ami had been devastated and hadn't left the room for days after Nana's death. We all knew how close she was to him. Uzair Uncle had phoned from Canada, but he didn't visit. He had married someone there, and I finally started sleeping at night the day I found out. I knew that chapter was finally closed.

As with all typical Pakistani arranged marriages, the approval to talk to a boy came, and Arsalan and I started talking to each other. Both families had mutually decided to skip the engagement altogether, and we were to get married within the next four months.

Those were good times. I felt important. Uncle and Aunty would shower me with lavish gifts now and then. I had never received so many new gifts in my life. Arsalan was very generous too. He would surprise me with flowers and chocolates, and we spoke daily. I felt important and thought that my life had finally turned a corner. I would be happy for the rest of my life.

We had shared interests, discussed books and films, and shared life experiences. It was easy to be friends with him. He was unassuming, not demanding, and our relationship felt easy.

I wondered why I was the only one calling him or making plans to meet. But then I told myself that he had a nine-to-five job, and I had just finished university and had all the time in the world. Sometimes, I would find him short-tempered, but then

I knew I could be relentless about some things, too, like acting out if a meetup plan got postponed. He was the object of my affection, and no amount of attention was enough for me. I often had a strong impulse to tell him about Ami, but then something would stop me. What would he think about me? He would think I was like Ami too, that I was vulgar, and would judge me.

I sometimes had a strong impulse to hug him when we met, but I was too nervous to ask, and he never offered to. Or to hold his hand, but he never did that either.

Once, we were heading back from dinner, and I turned towards him in the car. 'Why don't you hold my hand?'

He looked startled and shook his head. 'I thought you wouldn't like it. You're shy.'

'I know, but…' I leant forward and held the hand that held the gearstick.

He smiled and squeezed it hard.

A few minutes later, he let go of my hand and played music. I found that odd. All the way to home, I kept thinking, *don't men like doing such things more than women?*

After he dropped me home and I had changed and was getting ready for bed, something triggered me, and I called him.

'Why did you let go of my hand?' I felt angry.

'What is wrong with you?' His voice mirrored my emotion.

'What is wrong with me? Are you serious?'

'Why are you picking a fight with me?'

'You're changing the topic. Why didn't you continue to hold my hand?' I wasn't ready to let go. I needed an answer.

'Go fuck yourself!' he shouted and hung up on me.

I was shocked. I couldn't in my wildest dreams have imagined that Arsalan, of all people, would speak to me like that. Tears welled up in my eyes.

I wanted to call him right away, but something warned me not to. That night I couldn't sleep. I kept checking my mobile to see if he would send me an apology, but there was none.

Finally, in the morning, I called him when I could no longer hold in my anxiety. 'Hello, Arsalan.'

'Why are you calling so early?'

I started crying.

'Yaar, why are you crying?' His voice warmed up.

'I didn't like how you spoke to me last night. And you didn't even say sorry.'

'Are you serious, Saniya? You owe me an apology for the way you were interrogating me.'

'I wasn't interrogating,' I whispered, tapping my finger against the phone.

'I never held your hand out of respect, and you got mad. It's disappointing.'

Shame travelled to every part of my body at his words. What the hell was wrong with me? How vulgar of me, and what kind of an impression was I giving him?

'I'm sorry, Arsalan. *Aaap theek keh rahe hain.*'

And that's how the relationship started. I believed his excuses, and I thought I made him angry. The blueprint of my marriage was in my face, and I missed all the red flags. I felt intimidated, and I started to lose my voice in the relationship.

Never had I imagined during that time that one day I would stand up to the husband who scared the daylights out of me in his fits of rage, that I would threaten to leave if he didn't stop, and carried a deep belief that I could walk out one day. And neither had I envisioned that I would fall for another man who would bring me to the most challenging decision of my life.

18   *Woman*

Was your trip good?

Gordon's name on my phone screen sent a current through me. Arsalan was busy with work as usual, which was convenient for me. The morning of our flight, he had acted normally, as if what had transpired between us the night before was a false memory. This was his habitual behaviour, something I had grown familiar with over the years. Denial was my favourite defence mechanism, but now, I felt I couldn't do it anymore. This strange wave travelled within me at the most inappropriate times, at the speed of lightning, with pain attached to its every fractal. It would pass quickly, but the aftermath of it would leave a dull, aching pain that I felt had now settled into every fabric of my being.

I was deeply hurt. I was hopeless. I was angry... lost in some unidentifiable abyss that I kept falling into and was unable to get out of.

I had only been responding to Arsalan about necessary things since the trip. He tried reaching out a few times, between his work and golf, with an invite to a dinner or trying to hug me at night, but I moved away and kept moving away. Whether he noticed or not was another matter. I just knew that I resented him with every fibre of my being.

For his neglect.

His abuse.

For carrying no remorse or ever offering a sincere apology for the pain he had caused me.

And I hated him for teaching me to scream as loudly as he did, if not more. The only difference was that he couldn't hear my screams. No one could hear them other than me.

For the first time, I thought, *why do I have to continue being married to him?*

I started considering a possible escape from the marriage, but deep down, I knew that I couldn't financially support my children alone. Ami would never welcome me back, so I might as well be on the streets. However, Arsalan's care meant nothing when he made me feel like nothing. I was reduced to ashes when I was called a *bitch* and a *whore* and *pathetic* and other things. My husband ruthlessly extinguished my spark. I had experienced self-hate; I had lost my self-respect for being a woman who stayed in an abusive marriage.

Yes, I could finally call it what it was: an abusive marriage. I was done lying to myself. I could no longer deny my issues because I had taken ownership of them, whereas he was stuck behind his defences. He had gaslighted me for so many years, never realising how heartbreaking it was.

I hadn't responded to Gordon for a few days. I just wasn't ready to speak to anyone. I extended my time off from work too. Pain and anguish were too much for me to process, my own or the clients'. I didn't feel like taking therapy either. I was angry at Yasir for encouraging me to hope again, to go on this trip with Arsalan and give my marriage a shot. How many times was I going to hope? How many times? Couldn't anyone see how tired I was? How tired every fragment of my body was? I couldn't fall so often and get up again, especially on my own.

I don't want to burden you... I felt like I would choke on my pain as I texted the words to Gordon. He had asked me why I was low. I could never understand how he could sense that.

As I noticed the two blue ticks indicating that he had read my text, he called.

'Saniya. You're not a burden for me,' were the first words that came out of his mouth.

And I couldn't hold the tears back any longer. I started crying hard, unable to speak. He didn't say anything as I continued to cry and then said in a soft tone, 'Meet me.'

'Okay. I want to.' The words rushed out of my mouth before I could stop them.

I didn't care anymore about anything. And if Arsalan could have so many female friends, then why couldn't I have male ones?

'Let's talk face to face then, okay?' There was so much kindness and care in his voice that it was all I could do not to burst out crying again.

The next day I was a nervous wreck. I regretted saying yes to him. What if someone saw us? But then, what would they see? Two adults could have a cup of coffee together. There was nothing wrong in that, but I was still conflicted. I felt guilty because I was excited. I hadn't met up with him since first meeting him at the party, and I thought I was crossing a line, but not meeting him now was unimaginable.

The children were at Ami's, and Arsalan had gone to Karachi for a night. At least my thoughts were not muddied by external chaos and the presence of my family to amplify the blinding guilt.

I took out a plain white shalwar kameez and was ready half an hour before I was meant to leave. We were meeting at a quaint little coffee shop hidden on Upper Mall Street. He had suggested the venue, and I was grateful I didn't have to share my concerns about going to a very public place. He'd thought of everything, hadn't he?

I entered the coffee shop with a heart beating so fast, it threatened to make my legs give away, and I tightly clutched the leather tote hanging on my shoulder. I arrived a little early, so I could run away if I felt too uncomfortable.

Luckily, the coffee shop was empty except for a single table that was occupied by a bald man and a middle-aged woman. Were they out on a date too? I suddenly felt horrified at my thought. This was not a date. We were friends. I was contemplating where to sit when I heard his voice from behind me.

'Hello, Saniya.'

It was too late to run away.

'Hi, Gordon.' I turned around with a confident smile and dug my nails further into the strap of my bag.

He looked good. Wearing a black T-shirt and jeans, he might not have been classicly handsome, but he was much more than that. He had an energy so powerful that I felt completely engaged with him, not distracted by the world around me.

I followed him into a tiny alcove at the back of the coffee shop. It was next to a big glass window that opened into a lovely garden thick with overgrown and neglected plants – the perfect spot. This place had an air of calm to it, unlike most of the coffee shops in Lahore that were always heaving with people.

We decided on coffee and a slice of cheesecake since we weren't very hungry. To distract myself, I looked at the green plants outside. I didn't know their names, but I liked looking at them. What was I doing here? What if someone saw us? I'd never met a man other than Arsalan in an intimate setting.

'How are you doing?' he softly asked, and I turned towards him.

Too close. I leant back in my seat.

'I don't know. I don't know anything anymore,' I admitted in a mere whisper, but I knew he heard me with or without the words. I couldn't pretend anymore. I was tired.

He stayed quiet but kept looking at me.

I took a long, deep breath and started talking. 'I'm not happy in my marriage, Gordon. I'm not. I'm not sure I can go on anymore.' As I said the words, I felt a sob escaping me and I covered my face with my hands.

'It's fine, Saniya. You're allowed to cry. There's no one here. Just me.' The warmth in his voice was like a balm on my aching soul.

I pulled my hands away in case I reached out for his and looked at him. 'Why do you care, though? You don't know me from Adam.'

He smiled. 'I don't, but you and I know what we share is beyond how long we've known each other.'

'What do we share?' I needed clarification. The waiter came at that moment with our orders.

A few minutes after he had left, and as I took a small bite of the cheesecake, Gordon's voice filled the silence.

'We have a special bond, don't we? We don't know why we care, but we do.'

I nodded. That's exactly how it was and the affirmation of how I'd been feeling without asking for it was a first of many.

In bits and pieces, I started sharing the narrative of my marriage. I didn't censor anything, and it felt right to tell him everything. I was a very lonely woman who felt unwanted and undesired by her husband. I don't know how long I spoke for, but I knew I couldn't stop. Now and then, I would sneak a glance at him and see a pair of the kindest eyes looking at me, an expression that said, *I hear you. I hear your pain loud and clear, my friend.*

He was my friend. Yes. He was my best friend.

I suddenly stopped and smiled. He smiled back. As if he knew, just like me.

'You're my friend. My best friend.' I bathed in the moment.

'Yes, I am, and you are mine.'

'But you never tell me anything about yourself. We only talk about me,' I said.

'Yeah, we do, and we need to, don't we? Someone needs to hear you out. It's high time.'

I felt tears rushing into my eyes as he said that.

'It's not that bad. I have good friends, my sister, and my therapist.' I looked away. But I paid my therapist to listen to me. Is that how my clients felt, too? I wondered if my care for them was for sale, transactional.

But I genuinely cared for each one of them. I did. People fascinated me.

He didn't respond for a moment. I think he knew that he filled some vacuum in my life that none of the people I'd mentioned did. Otherwise, I wouldn't be sitting in this coffee shop, opening my heart full of pain to a man I was meeting for the second time in my life. A man I had barely known for a few months.

'I'm tired, Gordon.' It felt liberating, just saying it out loud.

'Have you tried talking to your husband?' he enquired.

'I have now and then. I don't feel like it anymore. And, in all fairness, he doesn't get as angry as before.'

I assumed the defensive position I always did when it came to Arsalan. I knew somewhere hidden in that defence was the love for him that I no longer felt. It hurt to love this man. It hurt, and blocking him out of my heart was the easy way out.

'I have better boundaries now. But I'm lonely, Gordon.'

I brushed the forlorn tear I could feel sneaking out of my eye again. I seemed to have a reservoir of unspent tears.

His hand reached fowards and I withdrew mine. I wasn't willing to cross that line for anyone or for anyone to cross that line with me. That was a no-go area. He withdrew his hand with an expression that said, *I understand.*

'Saniya, it's been tough. You have such a loving heart, and it simply wants to love freely and be reciprocated.'

This man made me want to love every inch of me. Was that even possible?

'How do you know I have a loving heart?' I whispered.

'Is that even a question?'

'Yes. How do you know that?'

'A woman who chooses a healing profession out of love more than anything. A mother, a wife who stays in a difficult relationship, to say the least, is nothing but loving.'

'You make me sound like a saint. I've played my role in this marriage too.'

'Okay, you are the devil, woman.' I loved his smiling face.

I smiled back. 'I'm not the devil either.'

'Saniya, I'm not challenging that you had your role to play. It still doesn't justify his verbal abuse of you. There is no justification for it. Full stop!'

'Yeah, I know there isn't. I can say that, Gordon, but I can't do much about it.' My voice dropped a little, perhaps aligning with the helplessness I was experiencing.

'Why can't you?' It seemed like he was challenging me.

I shook my head, brushing a tendril of hair from my face. 'I don't know. I mean, it's better than before, but it takes one incident for me to go back to being the woman who has to listen to her husband swearing and shouting at her. I don't like being her.'

'I hear you.'

As we sat sipping at our coffee, I attempted to steer the conversation in a different direction. 'So, tell me about your family, Gordon.'

Gordon shrugged as if his own story was inconsequential. 'Well, I'm single, as you already know. I was in a long-term relationship for a few years, but we drifted apart...' He seemed to become sombre as he said it.

'That must have been very hard for you.'

He blinked, once. 'It was. I'm over it now, however. The past few years have been all about work. I'm also working on my first book.'

The coffee burnt my mouth as I took a sip too quick. 'Are you serious?'

He nodded. 'I'm writing about consciousness and motivation, and what it means for the mind-body system. The challenges of it and more.'

'That's… that's wonderful, my friend.' It felt awkward when I said 'my friend', but what the hell?

He picked up on it and had a bigger smile than before on his attractive face. 'I'm happy to have met you, Saniya. Feels like I've always known you…'

I was smiling too. 'That's exactly how I feel, Gordon, although I'm pretty tricky. I'm warning you now…'

He bowed his head. 'I stand warned. Be as difficult as you'd like to be. Bring it on, woman.'

I laughed at that. 'Well, if you're going to be my friend, you better keep up…'

'Aren't we already friends? What else is it that I need to know?'

'Well, for starters, I don't like it when people don't respond to my messages or call me back.'

'Why don't you like it?' he enquired.

'I just don't,' I quietly admitted.

'You feel you don't matter, don't you?'

I felt a sharp pain in my tummy. He'd gone for the jugular. 'Yes, it hurts me that I don't matter.'

'You matter to me. Your friendship is one of the most precious things I have found recently.'

It was a heart-warming moment. I felt safe. For the first time, I thought I had someone who cared for me unconditionally.

'Stay then, will you?' I asked, holding my breath, my entire being unsafe and insecure as I looked at the possibility of care and love before me. It was love but a different kind of love. It was so new and unfamiliar.

'I'm here for you. And I'm not going anywhere.'

He looked straight at me, and for a second, I dared to hold that gaze, and I finally felt I mattered. This time when he reached out for my hand, I involuntarily grabbed it and clutched it hard.

Something changed after that. We started talking almost all the time between work and home life. It had been two weeks since coming back from Dubai, and for the first time, we had started meeting up too. I was curious to know what had changed. Was it the rebel in me that pushed me more towards Gordon, or was it that the more I got to know him, the more I was attracted to him? There was an energy between us that was new and raw and sent weird sensations through my body.

For the first time, we went for a drive together. It felt risky, and the intimacy of that closed space was thrilling and scary at the same time. Arsalan was travelling, and after putting the kids to bed and reassured that Zubaida Maasi was with them, I had driven over to a failing café at the corner of Upper Mall Street that no one I knew would ever visit and had hopped into Gordon's car for a drive. We had driven around for an hour on the less crowded roads shooting from Upper Mall Street. It was a weekday, and oddly, the ever-awake city of Lahore seemed to be taking a break, like a tired traveller seeking respite under shade after a long journey in the sun.

I had sensed the sexual energy in the car that day – a sort of tingling sensation in my belly. I wanted to hold his hand, which was resting casually on the gearstick. I wanted to put my head on his shoulder. I wanted to kiss him and touch him. I didn't want to think more. But this growing attraction was different from my emotional attachment to him. Had he not started to look at me more intently than before? Was it a figment of my imagination when I thought he was staring at my body for longer than he usually would?

Whatever was happening was making me aware of myself in a very different way. I felt pretty and desirable and perhaps not the girl next door anymore. It was exhilarating thinking of what to wear when I would meet him again, and the anticipation of his appreciative gaze, which I could recognise now, and the text that would follow post our meetup.

You are gorgeous... how can your husband keep his hands off you?

I had started sharing more with him since the Dubai trip, and we met at any given opportunity. I ended up sharing the reality of my marriage. I told him about Ami. I told him about Arsalan's lack of desire for me. I told him about every detail of my life. Every painful event, every moment of despair, unspent anger, helplessness in the face of a life that kept throwing one curveball after another. For the first time, I felt I was not alone. I could reach out to Gordon whenever I wanted to. He had given me the space to say whatever I wanted to.

We would meet in unknown cafés and lonely parks or drive around. Two people in a busy city, sharing unknown and known feelings and thoughts without slowing down to see what all this meant for them.

What was happening?

Initially, when he wouldn't immediately respond, my abandonment anxiety would get triggered, but with time, I started to trust that he would respond when he could. I began to trust his care for me, and I knew I finally had someone who would always be around. Gordon was my best friend and perhaps more.

I often played a fantasy in my mind, where he would tell me he loved me or ask me to marry him, and I would say yes. I would imagine the life we could have, full of love and passion, two people who understood each other even in silence.

In those days, I was blinded to, or had turned a blind eye to, my husband and children. I, like a robot, performed all my duties, but I no longer felt any guilt for seeing Gordon every chance I got or for talking to him for hours at night. I believed that I owed it to myself; anytime the familiar responsibility came up, I would feel anger like I'd never experienced before.

A week later, a session with a couple triggered me to move something deep within me.

The minute I walked into the room to meet the couple, I felt this tightening in my belly. It was a young couple seeking marriage counselling for the first time. The guy was thirty, tall and broad, unkempt and messy. He wore a shalwar kameez that hadn't been appropriately ironed with Hush Puppies chappals. I felt an instant dislike for how he was dressed. The girl was in her mid-twenties, a petite, skinny girl covering her head with a scarf around her pixie face and wearing a pale pink shalwar kameez and khussa shoes on her feet. I noticed her timid nature and the vital air of anxiety around her. Her legs shook slightly, and I needed to walk up and hold her.

They had been married for three years. The guy stayed at home and did social media marketing assignments covering their minimal bills. The girl worked in the development sector and handled the home expenses.

'What brings you here?' I asked, attempting to break the ice.

The guy, Junaid, turned to his wife, Huria, and said, 'Should I start?'

'Yes, you should,' Huria replied.

'Okay. So, ever since we got married, she keeps complaining about something. Nothing makes her happy, and I'm tired.'

I didn't say anything. Silence always created pressure for impulsive behaviour. The most important information came out impulsively.

He carried on as his right leg started to shake. 'If I'm with my friends, she calls me repeatedly. If I'm watching a film, she has an issue. Then I end up losing my temper, and I become the bad guy. How is it fair, aap batain, madam?'

I felt a protest build in my body. He was so loud.

'Junaid, I don't like it when you—' Huria began but he cut her short.

'Yaar, you don't give me space to breathe.'

I felt like getting up and punching him. 'Will you please let her finish?'

I turned towards her. 'Take your time, Huria. Tell me what you don't like?'

She started crying. Silent, meek crying. She looked so small.

He was about to repeat something, but I stopped him with my hand.

'He hits me very often now,' Huria began. 'He shouts about every little thing. I don't think he's happy with me anymore.'

I knew it was coming, but I was hoping I was wrong. Sitting across from a male client who was abusive towards his wife was the hardest thing for me. At that moment, I became the wife, and I felt many emotions in my body, so many of them, hers and mine combined.

'How long has it been going on?' I asked, desperately trying to keep my voice measured.

'Since we've been married. He has anger issues.' She stole nervous glances at her husband.

'What do you expect? *Dimahg kharab ker diya hai tum ne!*' He turned towards her, his face contorted into an expression that wasn't unfamiliar to me. 'I need to tell my story too. It's so easy to use these words, like "anger issues". You don't let me breathe.' He seemed agitated and was red in the face.

Throughout the session, there was a scream inside me.

Leave him! Leave him!

The fact that she didn't have children made it even easier for her to leave.

'I don't judge people, Junaid, but I do judge behaviour,' I finally said. 'Do you think hitting and verbally abusing her is wrong?'

I had challenged him, not caring if I sounded empathetic.

For a moment, Junaid seemed wrong-footed. 'Ji, sure. But she gets furious too. She has lots of issues.'

'Junaid, you hardly come home till two in the morning,'

Huria said. 'You don't pay for anything. I only ask you to pick me up, and you don't even do that.' She was pleading with him, and my blood was boiling.

I took a deep breath. I needed to step back. I was feeling too many emotions of my own. I let them talk to each other and observed the dynamic between them. But this session reminded me of my life like a harsh slap on the face. I knew what I had to do. For my sake. For Huria's sake. That was a life-defining moment for me. One of many.

It had taken me a long time to get there. Gordon's care and support, and compassion, had made me see myself differently. I had started to fall in love with myself. Our conversations moved from politics to films to abstract ideas about ourselves, and I had never felt so alive. I had spent many, many years playing dead, hadn't I? A corpse that smiled, talked, and cared enough to offer the possibility of healing to clients but remained invisible herself.

This kind man saw it all, and slowly, he had brought me back to life. When he checked up on me after I'd told him that I had a headache, his care made me feel like I was born again, deserving of love and taken care of. I felt less alone than ever before. Anytime I felt a stirring inside me, a deep pang of loneliness, an ache that was too stubborn to move away, a few words from him sorted it out.

Was it love?

Maybe.

Was it the sort of romantic love I didn't know of? Did I feel my insides shivering with the fear of not hearing from him? Yes. I was so scared of losing him. But did he ever make me think that I would leave Arsalan? I needed clarification. I didn't want to label my feelings. They were just too precious. Many men over the years had looked at me with desire, and it would make me angry but validated at the same time.

Why them and not my own husband?

Gordon made me feel desirable; it never felt cheap. It never felt dishonest. There was integrity in him, commenting on my Instagram pic with, 'You're so beautiful'. I was surprised by that for the first time because, despite fighting with my husband over our sexual problems all these years, I felt I made an issue out of it. I had never really felt the need for it until the last year or so when my exposure to men and a random comment here and there made me want to feel feminine and desirable.

Was I ever tempted to cross the forbidden line? No. Was I ever tempted to cheat? No. I remember my friend Maria from Healing Matters saying once, 'How can you cheat on something you never had?'

I remember how powerfully those words had hit me. But I respected the sanctity of the marriage and believed I should leave or look at other choices. But if I stayed, I didn't want to cross any boundaries.

I often asked myself why I stayed in the marriage. Why did I continue to stay in a marriage that offered its convoluted version of love but missed perhaps the most crucial space shared by a husband and wife?

And yet I stayed. Why?

Honestly, I never knew there was a choice, not until now. Arsalan was home, and I had no other home. Maybe if I'd had parents who offered love and safety, I would have questioned and protested more loudly. Perhaps they would have seen my pain on their own then, and I wouldn't have had to contemplate and worry as I could have told them out loud that I was unhappy. But to say I was depressed wasn't true. Despite those heartbreaking moments when I felt I didn't exist, the affection and friendship between Arsalan and me did numb the pain somewhat. My journey to finding myself had just made everything so much more real.

Two days after he returned from another one of his business trips, I told Arsalan that I wanted to talk to him. Maybe it was the seriousness of my tone or how I'd avoided him since that night in Dubai, but for the first time, he took my need to talk very seriously. I had sent the children to Ami's house for the day. It was a weekend anyway, and Ami had asked us to have dinner with her that night. I wasn't sure if we would be in an apprpriate state of mind to do that, so I made an excuse and told her that I would attend, but Arsalan wouldn't be able to.

'Haan. What's up?' he casually asked, grabbing his tea as he relaxed on the sofa in the living room.

I felt nervous. But I had to do this. I needed to for myself. I needed to for my children. The abuse had to stop.

'I want to talk about us,' I said.

'What about us?'

'We have problems... I—'

He cut me short. 'What problems?'

'I'm not okay with the verbal abuse anymore. It's not acceptable.'

He put the teacup on the table and sat up, his face changing its colour, but this time to an unfamiliar one. I could feel my heart thumping, and my palms started to feel cold, but I knew I wouldn't back down today.

'Do you think I like doing that? It's only you who makes me that angry. I've never raised my voice to anyone else!'

This narrative rubbed me up the wrong way. I felt angry, and that anger made me feel empowered. I was so done with this bullshit. 'I don't want to hear how I bring out this ugly side in you. This abuse has to stop, or I will walk out.' I felt scared by what I had just said. For a moment, I wished I hadn't said it. What if he ended up leaving me right at that moment? I didn't want that. But it was too late now.

I didn't look away. He was quiet.

'What are you saying?' he asked quietly. Was that a good sign?

'I am willing to change whatever needs to change in me. You can say whatever you feel like, but you will not raise your voice and will not swear at me.' I lifted my chin and looked him straight in the eye. 'If this goes on, I will file for divorce.'

Somehow, some inner strength had made me stand up to him as I made this statement, with ramifications I didn't fully understand. I mattered. I came first, and I would always come first from this moment.

'*Kiya hogaya hai*, yaar...' He got up and came towards me, trying to hold my hand.

I pulled it back.

'I need you to listen to me carefully, and I need you to acknowledge what I'm saying. I mean it, Arsalan. I will leave if you don't stop. I am done.'

'You're acting as if you have nothing to do with this?'

'I have always taken responsibility for my issues and continue to work on them. You know that.' I started to walk away, but then stopped and turned towards him. 'But I have nothing to do with this. You have no justification for screaming at me and verbally abusing me. I'm not even bringing the other issues to the table.'

'Other issues? What other issues?'

He was feigning ignorance which infuriated me even more. 'You seriously want me to spell it out? Are you fucking kidding me?' I was feeling so angry that I felt like breaking something. It reminded me of that day a couple of years back when I had a nervous breakdown. But this anger was different. I wasn't blinded by it; it didn't drown me in pain that made me collapse. I knew I had to get my message across.

'You do not desire me as a wife. You don't care how it's killed my femininity. How frustrated I feel.' I started crying at this point, overwhelmed by my anger.

Surprisingly, he stayed quiet. After a few minutes, he said, 'I work so hard for you and the children. Look at this luxury we live in, and instead of gratitude, you have a box of complaints?'

He looked dejected.

'Arsalan. I don't care about sex anymore. I don't care what you do or do not do. For the last time, if you ever raise your voice at me or use bad language, I will leave, and I won't even inform you.'

I left the room without waiting for him to respond, glancing back only once. He was quiet and had an odd expression on his face. I grabbed the car keys to get the kids, slammed the front door hard behind me, and walked out.

I realised something at that moment. He no longer seemed handsome to me. He looked so ordinary, and it hit me that it was a flicker of fear on his face that I'd just seen. Something had shifted between us in that moment. I wondered if I had been attracted to him because of his powerful persona; had that power masked a misogynist attitude? Over the years, he had gained weight and belly fat and had a receding hairline too.

Today, I knew that I was no longer the Saniya he knew, and I could never return to being her.

19   *Student*

It was during my last year at Healing Matters that we were assigned clients to work with. It was a terrifying moment when I was told that I was being given a client with whom I had to schedule a session for the next day. Whilst I was proud of myself for being the first in my class to be permitted to start seeing clients, my performance anxiety had also kicked in, and I was shit scared of failing.

I had always excelled at school and university, and it had continued in my professional journey. But every milestone I achieved only amplified my extreme fear of failing. Baba was there with me in those moments. I was scared of disappointing him if I didn't have those achievements under my belt. I remembered how happy he would be when I did well in school, and that was the only time Ami smiled and was pleased with me. I also knew I worked hard to compensate for not feeling good enough about myself. My self-esteem plummeted after getting married. If someone saw me, they would have laughed at my insecurities. I was fairly good-looking, spoke confidently, managed to make more good jokes than bad, could make friends easily, and carry a conversation with a random stranger with ease and aplomb, and yet deep down, I was a hostage to deep and blinding insecurity and a conviction that I could only be rejected, and no one would ever walk my way.

I was always consumed by triggering questions: did I matter? Was I loved? Was I wanted? And life had thrown enough experiences my way to leave those questions answered in only one way. My mother and my husband, two peas in a pod, had done enough damage to keep me stuck in a place within myself where I felt unloved and unwanted by everyone around me. I had good friends and lovely children who loved me to bits, but I was always drawn towards rejection rather than acceptance. I wondered if I was permanently stuck in a victim position and needed to take life with a pinch of salt.

And so, as I got ready to meet my first client, I had the same question: would the client want me as a therapist, or would they ask for another referral, as many clients did? Contrary to the common perception that the therapist had all the power in the room, I felt we were so helpless to clients who invited us into their inner world and could choose how long we could stay there.

I had arrived in the therapy room fifteen minutes before the session, that's how nervous I was. I was wondering how I was going to greet him, when I realised that my arms were folded across my chest. I unfolded them, knowing it was a defensive stance. I had chosen a pair of black trousers and a pale pink blouse for the session, hoping this would make me look professional.

I put my phone on silent and turned towards the door as the client entered.

'Hello.' A very tall, skinny guy entered the room.

Damn! He's tall.

'Hi,' I said.

He was dressed in blue jeans and a white collared shirt. What stood out for me were his intense eyes, which did not waver. I started playing with my hair and then stopped, worried he would figure out my nervous habit. This was the first time I was sitting across from a man in an intimate setting, and I was finding it hard to maintain eye contact. He seemed a few years younger than me and was nice-looking with his five o'clock shave and attractive features.

'My name is Saniya, and I am your therapist.' I tried to smile as I introduced myself, talking slowly and as clearly as I could.

'I know that.' He had a confident smile that was a tad patronising.

That was stupid of me, but it was too late.

'Tell me about yourself,' I asked, a feeble attempt at covering the foot in the mouth.

'My name is Mansoor, and I am your client,' he said.

I laughed out loud at that. 'So, what brings you here, Mansoor?'

'I might be addicted to drugs, and I want to get clean.' Just like that. Direct and abrupt but his eyes blinked rapidly as he said it.

I felt shocked to hear that. Drugs? I didn't know how to work with that.

'What kind of drugs?' I asked.

'Cocaine.'

He was casually sharing all this as if talking about a random benign activity in his life.

'Is this your first time in therapy?' It was getting uncomfortable. I didn't know how to move forward, and I wanted to tell him that he needed to see a more senior therapist. Another part of me didn't like that and wanted to try my best and make this work.

'No. I've been to many therapists before.' He stretched his legs and put his arms behind his head.

'And how long have you been using drugs?' I enquired as my mind tried to formulate the next question.

'Since I was sixteen.' His gaze was unwavering, and I felt like I was in an examination room.

'And how old are you now?'

'Twenty-nine.'

I felt stuck again. I took a minute and found my bearings. 'Tell me about your family?'

'Why are you nervous?' he asked, leaning forward and cradling his face in his hairless hands. His long legs filled the small therapy room, and I felt awkward. I leant back and pulled my legs in even more. He saw me doing that and smiled.

'What do you mean, nervous?' I had read somewhere that when you were unsure what to say, you should answer a question with a question.

'Are you nervous?'

I took a deep breath and went with my instinct. 'I am,' I quietly replied.

He looked at me, and I held his gaze. I suddenly felt very vulnerable.

'I appreciate your honesty,' he remarked. 'Why are you nervous?'

'It's my first session. I'm a therapist in training, not experienced. Sorry.' I felt guilty for some reason and laughed awkwardly.

'I already knew that.'

'Did you?'

'Yes. I asked, and they told me, you don't have any experience.'

'What made you...' I frowned, confused with the way the session was unfolding. 'What made you choose me, then?'

'Well, to care and not judge doesn't require experience, does it?' Somehow, his words made me feel held. 'I saw you yesterday in the lobby, and I just felt I wanted you to be my therapist.'

I was quiet. I felt like he was the therapist and I the client. 'Well, I do care, and I try not to judge. I can promise you that I will say so if I judge.'

'Honesty is all I'm looking for. People have always lied to me, Saniya.'

'Who are these people?' I asked, looking into his eyes and noticing for the first time they had loss and emptiness in them.

He scratched his chin as his voice almost dropped to a whisper. 'My parents.'

'That must hurt a lot.' I felt sad for him.

He told me how his parents had had an ugly marriage until they got divorced when he was nine. He was an only son and had grown up very lonely. I kept nodding, trying to remember everything he was telling me.

Towards the end, when there were a few minutes left, I made a call and decided to share it.

'Mansoor. Drug addiction is serious, and I admire that you want to get clean. Have you considered rehab?'

His face changed at that suggestion. It suddenly transformed into an angry red.

Had I said something wrong?

'No!' His voice was louder than ever, and I bit my lip until it hurt.

'Hmm, okay.' I didn't want to push for it. 'Would you like to come at the same time next week?'

'No. I won't be coming.'

My heart dropped. 'You're not planning to continue therapy?'

'I didn't say that.' His tone was so severe that I felt reprimanded. 'I will continue therapy but not with you.'

How awful. In my first session, I had pushed a client away.

He looked at me and, after a few seconds, said, 'Have I made you feel rejected?'

I felt like crying. My hands were clutching the sides of the sofa seat tightly. *Do not make a fool of yourself*, I warned.

'Yes, you have.' I didn't know how to lie.

He kept looking at me and said, 'Well, see you same time next week?' And without waiting for a reply, he got up and left.

A few days later, I discussed this with my tutor, who

supervised our client work. If we had any issues, we could talk to him about them without naming the client. Of course, maintaining the confidentiality of the client took precedence.

After listening to everything, he said, 'Saniya. Being honest and sharing that you felt rejected by him gave him the power. And he's someone who has felt helpless all his life. He felt he mattered too, and maybe that made him stay.'

That was validating for a newbie therapist like myself. After my first painful experience with Ahad, I hadn't gone into therapy for many months. I couldn't imagine opening myself up to anyone again. Even in class, I had stopped the little personal process I had attempted to try, other than that one workshop session with Ross. However, now that I was a therapist myself, I knew I had to seek therapy for my own issues. It was one of the most challenging experiences of my life.

Sara was a middle-aged experienced therapist referred to me by a friend. I clearly remember my first session with her, which was also the last.

The first hitch was that she made me wait. The session was at her home, and in what seemed like the drawing room. The sheer size of it was the first thing I noticed. Too many decoration pieces was the second. I felt small in such a big room.

'Hello!' I heard a chirpy voice before I saw her. A plump woman with a beaming smile and jet-black hair cut in a short bob. She wore a blue-collar shirt with white trousers and seemed very comfortable in her skin. She plopped onto the sofa opposite me.

'Hi, miss!' I said, before biting my tongue. Why did I call her miss? It wasn't like I was a teenager.

'How are you doing?' She picked up a notebook and jotted something down.

I told her I was well.

'Tell me about yourself...'

The customary beginning, I thought. I felt a slight irritation. What was I expecting? A grand opening to a Broadway show?

258

'Well, I'm a therapist in training. Mother of two.'

'That's great. Do you enjoy training as a therapist?' She wasn't smiling anymore.

'Yes, I do.' Duh. What an obvious question.

'So, what brings you to therapy?' She got up to pick up her dark-rimmed glasses from the coffee table between us.

'Well, we need therapy as a requisite for our training.' I heard my mobile ringing in my bag. 'Sorry.' I fumbled in my bag and put the phone on silent.

'It's better to put it on silent before the session.'

The irritation went up a notch. Why did she have to say that?

Sara arched an eyebrow. 'So, you're only taking therapy because it is required for your training?'

I heard criticism in her voice. We seemed to have started on the wrong foot, and I couldn't shake off the irritation growing in me with every minute.

'Of course, I want to increase my self-awareness.' At this point, I wanted to leave.

'What would you like to talk about?'

I tried very hard not to roll my eyes. 'Hmm, I'm not sure.'

She stayed quiet. I stayed quiet. The silence seemed unbearable to me, the air thick with resistance. Mine or hers? The walls felt closer than before, and I felt the sweat gathering in my armpits.

'I'm very impatient with my children sometimes. I would like to work on that.' I felt relieved. We could talk about that.

'And how do you express that impatience?'

'Hmm, I end up shouting at them. I don't hit them.'

'I didn't say you did.'

'And I very rarely shout, either, but I would rather that I didn't at all.'

'What or who are you angry at?' She asked the question but was looking down at her notes.

I experienced shock at this question. 'I'm not angry at anyone. Why do you ask?'

'You tell me?' She looked up at that moment, and all I wanted to do was shout at *her*.

Instead, I took a deep breath. 'I get tired of work. And there is a lot to do at home. All mothers lose their patience now and then, don't they?'

'Then what's the problem?'

'What do you mean?' I was confused, and my irritation had turned into anger. I didn't like her. I didn't like her at all.

She shrugged. 'You said you see your impatience as a problem. Just now, you said you think it's not, as all mothers lose their patience now and then.'

I wanted to get out of this ugly room. She was so critical!

Shifting on the sofa, she turned to a new line of questioning. 'So, tell me about your family.'

Great. Now she wanted details.

'Well, I'm married,' I replied. 'Have two children. A boy and a girl.'

'And your parents... siblings?'

'My father died when I was young. A mother and a younger sister.'

She tutted. 'That must have been hard.'

'Hard?'

'Losing your dad.' She didn't look as if she cared. Empty words!

I hesitated, fiddling with the hem of my shirt. 'Yes, it was.'

'Are you close to your mother?'

'Everything is fine.'

She chose to stay quiet at that moment. I knew what she was asking. I knew where she was taking me. I wouldn't go there.

'What is your relationship like with your husband?'

'It's good,' I replied without a moment's hesitation. Was she going to pick on that?

She smiled, then. 'Well, you seem to have lived quite a happy life, then.'

'Yes, I have been blessed.' I attempted to smile as I said it.

'So, what makes you so angry, then?'

And there it was again. 'I don't understand...' I began, frowning.

'You don't understand your anger?'

God! What the hell is wrong with her?

I threw up my hands. 'I'm not angry! You're assuming a lot here.'

'Anger is not an unhealthy emotion, Saniya.'

'I know that too. It's okay to be angry, but I'm not.' How could she make such big statements in the first session?

I could feel the tension in my neck. My face felt warm. This woman... *ugh*! How could someone I'd just met evoke such a reaction? I had a fantasy of screaming at her.

What the hell?

'How long have you been practising?' I asked, wanting to ground myself, even though, at this point, I didn't care to know anything about her. I knew I would never come and see her again. She was harsh. There was no empathy in her.

'Over ten years,' Sara replied in a level voice before adding, 'what made you choose this field, Saniya?'

Okay. Finally, a sensible question or a safe one.

I cleared my throat. 'It was just a coincidence. I initially just started this self-awareness course. But then I realised I liked psychotherapy, so I continued.'

'What do you like about it?'

'Well, it's a great feeling to help someone hurting, right?' I invisibly patted myself on the back for this innovative, intelligent response.

'And especially someone who may have experienced pain closely so they can better understand the pain of others.'

Tears suddenly came up in my eyes. Damn! That's the last

thing I wanted. I would rather die than let this woman see my tears.

'I will have to leave a bit early today. I have to pick up my daughter from a play date,' I fibbed.

She didn't respond immediately but got up to hand me the box of tissues next to her seat. Why did she not keep them on the table in front of the client?

'Sure. It's your call. How long have you been running for?' She had the same playful smile on her face.

What the fuck! I was sick of her twisted questions. I had never instantly disliked a person so much in my life.

'I don't know what you mean.'

'Sure.' She didn't press the point.

I picked up my bag and took out the envelope with her fees. 'Thank you for your time. I will let you know when I can make it next time.'

Sitting in the car, I felt breathless with a tsunami of questions. Why was I reacting so badly to her? Suddenly I remembered the thought I'd had inside.

I would rather die than let her see my tears. Where had I heard these words before? And then it hit me!

Ami! That's whom she reminded me of! Wow. It made so much sense now. She was like a harsh, critical parent. An examiner who had already decided that she would fail me. I felt uncared for and knew this wasn't the space to show my wounds.

Transference. That's what it was. Now that I was out of that room, my internal therapist brought it to my attention.

We had been introduced to the concept of transference this year, and it fascinated me how we unconsciously transferred feelings from an experience or a person onto another person in the present.

Sara reminded me of my mother. I also felt a moment of pride for realising that. I wouldn't have if I wasn't a therapist. After learning about transference, so much had started to make sense. Later that day, I called my classmate, Saqib. He and I talked now and then and always shared more than planned.

'*Kia haal hai,* Saniya Bibi?'

'*Aaap batain, waqeel sahab.*'

We always started this way, and today was no different.

'Well, I finally went to therapy, and—'

'That's awesome,' he cut me short mid-sentence.

'Hold your horses, bro.' I got up and closed the bedroom door. I could hear the children watching TV. 'It was a disaster.'

'Oh really! Why?'

I told him what had happened during the session.

'Whoa!' he exclaimed. 'Such strong feelings in the first session? That's something.'

'I don't know. I didn't like her.' I wasn't ready to tell Saqib who Sara reminded me of.

'Chalo. Let me think of another therapist for you.'

'Yeah. I would prefer a male. I'm not fond of women.' I laughed at this admission. I realised how absurd it sounded.

I was a difficult client, and I knew I would meet many therapists with whom I would experience negative transference. We were taught that many clients would terminate therapy because of the unresolved conflicts and traumas they had projected onto their therapist. At this moment, I was a client looking for a therapist who could unconditionally care for me and with whom therapy was not another relationship I had to put work into.

20 *Woman*

I left the marriage in spirit, although I was physically present to carry on the farce as best as possible.

That flicker of fear I had seen on Arsalan's face after the trip to Dubai changed our dynamic. I discovered a new power in myself as someone who had a voice and could stand up to him. For the first time in my decade-old marriage, I could almost hear myself telling him, loud and clear, that if he couldn't value me, I'd have no qualms about walking out.

My body would sometimes betray me, fearing the impending outbursts that usually followed any such conversation. Still, the anxiety stayed within my body, and I tried my best not to let my face or voice give any hint of what was transpiring inside. I knew it would take years for me not to be pushed into a fearful position habitually, but I also knew that I was changing.

Deep down within my darkest corners, I knew I would hold my ground now. I had come so far in so many ways, and there was no way I was returning to being the same woman who would beg Arsalan not to scream or abuse her.

I was no longer the woman he had married. I was no longer the daughter Ami had raised. I was no longer the person I had set out to be. I was evolving with every breath I was taking. Many people and experiences had brought me to this place, but Gordon stood out more than others.

My friend.

My best friend.

I didn't care how society saw a platonic relationship between two people. I didn't care how anyone would react to him being my best friend. But for the first time, I had someone who cared. Someone who didn't shame me for being 'needy', someone who showed me the possibility of healing.

Throughout the day and night, anytime I felt like, I could text him about anything and everything under the sun. About how tired I was after five sessions that day, how much Nyle and Neha had started to fight, or how Ami's criticism was beyond my window of tolerance. I finally found the courage to tell him about Ami and Uzair Uncle. It was a difficult conversation. I was sure he would start seeing me differently. It was one of the scariest moments of my life. But Gordon being Gordon did none of that, and he held the space with the same love he always did and reminded me loud and clear that my mother's actions had nothing to do with me.

I struggled with guilt for some time. I questioned myself as to whether I had become like Ami. I was emotionally dependent on a man who wasn't my husband. I talked to him day and night. How was I different? And on those days, I abruptly withdrew from Gordon; the guilt was just too much to bear. The last thing I wanted to be was my mother; the thought haunted me and kept me awake at night. But I was her, wasn't I? The apple didn't fall far from the tree.

Gordon reached out daily with a call or text, but I didn't respond. One day, unable to contain the pain, I picked up the phone.

'Saniya.' He said my name in the gentlest of voices, which surprised me. I was expecting him to be angry.

'Yeah…'

'What's happening? Talk to me.'

'Why are you running after me?' I bit my lip hard to stop myself from breaking down.

'I promised you that I would, didn't I? I won't let you run for long.'

'Gordon…'

'Yeah?'

'I've been struggling with something. I'm sorry I was so rude.'

'Don't worry about that. I'm here for you, okay?'

'I don't know…'

'Don't know what? Tell me…' he asked, his voice bringing out the calm in me.

'I'm not my mother. I'm honest.' I found the defiance in my voice, the last attempt to convince myself I was not, my moral anxiety kicking in.

'What makes you think you might be?' His voice seemed a bit guarded. He knew what a sensitive topic my mother was for me. He always knew everything, and then I realised I was idealising Gordon like I had idealised Ahad and Arsalan. I tended to attribute more to others than they deserved and, eventually, they fell short of my expectations.

'I'm not a cheat. You hear me?' Angry tears welled up in my eyes.

'Of course, you're not! What makes you think you are?'

'I should not be friends with a guy. How am I different from her?'

The anger dissipated at the softness of his voice. 'Are you hearing yourself? You and I are just friends. We emotionally support each other. We are not in a relationship. We are not sleeping together.'

For the first time, I sensed a bit of anger as well. I didn't want to lose him.

'I'm sorry.'

'What are you sorry for?'

'I don't want to lose your friendship,' I begged. I couldn't imagine my life without him.

'Why would you lose it?'

'Because I'm insinuating wrong things…'

'No, you're not doing that. You're sharing your worst fears out loud.' He adopted an even gentler tone. 'Listen, you are not your mother. You have not had a relationship with a man for years in your home. You have not been fucking anyone.'

I felt a jolt at his blunt words. My first reaction was from the protective part of me that automatically wanted to defend my mother. It wanted to scream at Gordon for using such harsh words. But they were true. But the second reaction liberated me from the guilt I had been experiencing for some time.

I wasn't sleeping with anyone. God knew I had every reason to. But I believed in the sanctity of marriage, even if it was a shitty marriage. My turning towards Gordon was just an act of defiance. In a way, it had started as a response to my husband's infidelity. Maybe he hadn't slept with any of those women. All I knew was that he didn't make me feel like a wife in more ways than one, and his repeated attempts at seeking someone outside of the marriage left me broken in many places.

I also wondered if it was his way of seeking something that was lacking in me. Then I also felt like a hypocrite as I was doing the same.

But then, if my husband had treated me like a wife, I would never have turned to another man for care and support. And that care still didn't compensate for my unmet physical needs. I was still unfulfilled in so many ways. But after a lifetime of feeling unwanted and unloved, I had thrown caution to the wind, and I, with both my hands, wanted to take whatever scraps of affection I was receiving. Was that why Ami turned to another man? I had started to question if Ami was, indeed, the villain in my life. Maybe I didn't know the complete story, but even so, nothing excused the abuse. She could not be forgiven for that.

Gordon's strong statement helped. I was not my mother. I had not crossed any ethical boundary that was defined in a marriage. I had not made my children's home unsafe for them.

I had given, with love and sincerity, the prime years of my life to a man, only to be deprived of my rights and be abused.

But you do want to have sex with him? a voice whispered in my head. Who was I fooling here and what was I trying to prove? That I'm not like Ami? Would I be able to say no if Gordon held my hand and invited me to cross the line?

Could he tell that, even though I knew I wouldn't sleep with him, for the first time I was turned on by a man? I did fantasise about having sex with him more often than not. To be kissed and touched by him. Did that not count?

The next day, 26 April, was my birthday. Even though I hadn't celebrated many birthdays as a child, I had started to take my friends out when I started secondary school. Arsalan wanted to take me out for an intimate dinner on my birthday, but I didn't want to go. His presence made me angry.

All that unspent anger seemed to have broken free of the tight reins I had kept it on. It wasn't just a wife's anger. It was also a child's anger towards her mother. It was towards her father, too, for leaving so soon and not protecting her while he was alive, for being weak. There was so much of it. No matter how hard I tried, I could not see Arsalan as the man I had deeply fallen in love with anymore. I questioned now if it was love or attachment or a rebound relationship of sorts from the one I had with my mother. The children had planned a little surprise for me around midnight. I was asleep when I felt little hands waking me up.

'Mama! Mama! Come to the lounge.' I felt Neha's soft hands on my face. I opened my eyes, half drowsy.

'Okay, baby. Give me a minute…' I got up to wash my face.

Arsalan popped a party popper when I entered the living room, and the loud noise sent an angry shock through my body.

'Yaar, for God's sake!' I had no patience for loud noises. I was about to say more when I saw Neha and Nyle's faces, and I stopped. I put on a big smile. 'What's all this? I had no idea!'

The room was full of silver and black balloons. There was a chocolate cake with candles on, already lit. A few packed gifts were placed on a side table.

'Come, Mama! Cut the cake before the candles melt.' Arsalan was as excited as the children, and I felt the protest build within me.

I cut the cake for my thirty-sixth birthday as the children cheered. I avoided making eye contact with Arsalan and hugged the children. They had both got me little gifts. There was an 'I love you, Mama' mug, cards, and chocolates. I was surprised because I knew Arsalan was behind this effort.

'Give Mama's gift,' the children screamed at Arsalan; the excitement on their faces was heart-warming.

I insisted on taking them to the dinner with me. I was finding it increasingly difficult to be alone with Arsalan now. My anger, hurt, and unimaginable pain had constructed an imaginary wall he was trying to break between us, but I built it even higher every time he did that. Sometimes, I wondered if Gordon's name was written on that wall that refused to break. But, when I looked back at the years I had wasted, I felt blinded by snapshots of anger and hurt and an inner scream asked why.

Why did you not fulfill my rights as a wife?

Why did you reject me so many times?

Why did you verbally abuse me, scream at me, and justify to yourself that it was the only way to get through to me?

Why did you seek friendship outside of marriage?

When I looked back, that's all I could see, and I was done. A part of me was waiting for him to abuse me again so it would give me the courage to run and never look back. Another part feared that the firm boundary I had drawn with him meant nothing, and I would, other than shedding some more tears, still be around, losing more respect for myself. His efforts to get my attention were confusing me, though. Had he started to see me? But then, I didn't trust that he could see the person I was now.

For now, I was pushing Arsalan back as hard as I could. I was rejecting him as much as he had denied me and more. I felt I had become mean, but I still couldn't bring myself to care. On the way back from dinner, he tried holding my hand. Without a word, I pulled my hand away.

'Why are you behaving like this, Saniya?' he asked.

'I don't want to talk about it.' The children were sleeping in the back seat, tired from the excitement of the night before and the day that followed.

'You asked me to control my anger, and I have. Why are you behaving like this?' he repeated, his face looking sad.

I was about to answer when my silent phone alerted me to a message. My heart skipped a welcome beat.

Gordon.

'Why can't you be normal?' he continued.

I started laughing. 'Normal? Seriously, you did not say that.'

'What do you mean?'

'Is there anything normal about our marriage?'

'I don't understand.' His voice was atypically calm despite the irritation in it.

'Exactly. You never did, did you?'

'I'm not into guessing games here.'

'Neither am I. So, tell me again, when was the last time we had sex?'

'You know I've been busy.'

'A month since Dubai, and before that, it was almost four months. And let me see, an entire year every time I was expecting the children and months after that because you chose to sleep separately. Should I go on about our normal marriage?'

'Is our marriage all about sex? Will you take no responsibility for your actions? Are you telling me that you're a victim here?'

270

'Yes! Yes! I am a fucking victim here!' I took a long, deep breath. I couldn't carry this on.

'How can we fix this? I don't like how things are,' he murmured.

Somehow, this side of him where he was trying to make amends was making me angrier and making me withdraw even more.

'Please let me be. I need space.'

'This therapy thing has changed you.'

'It's not a thing. It's my fucking profession and something I have worked hard for.'

'And your language...' He carried on as if he hadn't even heard me.

'My language? Really?'

'I was the one who used to say the F word.'

I leant forward and put the music on. Some unknown song was playing on FM 89, maybe only to me; I didn't know who the singer was. I turned around and saw that the children were still sleeping. The last thing I wanted was for another child to get exposed to a lifetime of internal chaos and confusion. I needed to protect myself, and I needed to protect my babies, and I knew I wouldn't let anyone come in the way of that.

In the following weeks, I withdrew more and more from him. I felt trapped like never before. I did feel less helpless, however. My work came alive, and I felt more grounded within myself, and it was all down to one person.

Gordon.

I was attracted to his smiling face, the twinkle in his eyes, and his brilliant mind. Our conversations were engaging and moved from one space to another. I would be drowning in pain, and he would say something funny, and I would laugh out loud with joy and abandon, and in that moment, nothing mattered. I would send my photos, and his compliments would make me smile, even during work. I told myself it wasn't typical romantic love, but then what was it? It was something profound that was growing as time passed. I couldn't imagine my life without him.

I worried that he lived alone. I worried about his well-being. His success at work made me immensely happy. I fantasised about what life could have been like if I had been with someone who was into me, noticed me, and made me feel beautiful and worth seeing. I was falling in love with myself, but was I also in love with him? I wanted more, and although I kept reminding myself that I would never act on my feelings, a part of me badly wanted to.

Badly.

That part didn't care that I was like my mother. It yearned for Gordon.

The truth was that I wanted more with him. I wanted to have sex. My body had never been more alive to his presence. I knew I was idealising him, but my heart trusted that he had earned that.

A few days later, we met for coffee at our regular spot. Winter was just around the corner, and strangely, I felt colder than usual. Standing at the make-up counter, I realised that I had stopped seeing myself as a feminine woman over the years. I hardly felt like dressing up. A man had so much power to make a woman feel beautiful. Bit by bit, my feminine side had shrivelled. Once I became a therapist, I started to learn how to love myself and see myself beyond just a wife. It wasn't until I found Gordon's friendship that I realised that love was the best cure for an aching heart; he made me feel alive. And that love didn't have to come from an intimate, romantic place. It was about being cared for. I knew that I mattered to him, no matter what.

I wore a pale blue woollen top that I had bought from Marks & Spencer a couple of years back on one of our trips to London. I wore it with my favourite black trousers, which I was addicted to, along with my black Nine West pumps, pulling my hair into a bun. I had recently learnt how to do make-up on YouTube and went for a minimalist look, although it included everything. It was the first time I had bought make-up since my wedding.

Gordon was already at our corner next to the window with the big plants.

'Hey.' He got up and waited for me to sit down. Chivalry was so charming. 'You look lovely.'

I blushed at his compliment.

After exchanging pleasantries, I told him about a minor altercation at the grocery shop.

'What happened?' he asked, concern in his eyes.

'Oh, well, I slapped a guy!' I started laughing.

'Are you kidding me? Why did you?' He looked incredulous.

'Well, he touched me inappropriately, and without thinking, I turned around and slapped him. And, of course, I asked him to acknowledge what he did and apologise to me.'

I smiled with a triumphant expression.

'You walk into the hero's archetype, don't you?'

'Well, I believe in raising my voice if I see unfairness,' I replied.

'And your hand, in this case!' he teased.

'Yes! Would do it again if anyone dares to take advantage.'

Gordon smiled. 'You go, girl! But tell me, are you doing better?'

'I am. It feels good to be heard and taken seriously for the first time, Gordon.'

'Is he behaving himself?'

'Yes. No more shouting or, you know…'

'Yes, I know. I don't ever want to see that man.'

'Why not?'

'Why not? The way he has treated you makes my blood boil. You don't speak to a woman like that. Full stop.' His voice had an angry tinge to it.

I stayed quiet. Breathing in the care and protection that Gordon offered me. It was so rare. No one had ever stood up for me like that, and somehow, it was giving me the courage to speak up for myself.

'Thank you,' I murmured.

'You have nothing to thank me for. I'm just happy that you're standing up for yourself.'

'I am! I am!' I made light of the moment with a smile on my face.

'You are! You are!' He smiled back.

We looked at each other until I looked away. It took a lot of work to keep looking. There was so much of I wanted right in front of me, but was it mine to take?

At that moment, I had a strong impulse to hug him. I felt a deep ache in my body for it, but I held back. I had to maintain this boundary. But then he just reached out and held my hand, and without realising what I was doing, I held it tightly and kissed it.

At that moment, something shifted between us. I felt it. Or maybe just within me. He didn't say a word. I didn't say anything. A man and a woman. Two hands. A connection that had no words to describe it.

As I lay in bed that night, I wondered if Gordon had ever been married or was with someone. Once again, I felt overwhelmed by the fear of losing him. I needed his presence in my life, whatever way it was offered.

He'd told me about his failed relationship, but surely, a man like him couldn't stay single for long. Somehow, the thought of him being with someone unsettled me.

I felt possessive. I wanted his attention just for myself. I realised the child within me, the teenager, and the woman all needed him. A huge part of me unreasonably wanted him to make up for all the hurt and pain caused by others. He felt like my family, and the thought of someone else in his life intensified the fear of losing him. For now, I thought I had him. I could reach out to him whenever I wanted. He always responded.

Over the next few weeks, I got used to someone in my world who cared enough to respond to me all the time. I shared anything and everything. We laughed, pulled each other's leg, and shared our emotions. It was magical. As I grew emotionally attached to him, my body felt more alive. It would start tingling even as I thought about him. We were reaching dangerous territory, and I didn't know how to stop it or if I even wanted to.

I asked Gordon to hug me and was deeply hurt that he never offered to. I realised that this mirrored what it had been like initially with Arsalan and the thought alarmed me, but this time I didn't want to keep these thoughts to myself, so I asked him. To my surprise, he said he didn't want to cross a line, and hugging me made him desire me more, although he had been dying to. His response sent tingles down my spine; the idea that a man didn't want to touch me because it turned him on was like a homeless person being offered a warm blanket after being left out in the cold and rain. The irony of the moment brought pain too. One man didn't touch me because he felt nothing, and another chose not to because he felt a lot.

I insisted that Gordon touch me, and so every time we met, he would hold my hand and offer a hug. It felt as good as I had fantasised it to. I felt safe and learnt to trust again.

It was as if there were two of me who were breathing. A woman who felt alive and herself with Gordon and a woman who, like a B-grade actor, played the role of a wife day in day out.

Arsalan made things worse. He was different, and it left me confused and angry. He was less angry. Even when provoked, according to him, he was less angry. He was making an effort to come home early. I felt panicky when I saw him making those efforts. He was knocking repeatedly on the door, soft knocks, but I was no longer interested in opening the it. I took it to therapy and now vividly remembered part of our conversation.

'What triggers you?' my therapist asked me when I told him I felt triggered more often than before.

275

'When I see him reaching out to me,' I said, looking down, almost ashamed.

'Why would that trigger you? Isn't that what you always wanted?' Yasir's casual tone belied the curiosity in his deep voice.

'I don't need it now. It's too late.' I felt angry at his question. Whose side was he on?

'Is it too late, Saniya, or is this about something else?'

I shook my head slowly. 'I don't get your point.'

'Do you think you might be feeling this because of Gordon?'

'Are you serious?' I could feel my face heating up with anger.

'Yes, I am.'

'Gordon? Really?'

'Yes, your attachment towards him might make you lean away from Arsalan.'

I laughed out loud, but it rang false. 'I have been with a man who hasn't desired me like a wife for ten years. Who made me believe there was something wrong with me... who provided for me, sure, and was my friend, but he would also take it all away when he'd call me a bitch and a whore, and instead of feeling remorse, he'd tell me I asked for it. And you have the nerve to tell me it's because of a man I have just made friends with.'

I felt sad. I felt unsafe. Yasir had become like every other Pakistani man at that moment. I knew my therapeutic space was gone.

He stayed silent.

'And Gordon only made me realise that I am worthy of being loved, and he made me feel alive. I can finally feel myself breathing. I see myself through his eyes. I feel like I matter.'

The room was silent after that. I was tired. I was so tired of explaining myself.

'Saniya, you assumed a lot on my behalf. I'm not judging you. I'm curious if he was the catalyst, that's all.'

'You should know better. You've been my therapist for over a year, and you know my story. You shouldn't have asked that question.'

He sighed. 'You might not like hearing this, Saniya, but this victim position you assume is the least interesting thing about you.'

'Are you saying I'm not a victim?'

'I didn't say that. You were a victim of a situation, but you have more choices in your life than many.'

I was disappointed in him. I felt the instant disconnection after he said what he did, a plug abruptly pulled out. But he got me thinking about how I might have a lens through which I only perceived rejection, and it kept me rooted in a victim position.

For the next few days, I felt triggered. I found my patience wearing thin with the children too. I shouted at both of them for no reason at all. I was avoiding Ami and Maheen's calls, too. My school friend, Asifa, who was based in Vienna with her husband, called a few times, but I didn't take her call. I was in some isolated alternate reality where I was functioning on autopilot as a mother, a wife, and a daughter, fulfilling my responsibilities. I only felt alive in my interactions with Gordon. Yasir's words had planted a seed of guilt for what I felt for Gordon.

I kept feeling panicked as the conflict grew in me. I was at a crossroads where I thought I had to choose between this life where I lived within the limited moments with Gordon or the one where I dragged my feet throughout the day. But I wasn't sure if I had a choice. I felt trapped and stuck in my marriage.

The conflict kept growing in me. A few days later, I had a panic attack in a session and felt I couldn't breathe. As I saw my client sitting before me, I was fighting a wave of despair and pain that was coming up, tears that threatened to spill over, and a loud warning in my head, *don't be unprofessional, Saniya, control yourself.*

And I could neither stop myself from temporarily breaking down nor hide all the chaos and confusion I was experiencing. Luckily, the client had been coming for three years, and we had a solid working alliance. He was kind enough to offer that we end the session before time. His understanding was important to me as I sat there struggling with the shame of not being professional enough.

His words were, 'Saniya, you are human too,' and he quietly left.

This experience initially made me feel guilty for not being able to ground myself. Still, his reminder of my 'human element' made me realise that I had to allow myself to be vulnerable. I could be strong and weak, and I didn't have to be stuck in one position for a client. To connect to your therapist at a primary human level was just as crucial as other experiences within the therapeutic relationship.

Somehow this experience grounded me and made me realise that the pain I had been running away from all my life was what made my work as a therapist so special. My journey, which I had seen as a burden I had been carrying for so long, took me to this place where my wounded self connected to my client's injured existence.

Gordon was a silent song playing in the background. I knew he was there, and mostly, that was enough for me.

Mostly.

The night before, he started teasing me when I asked if I was too much for him. We were texting, and when I asked if I was a burden, he replied by saying:

Oh yes, you are! But I get tax exemption for being nice to you!

Haha! Very funny! Fine, I hear you! I texted back.

Seriously, you are so difficult and challenging and smelly! he continued to tease.

Smelly? Are you kidding me? I protested.

It's okay! I don't usually care if people smell a bit, to be honest.

Do you think this is helpful? You are implying that I do. *I'm not going to see you again!* I added.

Yeah, right. I know you will. You're stubborn, but you're not that stubborn.

Seriously? You don't know me, then. I won't! I was smiling as I texted back.

Hell, if that's what you want, Gordon replied.

You have many other friends already. All lovely and smelling like fucking roses. Meet them. I don't care.

Yeah, sure, right, x! he responded.

My heart jumped at the 'x'; this little symbol of affection that made me feel cared for.

The next day it was Sunday. Arsalan was in Islamabad, and I woke up with unease in the middle of my belly. *What's this?* I wondered. Being stuck in my marriage and expecting to stick it out felt like someone was cutting me. More than ever, I started to explore the possibility of ending it. It seemed too late to recover it. I imagined the possibility of a known companion, someone like Gordon, who could catch me when I fell, who could push me towards life. I needed love, intimacy, laughter, and tears. More than anything, I wanted someone to walk my way. I was tired of running after Arsalan all these years.

The call came around 7:00pm.

I was watching *Full House* with the children. I had got DVDs for the children of my favourite show when I was little. That was a good childhood memory when Maheen and I watched *Full House* weekly with Marie biscuits and milk. Life almost seemed normal at that time.

'Mama, why do you like this show?' Neha asked me. Her head was in my lap, and even though I knew it wasn't good for her eyes to watch TV like this, I enjoyed running my fingers through her soft, dark hair. Nyle was leaning on me, with his head on my shoulder. It was a strange day. Since the morning I had felt uncomfortable, and the children were quieter than usual.

Arsalan was arriving around dinner time, and I had asked the cook to make mutton karahi and daal for him. The children had ordered pizza and were waiting for it.

I heard my mobile ringing in the bedroom. I was too lazy to get up. I didn't care to pick it up.

After a few minutes, it started ringing again.

'Yaar, *kon hai*,' I said out loud. 'Nyle, get my mobile, please.'

'No, Mama! I wanna watch!' But he still got up to fetch my phone, anyway.

I paused the programme, and Neha started to scream. 'Put it on! Put it on!'

'Stop shouting, baby! Let bhai come back!'

It stopped ringing by the time Nyle brought my phone. I switched the video back on and was about to check who was calling when the call came again. It was an unknown number.

I picked up the call. And everything changed. Once again.

21 *Daughter*

Maheen was visiting, so I decided to take a week off and spend time with her. Staying at Ami's was not something I enjoyed but the children loved being there, and I wanted to spend some quality time with Maheen. Ami had also calmed down with time and age. She no longer questioned my work or criticised my lifestyle or parenting as much as she used to. She would comment occasionally, but it was just a habit, and I didn't react by arguing or expressing my frustration. Over the years, personal therapy had helped me change my dynamic with Ami, and I was mostly indifferent to her. I would go quiet, and the moment would pass.

We sat and talked after dinner. The kids had all gone to sleep after a long day at the zoo, followed by lunch and a water fight that, to my surprise, Ami thoroughly enjoyed while laughing and cheering the kids. There was a free child within her that we never saw playing with us, but at least our children were a witness to it.

There was a moment of silence when Maheen spoke up. 'Ami, why wasn't apa happy when she was younger?'

I looked up in shock. Where had this come from? I looked at Ami, and she looked as taken aback as me.

'What are you talking about, Maheen?' I scolded her.

'Let me talk, apa.' Maheen's voice was assertive. 'Ji, Ami. Why was apa so unhappy?'

'I don't know what you're talking about,' Ami replied, putting her half-filled teacup on the side table and fixing her dupatta, which had slipped from her head.

'Ami, she was miserable. Still is. I don't think you treated her well.'

I started to feel anxious, imagining the conversation going to places I never wanted it to go to. Any time anyone had suggested confronting Ami with what she did, it filled my entire being with a horrible panic.

'I don't know what you're talking about,' Ami repeated, but there was a shift in energy in the room. It was tense. No one was smiling. The air was thick with difficult questions whose answers perhaps Ami didn't have either.

I tried interrupting again, but words were not forming. I wanted answers too but had lacked the courage to ask. Maheen had done the impossible for me.

Suddenly, Ami turned towards me, and in that instant, our eyes locked. Something strange happened at that moment. Neither Ami nor I could look away. I started to feel breathless as I looked into my mother's eyes, a moment that communicated so much without any words, and it hit me that she knew that I knew. Ya, Allah! Ami knew that I knew how she had treated me. I looked away but suddenly felt Ami's hand on mine and her words.

'Forgive me.'

I felt shocked. I felt numb. I abruptly pulled my hand away and started feeling choked. *No, I don't want her to see me crying. I cannot let that happen.* I had to do something.

'It's okay, Ami,' I turned towards her, and for the first time, the three-letter word 'Ami' felt real, and my heart felt all the unspent love I'd had for over three decades.

'Hug her, apa,' Maheen said, tears running down her face. 'She won't bite.'

We all started laughing. I didn't know how to hug her, and Ami didn't either. But one day, I knew she would, and I would.

For now, something profound had moved between us, and I wanted to soak up this moment where I felt I had a mother for the first time.

That interaction changed me further, and I started to accept life for what it was now. I stopped feeling sorry for myself. I started to feel grateful for my life and saw my marriage as a part of my life, not my entire life. I stopped, or at least tried to stop, feeling sorry for myself. This was life, and it was real, and we had all our trials. Gordon played a significant role in this process, and while I started to accept this, I started to think about how Gordon could become a permanent part of my life.

22   *Wife*

I picked up my phone to answer the call that would change my life.

'Is this Arsalan Ahmed's residence?' A low male voice asked.

I felt it before I heard it.

'Yes?'

'Madam, Arsalan Ahmed has been in an accident. Can you come to National Hospital?'

I didn't remember anything after that. I faintly remembered rushing the children to put on their shoes, grabbing my bag, before running out of the house. I remembered needing money, so I returned, took out my hidden stash, and ran out again. I was numb and just kept moving.

On the way to the hospital, I called Zoya and asked her to come and pick up the children. Before she could ask any further questions, I hung up. My hands were trembling as I tightly gripped the steering wheel.

'Mama, where are we going?' Nyle asked. Neha was quiet too. Somehow their psyche had picked up that their world might drastically change.

Please let him be alive, I silently prayed. I felt I was about to break down, but I took a deep breath. I couldn't afford to let go.

'Baby, all is well. Zoya Khala will get you. I have to check on someone in the hospital.'

'Who, Mama?'

'No one. Just pray they are okay, will you?' A sob escaped me, and I put my fist in my mouth.

We couldn't live without him. We couldn't.

In the car park of the hospital, Zoya was already waiting. She gave me a quick hug and whispered in my ear, 'Stay strong. All will be well, inshallah!'

I thanked her and rushed inside. I didn't want to call anyone until I saw him myself.

At the reception, after a few minutes, someone pointed me towards the emergency room, and with a pounding heart and shaking legs, I ran in the direction they'd pointed.

The place was in chaos. I asked the duty doctor about Arsalan.

'He's not here anymore,' he informed me with a cavalier attitude as he checked some files.

He's not here anymore. The words pierced through my heart. Everything stopped.

'What do you mean? Where is he?' What was he trying to tell me? I found my legs giving way, and I momentarily blanked out as I tried to process what he was telling me.

'Relax, madam. He's fine. We've moved him to another room.'

I started crying with relief.

'Please tell me the room number. No, wait – tell me what happened to him.'

'He had an accident on the motorway, I think. Room 501.'

'Yes, he was coming back from Islamabad.'

'He has a few minor bruises and scratches. But his ribs are broken, and his forehead is bruised.'

I didn't wait for him to say more and rushed out. The lift seemed to take ages. I knew people were staring at me as uncontrolled tears spilled from my eyes.

'Allah behtar karega, beta.' I felt a hand on my arm but didn't look up to see who it was in this crowded lift.

Before I reached the room, I roughly wiped away the tears and took a deep breath.

He was lying down with his eyes shut. There was a big ugly white bandage on his forehead and some around his bare chest. His face was so bruised. I covered my mouth with my hand to stop myself from crying out loud. I slowly walked towards my husband.

My husband.

I gently touched his hand. He didn't stir. Was he okay? Why wasn't he opening his eyes? I left the room and went to the nursing station. There I found out that he had been sedated. I spoke to the consultant, who was luckily around, and he assured me that Arsalan looked worse than he was. He had taken off his seat belt to reach for something, and at that exact unfortunate moment, a car hit him from behind. The impact had thrown him again the steering wheel, and his head and upper body had suffered. Luckily, both cars weren't speeding.

I didn't want to imagine what the outcome would have been otherwise.

I sat next to him for the next hour. I knew I should be calling his parents, but selfishly, I wanted to be alone with him before the family came rushing in. There was anger and guilt for not saying goodbye to him properly before he left the day before. I hated myself for not replying to his text a day earlier. What if he had died?

I felt a hand on my head. I hadn't realised I had put my head down next to his and dozed off.

I immediately looked up. He was up and smiling.

I started crying.

'Relax, I'm okay.'

I grabbed his hand tightly.

'I'm okay, Saniya.' He gently held both my hands. 'I'm fine. It looks worse than it is, I promise you.'

I wanted to hug him badly, but the bandage around his ribs stopped me. 'I'm sorry. I'm sorry.'

'What are you sorry for? You didn't hit my car,' he joked. 'Relax.'

He may not have known what I was apologising for, but deep down, I knew.

'Are you hurting a lot?' I ignored the question I didn't have an answer to.

'Yeah, but right now, the painkillers are working.'

'Do you need anything?'

'No, I'm good. Have you told Dad and Ami?'

'Not yet.'

'Acha! They are going to be worried if they hear from someone else.'

I nodded. 'Okay. I'll call.'

He closed his eyes again.

'Kia Hua?'

He shook his head once. 'Nothing. Feel drained.'

'You were sedated. Try sleeping more.' I gently ran my fingers through his hair. Unable to control myself, I leant forward and kissed him lightly on his cheek. He slightly smiled, or maybe I imagined it.

Ya Allah tera shukar. I didn't want to imagine how the children or his parents would have tolerated this loss. How would I have felt? I didn't want to imagine that either.

As I picked up my phone, I noticed multiple WhatsApp messages. As I opened them up to see, Gordon's message stood out. I felt my heart skip a beat.

Not now. I ignored the messages and called Arsalan's parents, who were stricken to hear about the accident and rushed to the hospital within the hour.

The next few days were spent in a frenzy. Arsalan didn't want the children to see him till his face looked less bruised. Between home and the hospital, I had lost all sense of time. I had asked Ami to move to my place as I needed to stay in the hospital at night, and I had no time to shower, let alone drop the children at her house.

For the next ten days, I took a break from work and dedicated all my time to caring for Arsalan. I helped him change, fed him, and handled tasks like bank payments. My fight mode was fully activated in this situation. I didn't know what the force was behind this care. It just happened. Everything I had felt for him, all the anger, seemed to have been suspended for the time being. Maybe it was overriding guilt because of my attachment to Gordon, but I just knew that I wanted to take care of him.

I briefly told Gordon what had happened and asked him not to contact me. I needed some room to breathe. These last few months had been overwhelming in so many ways, and for now, I just needed to ground myself in caring for my husband. I didn't want to wear any other hats. All I knew was that all these years of our marriage demanded that I be there for him in this difficult time.

Arsalan's attitude left me confused. He was different in a way that was good but difficult for me to process. He was gentle. He kept thanking me for little things. Reflective. I would find him holding my hand now and then and hugging me despite his hurting ribs. I didn't know what to make of all this. Had he changed? Had the accident changed him? Or was I finally standing up to the bully in him? Whatever it was, I was like a zombie, just responding to everything happening around me.

He would reminisce about our earlier days. Stories that I needed to remember. We used to go for long walks on our trips, holding hands, how he laughed at my bad jokes or how proud he was of my resilience at the birth of both our children. How proud he was of how I managed the home so well and took care of his parents.

I was numb and confused. Who was this man saying all these things to me? It was the most peculiar feeling in the world.

He asked me to lie down on the hospital bed next to him one night. I made an excuse, saying that I could hurt him, but he refused to take no for an answer. As I lay down carefully next to him, my body tight, ensuring I didn't hurt him or myself, it was so easy to let go and start hoping again. I was so close to it.

'I want to apologise to you, Saniya.'

I was shocked. I wasn't prepared for this. I didn't say anything.

'You are a wonderful wife, and I've hurt you with my words, and I've hurt you with my actions. I want you to give us a chance.' He kissed my forehead as he said it.

I couldn't hold back any longer, and I burst out crying. How I had longed for these words. Some acknowledgement of my pain, my sacrifice. Something.

'I also want to say that you were right. I realise I don't have a high sex drive, and I blamed you for it. I didn't want to own up to that.'

'It's okay. Please don't blame yourself,' I said between tears.

'No. Let me say it. Maybe it won't change, and we won't have a typical husband-wife relationship. But maybe it will change. But until then, I don't want you to give up on me. Give up on us.' His voice seemed choked. I had never seen him this emotional.

'It's okay,' I repeated. I felt emotional. I felt something. But I needed some space. I got up and went to the bathroom.

Some of me wanted to leave this hospital room, hide in a corner, and reach out to Gordon. I missed him and felt guilty for missing him every time Arsalan smiled at me or looked at me with an expression that looked like love. I couldn't feel it. I just couldn't. I wanted to talk to Gordon and feel him silently listening to everything I was saying and not saying. I missed my friend. Was it possible to care for two men at the same time?

I was overwhelmed with emotions. How long had I wanted to hear Arsalan call out to me? To call out to me as he did today.

I was tired of running after him, but I knew he wouldn't walk towards me if I didn't. I was curious if I was ready to receive all he offered today. Maybe it was too late. Maybe?

But, for the first time since I had withdrawn from the relationship, I saw him walking towards me. It left me thinking about how changing myself brought out the change in him. And I believed in that and advocated the same to my clients. It just took some time for me to realise it about myself. It was hard to trust this gentle voice. And it was a little too late. I could no longer convince myself that, other than his abuse and lack of desire for me, the rest was all hunky-dory, and I should be grateful.

No, I wanted more, and now that it was coming my way, I didn't know what to do with it. What if it was only until he was helplessly lying in this hospital room? It was hard to trust him.

I came out of the bathroom. 'I need to go,' I announced. 'I'll stay the night at home. Aunty will stay with you tonight.' And after taking one look at his face, I rushed out of the room, not wanting to look back at that odd mixture of hope and hopelessness on his face. Maybe he also realised it was too late, yet he hoped, as I had for years.

I felt torn to pieces. I had finally shut my heart to my husband. A heart that had been battered and bruised every time I had granted it permission to hope again. Whenever I had allowed myself to be vulnerable again, the wounds had only got deeper and bled more. And these past tumultuous weeks, I had found myself in so many places besides my marriage. I had understood that marriage was a part of my life and not the whole bucketful of paint that covered an entire wall. I loved my work and felt passionate about it to the core, and I could see now that I was good at what I did. I had a sense of purpose in life. All these clients who walked through my life made me feel cared for and visible, just like they let me into their inner world. We were mirrors of each other. I was a wounded healer for them. Many times, as I sat in the therapy room with my wounds hurting me and wanting me to scream, rather than making my work difficult, my clients allowed me to step deeply into their world. Our stories were different, but the pain that bound us was the same.

I saw that I could find love in the oddest of places. I found it in my work when a client would sit before me and acknowledge with love and gratitude how my presence in their lives had changed the landscape of their existence. How they were broken, and I had helped them put together those broken pieces.

I found love within myself. I had started to fall in love with myself, and rather than look to others for validation, I looked within myself and found all I needed. I could take myself out for lunch, sit there, breathe, and feel content.

Gordon.

I found a form of love in my dearest friend. He felt like a father, a mother, a long-lost sibling, a partner, and so much more. He made me look at life differently.

It only ever took one person at a time to show us the possibility of finding love in the most unexpected places. I found it in myself. Who would have thought?

That night as I tried to make sense of this unexpected growing change in Arsalan, I texted Gordon. He asked me to meet him the next day, and without thinking, I said yes. I needed a break from the frenzy of the last few days. And I was missing my friend. I asked Aunty to go to the hospital and told her I had some work.

We met at our usual spot, and he was waiting for me this time.

'Hey, stranger.' He greeted me with a smile and got up from the chair until I sat down.

'Yes. Tell me about it!' I sat down and put my all-purpose bag on the next chair. 'I'm starving!'

I suddenly felt so hungry. I had been surviving on coffee for many days and had lost my appetite. My relationship with eating had always been dependent on my emotional state. When I felt helpless, I controlled the only thing I could – myself. And to stop eating and lose my appetite was my go-to mechanism.

We ordered paninis and coffee.

I was quietly looking outside at the plants from my favourite window. He didn't say anything. Somehow, he knew I needed space for something. And he never tried to rush me out of there.

'I missed you.' I looked at him and felt the tears in my eyes, but unlike before, I didn't feel shame for them or try to cover my face with my hands.

'I missed you too. It's been quite tough, hasn't it?'

'Yes, it has been,' I replied. 'I don't want to imagine if he had been more hurt…'

Gordon sat with his arms folded on the table. 'I hear you. How is he now?'

'He is much better.' I noticed how both of us avoided saying Arsalan's name. Did I wonder why? I knew why. We were friends, but the possibility of being more was present between us, a strong force, an extreme case.

'How have you been?' I finally asked. 'How are your workshops going?'

Our food arrived before he could answer. After a minute or two, he replied, 'The workshops finished last week. I'm done for this term. I've been swamped trying to sort my flight back.'

I felt my heart drop. I stopped eating. 'What do you mean?'

'I have to go back home. Dad isn't doing well.'

I felt my heart sinking even more. 'How long will you be gone for?'

'I think a couple of months. Have a few workshops lined up there, and then I'll be back.'

I felt the sudden rush of tears. I looked away, but he saw them. I wasn't ready for this.

'Saniya, we are going to stay in touch and talk. And I will come back. And you have to come to see me too.'

'Sure. It's fine!'

'I care for you. You're important to me, my dear friend.'

Friend. Why was this word pinching me? He was just a friend, wasn't he?

I nodded, blinking back more tears. 'I know. You don't need to say it.' After a moment, I stood up. 'I need to use the toilet. Can you order more coffee?'

I quickly left the table and dashed for the ladies' room. Lots of emotions were coming up, and I needed some time away from him in case I ended up making a fool of myself.

I opened the tap and washed my face with cold water. I looked up and saw a distraught face with drops of water running down. My eyes were wide with confusion and there was a haunted look on my face.

You are married. You are married, I reminded myself again. *He is just a friend.*

I took another deep breath, and with a smile that was hard to muster, I walked out.

Gordon watched me as I returned. 'Saniya?'

'Yeah,' I said, sliding back into my seat, hoping my face looked more presentable now.

It seemed as if he wanted to take my hand, but instead he lowered his hands to his lap. 'You are important to me. And nothing would make me happier than you being happy. You believe that, right?'

'Yeah...'

'I will try to come back for a visit as soon as possible. I also want to talk about us.' And that was when he grabbed both my hands. 'I want more.'

I looked up at him, and I got the confirmation I had been looking for. There was an us. But was I ready to explore that?

I missed him already. We hardly met up, but knowing he was in my world and city helped. But I knew that if he said he would visit, he would. I could, too, but...

'I need to go.' I didn't wait for his response and ran out.

When had I started to believe that Gordon would be a part of my life forever? What a fool I was.

On the way to the hospital, I felt more conflicted than ever. Leaving my marriage was a challenging option. Was it even an option at this point? I could no longer think as an individual. My children came first. I felt my hands tied behind my back. But my heart? I had complete control of my heart, didn't I? But who did my heart belong to? Did it belong to my husband, who could still pull at my heartstrings? Even when these strings were so highly strung. There was some power in the marriage bond that made one hope that one might find love in the same place it started. But I could also see how much things had changed. I had outgrown my spouse. I felt I no longer knew him as well as I did all those years ago.

And then there was this new space with Gordon that made me feel all these new things that sometimes pushed me so hard to act. My head was spinning with all these overwhelming emotions.

My marriage had been a bittersweet experience, more bitter than sweet, and all these years, I didn't know which one to trust. The many sweet moments spent with Arsalan... moments of friendship and travel and family time and children and more... or the bitterness of harsh words slapped on my face at impulse or the rejection of my sexual needs again and again and again...

No matter how many hours of therapy I took or how much I tried, that bitterness remained. When I would sit before a female client who would tell me that her husband, despite their differences, always initiated sex and was moving towards her in the intimate space, I'd feel a piercing pain in my gut. I'd go back home, look at myself in the mirror, and question: *why not me?*

I knew Arsalan had some issues around sex, and he had only just admitted to them. What I wanted to ask myself was if I was ready to accept the limitations of our relationship. Was I willing to forgive him and move on and accept that, at best, we were friends and could love each other as friends?

Was I ready to let go of Gordon too? Because I knew a part of me denied how his presence made me withdraw more and more from Arsalan with each passing day, until this accident had jolted me out of the world I inhabited with Gordon, a world where, when we were together, nothing else mattered.

Was I ready to let my guard down again and invite my husband back into my heart?

He was trying, and trying very hard. If we continued to connect the way we did, we could translate this into our physical space. I also asked myself why I couldn't look at Arsalan with the same empathy I showed my clients. I didn't know how he'd acquired his wounds. He didn't know of mine either. Maybe one day we would show our wounds to each other. Who knew?

I knew it was different with a client whom I met once a week for fifty minutes. I also knew that they didn't directly impact me. They didn't directly affect me. I was also a champion of self-change and firmly believed that, as adults, we should take ownership of our actions that hurt our loved ones. I had changed so much myself. I was no longer bothered by Arsalan's interests outside the marriage. I did not impose myself, although I never thought I had. I'd given him as much space as he'd wanted and didn't nag him as he would complain, the nagging being a call for attention.

Once again, the question remained whether I would give him another chance.

Give us another chance.

Or would I give Gordon a chance?

23   *Woman*

I sat on the front porch of Ami's home. She had hosted a brunch for us and Arsalan's parents. Maheen was visiting. The house was packed.

Hafsa Khala had moved back a couple of months ago as well. It was a cool November morning, perfect for brunch, and everyone seemed to be enjoying themselves. Ami had even gone to the trouble of hiring a catering company for the event. Nyle and Neha along with their cousins, were jumping on the trampoline that Ami had purchased a few months ago for them, and there was screaming and laughter that brought a smile to my face. I wanted to soak in this scene before me. All my loved ones were in the same space.

I needed to figure out how to describe the last year. So much had happened. From the outside, it seemed like nothing had happened, but a lot had changed inside me.

I looked at Ami and smiled gently. I finally felt that I could forgive her. I had more space in my heart to love Ami. I had been drawn to another man outside of my marriage. I had not crossed boundaries like Ami had or made my children's home unsafe, but I had new feelings like little buds pushing to blossom in my heart. And it had been the damage and hurt by my husband that had made me look towards another man. I saw Ami as a woman for the first time and not as a mother. I wondered what her relationship with Baba had been like. I started questioning what had drawn her to Uncle Uzair. What unfulfilled needs made her take that step? A part of me could never forgive her for the price I paid as a child, but I was willing to let go. I was learning to let go.

My boundaries with her were as intact as with Arsalan and the rest of the world. She thought twice before attacking me or criticising me. We weren't the perfect mother and daughter, but we were perhaps two broken souls who met somewhere, and that was enough, for now; that moment of her asking me to forgive her had changed and healed something broken between us.

I looked at Neha as she laughed so freely, my spirited daughter. I silently vowed to continue to aspire to be the mother I had always wanted. My daughter would make the choices she wanted, and I would be her guide and support and show her those choices, but she would get to choose and take the risks that came with them. If she staggered, I would hold her and be proud when she sprinted.

Nyle was already a little man, and nothing made me happier than the fact that he was polite and gentle. He couldn't hurt a fly if he tried. I'd made him sit down with me time and again, and we'd discussed Arsalan's behaviour that he'd witnessed, more so because he was the firstborn. I realised that addressing the elephant in the room – his father's abusive behaviour – was essential. He could then separate the behaviour from the person, and it was an important lesson for him that his father, whom he idealised, wasn't perfect. But he was trying to change, which was my son's most important lesson. We kept trying to look within ourselves and do better for ourselves and others.

Gordon and I continued to stay in touch, but as time passed, he started receding into the shadows, and Arsalan came more and more to the forefront. After his accident, he was a changed man. We didn't have a healthy intimate space yet, but he was open to seeking help. We were taking baby steps, and maybe that would change too. He had stopped abusing or taking his anger out on me as he did before, which made me hope that anything was possible.

I missed Gordon now and then, but other than staying in touch occasionally, our space had shifted. A part of me was his, for now, filled with love and gratitude. He came for a purpose. He made me fall in love with myself. He taught me how to stand up to Arsalan. He made me feel feminine and womanly; no one could fill that part of my heart. I sometimes missed him so much that I thought I couldn't breathe. He had made me feel alive and had brought me back from the dead when I thought I was always dragging a corpse with me. And he had made me see a snippet of what love could look like in its purest form, but I had to choose between the possibility of an almost perfect kind of love and one that was broken.

I chose Arsalan. I chose my marriage. My family.

But most importantly, I chose myself, because all the other choices that followed were my choices. I was in a place where I knew that if I had wanted to leave, I could have. I would have left. So, staying was my choice, and I was happy with it.

Did I stop hurting? No. Now and then, the pain of all my past traumas came knocking, and I always opened the door to it. I liked sitting in my pain. It reminded me of my courage and strength, the rocky roads I'd travelled, drowning in solid currents, joy and hurt, or ruptures and repairs. And how empowering was that? I could sit with my pain, smile through my tears, and sometimes cry whilst I smiled. I didn't get attached to outcomes anymore. I welcomed both the days when I felt still within myself and those when it was stormy... I just liked moving. Sometimes, I thought I knew myself much more than before, whilst at other times, I didn't know myself at all.

Arsalan. I looked at him, and I felt warm and content. He would suddenly look up from his phone and smile at me. I smiled back. This was another form of love. It could have been better. It was broken. But in that brokenness were some pieces that could fit well together. We had moved to a good space. We were getting to know each other again in new ways. Did I feel the hurt that he had caused me? Yes, I did. Did he feel the frustration I caused him? Yes, he did. But we were beginning to see that hurt could sometimes pave the way for healing. I was learning to settle, and holding his hand at night was sometimes enough. Some nights it was frustrating. I allowed myself both. I allowed myself to feel that whatever existed was good enough and permitted myself to feel the occasional frustration and longing. But I was no longer waiting for anything. I had stopped walking and running after Arsalan.

I stayed where I was and welcomed him if he came my way. And didn't fall in despair if he did not. I felt no shame when Gordon's smiling face popped into my mind during the most unexpected moments. I smiled inside and felt gratitude for knowing such an incredible soul. He was an explorer who travelled from country to country, motivating the world towards life. And he had taught me how to explore too. The exploration within, which had taken me to exciting lands and war-torn areas of myself.

'Saniya! Sit with us!' Arsalan called out.

'Yes, apa! Stop ignoring us.' Maheen was laughing.

I walked towards them.

Every relationship is different and there is no textbook marriage. I understood that Arsalan and I were two broken souls whose wounds had bled onto each other, and it had taken us time to find a way to learn how to start healing each other.

This was reality.

Life.

I walked towards life as it was now… I had forgiven the past, and I didn't dread the future…

This moment was all that mattered.

I walked towards that moment.

Acknowledgments

Deep gratitude to Abu who pushed me throughout my life to stand as tall as my brothers, be it through studies or teaching me how to play hockey and most importantly, turning me into a reader first and then a writer for life.

Mama, for the power of her constant prayers that reaffirm my faith in myself.

I wish to deeply thank my mentor, whom I connected with at the time this book was a rough sketch in my mind. Through the next few years, he played a pivotal role in my journey of inner growth and change, inspiring me to view human relationships from a different lens and transform that awareness into this story. I am grateful that you continue to teach me a thing or two.

My girl gang; Mariam, Naima, Zara, Hajira, Hafsa, Natasha, Saima, Farah, Saman & Arshia who unconditionally held the space for me to 'be' with empathy and a few necessary kicks now and then.

A special note for Awais Khan, a wonderful author and friend who has supported and encouraged me at every step of the book.

Zara M is a psychotherapist and a freelance writer from Pakistan. *Saniya* is Zara's first novel and combines her passion for psychology and writing.